Meera Syal is an actress and writer. She has written a number of successful TV and film scripts, including *Bhaji on the Beach* and the multi-award-winning *My Sister Wife*, in which she also starred. She co-wrote and starrred in BBC2's hit comedy series *Goodness Gracious Me*, and is co-writer and star of the hugely successful series *The Kumars at No. 42*. Her first novel, the bestselling *Anita and Me*, won a Betty Trask Award and was shortlisted for the Guardian Fiction Prize, it has also been made into a successful film. *Life Isn't All Ha Ha Hee Hee*, her second novel, was acclaimed by critics and is now a major BBC production. Meera Syal was awarded the MBE in 1998.

By the same author

ANITA AND ME

LIFE ISN'T ALL HA HA HEE HEE

Meera Syal

BLACK SWAN

LIFE ISN'T ALL HA HA HEE HEE
A BLACK SWAN BOOK : 0 552 77187 2

Originally published in Great Britain by Doubleday,
a division of Transworld Publishers

PRINTING HISTORY
Doubleday edition published 1999
Anchor edition published 2000
Black Swan edition published 2000

7 9 10 8 6

Set in 11/13^{1}/2 pt Sabon by
Falcon Oast Graphic Art.

Black Swan Books are published by Transworld Publishers,
61–63 Uxbridge Road, London W5 5SA,
a division of The Random House Group Ltd,
in Australia by Random House Australia (Pty) Ltd,
20 Alfred Street, Milsons Point, Sydney, NSW 2061, Australia,
in New Zealand by Random House New Zealand Ltd,
18 Poland Road, Glenfield, Auckland 10, New Zealand
and in South Africa by Random House (Pty) Ltd,
Endulini, 5a Jubilee Road, Parktown 2193, South Africa.

Printed and bound in Great Britain by
Cox & Wyman Ltd, Reading, Berkshire

Papers used by Transworld Publishers are natural, recyclable
products made from wood grown in sustainable forests.
The manufacturing processes conform to the environmental
regulations of the country of origin.

*For all our mothers and daughters
And the East London 'kuriyaan'
You Know Who You Are.*

1

NOT EVEN SNOWFALL COULD MAKE LEYTON LOOK LOVELY. Sootfall was what it was; a fine drizzle of ash that sprinkled the pavements and terrace rooftops, dusting the rusty railings and faded awnings of the few remaining shops along the high road. They formed a puzzling collection of plucky bric-à-brac emporiums (All the Plastic Matting You'll Ever Need!) and defeated mini-marts (Cigs 'N' Bread! Fags 'N' Mags!), braving the elements like the no-hopers no-one wanted on their team, shivering in their sooty kit. Grey flecks nested in the grooves of the shutters of the boarded up homes, abandoned when new roads were put down and old ladies died; they settled silently on the graves in the choked churchyard, giving grace and shadow to long-unread inscriptions – Edna, Beloved Wife; Edward, Sleeps with the Angels – and dressed the withered cedars in almost-mourning robes of almost-black. Pigeons shook their heads, sneezing, blinking away the icy specks, claws skittering on the unfamiliar roof which had once been the reassuring flat red tiles of the methodist church and was now a gleaming minaret, topped by a metal sickle moon. The moon at midday, dark snow and nowhere to perch. No wonder they said Coo.

An old man picked up a frozen milk bottle from his front step and held it up to the light, squinting at the petrified pearly sea beyond the glass. He'd seen an ocean like that once, in the navy or on the TV, he couldn't remember which now.

'You waiting till the whole bloody house freezes then?' his wife called from inside. A voice that could splinter bone.

And then he heard them. Nothing more than an echo at first, muted by wind and traffic, but he felt the sound, like you always do when it brings the past with it. Clop-clop, there it was, no mistaking it. And then he was seven or ten again, in scratchy shorts with sherbet fizzing on his tongue, racing his brother to open up the coal shute at the front of the house before the cart drew up and the man with the black face and the bright smile groaned, his sack on his back, freeing swirls of dust with every heavy step.

'Come here!' the old man shouted behind him. 'Quickly! You hurry up and you'll see a . . . bleedin' hell!'

The horse turned the corner into his road, white enough to shame what fell from the sky, carrying what looked like a Christmas tree on its back. There was a man in the middle of the tinsel, pearls hanging down over his brown skin, suspended from a cartoon-size turban. He held a nervous small boy, similarly attired, on his lap. Behind him, a group of men of assorted heights and stomach sizes, grins as stiff as their new suits, attempted a half-dance half-jog behind the swishing tail, their polished shoes slipping in the slush. A fat man in a pink jacket held a drum around his neck and banged it with huge palms, like a punishment, daring any-one not to join in. 'Brrrr- aaaa! Bu-le, bu-le bu-le!' he yelled.

The old man understood half of that noise, it was brass monkey weather all right, but what did he mean by that last bit? They couldn't like the cold, surely.

'Another of them do's down the community centre then,' said his wife, sniffing at his shoulder.

Other neighbours had gathered at windows and doorways, the children giggling behind bunched fingers, their elders, flint-faced, guarding their stone-clad kingdoms warily, in case bhangra-ing in bollock-freezing weather was infectious.

Swamped, thought the old man; someone said that once, we'll be swamped by them. But it isn't like that, wet and soggy like Hackney Marshes. It's silent and gentle, so gradual that you hardly notice it at all until you look up and see that everything's different.

'Like snow,' he said, out loud.

Trigger, the horse, was enjoying himself. Anything was better than the dumpy pubescents he was forced to heave around paddocks in Chigwell for the rest of the week. This was an easy gig, a gentle amble past kind hands and interesting odours. Early this morning, he'd been woken by an old lady in a white sheet breaking coconuts beneath his hooves. She had sung for him. She smelt of pepper. There was none of the kisses and baby talk the stable girls lavished on him to impress the parents, but her patient worship had made him snort with joy. He stepped lightly now, considering he was carrying a heavy-hearted man on his back.

Deepak had noticed the hostile onlookers, albeit in fragments through the shimmering curtain that hid him from the world, but the cold stone in his chest, hidden beneath the silk brocade of his bridal suit, made them unimportant. He had explained his dank foreboding away many times, over many months now, using the dimpled smile and the mercurial tongue that had made him a business success and rendered matrons in the neighbourhood giddy with gratitude when he graced their kitty parties. Fear of commitment, he'd said to the stone in the spring. Any eligible bachelor taking the plunge is bound to feel some pangs of regret. She is as sweet as the blossom outside my window, and just as virginal. Fear of failure, he'd told the stone as he'd eyed up the passing girls from his pavement café, pluckable, all of them, bruised by summer evening blue. She doesn't need to prance around in thongs and halter necks, her beauty is beautiful because it's hidden and it will be mine. Fear of becoming my father, he'd smiled at the stone as he tramped through new-fallen leaves, recalling his parents' amazed faces as he'd confirmed his choice of bride. A Punjabi girl! They had almost wept with relief, having endured a parade of blonde trollops through their portals for most of their son's youth. Marrying her does not mean I will become my father, take up religion, grow nostril hair and wear pastel-coloured leisure wear, he told the stone playfully. We have choices. Wasn't that the reason his parents had come here in the first place? And now it was winter and the stone refused any further discussion on the matter. It was done.

And there they were, waiting. Ahead of him, the bride's welcoming committee stood in the doorway of the crumbling hall, garlands of flaming marigolds in their hands. His own Baraat, the menfolk from his side who were his companions on this journey from callow youth to fully paid up member of the respectable married classes, roared their arrival. Bow and be grateful, the man who will take your daughter off your hands for ever is here! His future mother-in-law teetered forward, her face shining; brown moon, white horse, grey snow. Deepak drew his tinsel curtain back over his eyes and felt the warm horse rumble and heave beneath him.

*

Chila looked at his toenails and felt a strange sense of dread. His feet were fine; brown, not too hairy, clean enough. But she could not tear her eyes from his toenails as they walked round the fire (about to be wed, head bowed submissively just in case anyone might suspect she was looking forward to a night of rampant nuptials). Ten yellowing, waxy nodules crowned each toe, curled and stiff as ancient parchment, a part of him she had never noticed before, feet that demanded attention because of their glaring imperfection, the feet of a man who might read *Garden Sheds Weekly* every evening instead of loving her. Chila told herself off. This was unfair, sacrilegious even, on your wedding day.

Or maybe it was just being prepared, like her mother was. Her mother who had handed over a parcel of brand new and frilly pink lingerie which she had bought as part of Chila's trousseau, ready to wear when her daughter finally moved in with Deepak tonight, man and wife, all official. Her mother who had coughed with embarrassment as Chila discovered the sprinkling of rose petals hidden amongst the Cellophane, shyly folding in on themselves like her own fingers were doing now. 'Sweet, Mum.' Chila smiled, ignoring the subtext in her mother's eyes, My poor baby will have the dirty thing done to her tonight. Chila had not had the heart to tell her the dirty thing had already taken place many months ago in a lock-up garage just off the A406.

'Move, didi!' her brother Raju hissed, pushing her round the holy fire. She could not look up even if she wanted, weighed down by an embroidered dupatta encrusted with fake pearls and gold-plated balls. The heavy lengha prevented her from taking more than baby steps behind her almost-husband to whom she was tied, literally, her scarf to his turban. She would have liked to wear a floaty thing, all gossamer and light, and skip around the flames like a sprite, blowing raspberries at the mafia of her mother's friends whose mantra during all her formative years had been, 'No man will ever want that one, the plump darkie with the shy stammer.' But she had shocked them all, the sour-faced harpies, by bagging not only a groom with his own teeth, hair, degree and house, but the most eligible bachelor within a twenty-mile radius.

She stole a sneaky glance at Deepak, who was checking his profile in the fractured reflection of the silver mirror ball above their heads, each winking pane with its own tiny flaming heart, a thousand holy fires refracted in its shiny orb. Bloody hell, he was fit and he was hers. She wanted to celebrate. But instead she was mummified in red and gold silk, swaddled in half the contents of Gupta's Gold Emporium, pierced, powdered and plumped up so that her body would only walk the walk of everyone's mothers on all their weddings, meekly, shyly, reluctantly towards matrimony. Chila tilted her head with difficulty and took in a deep gulp of air before she began the next perambulation, glad of the momentary rest while Deeps adjusted his headdress. She locked eyes with Tania, sitting straight-backed on the front row. She's looking a bit rough today, thought Chila, with an unexpected tinge of pleasure.

Tania shot Chila a reassuring wink and just managed to turn a grimace of discomfort into an encouraging smile. She ached all over and the new slingbacks she'd bought in five minutes flat yesterday had already raised blisters. She was squeezed between two large sari-draped ladies, fleshy book-ends who exchanged stage whispers across her lap, giving a wheezy running commentary to the great drama unfolding before them.

'You see, how nicely she walks behind him? She will follow his lead in life. That is good.'

'Oh, now the father is crying. About time. Daughters

are only visitors in our lives, hena?'

'Hai, they are lent to us for a short while and then we have to hand them over to strangers like—'

'Bus tickets?'

'Hah! But then where does the journey end, hah?'

'Hah! Yes. Only God knows, as he is the driver.'

'Now the sister is howling. I'd howl if I had a moustache like hers . . .'

Tania leaned forward pointedly, hoping to obscure their view of each other and save herself another half-hour of homely wedding quips in stereo. But the women merely adjusted themselves around her, heaving bosoms into the crevices of her elbows. She suddenly remembered why she had stopped attending community events, cultural evenings, bring-a-Tupperware parties, all the engagements, weddings and funerals that marked out their borrowed time here. She could not take the proximity of everything any more. The endless questions of who what why she was, to whom she belonged (father/husband/workplace), why her life wasn't following the ordained patterns for a woman of her age, religion, height and income bracket. The sheer physical effrontery of her people, wanting to be inside her head, to own her, claim her, preserve her. Her people.

Tania checked her watch, angry at herself for hoping that the wedding might be running to schedule. Indian time. Look at the appointed hour and add another two for good measure. Memories of family picnics, outings to relatives' homes, rare but treasured cinema visits, where she would bring up the rear, mute with shame at her clan's inevitable late entrance. 'So what if the food's cold/the park shuts in ten minutes/the film has started?' her father would boom. 'Nobody minds, hah?' Tania minded so much she got migraines. She closed her eyes as the priest began another mantra, willing the familiar words to take her back in time and get rid of the small voice that chanted in time with the distant finger bells, the voice that said, You don't belong.

Sunita slipped into an empty seat at the back of the hall, just as Chila and Deepak were making their final round of the fire. Nikita stood at her side, shivering in her pint-size silk suit, so cute on the hanger and sodding useless in the snow.

'Come here, Nikki,' Sunita whispered, pulling her daughter close to her and moving her sleeping son to the other arm, plumply snoozing in his rabbit-eared Baby-Gro. She rubbed Nikita's hands and face until she felt the glow returning, and heaved her onto the remaining inches of lap. The pristine magenta suit she'd squeezed into this morning was now a map of motherhood, marked out by handprints, chocolate streaks and a recent vomit stain which bloomed from her breast like some damp crusty flower.

'Look at Auntie Chila, Nikki! She's getting married, see?'

Nikita nodded dumbly, absorbing the fairy grotto effects around her.

This is where it starts, thought Sunita, a little girl at her mother's knee wanting to be the scarlet princess whose beauty lights fires. Sunita felt a green stab of envy, seeing Chila, dark, dumpy, dearest friend Chila, parading her joy like a trophy. Sunita had been a perfect size eight when she wore her wedding sari. Akash had kissed each of her fingertips that night, awed by their perfection. She used to paint her nails then.

'Mama looked just like Auntie Chila when she got married to Papa,' Sunita told Nikita with a kiss.

Nikita blinked. Disbelievingly, Sunita thought.

Deepak and Chila finished their seventh round of the fire and paused before the priest, who held his hand up dramatically, waiting for hush. Pandit Kumar was pregnant with his own importance at this solemn point, emphasized by his impressive belly, which strained the seams of his beige and gold-trimmed shalwar kameez. He often thought of Elvis Presley at this juncture in the wedding ceremony, how the King would possess the microphone, angle that profile just so to the watching cameras with a daring insouciance, toss that quiff and casually break a thousand hearts. At such moments, Pandit Kumar forgot he was bald, sweaty and bandy-legged. He had the stage, he held the futures of two young lovers in the palms of his hands and he had a god-given duty to put on a good show.

He shiftily checked that the squinty videoman had adjusted to close-up mode before he cleared his throat, swallowed a sizeable phlegm-ball and began: 'Ladies and gentlemen, now I will ask the bride and groom to swap their seating, symbolically showing that dearest Chila will now pass into the hands of dearest Deepak and his loving family. Her old life as her father's daughter has ended. Her new life as her husband's wife has begun. Chila, Deepak, please will you now be seated!'

Chila gathered her sari about her and did a clumsy do-si-do with Deepak, negotiating fabric and high heels and the coconuts hanging from her wrists until, at last, she came to rest on a seat warm with Deepak's body heat. She saw Deepak's mother grinning mistily up at her from the floor. Chila grinned back, suddenly light-headed, feeling her stomach trying to rise up and displace her heart. She realized, with a shock, what it was that had possessed her body. She was happy.

Deepak reached over and squeezed her hand. He stared from Chila to his mother and back again. So this is what it felt like, he thought, to belong, finally. He leaned into Chila and whispered something into her ear, which made her titter and blush, and precipitated a spontaneous round of applause which began at Sunita's seat, rippled through eighteen rows of smiling, satisfied guests and reached the platform in a wave of goodwill and joy. The videoman risked an ambitious wide shot of the hall. Pandit Kumar raised a funky fist in the air and shouted, 'All right! Let's hear it for Chila and Deepak! All right!'

'So what did he say, then?' Tania demanded, before lighting up a slim menthol cigarette.

'Not in here, Tania!' gasped Sunita, instinctively swivelling to the door of the tiny anteroom, ears pricked to the noises of celebration outside.

'It's locked.' Tania smiled mockingly at Sunita. 'Calm down, Auntieji, we will not let the evil fumes ruin Chila's reputation.'

'I'm thinking of Chila,' Sunita retorted, cheeks burning. 'Chila's mother-in-law's hovering outside.'

'She's still ours, though.' Tania exhaled. 'Officially, until the doli. So they can wait, hey Chila?'

Chila wobbled on one foot, trying to squeeze a leg into bright pink silk pyjamas.

They made an odd threesome. Tania was svelte, sharp-featured, with long-lazy limbs and a leonine mane (never cut, odd for a Modern Girl), dismissive of the beauty that was her passport out of East London and into cosmopolitan circles where she was now termed merely exotic. Sunita and Chila had feared they might lose her, when Tania broke loose from her traditional moorings and drifted into an uncharted ocean with her English man and snappy Soho job. But they also knew, when she did return, it was always for them. And they forgave her, for when she did breeze in smelling of leather office chairs and tangy perfume she seemed to drag the world in with her, full of possibilities, on spiky heels. 'Here I am! Back with the pindoos,' she'd trill, back with the village idiots, she'd joke, although, Sunita noticed, Tania still sat like one with them, crossed legs, shoes off, unknotting herself in a way that suggested, despite her protestations, that part of her still responded to them like Home.

Sunita, they had all three decided, was always the one Most Likely to Succeed. She'd sailed through school and college with straight As, and was halfway through a law degree when she'd met Akash. He'd called her a scab as she'd entered the university refectory to buy a pasty and lectured her right there on the pavement, in his open-toed sandals and fraying jumper, about the oppressed canteen staff within, who relied on their support for their ongoing work-to-rule protest. Sunita barely took in a word. She was trying to work out what planet he'd landed from, this man full of fizz and fury with Medusa-messy hair, and why the hell hadn't she known that there were Asian men around like this one. She failed her finals, unsurprisingly really, as most of her revision had taken place on Akash's bedsit mattress. Ten years on, the fledgling battling barrister had a comfy desk job at a local Citizens' Advice Bureau, and the children of the revolution's children held them, comfortably, together. Sunita's delicate, doll-like features were now softened by the fleshy mantle worn by married Indian ladies in their mid-thirties. It was like a uniform, the designer silks, the ostentatious gold jewellery, collected on booty trips to Bahrain, the rippling belly rolls escaping from painted on sari blouses. No guilty aerobic sessions for them. The old rules still applied; coming from a place where starvation was a reality rather than a fashion statement, fat meant wealth and contentment. So Sunita could claim her cellulite was a political stance, rather than something, like many other things in her life, which had crept up on her unawares.

And then there was Chila, wrestling with fuchsia folds.

19

Known as Poor Chila for years, while relatives and educationalists alike mistook her innocence and unworldly joy for stupidity. First she was slow, then thick, then sweet, and finally, concluded her sorrowful parents, unmarriageable, for didn't the boys nowadays expect smart yet domesticated women with both culinary skills and a Ph.D.? But Chila's close friends knew better; Tania and Sunita had noticed early on the cinnamon smiling girl standing by herself in the corner of the playground. They had even briefly joined in with the mob teasing of all the unfortunate rejects who were herded into the prefabricated hut reserved for the Special Children. They had watched through the hut windows, giggling, as Chila and her classmates, mostly black and Asian children, cut out pictures from catalogues with blunt scissors, tongues out in concentration, and wondered why she never got angry or embarrassed at their gawping. And one day, suddenly, Chila appeared in their classroom, clutching her folder nervously, and was shown to the empty desk behind them. The news spread that Chila had entered an essay into a schools' competition and won. The school had assumed that the recent refugee from East Africa could not speak a word of English, never mind compose a lyrical treatise on the joys of spring. Chila's essay was pinned up outside the headmaster's office. It was full of violent African blooms and flame-coloured birds, a different kind of spring that briefly inhabited a musty corner and made those who read it sigh longingly and wish for the sun. Chila never wrote anything as good again. In fact, she consistently failed every exam going, as if that single swansong had depleted any formal intelligence she may have possessed. But by then Tania and Sunita had adopted her and discovered that the girl they'd once tagged the Dark Dumbo was funnier, sweeter and kinder than anyone else knew. They kept the secret like they kept each other's friendship: close, to themselves.

Tania picked up the top half of the suit and wrinkled her nose. 'Is this what his side have given you to wear for your exit?'

Chila nodded, hitching the trousers up quickly and tying the cord with trembling fingers. She couldn't understand why she felt shy in her underwear in front of her friends, the two friends who'd seen her through mammary growth, menstruation and men problems. Maybe it did all change once you got married. She'd already had the lecture from Tania about how pathetic those women were who acquired a wedding ring on one hand and dropped all their female friends with the other. That was not going to happen to them, especially as Chila was the last of the three to get a man. If it all fell apart now, it would be Chila's fault. Definitely.

'It's . . . a bold print,' ventured Sunita, eyeing the spangly top which Tania dangled from a manicured finger.

'Bold? It's positively Bolshie!' laughed Tania. 'What is it about the bloke's family and the doli suit? You've got Chanel designing catwalk Indian suits and they go to Mrs Patel's bargain basement bin for the loudest pindoo suit they can find, to bring their new daughter-in-law home in.'

'God I know,' Sunita said. 'I got some frothy lemon yellow thing with bells on the scarf from Akash's mother. When the DJ asked for requests for our first dance, someone shouted out, "Have you got 'My Ding A Ling?'" I could have died.'

Tania choked on her cigarette, giggling out fumes from her nose. Sunita patted her on the back, before stealing a quick drag and blowing a blissful cloud right into Tania's face, which made her choke all over again.

'Tut tut! Bad Indian woman,' teased Tania, wiping her eyes. 'Thought you'd given up.'

'I have,' Sunita said, 'I really have.'

'Go on then,' said Chila. 'How bad is it?'

She was standing in a pool of sunlight that had brazenly, unexpectedly spilled through the dirty single window. The gold at her ears, throat and wrists caught the light and threw it back in dancing darts, the dark brown of her skin softened and glowed, the dreaded pink suit flamed around her in rosy benediction. She had stopped the snow in mid-fall. Her watching friends' hearts contracted in unison; they had never assumed Chila would get married, that any man would understand or recognize her hidden, fragile charms. And now they saw her beauty in full bloom, they worried for her and about him.

'Chila,' breathed Sunita. 'You look beautiful.'

Tania smiled tightly. 'It's better on, for sure. What did he say, then?'

'Who?'

'Who? Dreamboat Deepak. You know, when he whispered something and you went all girlie and the pandit went gospel for a moment . . .'

'Oh, it was nothing. Bit weird, but nice.'

'Something romantic, I bet.' Sunita grinned. 'From the movies. Your hair is like the black monsoon cloud, your eyes like the startled faun . . . hai hai.'

'No. He just said, "Thank you." '

The moaning began as Chila fell into step behind Deepak, who strode manfully towards the glass swing doors. The guests gathered either side of the exit, spilling out into the courtyard and around the silver Mercedes, whose bumper sported two shrivelled balloons. CHILA WEDS DEEPAK the balloons said, or rather whispered, in deflated, croaky voices.

Sunita had dragged Tania to a prime spot, next to the back seat of the car, arguing that their faces should be the last Chila saw before being chauffeur-driven off to her new life. Sunita was already sniffling into a shredded tissue, glad she had left the children indoors with a vague relative. She didn't mind them seeing weddings, but the doli was too upsetting, at least for her. She looked up at Tania, who was standing stiff-backed against the breeze, obviously bored. Of course she doesn't understand why this is so painful, Sunita concluded. Unmarried women never do.

Tania thought it was a swarm of bees at first, wrong-footed suddenly, wondering how they had amassed and appeared in the middle of winter. Then the swing doors flew open and the hum became a keening, a mournful wailing with no end and no pauses for breath, taken up by one throat and then another until the sound enveloped them all. There in the quiet eye of the storm was Chila, head bowed, face contorted, black trails of mascara running down her cheeks, with her father clinging onto one arm and her mother to the other, wide-mouthed, emitting this awful endless moaning, broken with pleas in Punjabi to 'Please God, don't take our daughter from us, our baby leaving us for ever, please God, keep her safe . . .' Other members of Chila's family followed in a hysterical wake, raising impassioned eyes and arms to the sky, towards Deepak's family, towards Chila's parents, the all-purpose Indian gesture of 'Life's crap but what can you do, huh?'

Tania bristled with irritation at the sobbing around her, watching Chila being push-pulled slowly towards the open car door, where Deepak's family stood now with the sorrowful but resigned air of funeral directors, saddened by their unpleasant duty to remove this woman from her grieving family but determined to fulfil their role with dignity and, if need be, a gentle shove.

'For God's sake,' Tania whispered, 'she's only moving to

Ilford. She's not being kidnapped in a bleeding bullock cart to a distant village, is she?'

'It's not how far you go,' Sunita said, 'it's who you're going with. She's his now. Her parents have got to let her go.'

'Well, they should be having a laugh then, the number of years her mum's bent my ears about Chila not getting a decent bloke.'

'Not now, Tania.'

'They spend half your life nagging you to get a degree and keep your hymen so you'll bag a husband, and beat themselves up at your wedding because you have.'

'Tania, that's it, shutit now.'

Tania had a comeback all ready, tart on the end of her tongue, because she loved winding up Sunita more than anyone else. And then, despite her best intentions, she looked at him. Deepak stood in the centre of this circle of grief, the lone male in an ocean of heaving female flesh. The other men had regrouped in awkward clumps, giving the women space to grieve, exchanging rueful glances, scuffing their shoes guiltily in the melting slush. For hadn't they all done this once, pretend cavemen for a day, dragging their women away by the hair, parping their victory on their car horns? Deepak's face was a mask of calm, almost ennobled by the task ahead of him, to protect and nurture this weeping woman. And his serenity, his certainty were what helped Tania understand as she scanned the keening women at his side. They knew what lay ahead, they remembered their own dolis and wept for what they didn't know then, and what they knew now. They wept symbolically for Chila and noisily for themselves. Unexpected tears pricked Tania's eyes. She let out a long shuddering breath, which Sunita noted with surprised satisfaction.

As Chila was finally bundled into the back seat, eyes

downcast, nose streaming, headdress awry, Tania pulled Sunita forward so they were right up against the door, only a millimetre of glass separating the three friends. Tania knocked on the window and forced a manic grin, nudging Sunita to do the same. Chila looked up and blew her nose pathetically. Impulsively, Tania kissed the window, leaving the lipstick imprint of a rueful, lopsided smile, which she later thought most appropriate. Sunita mouthed 'Love you' between hiccuping sobs. Then Deepak slid in smoothly next to Chila and tapped the driver to move off. As the car edged forward, Tania looked straight into Deepak's eyes and told him silently what she had wanted to tell him since she had found out about this wedding. Look after her, she warned him and then, with an arch of an eyebrow, added a PS, Better than you looked after me.

Pandit Kumar threw a final handful of petals at the car bonnet with what he hoped was a Goodnight and thank you Vegas flourish. Ladies and gentlemen, the newlyweds have left the building . . . Tissue-clutching matriarchs re-attached themselves to harrumphing husbands, reaffirming their bonds to each other and the watching world. Single girls clucked in feverish groups, high on the drama of the departure, tossing their fancy dupattas at the single men, torn between the horror and the longing of it all. The single men back-slapped each other, their ushering and whisky-serving duties over, loosened ties while they felt themselves pulled along by the girls' invisible embroidered scarves. It was a game the young singles all played at weddings, regardless of the secret lives and liaisons outside these rarefied hours. For now, they could flirt as their forefathers must have done, brush up their smouldering technique, pretend that their futures were arranged at such venues under the eyes of their parents, rather than on their mobile phones on the way home.

The few English guests stood in a confused huddle, wondering why such a splendid day, replete with aching colours, mountainous piles of delicious food (much better than you get down the Viceroy), embarrassing hospitality, ear-splitting music, wild and strange folk dancing (a bit like jive, this Indian business, once you get the footwork going), inhibitions peeled off with second-best jackets, had to end with such a tragic performance. They had all got through the occasion without making an awful *faux pas*. Now what were they supposed to say to Chila's slumped and tear-stained family? Thank you for a lovely day?

For everyone else, it had been, despite the weather, a lovely day. A perfect day, because rituals had been observed, old footsteps retraced, threads running unbroken, families joined, futures secured. 'Bas! Now they are settled,' the women said, satisfied, their biggest worry over, blissfully unaware that some settled things can melt away, as easily as snowfall.

The car engine backfired once as it sped down the high road, scattering the pigeons from the mosque roof, who took to the sky in startled flight, momentary scudding shadows across the watery sun.

Chila

THEY WEREN'T REAL TEARS, YOU KNOW. WELL, BY THAT I MEAN, I did feel sad, heartbroken even, but it was like being at the cinema, when you're right there in the story, watching Clint in *The Bridges of Madison County* watch Meryl, with the rain plastering his hair to his forehead, and he's saying goodbye, because he loves her enough to understand he's got to let her go back to her boring husband, and you're choking on your popcorn and screaming, Jump, Meryl, before he goes for ever. You're there completely and then the lights come back on and you're embarrassed because there's snot down your top and you've got to get to Sainsburys before it closes. Well, Deepak was my Sainsburys, waiting for me at the end of the story. And I love a good cry, always have done. Like my mum's always said, Life isn't all ha ha hee hee, so if you know there's going to be a few tears, you might as well try and enjoy them.

And the other thing was, of course, that I knew everybody was watching to see how upset I was, because apparently, a girl who doesn't cry at her doli is considered a hard-hearted bitch on wheels who must be glad to leave her family. Sick, isn't it? I've heard of some girls who actually arrange for friends to slap them around a bit in the changing rooms beforehand or tell them a really tragic story, just to make sure they don't look too satisfied when they leave their weddings. Nowadays, with seventeen video cameras following your every move, you can't be too careful. You know that video is going all round the world to all the relatives who may never meet you, but will decide from the telly what sort of a wife and person you are. 'You see that, Bunty? The trollop almost smiled at the camera. May she only bear daughters, the hair-dyed hussy!' (That last bit is what I actually heard an old woman spit at one of my mates in Stratford Shopping Centre. Sad really, because that old woman must have been someone's daughter once upon a time.)

So I didn't attempt a fainting fit or rip off my clothes like a crazy woman, because actually I didn't have to try too hard. Seeing my dad blub sets me off anyway, and I was so knackered by the whole day and fed up of being stared at and seeing the surprise in people's faces when they looked from Deepak to me then back again that I just gave into it. Even the pandit put in his two pence worth. He actually asked one of my aunties if he was marrying the right couple. (And I know he had his eye on Deepak for his daughter a few years back. He reckoned you couldn't do much better than marrying the seed from a man of god, that's if you don't mind the fact his curie has a squint and breath that could melt paint.) Anyway, he says to my auntie, 'Well, I have known Deepak's family many years and I think they had higher hopes for their only son. But if he loves her tender and she doesn't have a wooden heart, it may work.' He's a weird bloke but he did do a lovely ceremony, even though the pelvic thrusts and his air guitar riffs didn't go down too well with Deeps' family. They were quite sweet to me. His mum kept bursting into tears every time she saw us together, which Deeps said was a compliment, as she's not one to show much emotion. And his dad just kept patting him, saying, 'Be happy. It's done now. No mucking around any more, OK?' His sisters are still a bit frosty with me but they'll come round eventually, I reckon.

There was a time, just after we announced the engagement, when they kept sending round their single girlfriends to Deeps' place. All these gorgeous long-haired women in designer suits would just appear on his doorstep with a casserole of his favourite dish and ask if they could pop in and do a bit of ironing. (Deeps told me all about it, he thought it was pathetic, although he kept the food sometimes and we ate it after, giggling together like naughty schoolkids.) It was like the more his family didn't want me, the more he did. Like being with me was something he had over them. 'I could understand it with the white girls,' he said, 'but on paper you're perfect. Apart from the qualifications bit.' Anyway, like his dad said, It's done, and like my dad said, Thank God, now we can die happy. I'll get Deeps' family round soon and cook them a slap-up dinner, so they can see how it's all worked out.

He was so sweet to me, Bichaara. As soon as we were on the North Circular, after we'd driven off from the hall, he got out his hanky and wiped away the panda rings from under my eyes. We both took our shoes off, he undid himself from the hanging gardens on his turban and we got Riz, his mate who was driving, to pick up a Kentucky bargain bucket, as neither of us had eaten in all the excitement. By the time we got to the honeymoon suite at the Garden Palace in Theydon Bois, all we fancied was a nap. Course, I got teased rotten by Sunita and Tania when they rang up the next day, wanting details, positions, number of times and what language he got excited in. I told them, It wasn't our first time anyway, so what's the big deal?

Except, and this is the weird thing, when we did eventually get round to it, it was like the first time somehow, because when we were going out together, it was impossible to relax; where, how, will anybody notice the windows are steamed up, will a vanload of people I know decide to have a midnight picnic in Epping Forest and park next to our car? Believe me, for single Asian girls, there is no such thing as safe sex. When you ask a guy if he's got protection, what you mean is, has he got tinted windows, safety locks and a baseball bat in the boot, in case of passing brothers? Of course, you learn to be imaginative, because of space, cramp and because you're scared of coming back in the next life as something with fur because you're doing something you're not supposed to.

The first time, if the truth be known, was sweaty, painful and messy. Deeps had arranged for us to spend an afternoon at a mate's house whose parents had gone to Kamla Warehouse for the day to stock up on tinned tomatoes. (He did have his own place, this gorgeous detached house, but he said his cousin was over from India staying with him and the lazy sod hardly ever went out, so no joy there.) So this mate's promised him they'd be away at least four hours, what with the rusty lock on their van and the roadworks on the M11 link. Anyway, we get down to our undies and of course, the van pulls up in the driveway, so we leap through windows and climb over fences until we end up in an alley-way running behind the houses, and eventually, after deciding we had been planning this for weeks and we should stick to it, on a mattress in Deep's lock-up garage. So it was over pretty quickly, with both of us being nervous, feeling disappointed and foolish, and he asked me if I'd liked it and I said yes because he'd gone to so much trouble.

I never told him it had been my first time. For a start, he wouldn't have believed me. I mean, how many thirty-two-year-old virgins are there in East London? And then he would have wanted to know why, and I couldn't have explained that without it sounding like there was something wrong with me. Which is just one of the rumours I've had to put up with round this manor.

It started at school, the rumours, the relatives and neighbours whispering about soft-in-the-head Chila. I suppose it didn't help that my education was spent in the prefab hut at school cutting out stuff from old Argos catalogues. I always did the same picture: My Perfect House. I'd cut round beds and dining tables and pine kitchen units and pink chaises-longues and I'd arrange them all into rooms and I'd always leave a space in the hallway for me to stand. Just me. And a cat if I could find one, though I was never very good with cutting round the ears, really fiddly. I liked it in that hut. The United Nations for dumbos Sunita had called it, and said it was a conspiracy to keep anyone foreign down, but I felt safe in there. It was when they took me out that all the trouble started. I was always going to be a cut and paste girl. I would have been just as good at it in Africa. That's what I told Mum and Dad when they threw fits about me failing yet another exam and how they had given up paradise to get us girls an education.

Then the visits started from the aunties and their witchy friends. They'd come round with cooking pots full of brain food which looked like scrambled rats and smelled like old pants, and home-made spells, or lockets with something hairy inside I would have to wear in my sleep, or mantras I'd have to learn and then be sent out into the garden to chant to the moon while throwing chicken bones over my shoulder. God knows what the neighbours thought. 'Seen that slow fat girl standing in the bushes talking to a chicken

31

leg?' I had mustard oil massages from an old man in bottle glasses who spent a lot of time looking for my missing brain down my bra, for some reason. I had scalp examinations from a blind Bengali woman who charged my mum fifty quid to poke in my hair and then gave me a bottle of dandruff shampoo. I even got dragged off to a visiting guru from India who had taken over one of my aunties' houses in Harrow for a month. He had come over here to spread the divine message to the rootless Indians in the West and save them from spiritual exile, at least that's what it said in his leaflet. He said some really nice poetry to me, something about the wisdom of the heart being more important than the knowledge in your brain, asked Mum for a donation to his ashram and went upstairs to play on my nephew's Sony Playstation. The only thing that made Mum give up was visiting a few astrologers. After the fifth one had done my chart yet again and told Mum what they all said, that I would marry soon and marry well, she stopped and left it to Fate.

I know that was her way of saying she had given up, but I was OK about it. The teasing wasn't too bad because I always had Sunita to argue for me and Tania to beat people up for me, but I never minded if someone called me slow. By then I knew that it was just the rest of the world was too fast and one day we'd catch up with each other. So I cut and pasted and dreamed and hoped and waited for Deepak to come and find me. I mean, I didn't know exactly it was going to be Deepak, and most people had paired me off with Uncle Madhan's son who works on the petrol pumps in his dad's garage and has a withered arm. (They always try and match you up with someone who they think has got similar deformities to you. 'Boy with club foot seeks similar'; 'Girl with acne will consider short, balding man with no prospects', according to the matrimonial column in our local Hindi paper.) But I knew it was just a matter of time before Someone would want me and all I needed was that one chance, to make that Someone never regret it. That's what I wanted to tell Deeps, there on that mattress in the garage. Anyhow, I let it pass, flow away, with my blood. Some things you never get back.

So when it came to honeymoon night, we were lying on a different mattress of crushed flowers, squashed tinsel and finger-lickin' crumbs. We both knew this should have been our first time, if we'd done things the proper way. Maybe blokes don't feel guilty about stuff like that, but I did. I wanted it to be special, to be proper. It's how I was brought up. I mean, of course I'd done loads of things I shouldn't have, like wearing blusher to school, and later on, skipping lessons to go to those midday raves in town with Tans and Sunny. They thought this was the height of excitement, but I always ended up feeling a bit stupid, squashed in a dark corner with some strange bloke's tongue in my ear. It's not like you can have a conversation. His mouth is full and you can't hear anything, and then there's that awful moment when you get home from school, back in your uniform, and have to pretend you got those marks on your neck from a falling dictionary in the library. But I always worried about what I was throwing away, all the rules my parents had given me I seemed to be chucking out the window. Because a lot of the time, you don't know what you might need until it's too late. It's all gone into the skip and then you think, Oh, I could have done with that crochet top, now it's back in fashion. That old lamp only needed a polish and who knows, there might be a genie inside. Some of the old rules hold you up; trouble is, you only find that out when they're being carted off in the rubbish van and you're left on the pavement in an embarrassing nightie wondering who's going to tell you what's right now. At least, that's how I felt then.

He unwrapped me like a present on our wedding night, our proper first time together as man and wife. That's how I felt; a longed for, favourite present he'd been asking for every Christmas since he was a kid, and finally, there I was under the tree with his name on my forehead. There was so much to take off; a billowing suit with fiddly hooks, nose rings, heavy bangles, not to mention the coconuts on each wrist. He looked straight into my eyes as he opened me up slowly, layer by layer, until it was just me and him and nothing between us any more. I've never been so frightened and so excited all at once.

He talked all the time, soft words, some in Hindi, not really to me but about me, my eyes, my hair, my fingers, my bwoti, my Chila. He discovered moles I didn't know I had, found bumps and crevices I'd never counted as part of my body. I'd never realized how dark I was until I saw his fingers on my skin. And when he . . . it wasn't the Dirty Dreadful Thing I'd been warned about, it wasn't the Fumbling Messy Thing we'd shared before, it wasn't even the Boring Back-Aching Thing I'd heard my mum's friends discussing in hushed whispers when they'd had a Babycham too many at some party: 'It's quick and he's nice to me after so, bas, I let him in sometimes.'

For me, it was a letting go. I fell into him and he caught me. I think he got a bit teary afterwards. His voice was all furry in the dark. And he thanked me again. All I could think of was how much I'd been lied to, all the years and horror stories spent on scaring us off what we'd just done. But at least I understood now why everyone spent so much energy stopping women doing it. It's bloody brilliant. It's the best kept secret in the whole bloody world.

It's a good job that I'm thick, I reckon, because my world is small, tidy and hoovered and I like that. Once I'd flunked school and Tans and Sunny had gone off to college or whatever, I knew it was time to pick myself up and make something of my life. I had relied on them for so long, I felt like a baby bird pushed out from the nest. So I got myself the job at Leos on the check-out, after considering some other offers (Sainsburys was too far and Safeway overalls are downright unflattering), and I was good at it. I'm good with people, always there with the chat, smiling at the kids who have eaten half the trolley before they reach the till, the old people with bent fingers who pay in loose change and the Care in the Community lot who know the price of everything and sing Beep! along with the computerized swipe. And especially the old Indian ladies who know I'll let them prod the aubergines for freshness without glaring at them and chat to them in Punjabi or Swahili about their good-for-nothing kids who leave them all day in unheated houses with piles of vegetables to cut for dinner. All life is in that supermarket and, watching it go by with the tins and packets, I knew I'd found my place.

In fact, I was up for promotion just before I got engaged to Deeps but he said no wife of his was going to work if she didn't want to. (I did want to as it happens but he forgot to ask me that bit.) I reckon it was more that he was a teensy bit embarrassed that his fiancée swiped cans of beans for a living, especially since I've met some of his friends' wives who wear sequinned tracksuits and spend one morning a week helping with their husbands' businesses and the rest of the time doing interesting charity events like Bhangra Nights for Bengali Flood Victims and posh dinners for Famine Relief.

I met some of them about a week after we'd got married. Laila, I think her name was, threw me a party to welcome me into their club. Her house was gorgeous, some mansion out in Chigwell, leather suites in cream silk, chandeliers and a little foreign waitress serving snacks. Actually, she was called Lenka, she was over from Prague because her husband had run off with their two kids and she was trying to get enough cash together so she could hire a lawyer to find her children. We got on really well, which was fortunate as I didn't talk to the business wives much. I mean, I tried but we didn't seem to have a lot in common and they'd go off in corners giggling and jingling their jewellery. Deeps said I just needed to get to know them better. I have invited them all over but it is the charity ball season apparently. I'm sure they'll visit soon.

So anyway, six months as a married woman and it's all going as expected, which is how I like it. We've settled into a nice routine, now I've got the house the way I wanted. You know, organized all my cupboards and drawers, found homes for my glass animal collection and his badminton trophies. Deeps is home regular as clockwork, except on the few days a month he has to entertain clients. He always offers to take me along but I'm happy catching up on the chat shows I video off cable and doing the little bits that make a house into a home, you know, lining all the drawers with scented paper, scraping the limescale off the bathroom tiles, with Sunrise Asian radio on full blast. I still listen to the Sunday matrimonial phone in (even though I don't have to now! It seems to have got so much more ... complicated). All those confident parents who ring up wanting a match for their kids, swearing their Bunty wants a religious graduate while you can hear their kid in the background shouting, 'No, I don't! I want someone in the media with a nice arse!' And all those divorced men with angry voices who say their wives didn't understand them and could they start again with someone who's about twenty-two ... (Funny though, you never get any divorced women ringing in ...) And the ones who really break my heart, the thirty-something single women, who start off all brassy and bright, they've all got degrees and they all know exactly what they want in a bloke: he's got to respect their parents but also know his own mind, be modern enough to load the dishwasher and traditional enough to swear in Punjabi, earn at least fifty k a year and also know the value of a walk in the moonlight, Western enough to be trendy, Indian enough to be pukka. By the time they've reached the end of the list, their voices are small and hopeless, like they've realized as they're saying it all how silly they sound. I mean, it's good to have standards, but how choosy can you be at thirty-four? You can't arrange a marriage and then expect to find perfection.

We have only had one argument during all this time. It wasn't even a row, just a silly tiff, when Deeps asked me why I had removed the plastic covers off the settee and the hall carpet that his mum insisted we should keep on, 'So it will last for ever, beti.' So I told him, Carpet isn't supposed to last for ever. Important things are, like good mates, and love. And I've waited so long for all of this that I don't want to save anything for Later On. I want it now, out of its wrapping, fresh.

So I get up with him at half past six, even though he says I don't have to. It's so nice, just making him some tea and toast in the morning and watching the sleep flake away from his eyes. Me in my kitchen with my man. Tania would kill me if she heard me say that. She always said I was too grateful. Beautiful women like her always say that, because they've never had a moment's worry that there isn't someone ready to open their doors or kiss them till their teeth hurt. But I am grateful, I admit it, especially for the little things. Like morning tea and seeing him off with a kiss and his briefcase, and planning what we'll eat when he comes home. And my favourite bit, when he wipes his plate round with that last bit of roti, stifles a burp and pats his knee. He doesn't have to say anything, I'm there, in his lap, and he just holds me, not so tight now, and I've managed to stop him saying thank you all the time because it was making me feel funny. I asked him, during the first week it was, why he kept thanking me and he said, 'You saved me.' But he won't tell me from what. Maybe he doesn't know.

The best advice my mum ever gave me was not to expect too much (the only thing she could say to me when I was growing up and messing up everything I touched). And it really works, you know. I've never been disappointed because everything good about Deeps is a big fat bonus. Every little lovely thing he does is a wonderful surprise. And I know that at some point in the future he's going to severely piss me off, but I'm ready for it. I look forward to it, funnily enough, because it's all part of the plan. You find someone, they love you, they hurt you, you forgive them, you carry on, because there's no question you'd give up on someone just because they've turned out to be human, is there?

I once tried to explain to Tania about how I felt when I was in that hut, with my catalogue and scissors and dizzy with happiness because I knew what I had to do and how to do it and that every day was the same and she looked at me like I was mad.

'Well, what about spontaneity?' she said. 'And adventure and fun and . . . you know, the thrill of things that you don't expect, that just happen? Why are we lot so hung up on having everything predictable and . . . decided?'

I just smiled at her, so full of love for her at that moment, so glad I wasn't in her head.

And then she shook all that hair, black cloud around a puzzled sun, I remember thinking, and she said, 'God, you're so bloody lucky, Chila.'

And it's sort of true actually. Compared to her and Sunita, I think I really am.

2

TANIA CURSED QUIETLY TO HERSELF AS THE LIGHTS CHANGED from green to amber and drew her jeep smoothly to a halt. A waddle of ancient Indian women in white widow's weeds creaked slowly across the zebra crossing, oblivious of the impatient honks of the traffic building up behind Tania. One of them, intriguingly, was carrying a large carrot which she proudly displayed to her friends, who paused to examine this fine specimen of root vegetable and congratulate their compatriot on her cunning at obtaining it. Tania jumped as the car behind her emitted a ten-decibel version of 'Colonel Bogie'. Early twenties Punjabi lad with goatee beard, gold earring, over-gelled hair and I Heart Khalistan stickers on his souped up Cortina, Tania bet herself, confirming her guess with a quick glance in her rearview mirror. The predictability of it all depressed her suddenly and she revved up impatiently, feeling, as she always did on this stretch of road, that she should have brought her passport.

There was border control, the Victorian police station on

the corner which separated the Eastenders from the Eastern-Enders; on one side, auto-part shops and a McDonald's, on the other, Kamla's Chiffons and the beginning of two miles of sweet emporiums, café-dhabas, opulent jewellers and surprisingly expensive Asian fashion boutiques. It was possible, literally, to stand with a foot in each world on this corner. In fact, she'd used this location several times in the many gritty documentaries she'd worked on, persuading some self-conscious presenter to stand legs akimbo, while they gravely intoned on the Scandal of Britain's Lost Urban Youth, the Secret Trauma of the Schoolgirl Brides, the Tomato which Contained a Message from God.

As the old women finally reached the pavement, helping each other negotiate the dizzying six inches of kerb, the car behind screeched in front of Tania, narrowly missing her bumper and the startled pensioners, and gave a final blast of horn before its driver sped down the broadway, spewing exhaust fumes in its wake.

Tania was used to being cut up by angry young men. She could feel them seethe as she drew up to junctions in her black and chrome four-wheel drive, feel them nudging each other, pointing, mouthing endearments and then obscenities when she refused, steadfastly, to respond. It had always been the same with Asian blokes; they didn't know whether to seduce her or slap her. Oh, she had played the game when she was younger, learned how to tread that fine line between tramp and tease, flirting just enough to make the boys feel flattered, but not too much, to make them think she was giving it away for free, training her eyes to promise what her body would not deliver, until she was married, of course.

She was rather good at it too. Even now, driving along the broadway of Little India, every corner held memories of a conquest, a secret assignation, a gently worded rejection, a humiliating heartbreak. The Lotus Café, with its all-year-round Christmas decorations, an island of yellow tinsel and red paper bells, where she had eaten cheese pakore and exchanged furtive greasy kisses with Jaz, the trembling sixth-former, who would blush the colour of tandoori chicken with one glance from her eyes. Pradeep's Sweet Mart, manned by a family of minuscule Gujeratis, spooky clones of each other, even the children and the grand-parents, all with the same pudding-basin fringe and doleful monkey eyes. They would stand in the kitchen doorway and stare sorrowfully at Tania at a corner table, whispering with her beau of the week. At hourly intervals, one of them would be despatched with another cup of tea or plate of chaat, banging it down pointedly, making the sugar crystals jump in their chipped, green glass bowls. Tania never looked directly at any of them. She was dizzy with her own beauty, drunk with freedom. If her parents didn't mind where she was, why should they? But every time she left, there they all were, arms folded, brows furrowed, huddled under a calendar of a fat, blue baby Krishna with his fingers in the butter churn, tiny simian judges, secure in their good-ness, revelling in her sin. Lahori's Kebab Hut, where Maz the would-be DJ had tried to grope her on the stairs and, after she'd refused him, informed anyone he met she was a desperate tramp who would give you a hand job for a free lassi.

The Delhi Silk House, where her mum would drag her at the beginning of every summer, the wedding season, insist-ing she would not shame the family by wearing last year's fashions. While her gasping mummy ran her work-worn hands over waterfalls of silks, mountains of beads, snow-storms of sequins, Tania would be out the back, giggling with the lads who worked at the halal butcher's next door.

On one occasion, her mother had actually suffered an asthma attack while perusing some hand-sewn sari blouses, probably brought on by the price tags, and Tania only found out when she finally went back upstairs and saw her mother slumped on the floor, still gripping her net shopping bag. For a moment, Tania had had the strangest sensation that the world had turned to stone, that Medusa herself had slithered through the rails of glittering fabrics, around the display cabinets gaudy with gold sets, intricate and heavy, smug in their velvet casing, swivelled her hissing head around the room of terrified matrons and gum-chewing teenage assistants and struck them mute and solid where they stood. Only when she came closer did she realize Mummy was sprawled at the painted feet of the shop mannequins, specially imported big-bosomed dummies with permanent beehives and sad almond eyes, gesturing uselessly to something on a far off horizon. 'Mama! Wake up. Why have they left you on your own?' Tania shouted, while her mother snatched shallow, raspy breaths. 'They . . . were . . . all . . . looking . . . for you,' she whispered, and slumped back, satisfied she had made her daughter feel guilty before she lost consciousness.

Tania blinked rapidly as a kaleidoscope of impressions danced across her windscreen, vivid and yet so removed, holiday slides flickering on a suburban wall; yeah, it was fun but you wouldn't want to live there. And once her mother had kept her promise that 'One day you will kill me, Tania,' and had keeled over at an engagement party, tired with the effort of having to breathe – always a struggle for a woman who'd donated most of her lungs to the laundry where she'd worked to feed her family – there was little reason for Tania to stay. Her father had chosen to move in with Tania's older brother, freeing her finally, though at that time, she was not quite sure for what.

She slowed down as she passed Riz's Music Mart, comforted by the group of teenagers that always hung around outside. This had been her favourite place. It had been a Saturday morning ritual, coming down here with Chila and Sunny, wanting to be the first to bag the latest Hindi film soundtrack, and later on, the bootleg tapes flooding in from Birmingham and Southall of the British bhangra bands. It must have been about fifteen years ago when Riz, the doped-out manager, had slotted a grubby-looking cassette into the shop's sound system and carefully turned the volume to bleeding ears level.

'You curies get a load of this band. British Punjabis, like us, recorded in one of their uncle's garage. Not those fat geezers in the John Travolta suits, swinging their medallions, singing about the bleeding harvest and birds in wet saris. This lot ain't much older than you.'

And the three of them were almost knocked back by the wall of sound and fury that came at them from the speakers. The drums they knew, their parents' heartbeat, folk songs sung in sitting rooms, the pulse of hundreds of family weddings; but then the guitars, cold steel and concrete, the smell of the Bullring, the frustration bouncing off walls in terraced houses in Handsworth, hurried cigarettes out of bathroom windows, secret assignations in libraries, hurrying home with a mouthful of fear and desire. The lyrics parodied I Love You Love Me Hindi film crooning, but with subtle, bitter twists, voices coming from the area between what was expected of kids like them and what they were really up to. Chila hadn't much taken to this new sound; she'd put her fingers in her ears and wandered off to the Lata Mangeshkar section, oblivious. Sunita had said 'Wow! Yeah' and possibly 'Wicked' (a new phrase that was just coming in, via their one and only black friend, Judith), but had decided not to buy the tape, not this time. Tania had practically begged Riz to let her take the bootleg home, where she played it for hours in her bedroom with the curtains drawn, until her father had banged on the door and threatened a beating with his shoe unless she turned down that howling from hell.

And now, what were they playing? Tania pressed a button and the jeep windows rolled down smoothly, allowing a blast of spiced air into the car, overlaid with car horns and the excited chattering of the teenagers on the pavement beside her. She recognized, with surprise, a line from one of her favourite old Hindi songs, but repeated scratchily, laid over jerky violins and a soporific single sitar note, with a pounding acid beat below it. She wanted to go with it, she felt a familiar tug and wanted to abandon herself to the sound, but she was wrong-footed, tripped up by the fractured lines of melody, alienated by the electronic thrum that throbbed like one of her migraines. She wanted to dance but didn't know the steps to this one.

The teenagers lounged easily against each other, girls in customized Punjabi suits, cut tight, set off by big boots and leather jackets, others in sari blouses twinned with khakis and platform trainers; one of them had placed bindis all around her perfect belly button. The boys favoured track-suit tops or kurtha shirts, love beads and pierced eyebrows; one of them had a turban, another wore his long hair in a thick plait that lay like some fat black snake on his back. Some of them smoked. None of them noticed Tania. They weren't looking over their shoulders, wondering who was watching. When did it become easier? Tania wondered, with a sharp stab of envy. She had a powerful urge to stick her head out of the window and tell them that they were standing on her street corner and if it hadn't been for her and all the mini-wars she had fought on this road, maybe they wouldn't be loafing around in their mix and match fashions listening to their masala music with not a care in the world. But once she realized she sounded like her dead mother, she turned the wheel sharply instead into Sunita's road.

Tania double parked, left her hazard lights on and negotiated the weeds and strewn plastic toys that led to Sunita's front door. The garden was a lush jungle, borders and beds overgrown years ago. The plastic recycling tub next to the front door was the neatest thing in the vicinity, bulging with carefully stacked Sunday supplements and a dozen red wine bottles. The posters tacked to the bay windows confirmed that the state of Sunita's garden was a statement rather than an accident. 'VOTE FOR MUHAMMED AZIZ, YOUR LOCAL LABOUR CANDIDATE' said one, the other advertised some benefit three years ago for Somalian refugees.

Sunita opened the door before Tania could ring the bell. Tania groaned inwardly, confronted with an all too familiar scene. Nikita was hanging onto Sunita's leg, whining sleepily, while behind them, Akash vainly walked a screaming Sunil up and down the cluttered hallway. Sunita was squeezed into a velvet dress which was already crumpled where Nikita had been holding onto it. Her hair was unbrushed and she had obviously had no time to apply make-up, as Tania could now see, for the first time, the greyish puffy bags underneath her apologetic eyes.

'I think Sunil's teething. He's been crying non-stop since I got home. Sorry, Tania—'

'Sunny! You can't do this to me again.'

'He won't settle, Tans. What can I do?'

'He's with his dad, isn't he?' Tania muttered, shooting a glance at Akash, who smiled thinly back.

He shifted his bawling son to his shoulder, suddenly aware of the hole in his jumper sleeve and wondered if the overhead light revealed his recently discovered bald patch.

Fleetingly, he remembered the article on Viagra he'd cut out from some magazine last night and hoped fervently it was not lying anywhere in Tania's vision.

'No. You go, sweetheart,' Akash said smoothly. 'He'll drop off soon. Or I'll go deaf. Either way, I'm happy.'

'I don't have to go you know . . .'

This was Sunita's mantra on the rare occasions she did venture out without a child surgically attached to her side. She looked pleadingly from Akash to Tania, begging acceptance from one, patience from the other. She searched Akash's eyes for any hint of disapproval, sensing his disappointment that she was leaving him holding the babies, when she knew he had a paper to finish that evening. She glanced quickly at Tania, hoping she would not pick up the wrinkle of distaste that had accompanied so many of their aborted evenings, Tania's reaction to the bad smell of motherhood that always spoiled their fun.

Sunita wondered if she did actually smell; she still had haldi stains on her fingertips and although she'd scrubbed and scrubbed her hands, garlic did linger, didn't it? Her breathing quickened. Small scrabbling insects began inching up her spine. She closed her eyes and forced herself to breathe deeply. What was it her yoga teacher had told her during pre-natal classes? In with the new air, out with the old air, bear down on the exhale, not too hard, ladies, as we don't want all those unwanted piles afterwards, do we? Sunita still had hers. That made her give up and open her eyes. Miraculously, Akash had gone into the kitchen. She could hear him opening the bribe cupboard where the sweetie stash was, while he murmured soothingly to Sunil in a baritone monotone. She turned to Tania.

'What did you do?'

'I just told him this was our first reunion since Chila's wedding and you were dying to see the pictures.'

Sunita picked up a hairbrush from the floor and hurriedly dragged it over her scalp. 'And?'

'And I said that only a man with a severe Oedipal complex and possible castration fears would stop his wife going out on the razz with her mates.'

Sunita stopped in mid-brush.

'It's always best to use the language they understand, Sunny. Now get your coat, you've pulled!'

Sunita grabbed her puffa jacket off a lopsided peg and only began laughing when she was sure the door was shut behind them.

Nevertheless Akash heard it. He handed Nikita another bag of Milky Stars and wondered if they were laughing about him.

'He's really getting into it, you know,' said Sunita, enjoying the smooth purr of the jeep and the faintly naughty smell of pristine leather. 'I mean, I thought when he gave up law, he'd go into this big depression because it was his childhood dream. You know, brown barrister in white wig overturning the fascist system. But therapy is such a growth industry, he says, and transcultural therapy, which he's so perfect for because he's bilingual, that's where the money is.' Sunita knew she was gabbling now, talking too fast and smiling too hard, but it was the only way she could push away the anxiety curdling her stomach. It always made her feel better to talk about Akash. She fondly imagined, hoped, that somehow, he would know. That he would pause at the kitchen counter and smile to himself, comforted that his absent wife was still thinking about him.

'And there was me thinking therapy was about helping people,' Tania said, smiling. She lit up a cigarette and handed it to Sunita, praying the nicotine would go straight to her friend's head and end the manic monologue.

'Well, of course it is, I mean, in the end, that's why he wants to do it,' Sunita said, pausing for a luxurious drag. 'To me, it's an extension of what he was doing before. Empowering the community, but this time, on a personal level. One to one. I mean, if he really wanted to clean up, he'd go into private practice, but he's already said, NHS referrals or nothing.'

She hesitated, suddenly light-headed. Indistinct particles swam before her eyes and then the world came back into focus but softer, less important. She beamed at Tania who was staring straight ahead, watching the road. Her pupils bloomed and shrank with the passing headlights.

She doesn't even blink, thought Sunita, suddenly transported back to a windy corner where she would stand holding Tania's duffle coat, a nauseous spectator to another playground battle. The opponents changed but Tania's strategy was always the same. As soon as she'd thrown her belongings at Sunita, Tania would wade in, arms swinging, talons outstretched, teeth bared, and always silent and unblinking. She wouldn't even flinch when Chila and Sunita took turns in wiping away blood and, on one occasion, trying to reinsert a large molar. 'Attack is the best form of defence,' Tania had lisped. 'Don't even give them time to think.' Catfights, the lads called these female bundles. They would stand around the edge of the skirmish, giggling at the hair-pulling and cheering any quick flash of a pair of school knickers when the girls were rolling around on the concrete. But when Tania fought, the boys didn't laugh. They stood in reverential silence, their hands unconsciously draped over their goolies. No wonder she didn't end up with an Asian man, Sunita concluded.

Sita, the good Hindu wife, walked through fire for Lord Rama to prove her purity. It was an image that had haunted Sunita throughout her childhood. If he had loved her, why didn't he believe her? It was only during the first few years of her marriage that she understood the subtext of that altruistic gesture. All those moments when she could have met fire with fire, risen to Akash's angry bait, let out the nine-headed demons to pull them apart. Instead, she chose to acquiesce, and he became putty in her hands, responding to her sweetness with immeasurable tenderness. Even now, after seven years, she could not remember one screaming match. Some long silences perhaps, some endless sulks, a few slamming doors. But they had not crossed that line, into the war zone where things were said and done which could not be undone. Not yet. A few burns on the soles of her feet were worth that, surely.

She could imagine what Tania's response would be to any man asking her to enter the flames for him; Tania would push him in and add petrol for good measure. And then invite her mates round for a barbecue. Sunita snorted loudly. Tania grinned at her, enjoying seeing her relax.

'And what about you? Still cleaning up after white trash, hmm?' Tania raised a perfectly arched eyebrow.

'Oh, we do get all nationalities coming in,' Sunita answered, a little too quickly. 'I know last time we spoke I was feeling a bit down about it. But there's a reason Citizens' Advice Bureau is abbreviated to CAB. Any prat can call in if you're for hire.'

Tania noted Sunita's defensiveness and let it go. She had seen the pock-marked desk in a gloomy corner where Sunny sat, day in, day out, dealing with the effluence of misery that washed in from the street. She'd once been trapped there for half an hour, having finished shooting early down Brick Lane, some documentary on the yuppie invasion of Bangla Town, and had offered Sunny a free lunch on the company. She of all people should have known there is no such thing. Her penance was to sit like some helpless contestant on *The Generation Game* and watch the conveyor belt of disaffection go by; see how many you can remember and take them all home with you tonite! The dead-eyed pregnant teenagers, the keening Romanian refugees, the bankrupt city boy still in his Gieves and Hawkes suit but with no place to sleep that night, the distraught father pleading to see his kids, the shaking mother desperate to get rid of hers. And finally, the shuffling old boy, snappy dresser, hanky in top pocket, spittle down his chin, raging against the bloody Pakis – er Pakistanis next door, while Sunita nodded soothingly and took notes with a Garfield pencil. Such a waste, Tania had thought. I should have been shooting in here.

'That would do my head in,' she said now. 'Having to advise some old git on how to deal with the curry smells wafting in from next door. Wasn't he going to press charges, that guy? Nasal harassment or some such bollocks?'

'Well, he was eighty odd, lived in the same house all his life, couldn't cope with a big Bengali family as his neighbours. I mean, they were noisy. I could sort of see his point. That's why it was so hard. I felt . . . disloyal. Both ways.' Sunita exhaled gently and watched the yellow neon lights above her flash past the car, fluorescent beads flying through an inky sky. 'It used to be simple, didn't it, Tans? Us and them. My job was clear. Defender of my people. Waving my flaming sword over their heads. I liked feeling useful. But some of them don't even say thank you. And most of them are so bloody angry.' She paused, squinting against the smoke, and handed the cigarette back to Tania. 'Maybe it's something to do with being a mother. You see everybody's point of view. I imagine some of the poor sods I meet as babies, gurgling on sheepskin rugs with dimpled bums, and I wonder what the hell happened to them between being on the rug and standing in front of my desk.'

'Oh god. Spare me the bad childhood crap. We're not just what's happened to us—'

'I'm not saying that,' snapped Sunita. 'I'm just saying . . . I'm saying I have to do this job because we can't afford for me not to. Not while Akash is still studying.'

'So you won't be moving to the mansion in Epping then?'

'Not yet.' Sunita sighed. 'But then, I never married him for his money, did I?'

'Tch! Did you learn nothing from your mother?' Tania waggled her finger at her mock sternly.

'Yeah well, at least I married a brahmin, unlike you, polluting your genes with a gora.' Sunita giggled. 'And what will your poor children be, hah? Crazy mixed up mongrels who won't know how to eat with their fingers.'

'No kids for me,' Tania said grimly, 'not unless they're scrambled and on toast.'

'And what does Martin think about that? He looks like good daddy material—'

'Martin knows the score,' Tania butted in smoothly. She began feeling around in the glove compartment. 'Now, what sounds do you fancy? Bit of nostalgic bhangra? Massive Attack? Blast of R and B?'

'I dunno . . . Educate me a bit,' said Sunita. 'Play some of this new fusion stuff they're all listening to. Is that what it's called? Indo-garage-funk-thingy. You know, you're hip and with it, aren't you?'

Tania paused for a second and then slipped *The Best Of Aretha* into the CD player.

'Ah, sod it,' she said. 'I'm off duty now.'

Chila stood in the doorway, flustered by the honking of Tania's horn. She glanced behind her at her new glass coffee table in the centre of the through lounge, groaning under the weight of plates of sweetmeats, freshly fried samosas and a just unwrapped Black Forest Gateau. Her surfaces were so polished they sparkled, just like the advert said. Maybe she had got it wrong, but she thought that they wanted to see her new house as well as her. She beckoned them over furiously, she mimed food going down her throat, she even rubbed her tummy and said Yum yum, which made Tania roll down her window finally, laughing.

'I've booked somewhere for dinner! Hurry up, Chila sweetie!'

Sunita tapped Tania apologetically. 'Er, don't you think we ought to go in for five minutes? You know, bless the three-piece suite and that?'

'Look, I was lucky to get this reservation. If we're late there's twenty other wannabes who'll just grab our table . . . Nice suit, girlfriend!'

Chila clambered into the back seat, panting slightly, her tailored Punjabi suit emphasizing her voluptuous bust and cushiony hips. 'Like the goddesses on the temples,' Deeps had told her last night. 'All woman, real woman. Stuff your pasty stick insects, eh? Men want a bit of meat in their sandwich!' She hadn't liked the last bit of that. It made her feel like she should cover herself with lime pickle and hand him a serviette. But she had kissed him all the same until her lips hurt. The yellow chiffon scarf settled around her shoulders, making her skin look almost black in the half-light.

'I didn't know we were going out. I mean, if I'd known, I could have put my Lycra on or whatever.'

'Nah, they'll love that look where we're going. Nothing like a bit of the genuine ethnic for their street cred,' said Tania, starting the engine.

'Where are we going?' Sunita and Chila said together.

'Soho. Innit?'

*

Tania led her brood right down the centre of Dean Street as the pavements were heaving with people, spilling out from restaurants and cafés, drinking in the balmy night air with their cappuccinos and bellinis, playing at Continental café society until the rain and frost reminded them they should really be indoors with a cup of cocoa and the TV guide. Behaving like a Brit is so dependent on the weather, thought Tania as she pushed her way through a group of bemused cagoule-clad tourists, cameras aimed at a couple of drag queens who were arguing dramatically in a doorway. At their feet, a bored young man in a parka shook a tin mug at them half-heartedly, perhaps hoping to catch a falling sequin. His mangy terrier lay with its paws on a hand-written notice that said 'The drugs don't work and I can't either. Please HELP!'

Shiny happy people laughed on every corner: office workers with their jackets on one shoulder and a girl in tan tights and a grateful smile on the other; the media wallahs in their uniform of distrait black and carefully unkempt hair, sending round wine bottles like Chinese whispers in their huddled smoky groups, greeting passing friends with loud joy, the joy that suddenly comes at those moments when life begins to resemble the film set in your head. Here we are in Soho and everybody knows me. Even a soundtrack was provided, the rasping melancholy notes filtering out from Ronnie Scott's, the parp of irate taxis and the windy blasts of cheesy show tunes escaping through swinging stage doors while actors in incongruous costumes snatched a quick between-acts cigarette. The only ones who seemed unaware that this was officially the centre of cool were the pre-theatre patrons up from the suburbs, men in shiny jackets and women in Jaeger twinsets, trying to mind their table manners with half an eye on the passing tramps and the other on the handbags under their seats, next to their matching shoes.

Tania strode past them contemptuously. This was her patch now. She did not want reminding that she once wandered down this street in a too-new suit, clutching photocopies of her mainly fabricated CV, envying the frazzled couriers and surly sandwich sellers who dashed in and out of various adjoining TV and film companies with the Bolshie haste of the permanently late. That was before media was a respectable profession for women like her. Now it had replaced pharmacy as the new aspiring Asian vocation and she was continually bumping into doe-eyed babes and mockney lads at industry gigs whose confidence reminded her how fine the line was between pioneer and has-been. She had been one of the first. That counted for something, didn't it?

She rang the buzzer of her club, tucked away between a patisserie and a fetish accessory shop, and bundled her charges inside proprietorially, half-expecting to see mittens on strings dangling from her friends' coat sleeves.

Sunita followed Chila up the narrow stairway which led into a bordello-like reception area, all red velvet and ironically tacky tassles, to a desk attended by two blonde women with icy smiles. She tugged instinctively at the hem of her velvet dress, knowing it was forming an unattractive shelf over her bottom. She felt overdressed and she could feel her tights beginning their inevitable sag around her crotch. She wondered why Tania's good nights out always felt like an audition. A plate of sag paneer and makhi thi roti in a local dhaba would have been enough for her.

'And two guests please, Sammi.' Tania smiled at one of the airbrushed Valkyries, who looked up for a moment and stopped, her pen in mid-air.

Chila was looking round with the wonder of a child in a department store grotto. She reached forward tentatively and held one of the gold tassles gently in the palm of her hand, letting the fringes dance a samba on her fingers.

'Did you get these from John Lewis?' she asked.

'I'm sorry?' said the receptionist politely.

'I think I've seen these in their luxury bedroom section. I was thinking of them for my bedroom. But in mauve. Gold's a bit showy, don't you think?'

Tania attempted an 'Oh you' chuckle and began moving up the stairs, beckoning the others to follow.

'My mum's got these in her sitting room, actually,' said the receptionist, her smile beginning to thaw into something approaching human. 'She calls it the Best Room. She makes me die!' The bored drawl had taken on a sing-song lilt that belonged in a suburban Midland parlour surrounded by chintz.

The other receptionist leaned forward and whispered, 'Loove your outfit, by the way. This stuff is really in at the mo. Is it DKNY?'

Chila looked down for a moment. 'No, Bimla's Bargains, Forest Gate, I think . . .'

They were still laughing about it two hours and three courses later, re-enacting the scenario with empty bottles and stained napkins, Chila good-naturedly taking up her role as idiot savant, pulling faces which made them clutch their sides and long for the bathroom.

Men paused at their table all evening en route to the bar or terrace, drawn by the three burnished moons floating in the half-light of Tania's favourite corner table. 'Jewels in an Ethiope's ear,' muttered one out of work actor as he fiddled with a stash of coke in his trouser pocket, hoping the mono-syllabic director he'd been schmoozing for three hours would still be there when he returned from the toilet, brighter and wittier than before. 'That's what I need,' mused another, as his yapping girlfriend stalked him around the bar, moaning that he had forgotten to book a table and it was their anniversary. He pictured the one in the lemon suit serving him a home-made korma and then leading him to a silk-lined bedroom, dropping veils as she went, and taking him through a few positions in the Karma Sutra before gratefully moaning his name as they drifted into incense-scented sleep. A couple of them attempted conversation, friends of Tania's friends, who sidled up with small talk and smiles.

Tania enjoyed seeing them witter, enjoyed the unspoken questions hanging in the smoky air. The sense of dislocation that dogged her like a shadow momentarily faded. She was used to not belonging anywhere totally. In fact, it was quite a relief to peel off the labels randomly stuck on her forehead somewhere around 1979, which read 'Culture Clash Victim – Handle with Care' or 'Oppressed Third World Woman – Give her a Grant.' She'd met enough people like her whose isolation was their calling card; being different, having an objective third eye, that's what her business wanted. 'All artists are lone wolves, remember that,' a producer had told her some years back, just before he had patted her knee and asked if she could operate a dictaphone.

Lately, though, something else was bothering her. She couldn't quite pinpoint what it was. The fatigue, well, that's what happened when you were swimming upstream all the time; the insomnia, that she'd suffered with since her teens. She took another sip of wine and watched Chila and Sunita whispering together, their hands linked unselfconsciously, and her heart creaked wearily in its cage. She was lonely. And it was only when she was with these women that she realized she was. She drained her glass in one swift gulp and banged it down on the table.

'Come on, Chila, let's get the photos out the way, then!'

Chila shook her head. 'Oh no, listen, you don't have

to . . . I mean, we can do it another time.'

'Photos! Photos!' Sunita began chanting, waving her serviette around like a celebration flag. Her face was flushed, she could feel cool air on her cleavage and knew her dress had given up the battle with her bust and let gravity do its work. On the spinning carousel in her head, she saw teething babies, grumpy husbands, unironed shirts, bathroom scales and the old man from her office float by. She waved them all on and drained another bottle of red wine.

Chila brought a small Cellophane-covered book from her bag and laid it carefully on the table. 'This is just the official ones of the reception. I couldn't fit the other twelve albums in my bag.'

'Suppose you've got a video too,' said Sunita, grabbing the album and flicking through it. 'Oh, look at you. Hai hai! Such a blushing virgin bride.'

'Yeah, about seventeen hours of video,' Chila sighed, 'all with Hindi love songs on them and those fancy *Top of the Pops* effects. You know, twenty little me's all swirling round on a glitter ball. Quite nice actually . . .'

'God, he's a bit of all right, your Deepak, isn't he?'

Tania looked over Sunita's shoulder at a glossy soft focus photograph in which Deepak stood stiffly behind Chila, his arm resting on her shoulder. Behind them was a garish rosy sunset over a golden beach. Just above the fringed palm trees was the logo 'Paradise Video and Photography Services, Barking.'

'You didn't go on honeymoon, did you?' asked Sunita.

Chila shook her head.

'Then what's with the beach?'

'Oh, no, the photographer put that on in his studio. It's really clever, innit?' Before Sunita could answer, Chila flipped over a page and said, 'And wait till you see what he's done with these.'

The first thing Sunita saw was Chila's head floating in the middle of a rose bush. She put down her wine glass and blinked slowly. No, it really was Chila's disembodied head in the middle of the blooms, in full bridal headgear, smiling uncertainly as if she was slightly embarrassed that the rest of her body had decided not to turn up. There was Chila and Deepak running towards each other, arms outstretched, the mountains of Simla behind them in glorious Technicolor.

'I love this one,' said Chila, pointing to a shot of the wedding car. In the middle of the Mercedes bumper were Chila and Deepak, or more precisely their superimposed heads, leaning towards each other for a kiss. It was obvious that this particular photographer had a sentimental streak, or maybe he wanted to try out a new pair of scissors he had just acquired, but the whole album resembled a collision between an Indian film from the early Seventies and Salvador Dali on his day off. Here was Deepak holding a rose to his face while fountains spurted knowingly behind him; there was Chila, in miniature, superimposed on a large red balloon hanging from the bridal canopy. Various guests and relatives made ghostly appearances on garlands, in shrubs and, in one instance, from the flames of the holy fire.

'Those are your in-laws, aren't they?' asked Sunita, too stunned to laugh by now.

'Yes, Deeps didn't like that one. He said his family looked like a row of kebabs. He hated this one too.' She pointed to the final photograph, a plate of food displaying the various sumptuous courses offered during the reception. And there, in the middle of the bed of rice, were Chila and Deepak, feeding each other a sweetmeat. 'I mean, I could see what he was trying to say,' Chila apologized, 'you know, here's the food and here's us eating. But I'm not sure it quite worked. Still, it's different, eh?'

Sunita and Tania carefully avoided looking at each other, aware of the tremor in Chila's voice. Protecting Chila was something they had always tacitly agreed on. 'Well . . .' Sunita began, clearing her throat, 'like I said, your hubbie's good enough to eat, so why not put him on a bed of basmati?'

Chila giggled, closing the book. 'Yeah, he'll do, as they say. Good job Tania's got such good taste in blokes, eh?'

'Pardon?' said Tania quickly, the hysteria of the photos suddenly evaporating.

'Well, I mean you did introduce us, Tans. Otherwise I'd still be sitting at home watching QVC and doing me toenails.'

'How did you know Deepak then?' asked Sunita, glad of an opportunity to steer the conversation away from Chila's album.

'Oh, you know, around,' Tania muttered, hunting for a cigarette, 'when I was looking for finance for this short film.'

'Deeps has seen all your programmes, you know,' Chila said smiling. 'Even got some of them on tape.'

'Got to go to the loo,' said Tania, getting up. 'Do you want to order some more wine, Sunny, while I'm gone?'

'Oh, I dunno. I should be getting back really.'

'They'll be fine,' said Tania over her shoulder. 'Just call home and check if it makes you feel better.'

By the time Tania returned, the table was empty. A waiter stood beside it, coughing slightly as he handed Tania the bill.

'They're in reception, I believe,' he said, his hand outstretched.

Sunita was sniffling into a paper tissue while Chila rubbed her back, crooning gently to her.

'She just phoned home. A neighbour answered and said Akash had to take Sunil to hospital.'

'I never should have left them,' Sunita sobbed. 'I just had a feeling . . . Tans, can you run me home?'

'I can't, Sunny, I'm over the limit. That's why I left my car in the office car park.'

'I've ordered her a cab,' said Chila calmly. 'I knew you were a bit merry. Do you want me to come with you, Sunny?'

Sunita shook her head. She was absent-mindedly shredding the tissue into flakes which settled like giant's dandruff on her black velvet lap. The two receptionists were fielding guests who had just arrived for a private party upstairs. The arrivals shoved their coats hurriedly across the desk and averted their eyes as they passed the three women in the corner.

Tania turned her back to the stairs. Tiny bubbles started bursting somewhere near her left temple and she swore to herself. It wasn't fair, getting the hangover before she'd gone to bed. She knew she could pick up the phone and ask Martin to come and pick her up but tonight she didn't feel like answering the hundreds of questions there always were, when she returned from a night out without him.

Tania felt a tap on her shoulder. She swung round to face her boss. Jonathan was in his usual uniform of cord jacket and faded denim, at odds with his slightly sagging jowls and neat side parting. He was swinging a bottle of Bollinger from each hand.

'Tans,' he gushed, planting a smacker on her cheek. 'Red Box are having a do upstairs, it's the wrap for the adultery doc for Carlton. You ought to call in, there's a few people you should meet.' It wasn't a request. Jonathan was already halfway up the stairs, following a couple of pert behinds in red Lycra.

Sunita was shuddering quietly now, taking in small shaky breaths. Chila was talking to the cab driver, who stood uncertainly in the doorway, assessing his cargo of misery.

'Jonathan?' Tania called, mounting the first couple of stairs. He poked his head around a banister, the grin wavering slightly. 'Um, it's just ... I've got a couple of friends with me.'

'Oh bring 'em all, Tans. More the merrier.'

Tania flashed him what she hoped was an alluring smile. 'That's sweet of you, but one of them ... well, she doesn't hold her alcohol like you do and I ought to get her home before she freaks out too much.' Jonathan straightened up. She had forgotten how tall he was and how, in certain lights, he resembled a slightly fanatic headmaster.

'Well the thing is, Tans, I thought we could maybe have a quick chat about your doc proposals for the *Cutting Edge* slot.'

Tania's neck prickled. She had been angling for a producer's credit and had worked for weeks on several ideas she considered hard-hitting and ballsy enough to warrant this step up in the company.

'They weren't what I expected, frankly,' Jonathan continued cheerily. 'And we have to get these in by next Monday. So see you up there, yeah? Good.'

Good. Excellent. Triffic. Jonathan had a list of friendly farewells which basically meant, Do as I say or prepare to remove this stapler from your arse. His reputation as a smiling executioner made everyone distrust him and long to work for him because he treated his staff like family and the competition as expendable vermin. Tania's palms sweated slightly as she descended the stairs, just in time to see Sunita being helped into her coat.

'You're sure you don't want me to come with you?' Chila asked, buttoning Sunita up briskly.

Sunita shook her head. 'I don't know how long I'll be at casualty. I don't know . . .'

Sunita was fortunately too preoccupied to catch the wave of relief that washed over Tania's face. Instead, she was trying to juggle the scenarios playing on a loop in her head. Sunil on an operating table, his small chubby limbs spread-eagled under a bright white light, Sunil bleeding on to his yellow Tigger pyjamas, Sunil lying blue-lipped and blood-less on a steel-topped table. She dived into her grief and discovered another layer underneath, a hot stream, slow moving and thick as lava, which bubbled its way up into her mouth and made her babble to herself on the long car ride home.

'The one night I go out . . . He couldn't look after them for one night. I leave them with him and he does this . . . I left their pyjamas washed and ironed on their beds, I left food ready on the cooker, I even left their favourite books out at the right pages for their bedtime story. I set the sodding video for his documentary on male rape in case he missed it while he was looking after the babies . . . our babies. Why did this happen when I did everything right?'

Somewhere a demon rattled its box and Sunita heard it. She let the thought that had been lying dormant, curled up and waiting in the only corner not filled with images of dead babies, speak to her. He does this on purpose. He does it so I'll be scared to go out and leave them again. Sunita pushed the thought away. She checked the chains on the box and sat on it for good measure. She felt calm. She got out of the cab in the hospital forecourt, paid the driver, walked towards the brightly lit Accident and Emergency sign, and vomited in the pansy-filled flower pots beneath it.

Two hours later, two long hours in which Tania had flitted

from table to table, her attempts at cheery banter so bright and brittle that she felt, at moments, transparent, Jonathan finally motioned her over. She made her way through the press of bodies, alcohol and smoke fumes shrouding them like a caul, briefly passing Chila who seemed deep in conversation with a group of people Tania didn't know. She couldn't see Chila's face, only the faces of those around her, animated with amusement, listening intently as Chila's hands made small graceful arcs through the blue haze.

'Not what I expected, Tans,' Jonathan began without preamble, handing her a glass of champagne. 'Bit samey, I thought. Touch of the earnest ghetto creeping into your ideas. Surprised me, actually . . .'

Tania watched the bubbles rushing madly to the rim of her glass. She scrolled through her proposal ideas: the new Asian underground music scene, the Harley Street scam in replacement hymen surgery for Asian and Saudi women, the balti kings of Birmingham. Not one mention of arranged marriages, for fuck's sake, no heavy exposés of mad Muslims, nothing involving hidden cameras. She had talked through all her ideas with Jonathan just two weeks ago and he had claimed to love them all. She wanted to ask the question that hovered at her lips during so many meetings where a panel of forty-something white men told her what was important and real. All those moments where she had sat tight-lipped and buttocks clenched as Rupert or Donald or Angus nibbled on ciabatta and explained to her what it meant to be Asian and British, at least for the purposes of television.

'I don't know,' she began, surprised at how steady her voice was, 'what you mean exactly, Jonathan.'

'Well, it's victim mentality TV, isn't it? Let's look at these strange brown people and admire their spunk or pity their struggles. What about the happy stories? What about the

Asians who like who they are, who just get on and do it and . . . live? Yeah?'

Tania cleared her throat. 'Well, the idea about Asian millionaires. Can't get much more of a success story than that. Or the balti kings, they've transformed the—'

'No more restaurant gigs,' Jonathan interrupted tartly. 'And no more chinging cash registers. We want the human angle now. How people love, who they love, that tells you more than a skipload of earnest statistics . . . Hi, David! Got over Edinburgh yet?'

Jonathan turned away but placed a proprietorial arm on Tania's back, telling her to wait. She felt herself stiffen in response. Her fingers curled instinctively into a fist and she wondered if she might hit him. She could not work out why or how he had suddenly acquired this streak of sentimental zeal. 'Political with a small p' was Jonathan's catchphrase. Usually, anything that reeked of sob TV was thrown out, along with papers, coffee cups and, on one occasion, a laptop computer, with the cry, 'If that's the best you can do, call up fucking Desmond Wilcox and give me a break!' She briefly mourned all the human interest stories she had proffered over the last year. Maybe it was the male menopause finally taking hold. He was showing all the classic signs, squeezing into inappropriate denim, quoting bits from *Loaded* magazine, finding topless calendars funny in a post-modern, blokey sort of way, acquiring a sudden and passionate interest in football . . . Who had he been talking to?

Jonathan turned back to her in mid-chuckle. 'What's wrong with not having a problem, innit?'

Tania blinked. 'What did you just say?' Everything fell into place, noisily, with a final bang.

Jonathan looked over at Chila, who was now on a low settee, her face open like a flower. 'She's a remarkable woman, your friend. Do you know how rare it is, how much people want to see and have what she has?'

'What, an off-the-peg Indian suit and a mock Tudor porch?'

'Innocence,' continued Jonathan. 'What a story, eh? Holding on for her Prince Charming, finding her soulmate through an arranged marriage. You couldn't make this stuff up.'

Tania swallowed what felt like a large fur ball. 'Let me just get this straight, Jonathan. You want me to do a doc on arranged marriage? That heads the crappy cliché list along with corner shops, long-suffering Indian waiters and smiling beggars whose gangrenous stumps hide a wisdom we will never understand.'

'I didn't say that. I said do something on her, and others like her. Relationships. The new religion of the millennium. Take a note of these buzzwords, Tans: curious, restless, landmark, a unique insight into ordinary people on an extraordinary journey. Got it now? Triffic.' He snaked off into the crowd.

Tania swung the other way, finding herself standing over Chila, who looked up at her warmly.

'Shall we go?' Tania said, feeling inexplicably betrayed.

Chila snuggled happily into her red velvet chair in reception, watching her clever and pretty friend on the phone. She liked watching Tania when she did not know she was being watched. She liked having a friend who made heads turn as they walked out together, who moved through parties like the one tonight with such grace and ease. Chila had been surprised by how easily she had managed to talk to people this evening. Tania was always going on about how shallow and cliquy some of this crowd were, but Chila had been amazed at how interested everyone had been in her, asking her millions of questions, laughing at her tales from suburbia, wanting to know about her family, where she grew up, her lovely husband.

Deeps had sounded a little strange when she had phoned him up on his mobile a few minutes ago. 'Why aren't you at home?' he had demanded.

'Well, neither are you, jaan.' Chila had wanted to launch into a detailed account of the glamorous folk she had encountered but he interrupted her sharply.

'You should have told me, sweetheart, that you were going out. I've been ringing home all evening, wondering where you were.'

'I didn't know we were going out,' Chila replied in a small voice. 'I had cooked and everything but Tania wanted to show me her club, so—'

'It's OK, baby,' Deepak said quickly. 'As long as you're safe.' He paused for a moment, the hiss of the phone filling the silence. 'So you went to all the trouble of cooking and they didn't even bother to come in, eh?'

'Yeah, well. It was only snacks, so . . . But I've had a really good time. Missed you though, jaan.'

Deepak chuckled. 'We can make up for that later.'

After he had promised to come and pick her up, and after she had made him blow her a kiss down the phone despite his protests that he was in a restaurant and everyone was watching, she spent a few delicious minutes anticipating their reunion in the soft furry darkness of their bedroom. She closed her eyes and imagined the way the door creaked slightly when he closed it, the soft pad of his feet across their deep shag pile, the pale yellow light criss-crossing the floor (he liked the curtains open and light off; natural ambience, he told her), the weight of him as he moved into her, the strong fingers entwined in her hair, the precipice between pleasure and pain on which she hovered as he held her too hard, loved her too much . . . In her reverie, a bedside light came on suddenly. Something was bothering her, something Deepak had said to her. Then she remembered. 'They didn't even bother to come in, eh?' How had he known that?

The receptionist called over to her. 'Your husband's here. Shall I buzz him up?'

Tania looked up from the telephone cradle. 'You go, Chila. My cab's on its way. You must be tired.'

Chila stood up uncertainly. 'Don't you want to say hello?'

Tania replaced the receiver carefully. 'Of course,' she said finally. She saw his hand first, curled round the banister, and noted with satisfaction that he still bit his nails. And then he was in front of her. She photographed him in hurried stills, pieces of him. Sharp suit, that soft female mouth, curious caterpillars for eyebrows, wedding ring, he needs a shave . . .

Deepak enfolded Chila in a bear hug and cupped his hand around her face, as if looking for signs of corruption. He saw the same eyes looking back at him, no questions being asked, no secrets glinting in corners. He avoided Tania's gaze for a few seconds, knowing she was doing the same, their agreement still in place and tacitly sealed with too many kisses he would rather not recall. Ex-girlfriends were not normally a problem, as he had usually been the one to walk away. These mutual it's for the best separations were the ones he hated, because if you left with good will, it meant it was never really over. Some sparks always lingered, fanned by the hand of friendship. He did not need any more friends, thank you. Marriage was a rebirth for him, a cleansing away of his sorry past, all his karmic junk thrown into the holy fire, taken away by a priest who thought he was Elvis.

'How you doing, Tania?' He smiled, holding tightly onto Chila, who had already burrowed her small hands into his pockets.

'Good. You?'

'Good.' Distant sirens filled the pause.

'You need a lift anywhere?'

Tania shook her head.

'Tans has got a cab booked,' volunteered Chila, 'but we should wait with her, hena jaan?' Chila's tender Punjabi endearment made Tania fumble for her coat.

'In that case,' Deepak said, making for the stairs, 'I'll go and check if it's arrived.'

'But the receptionist will . . .' Chila trailed off as Deepak swept out. She took Tania's hand, marvelling at how cold it was.

'She'll be OK, you know.' Tania nodded dumbly, understanding nothing. 'I've been thinking about her all evening as well. I was feeling a bit guilty, actually, enjoying myself and all that. But I phoned her house about an hour ago and the neighbour said they were on their way back home and he's fine.'

'Sorry?' said Tania finally.

'Sunil. Sunny's baby. He's going to be fine.'

'Triffic.'

Deepak appeared at the doorway. 'Your cab's here, Tans, and we ought to be off, sweetheart.'

Chila held Tania close. 'Don't be a stranger, eh?'

As the car accelerated between speed bumps, Sunita supported Sunil's head, tracing the livid yellow bruise across his temple with a gentle fingertip. His breathing was even, baby breaths, snuffles like a small animal. She tried to breathe with him, wishing she could sleep with such abandon.

'It was an accident,' Akash said quietly. 'I didn't leave him. I saw it happen.'

Sunita stared straight ahead at the ribbon of unfolding road.

'If it had happened when you were there, I wouldn't have blamed you,' Akash said, more loudly this time.

'I'm always there, Akash,' Sunita replied evenly. 'Except for tonight . . .'

'Oh for f—' Akash bit his lip rather too forcefully. He knew his son was asleep, but he was always alert to the power of the ever-vigilant subconscious. And if his son came out with the f-word at nursery, he suspected that unwitting autosuggestion would not be an adequate excuse. He unpeeled teeth from flesh and thought he tasted blood.

'Things happen, Sunita. Accidents happen. I know you spend most of your time trying to make the world turn perfectly and safely but some things you can't control—' He broke off to negotiate a junction, risking a quick glance over his shoulder. 'I only took him in to check he wasn't concussed. That's why I didn't ring you. I knew you would panic. I mean, have you ever considered how much you over-worry? That's why when things do go wrong, you get it all out of proportion. Don't you think that's part of the problem too?'

'Akash,' Sunita said wearily, 'I am not one of your clients.'

Akash crunched the gears angrily. He wanted to tell her about a visualization exercise he had done in his own therapy session last week. He had been asked to imagine that his conscience was a person or an object, to give a solid shape to the guilt and fears that he grappled with. And Sunita appeared in an egg-stained nightie with a child in each arm, looking pretty much as she did right now.

'Well,' he said shortly, 'I can recommend a number of good people if you want to see someone.'

Sunita closed her eyes. 'Piss off, Akash,' she said.

The car glided smoothly onto the A40.

'Now,' said Deepak, and he put his foot onto the clutch

as Chila changed into fourth gear for him. She had devised this dual-control driving game quite early on in their courtship and he indulged her willingly, adding it to the growing list of her unworldly charms.

At first, her child-like playfulness had worried him, alert as he was to the local whispers of the girl being a few chapattis short of a thali. Of course, Tania had often spoken about Chila, always with defensive affection, as if expecting him, or anyone nearby, to launch into a tirade of abuse about her funny, soft-hearted friend. But then, once Tania discovered that he was seeing Chila, she seemed to change tack, warning him off her, almost as if, and this only struck Deepak now, *he* was not good enough for Chila.

So naturally, he began to worry when Chila dragged him into the Disney store to coo over the Beauty and the Beast duvet covers, and when she gathered up fallen leaves, wondering at their colours, and later painted them with clear nail varnish to make a pretty yet handy bookmark. The faces of delight she would pull while eating ice cream, messily and with abandon, the kisses she would lavish on passing beasts and babies, her laugh, a musical honk, full of snorts and side-holding, the way she would grab his arm and cling on to it happily, dragging him along, anxious not to miss the next experience. Deepak was both repulsed and enchanted. If this was a clever tactic, playing the fluffy female to appeal to his manly instincts, it was skilfully done and annoyingly effective. It did make him want to protect her, teach her, and the paternal feelings she aroused bothered him greatly (until he argued with himself that, at thirty-two, she was no spring chicken). Which left the other less savoury option that the woman had suffered some early injury to the head and he would end his days either feeding her liquidized cabbage or accompanying men in white coats to rescue her from motorways and park benches.

It was only after a month or so, when he had been wavering between jumping her bones or a gentle let-down before moving on, that he finally understood Chila was no actress. He remembered the moment clearly; they were in some West End store, killing time before their film began, and suddenly Chila had disappeared. He found her in the fur department. She had somehow eluded the security chains and was sitting between a couple of mink coats, running her hands slowly over their surface. Her eyes were closed, her lips parted, she trailed her fingers sensuously through the fur, lost in the moment. Deepak's stomach did a Mexican wave. How could she be so erotic without even trying? She opened her eyes and whispered to him, 'They are so beautiful, and so cruel. Isn't that weird?'

And in that one sentence she summed up all the women who had gone before her in Deepak's life. Snappy witty women with low-fat bodies and high-maintenance demands, who sneered when he offered to open doors and snivelled if he didn't smile patiently while they wittered on about their problems. But as they fitted his criteria for a suitable mate, he had learned what to do to keep hassle at a minimum: go Dutch on dates unless it was a special occasion or he intended to make some unusual demand in bed later on, encourage time out with their girlfriends so he could spend an evening farting in front of the TV in his boxers, enjoying making a mess, and always use his family as an excuse if they ever put pressure on him to commit. It always worked with the white women and sorted out the stayers from the players. (With Tania, of course, the reasons for breaking up had been much more complex.) But in any case, at that moment, when he saw his Chila snuggled up in mink, he realized all the compromises he had made in previous relationships had been much more of a childish game than changing gears together on a dual carriageway.

He was glad he had hung around to check on Chila that evening. True, he had felt a bit stupid, parked with his lights off outside a neighbour's drive, pretending to read an old copy of the *Financial Times*. But that sudden rush of warmth that flooded his whole body, when he saw Tania shouting to Chila through the window of her jeep, well, that told him he had done the right thing. Checking up on Chila, that is. What else could that belly-churning feeling have been?

Chila squeezed his hand on the gear stick. 'What you thinking, jaan?'

'Kuch nahin.' He smiled and squeezed back, hard.

The car pulled up to Tania's flat and Martin was already opening the door, a mug of tea in his hand. Tania threw some notes at the driver and walked slowly towards the rectangle of light, feeling more exhausted with each step. She stepped into Martin's open arms and leaned her head on his chest, sniffing his familiar scent of toast, fags and soap, simple pleasures, Martin's smell.

'Hey,' he said gently, juggling tea and a free arm. 'Plum tuckered out, are you?'

Tania nodded.

'Hot bath and a stiff vodka?'

Tania shook her head, not knowing why she felt tearful.

'How about a good seeing to from a blond Adonis who's been slaving over a hot computer for hours and only produced some jokes that Jim Davidson would call unsubtle?'

Tania didn't move her head at all.

'Hey,' Martin said again, 'What's up?'

Tania did not know how to tell him. What was up was that she wished he would call her jaan.

Sunita

PAIN IS A RELATIVE CONCEPT. I USED TO BE THE BIGGEST whinger in the world when it came to doctors, dentists, cuts and scrapes as a kid. My mother would have to physically restrain me to apply water and Savlon, while the neighbours wondered if those Arabs at number thirty-two would ever stop beating their children. Later on, after we had moved from the village near Bolton where we were, literally, the local colour, to the East End suburb where, God, I still am, we acquired lots of new neighbours who, joy of joys, looked just like us. (That's when my dad stopped ordering a daily newspaper. He said if we wanted to know who was doing what in the world, all we had to do was pop next door.)

It was a shock, the lack of privacy, having been the odd-balls whom people left alone. Luckily I met Tania on my first day in the new school. As it happens, I was screaming my oiled and plaited head off, having squashed my finger in a door hinge, freaking out as I always did at the sight of my own blood. She shrugged, told me off for being a pathetic kid and warned me that showing any weakness pretty much guaranteed I would soon be fishing my satchel out of a toilet. And then she put my finger in her mouth and sucked the blood away. Always had a sense of drama, that girl. I didn't mind being boring fat friend though. You got hit less, which was fine by me.

Still, it was a good lesson, and even though I felt the pain as much as I ever did, I learned how to disguise it. I grimaced my way through inoculations, period cramps, occasional netball accidents, and that awful, terrifying day when I underwent my first bikini-line wax. (It's funny, but now it's politically OK to remove unwanted hair, I don't bother. Call it my contribution to reclaiming the rainforest.) Tania insisted that this skin-ripping torture was nothing compared to a broken heart, but as I hadn't had a boyfriend yet and she had already shimmied her way through most of the local youths, I had to take her word for it.

I got my own back when I had Nikita though. When Tans wafted in with flowers and pink teddy bears and asked how it was, I threw up my nightie and showed her my episiotomy scar.

'This was the bit my wimmin's group told me to call my womanly flower. Venus fly trap is more like it, eh?'

Tania went slightly green so I carried on. I described in exquisite detail the twenty-hour labour, the progression from planned water birth with Vivaldi playing to lying in stirrups, fanny to the wind, all hope and dignity gone as I pleaded for anyone with a steady hand to give me an epidural and/or kill me quickly. I left nothing out, not even that moment when my Irish midwife told me to be a good girl and push, with Akash crouching next to her, tears forming at the thought of his first beloved child about to enter the world, and how their faces changed from birthday card beams to silent film screams when I strained for Britain and produced nothing but a fat warm turd. (There's all these theories now that you shouldn't allow your partner to see you give birth as it destroys the mystery that is an essential part of eroticism. You don't say!)

I told her how the barn door forceps they eventually used had left ravines that would never close up and muscles so slack that wearing tampons would now be a pointless exercise. 'Cocktail sausage in the Blackwall Tunnel,' I tittered through the drugs. I mentioned in passing the cracked nipples that yielded watery blood mixed with my body's milk, the amusing ritual I had to undergo at every toilet visit, wrapping tissue paper around my hand and holding my stitches as I sat, in case they burst with the strain. And the really funny bit, the smiling visitor I got my first morning in hospital, having been too terrified to sleep in case this precious scrap of human being forgot she was no longer inside me and stopped breathing.

'Mrs Bhandari,' the kindly woman said, sitting next to me, avoiding my drip. 'What contraception will you be using when, um, relationships resume?'

I pointed to Nikita, swaddled in her cot.

'Her,' I said.

Tania reassures me that she had already decided she didn't want children before I told her all this, but tell her I had to. She knew I had been a physical coward all my life, hiding my eyes in her duffle coat while she had her weekly scraps, and I wanted her to know that I had stared pain in its fanged grinning face and survived. Now I knew what real agony was, I reckoned nothing would be as frightening again.

That's what I thought, until that night when Sunil was rushed to hospital and for the whole of the ninety-minute cab ride, I thought he was dead. Labour pain has a point. Otherwise why would any woman ever have more than one child? No-one would volunteer to pass their insides out of a small hole without knowing there was life at the end of it. That's what sustained me through Sunil's birth, which was, thank Vishnu, much quicker as I ended up having an emergency Caesarean. (My son wanted to hit the ground running and decided to try and emerge feet first. Akash cracked some joke about his lad showing early signs of playing for England but quickly apologized for his un-PC comment. Like it fooled anybody . . .)

But in that taxi I felt I was hurtling through the night along an endless tunnel towards a bottomless pit, and that the falling would be slow, dark and for ever. That is what you see on the faces of those parents on the news, whose children never came home. That is something I see in passing, just the shadow of the thing's huge black wing, on some of the faces who turn up at my desk, wanting me to paper over the Grand Canyon with a few legal placebos, when we all know my sad corner is often the last stop before depair. It is the hell of limbo.

I tried to explain to Akash that I was not being a neurotic woman, it was just that he knew what was going on and I didn't. It was just me and my imagination in that taxi, and we've never got on too well when left alone in dark places. All he kept saying was, 'You swore at me, Sunita,' and that was something I had never done before. Apparently. So Sita has an off day sometimes! I told him, although he didn't get the joke. Not that it was, really.

Any road up, as we used to say up North when we were trying to fit in, in the three months since Sunny's tumble off the kitchen counter (don't even ask me what he was doing up there holding a potentially lethal Batman car), something's happened. Or is happening. Maybe my thoughtless piss off has triggered some childhood trauma in my husband's teeming psyche, maybe when I tumbled into casualty with a dripping nose and bits of barf down my front, he decided to go off me (the final straw after seeing me give birth twice, put on three stone and regularly hunt for underwear in the dirty washing basket), but it seems he's finally decided to chuck me without actually saying it, or indeed doing anything much different. He still comes home at approximately the same time, still helps wash and feed the kids occasionally, still disappears into his study the minute they are in bed and sits at his computer with a glass of wine and his one evening joint (window wide open and towel stuffed under the door, in case illegal fumes give away the one bit of youthful rebellion we still possess). True, he doesn't offer to cook any more, but that began when he started this training course. We don't go out much as a couple, but as we don't have a regular babysitter, having fun separately and in shifts seems the only sensible option. (Not that I've gone out since the Accident. Not that I've been asked to actually, apart from Tans and Chila ringing me up about movies and occasional meals. And whenever I say I can't make it, they cancel the whole thing, as if it's my fault that I've ruined their evening. Why they don't just go out together is beyond me.)

So it is not as if Akash is behaving oddly. He still goes through the motions, but it is as if he has checked out for a holiday, leaving his body behind. As a good Hindu girl, I should understand this. I still have the calendar that Mum brought home from one of her religious knees-ups, which was entitled the Migration of the Soul. This colourful wall-hanging features a man tending his cattle in a lush green meadow, while a woman washes clothes at a nearby stream and a beatific looking priest with a shaved head lurks point-lessly behind a tree. On each of their breasts is a swirling fiery sun, on every tree and bush, on the foreheads of the cows and birds and insects and in the centre of the sun is the symbol for God, Om.

'You see?' Uncle with Patterned Jumpers blared in my ear. 'This shows us that God is in every living thing. Our bodies are just vehicles to carry round the soul.'

'Like your Datsun Sunny, Uncle?' I asked.

'Er, well, something like that, yes. So if the body is a car, the soul is the driver, you see? And if the car crashes and is broken beyond repair, the soul merely moves into another car, er, body. Like so.' He pointed to a caterpillar in the picture, reclining gracefully on a leaf. 'These are the lower souls, you see? Bad people become the lowly animals. And if you are a good caterpillar you might become—'

'A tree?' I asked hopefully.

'No, plants come under creeping things. Maybe a cow. And after a cow? If you are a good cow, what do you think you would come back as, Sunita?'

I scanned the various options laid out before me, and pointed confidently to the turbaned man holding a staff. 'The man next.'

'No no no, silly girl,' tutted Uncle, adjusting his psychedelic tank top. 'First a cow, then' – his finger moved over to the stream – 'a woman. Then if you behave yourself, you come back as a man, and then of course, top position, number one car is the priest. The Rolls-Royce of the karmic cycle, yes?' He chuckled to himself and glanced round, extremely disappointed that there were no other adults in the vicinity to applaud his wit.

I hesitated for a moment. 'But women can't become priests, can they, Uncle?'

Uncle stared at me for a second, then got up, said, 'Finish your dinner,' and walked out.

I suppose that was some sort of turning point for me, young as I was. I grew up with three older brothers, so was quite used to being alternately spoiled and lectured by my parents. But this was different. This was a blatant example of unfairness, and someone had to explain it to me. (It's always got to me, which is why I ended up doing this job. Except now I understand why Justice wears a blindfold. And on some days, I'd kill for her sword in my bottom drawer.) Anyway, asking my parents was not a good idea. It would only get back to Patterned Jumper Uncle and he would in turn blame them for raising a mouthy curie who questioned the word of an elder. (By then I knew how the mafia worked: they always defend their own.) So I ran through the grown ups I could possibly approach without it becoming a minor scandal.

There were too many aunties and uncles to remember their names, so I gave them my own titles, based on their most memorable characteristic. There were the obvious ones like Ginger Auntie (over fond of the henna bottle), Car Keys Uncle (hands for ever in his pockets jingling things, at least I hoped they were his keys), Halitosis Uncle (no explanation needed), My Bobby Auntie (never stopped boasting about her fat son who, incidentally, ended up serving time for fraud) and my personal favourite, Existential Uncle, a tall thin man who never spoke when spoken to, but would occasionally interrupt others' conversation without warning, with loud comments such as 'Why it is, huh?' or 'They spoil everything, bastards!'

I finally settled on Modern Auntie as my confidante. It almost felt wrong to bestow the auntie label on her as she was nothing like the overweight fussy women who seemed to live at my house at weekends.

Modern Auntie was beautiful, really beautiful, with sharp aquiline features and sleek black hair like a Mughal miniature, except her hair was cut short in a fashionable bob. And she wore make-up. But not the usual auntie warpaint of bright orange lipstick (much of it on the front teeth) and alarming smears of eyeshadow. She used it to give her face shadows and contours. On close inspection, I realized she employed three different kinds of powder on her eyes, a gold wash on her lid, a dark matt on her socket, and a shiny glittery shade on her browbone. She showed me her palette once. It looked as complicated as the controls of a tank and I asked her if it was hard to remember what went where.

'Beti, when it comes to looking good, you have to understand it is a war, which you will lose as you gradually get older.'

God, how I understand what she means now! And while the other women favoured bright sequinned clothes for formal do's, and haldi-stained Punjabi suits for informal at-home meetings, I never saw her in anything except sleek, subtle saris, no pattern except on the pullau and hem, and the simplest gold jewellery.

I noticed the way the room would often fall quiet when she entered, women coagulating into whispering groups and men smoothing stray hair over their bald patches and hitching up their trousers expectantly, and I always thought it was her beauty and poise that unnerved them, the way she held her head high, her armour on, ready for battle. It was only when I told her that I secretly called her Modern Auntie that I discovered the source of her strange effect on others.

'Is that how you see me, beti!' She hugged me warmly and whispered, 'Well, that's much nicer than the name everyone else has given me.'

'What name?' I asked, happy to be inhaling her expensive perfume and feeling her bangles sing against my body.

'Divorced Auntie, of course.'

It took a few minutes for this to sink in. I had never ever met anyone divorced before, anyone Indian I mean. There were two single mothers back in the village, but no-one in my family was the least bit interested in them. In fact, we were surprised there weren't more of them. Divorce was one of the English diseases my mum was afraid we would catch if we hung around Willis' Fish Bar too much, along with short skirts, bad skin and bland food.

I had only seen Asian divorcees in the Hindi films we would watch around Gadget Uncle's house, the one person we knew who owned a video recorder. They were fairly easy to spot; they would have names like Kitten or Junglee, and enter scenes on a motorbike in black leather catsuits, chain smoking. They would puff out smoke clumsily and say sentences in gruff Hindi with the odd Bastard! and OK cool cat? thrown in somewhere. Usually, they would try and steal the hero away from the heroine, who was always a pudgy-faced doll given to fainting fits and saying prayers at every opportunity. And naturally, Divorced Woman never got her man. Who would want shop-soiled goods? That was a phrase she actually used, Modern Auntie, when we had our girly chat.

'You see, Sunny, how the women hate me because I walk in looking good, instead of crawling in on my knees, begging for them to like me? Pity me. And you watch how many of your uncles come and sweet talk me when their wives aren't looking. They think because I have no man, I will be grateful for their scraps. It is OK to wipe your hands on shop-soiled goods, hena?'

She told me about her ex-husband. Or rather, she listed her visits to hospital: 'Five broken ribs, nose broken twice, broken arm, burns to chest . . . No low-cut tops for me, sweetie. And I am the whore for leaving him, apparently.'

I sat next to her, sweating, not wanting to listen to this, afraid of what I would hear next, all thoughts of a chat about reincarnation long gone.

I swear I remember hearing actual cogs whirring in my head, the clanking of machinery as I began to reconstruct my small friendly world. I began to notice things I had never noticed before. The way the men would enter the house and sit, playing cards, waiting to be served while the women ran in clucking circles around them. The way my brothers would waltz in and out of the house with their mates, rolling back whenever they wanted, not even seeing my mother waiting up for them at the kitchen table, their dinners reheated and ready. The stash of gold my mother showed me one wintry evening when all the men were out, hidden in a rolled up sari at the back of the wardrobe.

'My insurance,' she said, unfurling heavy yellow bangles, triple-stranded necklaces, filigree earrings. 'We don't have bank accounts so we have these. Just in case.'

Sitting next to Modern Auntie, I suddenly realized what the just in case meant.

'I hope he comes back as a slug,' I eventually said.

She laughed. She had a wonderful laugh, earthy, smoky with sadness somewhere. 'The slug, dear child, is living in a big house in Ealing with his new wife and two kids. Men can always start again, can't they?'

I am so ashamed to admit this but I didn't talk to her much after that. I mean, that's one of my last memories of her and perhaps she just moved on. Or was moved on. She fascinated me but also scared me more than anything else, even the impending TB jab at school. In fact, after I got up from the settee and went upstairs to the toilet, I had my first ever panic attack. One moment I was staring at a spot on my chin in the bathroom mirror, the next I was gasping for breath, feeling the whole world was about to crack and fall around me. Everything looked different: the familiar wallpaper with its blue and yellow squares, the toothbrushes in the cracked mug on the sink, my own face. I hated her for making me see stuff I hadn't noticed before. And later on, much later, I thanked her for it. I reckon that was my first baby step along the road that led me to read law at university. It was also the reason I warmed to Chila straight away when Tania pointed her out to me, the little fat girl carefully balancing along the white lines of the netball court in the playground. Someone else whose story hadn't been heard, who needed someone like me to shout it. I need to remember stuff like this. Especially lately. I need to remind myself that I started out with the best intentions.

I got called Auntie for the first time recently, by one of Nikita's little friends from nursery, a Pakistani girl. 'Say bye-bye to Auntie,' her mum scolded her, after we'd had a brief chat on the front step. I actually looked round, expecting to see some old lady in the usual uniform of winter coat over sari, man's socks and sandals, and a shopping trolley. And then I realized she meant me. I told Akash when I got home that night. He thought it was really funny and I laughed along with him, although I felt strangely depressed by my new title.

'So what sort of auntie would you be?' He grinned, knowing how I'd classified my relatives in my youth. 'I know, Messy Auntie!'

I suppose it could have been worse. He could have said Cellulite Auntie, or Crap at Job Auntie. Or even Gagging for it Auntie, given the number of times I've snuffled into his back hopefully in bed and he's pretended to be asleep. (Like I don't know!)

I gave him his name, though.

'Preoccupied Uncle,' I said, and shut the study door on my way out.

Oh, I know these are supposed to be the Dark Days of Marriage, this period when you're bringing up young children and trying to establish your careers. It says so in all of Akash's psychotherapy books that I fall over regularly in the hallway or by the bed. (Yes, I have flicked through some of them, at least the pages that fall open when I'm tidying up his crap.) And I've talked to enough friends in the same position to know that what we're going through, whatever it is, is normal. But this is what I don't get, I suppose. When we first met, when we were so desperate for each other that we would happily skip days of lectures to lie on his bed and drink wine and argue the relative merits of Plato versus Homer, or Muttley versus Scooby Doo, that was considered entirely normal too. Every self-respecting young couple in love was doing what we were doing. It was expected, walking bow-legged and bleary-eyed into the canteen, smelling of each other's most intimate juices; and how we pitied the ones who had time to iron or write essays. They were the abnormal ones, obviously.

I could get used to this normal, if I could forget the one we had at university. It's funny, but I never had panic attacks during those years. I had suffered a few at school, which Tania had talked me through, before exams, after fights, but within a few weeks of meeting Akash, they stopped. Of course, I took this as another sign that We were Meant to Be. How could you not marry the man who gave you back your breath?

God, I was besotted. Even now when I get a memory blast back to those days, a record comes on like Joni Mitchell's 'Case of You', or I smell that refectory odour of ancient pasties and roll-ups, I'm back there, nineteen again, stupid, skinny and in love. My spine straightens, I feel layers of dimpled flesh peel off my thighs, my cheekbones come back, I'm running down the road towards the union in my Doc Martens and black leggings (the FemiNazi Max Wall look, he called it), probably carrying a placard saying 'Reclaim the Night!' or 'Hands Off Our Bodies!', and I fling it down to fall into his, waiting on the steps with a lazy smile playing on those soon-to-be-mine lips.

A big part of the attraction was that it was so unexpected. I'd already given up on men, especially Asian men, who only came in two flavours as far as I could see, according to the selection available at our university. First, the Mummy's Boys, in their ironed trousers and neat hair, stalwarts of the Computer Soc and Asia Society, usually reading medicine or pharmacy. Their idea of a good night out was organizing a showing of some ancient Hindi movie in a broom cupboard, and then getting tipsy on cider while the girls handed out microwaved samosas and tittered at their obscure bilingual jokes. I'd joined Asia Soc out of a sense of duty. I mean, politically, I felt I ought to seek out my brethren and express my solidarity. I had imagined long evenings in front of a roaring fire, discussing the implications of the recent Southall uprisings, snacking on home-cooked sabzis and planning sit-ins for peace in one of the labs, or marches against the bride burning scandals in India. I did not expect to be cornered in dark corridors by dribbling teenagers who thought, because I wore men's shoes and smoked, I might be the ideal person to lose their virginity with. I made my mind up then. Just because we shared the same skin tone, I didn't have to like them.

And then there were the Rebels, a small select group of brothers who were dotted about in various unexpected departments, the rangy Sikh guy doing fashion and design, the scary-looking Bengali punk reading politics, a couple of cuteys doing languages, and the shy, plump South Indian doing research in phonetics. They were easy to spot, as theirs was often the only non-white face in their particular departments. And besides, I had a built-in antenna for kindred spirits. I could spot it in the way they walked, the books they carried, what they drank and smoked, what made them laugh. Always the same stuff about family and duty and the double lives we were leading. Always proud to be who they were, but not scared to push back the boundaries, to redefine what being Asian meant. We were making history. We knew it as we were living it. It made us feel special and lonely. Maybe that's why I sought them out.

I'd had one boyfriend before, a brief fling in my first term with a guy from Southampton reading French, but I got bored with having to explain stuff all the time. How come my parents came over here? What did korma actually mean in my language? What was that dot on the forehead? Why was my skin so beautiful? I felt like his social worker, not his girlfriend. I knew then this wasn't what I wanted or needed. I needed someone I could have cultural shorthand with, someone who would get my jokes. So I found the Rebels, and there was loads we had in common except for one thing, which *they* all had in common. White girlfriends.

I'm laughing now but bloody hell, the tears I wept over that. I mean, I got all the usual crappy arguments back from them: love has no colour (yeah, right, try telling that to Nelson Mandela), it was impossible to meet Asian women because of their family restrictions (well I was there, right in front of them, available), Asian women expected too much commitment too early (which, translated, meant they might not shag on a first date), and finally, amazingly, Asian women were just too heavy! Puh-leeze. And they weren't talking about weight here, because as I recall, Bengali punk's bit of fluff, who happened to be sitting next to him, bore a passing resemblance to a blonde Hattie Jacques.

The next thing I remember, I was throwing cruet sets around and shouting in what I thought was a female and empowering way, and I gave it to them straight: 'Angela Davis has got you lot sussed. It says in her latest book that the reason men of colour want white women is revenge. It makes you feel powerful, shagging the women of your oppressors. But how do you think that makes us feel, eh? Your women? Not good enough for you, eh?'

There was a long silence, broken only by someone putting on David Bowie's 'Changes' on the jukebox. Then rangy Sikh guy cleared his throat and said, 'See what I mean?'

They avoided me after that, probably because I'd hit a nerve and they couldn't deal with the truth, which suited me fine. And luckily, that happened to coincide with the period I got heavily involved with the Uni Women's Group, so I was far too busy picketing rugby players' socials or attending meetings like Examine your own Cervix. Speculum Provided! to worry about being single. It is still something that Tania teases me about. She's always asking for anecdotes about my life as a womb-an, and nowadays I laugh along with her, amazed at how good I was at the theory of being a strong female. So yeah, hands up, I admit it, I did it all, maybe because it was the only group around in which I could be a star. You see, when I joined the sisters, there were only two women of colour members, me and Yaba, a statuesque Nigerian, far below the acceptable multiracial quota the group felt was decent. And I had, if you'll excuse the pun, loads of brownie points over all the others. I was, well, Black, back then (anyone not white was given the honorary title) so I had plenty of skinhead-centred anecdotes with which to impress the group. I was working class, which gave me the edge over Yaba, who was unfortunate enough to come from African royal blood. I was pissed off (my rant in the refectory had made me something of an underground heroine), and I came, as I was often reminded, from a repressive culture in which women were treated like cattle. (I kept quiet about cows being holy, it would only have confused things.) If I ever wanted to win a point, all I had to do was start the sentence with 'As an Asian woman' and end it with 'You don't understand.' So I marched and put up posters and organized pickets and spent drunken evenings dancing along to 'I Will Survive' and even considered taking up lesbianism as it would have been a logical and convenient choice, given how I lived. Life was good, simple and mine. And then I met Akash.

To be fair, it wasn't just him. Yaba's dramatic exit from the group had unnerved me. She walked out after a fevered discussion about female circumcision, in which Angela, our protest co-ordinator, had argued, 'Well, we can't condemn it totally. After all, it might be a very ancient and precious custom which we're just too white to understand. Like nose piercing.'

Yaba threw some furniture and likened Angela to a portion of the female anatomy, which in other circumstances might have been an attempt to reclaim a rude word, and in this instance, was just rude, then turned to me, trembling, and said, 'You remember this, Sunita. Our ancestors were living in cities with drainage systems while they were still shitting in caves. They ain't got no culture, which is why they're trying to own ours. What makes you think they know the answers, huh?'

That's when I began thinking about the men, our men, a little more sympathetically. Sat in here, everyone with a pair of nuts was an enemy. Out there, all we had was each other. Maybe I felt I didn't want to subdivide any more. Maybe I was just, finally, growing up. Weird really, but now I look back, not one of those marches or demos or discussions came close to the kinship I felt with my sex when I gave birth. Strangely enough, it is also the one thing, the only thing that separates me, Tania and Chila. Chila, I reckon, will be dropping sprogs as soon as she's found the right wallpaper for the nursery. But Tania, not ever wanting kids . . . I can't get past that one.

Akash always wanted children, loads of them, he said. That was number five that I ticked off my perfect man list within a week of meeting him. (To justify being a feminist and wanting a man, I had a very long and complicated list.) He passed the first three requirements within five minutes of me handing him a flyer for an Anti-Nazi League benefit.

'Oh, I'm already going to that,' he said, ruffling his fingers through his mad hair. 'In fact, there's a bunch of us from the Law Soc who have hired a coach to go down for the concert in Finsbury Park. Wanna come?'

I almost fell off my wedged boots. 'You read law? I haven't seen you around ... but I've been really busy, actually,' I rescued myself, wanting to slash my wrists with my CND badge for missing this one.

'Oh, I just swapped courses from PPE. Too much theory, I want to be on the front line, you know?'

He was the right colour, politically aware, and doing a funky subject. So what about vital number four on the list?

'Actually,' he said shyly (number eight; I'm a sucker for blushing blokes), 'I wasn't around campus much last year. Got into a bit of a heavy scene with a girl.' I held my breath. 'Messy stuff. Was really doing my head in, did no work, you know the score.' I was still holding my breath and hoped my turning puce wouldn't put him off. 'So I finished it and ... here I am.'

And there he was. The best of East and West in one perfectly formed package and I knew how lucky I was to have found him before anyone else.

Soon after that I left the women's group, and two years later failed all my exams while Akash sailed through his. I wasn't going to be a barrister, but knowing I was going to be his wife made up for it then. He proposed when I was in my digs recovering after ... an operation. I wonder now if it was guilt that made him produce a ring pull off a beer can from his pocket and slip it onto my thumb. (My other fingers were digging into my palm. It was the bleeding, it didn't stop for days.) I mean, don't get me wrong, he didn't force me to . . . It was a mutual decision, the wrong time for a baby, what were we going to tell our parents, etc.

We could have timed it better. Four weeks before my finals was not the ideal time to blow both our grants on a quiet visit to a suburban clinic. Yellow wallpaper. Isn't that the title of a book? It's what I remember most about that place. That and the gas mask coming down like a slap. Akash says I was crying, shouting stuff – forgivememybaby. He still pretends I was referring to him, even now. Like he's the one who can't live with it. I don't think about it too much. My chest hurts and I have to be careful. If you can't be good, be careful. My old village neighbour trilled that at us as we trooped off to school. I didn't manage either, did I?

I was really worried that Akash would bring this up when we had our pre-interview interview with Tania for her documentary. I wasn't too keen on the whole idea, to be honest. For a start, she knows most of the dirt on me and Chila, like you do with old girlfriends. And I wasn't about to repeat any of it just so she had some good hard copy to show her boss. So we sat there, answering these really intimate questions with polite smiles. I thought it was totally pointless, but Tania seemed really pleased afterwards.

And then she explained, 'Look, Sunny, I'm not after shock horror scandal scoops, OK? This is going to be a really wide-ranging look at relationship alternatives, no narrator, letting people tell their stories the way they want to, and with as much or as little detail as they feel comfortable about.'

'Well, I wouldn't watch it, then,' I quipped back. 'Who

wants to watch loads of boring couples banging on about how happy they are?'

She didn't take it badly. She had her preachy face on, so I made sure I was sitting comfortably.

'But that's exactly why people will watch, Sunny! No more Jerry Springer fisticuffs, no more digging in the trash so we can all feel a bit better about our own sorry lives. Right now, what we all want to know is, how do you get it right? And as it happens, my two best friends have most of the answers between them. Course, I'll be interviewing loads of other couples, so no pressure. OK?'

I should have told her then. I almost did, honestly. I wanted to congratulate her at having perfect ironic timing. I wanted to tell her that she couldn't have picked a worse time to ask us how we maintained such a happy marriage. But I felt I was partly to blame. As close as we all are, I've never been able to admit things were anything less than perfect, at least with Tans.

Chila, I reckon, would sympathize, but God knows what advice she'd give back. 'Oh, just cook him his favourite dinner and snuggle on his lap. Works for me, Sunny!' Hoo-sodding-ray for her, then.

I also knew that Tans was really worried about this film. She'd gone on and on about how it was her first time producing and that's why she wanted to work with people she trusted, and Chila had actually taken me aside and told me that if this documentary didn't work out, Tania would possibly lose her job. At least, that's what Tania told her. Chila, bless her, couldn't wait to be a film star. She'd even had the house carpet-shampooed when Tans arrived, on her own, with a notebook, and then had to eat a banquet cooked for a whole crew that Chila had been expecting. She ate it of course, and took doggy bags home with her, because you do that sort of thing for your mates. Which is why, in the end, I said yes.

As it happens, Tans has become very interested in Akash, or at least his therapy work with Asian couples. He resisted her at first, muttered a lot about client confidentiality and how Anthony Clare had lost all respect when he became public property, but I could have told him that no-one resists Tania for long. It makes sense, of course. He's got the overview, the access to cases, the hundreds of files, the thousands of books, the joints they both enjoy smoking in his office when I'm trying to put the kids to bed. Actually, in a weird sort of way, I'm glad he's become involved. It's become a bit of a cosy routine over the last few weeks. Tans comes over with a vanload of papers and questions. Sometimes Chila will join us (only when her hubbie is working late, and she always hurries back before he gets home). And we girls have a good long chat over the meal we've cobbled together (I get something from the freezer, Chila produces an amazing home-cooked dish, Tans always brings a take-away), and off we go.

It was only after the second or third session that I realized we three hadn't really sat down and talked like this for years. Oh, we've kept up OK, but as our lives got busier, we forgot about the soul chat. Sometimes I go to bed with a head full of long-forgotten memories, and I turn them over and over in the dark, enjoying the smells and colours they bring back.

Akash leaves us to it. He's always been sensitive that way, understanding that we won't get down to the essentials if he's watching. And then after Chila's gone and I'm tidying up, that's when Tans goes up to the study. As I pass the door on my way to check on the kids, I hear them chatting inside, Akash's bass chuckle, Tania gabbing over it, and sniff the fumes of happiness which somehow escape from the rolled up towel wedged against the door. No, I'm not jealous. I still believe in the sisterhood enough to know that the most Tania will do is flirt, and the most Akash will do is let her. As far as I'm concerned, anything that brings back his enthusiasm has got to be good for all of us eventually. Talking about relationships endlessly might make him look at his own. He might even finish some of those books. I can wait. I have given up so much to be where I am now, it seems the . . . careful thing to do.

3

MRS WILKINSON WORRIED ABOUT THE TRAFFIC MOSTLY. SHE
had bought her flat after her husband died, hoping for a bit
of peace and quiet. It stood on a pleasant tree-lined avenue
off the main road, no shops or schools nearby, and even had
the added bonus of some cherry trees right in her view. That
was how she kept track of the seasons, since time had
turned from a regimented march into this slow meandering
contemplation. It was one of her greedy pleasures, waiting
for the tightly scrolled buds to unfurl and burst into white
and pink froth, almost overnight.

And then that blasted clinic had opened up right opposite,
right under her favourite tree, the one with the scarred
trunk and the most audacious blooms. She had protested,
with many of the other residents. She had even got her
motorized shopping trolley out for a march, or rather slow
conveyor belt, to the local council offices, to argue that
inviting a lot of loonies into the area would do nothing for
the mental health of the neighbours, to say nothing of the
effect on their house prices. Those officious red-tapers had

reassured them that the Tisdale Clinic was simply a therapy centre offering a range of services to perfectly ordinary people who just felt they needed a bit of extra help.

'No Care in the Community cases,' the pompous jobsworth had shouted in her ear, as if she was deaf as well as slightly gouty.

Stuff and nonsense, she had shouted back, ordinary people did not have the time, never mind the money, to be sitting around hugging cushions and harping on about what they didn't have when they were six. Ordinary people, like her good self, went through two wars, three dead babies, rationing, a husband with cancer and the reshuffle of Radio 4 without ever complaining that life had been unfair. And why did every Tom, Dick, etc. expect to be happy all the time anyway? Two spoons of salt for every one of sugar, she'd told him, that's the way it is. By then he'd gone back into his office and she had to ask a passing coloured lady for some help to find a lift. The lady was awfully kind, and yes, Mrs Wilkinson had been a tad upset that day because she had wondered if she was going to have to move house again.

At first, Mrs Wilkinson steadfastly refused to even look in the vague direction of the Tisdale Clinic. She was aware of bodies coming and going, the car engines and slamming doors saw to that, and just to show them, she moved her armchair from the window to the other side of the room and turned up the radio with her gnarled, knotted fingers. But gradually, imperceptibly, she became interested in the constant flow of human traffic which arrived and departed every day, with the swell and regularity of the tides. She could have set her watch by them, had she worn one.

Beneath the benevolent blossoms, a hundred times a day, couples met with tender embraces, or uncertain nods, or sometimes walked right past each other, one leaving the door to slam in the other's face. They climbed the steps slowly, as if their hearts were boulders on their backs, or briskly, as if business had to be done and done quickly, or sometimes, rarely, hand in hand like infants in a school play, they made their entrance with self-conscious pride. While the trees kept their promises, and sprouted shoots, exploded into flower and shed their fragile blooms with comforting precision at their feet, love fashioned some unlikely pairings. Mrs Wilkinson would never have joined the sour-faced bottle blonde with the sad jowly gentleman in a suit, nor the mousy hausfrau with her leathery, tanned medallion man. What made that scowling pretty boy walk out with someone old enough to be his mother? And why did that gorgeous couple, who arrived in matching sports cars, both on mobile phones, look so lost when they faced each other on the steps? Why did the wind decide to blow at that moment and unsettle a blizzard of petals which fell, cruelly, like confetti?

There were other visitors, too, who arrived bearing different burdens. The anorexics were easy to spot, inevitably dressed in huge, shapeless jumpers, whatever the weather, with their stretched bony faces poking out, tortoise-like, from the voluminous folds. They would always be accompanied by a parent or two, anxious middle-aged people, worn out from smiling too much, who would hover round their emaciated child, watching them take reluctant sparrow steps towards the clinic. Those girls, and they always seemed to be girls, never visited for very long. Mrs Wilkinson concluded that they were brought to the Tisdale for some emergency consultation and then taken away to what she hoped were pretty houses in the country-side where they could eat cream cakes in soft sofas and get out of that terrible knitwear.

The obese over-eaters did not dress much better (How

many ways are there of wearing a flowery tent? argued Mrs Wilkinson), but they seemed to enjoy life more than the skinnies. Mrs Wilkinson actually looked forward to their Monday night meetings when, she fancied, the pavement would begin shaking as they all rolled into view, chattering between frequent stops to catch their breath. They were a mixed bunch, men and women, although fat was a strangely democratic uniform and from a distance it was sometimes hard to tell. She had never before seen so much flesh in one place; it was mesmerizing, the heaves and rolls contained under fabric, moving around like tumbling animals under a blanket and, strangely, wonderfully comforting. These were the people Mrs Wilkinson would have chosen to be her friends.

There were others who made her want to close her curtains and weep. The beautiful haunted woman, in expensive clothes, who stepped smartly out of the entrance and pulled out fistfuls of coiffeured hair as she descended each step. The gangly boy, only about twenty, who left the building still waving a jolly goodbye and as soon as he reached the pavement, collapsed against the soothing bark of a tree and howled like a stricken beast. Too many to recall, the numbers pained her as much as her final impression of their faces. But by now, she was something of an expert at spotting who was going to make it and get better, and who wasn't.

It was all in the exit. No-one entered that building without hope; even the smallest grain of faith could yield, in time, a pearl. But how they left it, that said everything. Mrs Wilkinson's whole day could be ruined by a couple leaving the building in stony silence, a tangible forcefield around each of them, the static crackling as they said their stiff goodbyes. She wanted to open her window and tell them, silly fools, Don't you realize how quickly you will grow old? But those days when two people would emerge together, blinking in the light, and one, perhaps, would wait for the other patiently, to put away a tissue or adjust a scarf, those were glorious days. Only tiny kindnesses, but the ones that counted, the million little mercies we take for granted, the mundane gestures that keep us, tentatively, together. Those were the occasions when Mrs Wilkinson would pour herself a sherry and put on her *Countdown* compilation video tape. Living where she did, she had learned to celebrate even the smallest triumph over adversity.

She kept a close eye on the couple who were approaching the clinic. Handsome folk, Asian or Middle-eastern perhaps, good jobs, the clothes were discreet and well-made, although his choice of jewellery gave away some common origins. He strode up the steps without waiting for her. Not a good sign. She rolled her eyes but managed a small smile and followed him up. Mrs Wilkinson glanced over at the sherry bottle. She would wait on this one.

Akash plumped up some African print cushions on the sofa in his consulting room and placed a strategic box of man-size tissues next to it on the floor. He stood up sharply, hearing a familiar whirring hum at his back.

'Do you have to film me doing this?' he asked with a sigh.

Tania adjusted the focus on her DV hand-held camera and nodded wordlessly. She went in for a close up on the tissue box and then slowly panned round towards the bulging bookcase, going in on the titles in jaunty lettering on the pristine spines. '*Anger Management: A Crash Course, The Tao of Captain Pugwash, Sexual Symbolism in Eastern Religions, Now I'm Better, Why Don't You Like Me Anymore?*'

'Have you actually read any of these tomes?' Tania finally

said, after switching off the camera and carefully placing it on Akash's weatherbeaten desk.

'It's probably not a good idea to be brandishing that dinky toy about when they come in,' Akash said, irritated.

'They know I'll be here, right? They've given their permission. I've got the consent form right here.' Tania picked through the contents of a china fruit bowl on the side table. 'Are they NHS referrals, then? Or members of the neurotic rich?'

'They pay the minimum, as they know they'll be seeing a counsellor in training. And anyway, they asked to see someone . . . like me, sympathetic to their culture.' Akash tried to keep the defensive edge out of his voice. 'They've been coming to me for a couple of months actually.'

Tania was peeling a grape slowly, slicing delicately through the skin with her thumbnail. Akash was momentarily mesmerized by this – the precise incision, the glistening streak of juice, the translucent flesh beneath, vulnerable and exposed – simultaneously wondering if everything Tania did was for effect.

It became burdensome after a while, this constant silent commentary in his head. There were no spontaneous gestures left in the world; everything had a motive, deliberate or unconscious. Every human being was supposedly unique, a complex collision of inheritance and environment, and somewhere hidden, in a spark caught between snapping synapses, the unpredictable kink, which in a crisis sorted out the sane from the rest of us. Some people called it the soul, he supposed. Although it seemed to him the more he saw of people, the more they seemed, depressingly, the same.

Maybe it was his job, his vocation that had caused this temporary rift between him and Sunita. Maybe now it was impossible for him to see her clearly, to react instinctively, emotionally, to what was bothering her, because every time he looked into those disappointed eyes, he flicked through case files in his head, pages flipping like a metronome. After all, who enjoyed taking their work home? He plumped another cushion and wondered if gynaecologists had lousy sex lives.

'It's not a toy, by the way, this baby,' Tania said, patting her video camera proudly. 'State of the art, broadcast quality, used by news crews all over the world and yet still compact enough to fit into a lady's handbag.' She threw the rest of her grape up in the air and caught it expertly in her mouth.

Akash felt he was expected to applaud.

'I'm using the DV for all the counselling sessions,' Tania continued, rummaging in her handbag, which was actually large enough to contain a couple of cameras and a tripod. 'It will give them a nice grainy feel . . . hand-held shots, no individual mikes, just the atmos I pick up with the built-in one, like I'm another person in the room just listening. It will make it feel—'

'Authentic?' said Akash, a small hard smile pinching his lips.

'Hey, you're the one who wants to be Dr Ruth. I'm happy not to film you at all.'

The intercom buzzed and a disembodied voice informed Akash that his two-thirty appointment had arrived.

He quickly sorted through a haphazard pile of papers on his desk, breaking off to speak into the intercom.

'Do show them up, Maureen.' After locating the missing file, he added over his shoulder, 'You know exactly why I am doing this, because people like us need to know that there are other people like us they can talk to, if they need to.'

'Oh, I dunno,' replied Tania smoothly, 'I think there's nothing worse than being judged by your peers.'

'Yeah, you call it judgement, I call it justice, and that, my dear Tania, is the difference between us.'

Tania picked up the camera and winked at Akash. 'We make a great team, don't ya think?' she said, just in time to catch Mr and Mrs Dhillon walking through the door.

Fifteen minutes into the session, Tania's neck began to tingle. Something was going to happen, she could feel it. The introductions had been cordial enough. The Dhillons seemed unfazed by the camera, having been reassured that their real names would not be used and that Tania would only film them in wide angle. Why they assumed that this would preserve some anonymity, Tania did not know, but she was not about to set them straight. Akash had been more nervous, clearing his throat too much and fiddling with his pen, until Raj and Seema had finally forgotten they were being filmed and stopped being polite.

'She just does not try . . . anything to make this better,' Raj began. 'I know she's unhappy. I've tried, you know, the stuff you've been saying, talking more, more time together. I even bought her flowers last week without being asked. She's still . . . cold. Ice woman.'

Akash leaned forward. 'Seema? Is that how you feel?'

Seema shrugged and lowered her head.

'You see that? See that, what she did? That's what I get when I try to talk to her. Sod all!' Raj shifted in his chair, crossing his legs away from his wife.

Tania framed it beautifully. She was getting frustrated at not being able to go in closer. They were a photogenic couple. He had typically Punjabi features, aquiline nose, strong chin, thick, wavy hair, a grainy wash of beard shadowing his cheeks. Those molten eyes, always their best feature, she thought, with a needle of nostalgia entering a soft part of her. Now the wife, she was interesting. Not a looker but she'd worked hard on herself, made the most of her bedroom eyes and heaving cleavage. Maybe it was the way the light filtered through the leaves from the tree outside the window, dappling her with soft, shifting shades, giving her a glow that Tania could only achieve with an expert DOP and a large amount of glycerine on the lens, but she looked up suddenly, this silent wife, and was transformed.

Incandescent was the word that sprang into Akash's mind. This is not a defeated woman, he rapidly decided.

Different, thought her husband, a worm of suspicion entering his chest, she's done something different and I've only just noticed. The last time she looked like this was on honeymoon. No wonder I fell in love.

Tania could not find the word, but she knew. Every sinew in her body vibrated, rusty strings plucked again after so long, painfully picking out, note by note, an old, old song she had tried to forget. She could sing the harmony to this, the tune that hung in the air between her and Mrs Dhillon. She reached for the focus on the camera and slowly, discreetly, began to zoom in.

'Seema? Do you want to say something to Raj?' Akash asked again gently.

Seema sighed, the winds of the world, oh, how she regretted everything and nothing, not one damn thing. 'Yes. One bunch of flowers does not make up for years of . . . years of being shouted at . . . and ignored.'

'I've been working on my temper,' Raj said through only slightly gritted teeth. 'You know I have. I've had to . . . unlearn stuff, like you said,' he continued, looking at Akash.

Akash began to clear his throat and thought better of it. Instead, he slightly angled his profile towards Tania. 'Yes, we've had long discussions about your family, Raj. You told us how you grew up basically watching your father bellow at your mother and, as she never complained, you assumed this was normal behaviour.'

Raj nodded wordlessly, his eyes clouded over, scenes replayed through the veil of his mother's dupatta, doors banging, glass breaking, the vice of her fingers on his small arm keeping him still and mute, Fiker na ker bucha, don't worry, stand quietly, your papa's passing. He was always reminded that he came from warrior caste, khattri, born a soldier, so there always had to be someone to fight. He was tired now, and if putting his balls on a plate and handing it to his wife was what he had to do, well, at least his children wouldn't piss their pants when he walked past them.

'These are the hardest habits to break,' Akash continued, managing a reassuring smile. 'The old ones. All men have to contend with the example set by their fathers. But for us, we are also having to reassess our cultural habits, too.' Akash was flowing now. He loved these moments, when the theory became flesh, when it all fitted perfectly. 'It is extremely hard, having to dismantle your belief system. Because we . . . you are not only having to question your attitudes as a man, but more specifically, as an Asian man. It can seem like you're losing everything that makes you you, but we all know, at least I hope we do after two months together, that we are also the generation that can change things, redefine what being Asian and male or Asian and female means, without losing pride in who we are. Because culture evolves and changes, just like human beings.'

'Oh, yeah? And how do we do that, then?' said Raj, looking directly at Akash.

'You're doing it now, both of you, just by being here. Do you think any of our parents would have ever considered coming to a place like this, without seeing it as an admission of failure? You see, in our culture—'

'If you mention culture one more time, I might just throw up,' said Seema calmly.

Raj stared at his wife as if she had just acquired another head. Akash coughed nervously, swivelled his head and looked straight down Tania's lens. Chaos theory personified, thought Tania as she adjusted the focus.

'Um, Seema, could you—' Akash began.

'I could end up like my mother. I'm supposed to because everyone says she's a saint, but she's sixty-three and I'm thirty-three, and I've already had enough practice at being a good girl and keeping quiet and I've got lots more years to live and I'm scared of wasting them and I don't have any more time to wait until my husband gets kinder or sexier or . . . better, because I seem to have spent all my marriage waiting and I know I'm supposed to try everything and think of the kids but we don't have any because we don't have much sex and I've been taking the pill behind his back and anyway, what more can you try if you don't love somebody any more?'

Akash blinked rapidly. Raj seemed to deflate in his chair, his knees and arms shrivelled to stumps and the bones in his face dissolved, leaving a sagging bag pinpricked by two glittering eyes.

'I've met someone else,' Seema said.

Tania went in closer for a BCU of Seema's placid face and could not stop her fingers trembling. She was lost, the wife, Tania recognized all the symptoms, way down the rocky road to hell, hand in hand with her angel.

'Who?' whispered Raj.

'It doesn't matter. He's not you.'

Tania didn't see the chair but she felt one of the legs clip her ear as it flew past her head. The sound quality wasn't great, but the roaring and screaming sounded rather good when distorted, and the slipshod angles really worked, Raj's jagged profile whipping past camera, Seema's panicked eyes, the bone of her ankle as she cowered behind the table, Akash's bald patch visible as he emerged from his hiding place under the desk and wrestled with Raj, the scattered files, the unused tissue box, and finally a bull of a man sitting quiet as a child amongst the debris. The world in pieces, how else could you shoot a scene of two lives fragmenting?

Afterwards, Akash sat on his sofa, limp as a rag. Undone, all those weeks of work, all those reassurances, all those noises of encouragement, all shattered with a few well-aimed words. Why had he not guessed what was going on? It was a textbook scenario, the reluctant partner with a hidden agenda. What pained him most was that Raj had been making such remarkable progress. Akash had not held out much hope when he first assessed him, had already shoved him into the box marked Neanderthal Man. But week by week, layer by layer, Raj had unpeeled himself, exposing nerve endings to the air. For anyone, this was an achievement; for this recent cave dweller, a ghetto boy made good, it was nothing short of a miracle. He had every excuse in the world not to change; he could have attributed all his failings to racism, bad parenting and a lack of positive role models, had he been familiar with the vocabulary, but instead, he had turned up once a week to talk and bought his wife flowers. Bad timing. Human nature. Kismet. Karma. Whoever we blame, the shit smells the same.

Tania, meanwhile, was packing her equipment away, humming to herself.

'Are you going to put what happened in the programme?' Akash said eventually.

Tania didn't look up. 'Can't tell yet. Depends.'

'On what?'

'On what happens next.'

Akash closed his eyes. 'They won't be coming back.'

'No,' said Tania. 'Fancy some lunch?'

Martin's stomach rumbled so loudly that he wondered if downstairs' repulsive shih tzu puppy had managed somehow to break into the flat. He reread his opening paragraph, angling his computer screen away from the window. 'Ben, Matt and Tony are three thirty-something lads who share a flat above a betting shop in downtown Clapham. They consider themselves quite ordinary, decent blokes: they like football but hate Arsenal on principle; they think Page Three is a laugh but wouldn't leave it lying around; they get pissed occasionally but not to the extent that they'd barf in a mate's car, forget their names or sleep with their girlfriend's sister. Oh, and one thing I forgot to mention . . .' Martin paused. 'They're all transvestites. No. They're all in love with the same woman.' His stomach emitted another warning grumble. 'They are all originally from the planet Zark,' he typed, and switched off the computer without bothering to save any of his morning's efforts.

He had to eat. No, he had to tidy up first. He surveyed the collection of coffee cups and full ashtrays around the sitting room and knew they would have to be washed, wiped and back in their allotted homes before Tania came back. Which was a little unfair as she had left them there. Foolishly, he found her debris comforting, little piles of Tania around him while he worked.

He ambled over to the kitchen counter and picked out Madhur Jaffrey's *Flavours of India*, its cover stained in the traditional way with yellow fingerprints of turmeric. He flicked through and paused fondly at the recipe for lamb with palak, the dish he had tried to impress her with on her first visit to his flat. He had arranged everything perfectly: candlelight, incense sticks burning, a Ravi Shankar CD playing (Kula Shaker would have been too obvious and naff), and a couple of local taxi firm numbers prominently displayed by the telephone, so she knew he wasn't expecting anything on a plate.

He had been besotted the moment he had walked into the offices of the production company, half an hour early for a meeting, and saw her through a glass door arguing with someone he later discovered was her boss. So he looked up and . . . What did Richard Burton do when he first clapped eyes on Elizabeth Taylor? He laughed out loud, astonished at the absurdity of her beauty. Tania's face shamed every pale imitation he had seen, in photos of those huge carved temples, the pouty heroines on the film posters in his local Indian supermarket, the airbrushed maidens in the wall friezes of his local tandoori. (Not that he hadn't ever seen an Asian woman before, God no, he grew up in Slough after all.) They were all of a type these images, long-haired, sloe-eyed, hour-glass women, the ideal blueprint captured for posterity. He never thought he'd meet someone who rendered every cliché impotent. It was her paradoxes that ensnared him: the tailored suit and the leonine mane of blue-black hair, the delicate hands banging savagely on the table, that perfect face spitting fishwife bile.

So really, he shouldn't have been surprised when, weeks later (after she had been sacked), after the lamb palak and a couple of bottles of wine, just at the point when Martin reckoned it was time to wrap up this fragile exotic bloom and send her safely home, Tania rolled over, carefully ran her tongue over his lips and whispered, 'Now. Right now.'

He replayed the scene as he left the flat and walked briskly towards the high street, a tantalizing peep show of tangled limbs, discarded clothing, and the darkness of her, enveloping him. He had been too shocked to worry whether his breath smelled of garlic or if he was wearing the Road Runner motif boxer shorts he chose when he expected to sleep alone. He suspected he could have had galloping acne and a fungal infection and neither would have deterred Tania from her quest. Was he chosen? Or was she up for it and he happened to be in the vicinity? Two years later, he still occasionally asked himself this same question, worrying it like a loose tooth; delicious uncertainty was what kept them going, kept it all fresh and exciting. He knew he was the envy of his mates; there had been the usual Whey-hey gags about dusky maidens and their rubbery limbs, tantric sex a-plenty and possibly a nice back rub at the end of it.

'They're real goers, the good girls, aren't they?' his friend Joe had confided in him. 'I had a Greek girlfriend once, all demure in daylight but it was like she was some carnal vampire. The minute it was lights off, we were at it for hours. Catholic women, Jewish birds, all the same. Not allowed to do it, see, so it's all they think about. Thank Christ.'

Now the more obvious jokes had worn thin, and he and Tania were still together, his friends' envy had softened into a sort of grudging admiration. If a struggling writer like Martin could keep a high-maintenance totty like Tania happy, he must be doing something right. He just wished he knew what it was.

But then, he debated, as he strolled past the first parade of shops, pausing in front of the newsagent's window, maybe it was better to preserve the mystery of whatever unknown chemical kept them together. It was true, there was a part of Tania he would always find fascinatingly alien, and he did not know if that was a racial or a female thing. It was not, as people often asked, anything to do with her family, as she rarely saw them and talked about them even less. It was not ostensibly a cultural barrier: she understood basic Punjabi but didn't speak it; Martin had been to India and she hadn't; it was Martin who brought home the latest fusion CDs and had to prise her away from Frank Sinatra to listen to them; it was him who brought home fireworks for Diwali or booked tickets for a Dussehra festival, and her who always refused to join in. 'Ghetto groupie' she had called him, only half joking. Although nowadays, fashion victim would have been a more accurate term, as brown was indeed the new black, in couture, in music, in design, on the high street, judging by the number of plump white girls prancing around wearing bindis on their heads and henna on their hands. Martin couldn't understand it; the more the rest of the world found Tania's background fascinating, the more she rejected it.

'Sweetie,' she told him one night, as she watched him cook dinner, 'I am the genuine article and therefore I don't have to try. I just have to be. You, on the other hand, being middle class, white and male, have to try any passing bandwagon, because what else have you got?'

And she was right, as his fruitless efforts this morning had proved. Who wanted to watch a sitcom about three lads much like himself? What conflict could there be, except a fight about the remote control or a woman? Martin had been a great gag writer for other people. That's how he had established himself relatively quickly, writer for hire on sketch shows, news quizzes, opening and closing quips for chat show hosts, a very funny guy when pretending to be someone else. But when it came to finding his own voice, he changed from life and soul party wit into sad bastard in the kitchen folding teatowels and eating all the crisps on his own. Now if he had been born a black woman, a single mother on a council estate with an errant ex-partner, bossy God-fearing parents and a radical lesbian rapper for a sister, he could write something amazing. Not a comedy maybe, but something with soul, purpose, fire. He would have suffered, the first prerequisite for creating Great Art.

When he had said all this to Tania, she had not even looked up from her book. 'If you were poor, oppressed and desperate, you'd have more to worry about than writing a pissy little sitcom.'

He bought a copy of *Broadcast* and leafed through it as he ambled towards the park, depressed by the number of names he recognized doing better than him. He told himself it was just a matter of time before he found his niche. He could pick up the phone right now and get a gig team-writing soaps or medical dramas, but he feared becoming one of those TV battery writers, confined to their North London hutches, force-fed a diet of demographically agreed story-lines, creating characters whom you would only ever meet on a film set. Live first, write about it afterwards. That was the right way round. Of course, people like Tania could take the short cut; the snippets of her life she'd deigned to share with Martin made him salivate with envy. It was all so epic! The upheaval of emigration, the overpowering patriarchal father, a dying mother, the schizophrenia of her teenage years, the brother who made money and refused to have her name mentioned in his mansion.

'What is it you are supposed to have done to make him hate you so much?' Martin had asked her one evening, when the wind howled outside and they'd been in their duvet nest for nearly two days, just talking, eating, exploring.

'It's what I haven't done, really,' Tania said. 'I haven't been at home, feeding everyone, supporting everyone, smiling at everyone, keeping the family going, filling the hole.'

'What hole?'

'A mother-shaped hole. A bloody big one as she was eighteen stone with a wrestler's biceps. They were big women, our mothers, in all senses of the word. They had plans, boundaries, a place. Why would you think you were in prison if you never saw the bars? If I went outside now, I'd just blow away. Like cotton wool.'

It was the only time Martin had ever seen Tania cry. Mostly she got angry. She even cried furiously and would not let him comfort her, which was annoying as he enjoyed the sensation of helpless tears soaking into his T-shirt. Nowadays, there weren't enough opportunities for a man to feel, well, manly. Not that he complained too loudly, as they were both aware it was Tania's wage packet that paid the bills, and his that took care of the extras. For now anyway.

He reached the park gates and hesitated a moment. The park was a riot of blooms and verdant greenery, cartoon primary colours, and somewhere, an ice-cream van sprinkling the air with an off-key version of 'The Teddy Bears' Picnic'. The sunshine had spawned the usual rash of optimistic worshippers; pasty, half-stripped bodies lay on every available patch of green, their office clothes shed like old skins around them. There were couples everywhere, competing for the most in love title that good weather always encouraged in public places, feeding each other ice cream, finding ducks funny, sighing over the toddlers who wobbled past on fat eatable feet.

Martin pitied anyone in the park who was single. Fortunately, he hadn't been alone for longer than three weeks since his first relationship, although he had been a comparatively late starter at twenty-one. As a teenager, he wondered if he would be alone for ever, one of those sad bachelors you could spot at Tescos in the afternoons, poring over the additives in a curry for one, embarrassed at what their shopping basket gave away. The two potatoes, the two cans of beer, the individually wrapped cheese slices, everything packaged in small bites, stamped with co-ordinated sell-by dates. But strangely, all the qualities that branded the teenage Martin a weed – sensitivity, a sense of humour, the ability to listen, getting choked at adverts with puppies in them – miraculously transformed him into number one eligible bloke when he hit his twenties. That was the great thing about having a developed feminine side, women loved it.

Martin checked his watch. Tania would just be finishing off her filming. The sun was shining, his heart felt light as a kite and he wanted to see her. He walked towards the tube station, already smiling with anticipation. He would kiss her in the middle of the street and recite his favourite line from *When Harry Met Sally*, when two long-term singles finally meet their soulmates: 'Tell me I'm never going to have to be out there again.' And she would reply, on cue, 'You'll never have to be out there again.'

'Start from the outside and work inwards,' hissed Deepak.

Chila looked down at the battalion of knives and forks guarding her gold-rimmed plate, upon which sat three tiger prawns making V-signs at her with their feelers. 'This one?' she whispered back.

Deepak sighed, picked up the fork furthest away from the plate and placed it in her hand. 'But peel them first.' He smiled, and returned to his conversation.

Chila glanced round nervously, checking if she was being watched. Everyone else on the table seemed to be having a good time. Although she could now name all the wives of Deepak's business associates – Leila with the bouffant hair and discreet diamonds, married to no-neck Asif, Chandni, face-lifted and regal, married to Ram, silver haired, including the ones sprouting alarmingly from his ears and nose, and Manju, plump and dusted as a bon-bon, married to gap-toothed Manoj with his slightly sinister grin – she still could not think of much to say. She had begged Deepak to excuse her from this black tie luncheon, claiming she had a mountain of ironing and a compulsion to reorganize her spice cabinet, but he had virtually dressed her himself.

'You have to get used to these events. It's part of being a tycoon's wife, darling,' he had teased her, sweeping her hair from her back as he carefully zipped up her embroidered silk chemise. 'Besides, this is an A-list event. Every year, East-West PLC publish a list of the hundred richest Asians in Britain, and as everyone who is anyone wants to be on it, those people are all going to turn up.'

'Are you on it, jaan?' she asked, wincing as a piece of hair snagged on a steel tooth.

'Not yet, baby, but I'm getting there. Now go and pretty up. And wear the ruby set from Mum, it will set off your suit.'

Chila had stared at her reflection for a long time; he was right, the rubies danced like a circle of fire around her neck. He was always right. She so wanted to impress all his friends, to casually throw in murmured one-liners which would make them gasp and then laugh admiringly, throwing open their arms to let her in. She decided to practise a few before putting on her make-up. She tilted her head and laid a forefinger across her cheek. Yes, that made her look deep. She tried a laugh. No, that sounded like a donkey with wind. Maybe a snigger. No, too snorty, she sounded mean. She exhaled slightly, turning it into a chuckle at the last moment, hehhehheh, and sucked in her cheeks so dimples appeared like two commas, framing her mouth. That was it. She looked like she was having a good time, like she understood.

'You are too awful,' she said to her reflection, mimicking Leila's catchphrase. 'Manju, tell this man to stop being so naughty!' She looked OK when saying it, cheeky but not aggressive, but she would have to find her own motto. It wouldn't do to steal someone else's. She would think of one on the way there. Something that was all hers.

'Not hungry, Chila?' Leila was looking pointedly at Chila's untouched starter.

'I think it's such a nice change not to have desi food,' tinkled Manju. 'We go to so many of these things and they always drag out the chicken korma and the blasted lime pickle, as if we can't eat anything else.'

'Absolutely,' smiled Chandni, as much as she was able without pulling on the cosmetic scars behind her ears. 'Someone should really create nouvelle Eastern cuisine.'

Chila watched, horrified, as Chandni casually picked up a prawn with her fingers and ripped its head off with one quick snap. She looked down at the fork she was still gripping like a blunt instrument. Well, what was she supposed to use it for, then? She prodded a feeler hesitantly. The prawn shifted slightly and looked up at her with one sorrowful black bead of an eye.

'The Village Dhaba in Mayfair does something like that,' ventured Leila, who had upended her prawn and was scooping some horrible eggy stuff out of its stomach. 'It's basic khana, but presented in super small portions actually on the plate. None of those off-putting silver dishes on the table with everyone's fingers in it, helping themselves.' She deposited the frogspawn lump on one side and began prising the shell from its back. Small flakes of coral collected beneath her fingertips, but she didn't seem to mind.

Chila put down her fork as quietly as she could, laying it back carefully in its proper place. She felt hot suddenly, the back of her neck ached and she was desperate for the toilet. But the thought of having to get up and walk past everyone, when they would know where she was going and maybe talk about what she was doing while she was away, kept her seated.

'Not used to seafood, Chila?' asked Chandni, hooking an amused eyebrow at Leila. 'It is an acquired taste, I suppose.'

Chila swallowed, and placed her hands in her lap, clamping them together.

'I don't like eating anything with a face,' she said finally.

'What?' The three women all shrieked at the same time.

'Oh, but that is too, too funny!' Leila said, laughing. 'Don't you think?'

Manju clapped her hands loudly, now she had been given permission, and Chandni nodded vigorously, trying to register amusement while using as few facial muscles as possible.

'Darling boys, did you hear what Chila said? It was too awfully funny, really.'

The men swivelled as one, glasses halfway to their lips, tolerant expressions on their faces.

'Do say it again, Chila darling!'

Chila opened her mouth but Chandni butted in. 'She said, she doesn't like eating anything with a face.'

Manoj and Asif pointed at Chila, shook their heads and said, 'Very good' a few times, before resuming their discussion.

Deepak fixed Chila with a long, loving stare which calmed her immediately. He winked at her and gave her a subtle thumbs up, and she swelled with pride. Funny, she felt like she did when she wrote that essay at school about Africa and took it home to show her parents. Her mum had barely registered the two crumpled pieces of A4, but Chila's father had sat down in his armchair and read the whole thing carefully, his finger tracing the words as he mouthed them silently to himself. When he had finished, he looked up at Chila, his eyes brimming with tears.

'You remember so much about Africa, beti?'

Chila had nodded back, perturbed by his reaction.

'We had twenty acres, ten servants and sunshine, always sunshine. I was a fool to bring you here.'

This, Chila now realized, was probably the reason she had never dared write anything else again. She hated upsetting people. It was much better, in the end, to keep quiet and keep smiling.

'You really are too awful, Chila!' Leila nudged her, a little too hard.

Chila nudged back. 'So are you, Leila. Really awful.' A posse of waiters descended upon them and removed their dishes. Chila relaxed a little. She cheerfully helped herself to a bread roll, split it in half with her knife and carefully layered it thickly with butter. At least she knew how to eat one of these.

'You're really supposed to break the roll into pieces with your hands, and then butter each portion individually, strictly speaking,' Manju said pleasantly.

Chila picked up a buttered half and chomped on it boldly. This was a good opportunity to try out one of her lines, now that she had broken the ice.

'Well, it doesn't really matter how it goes in. It all comes out the same way, eh?'

'Indeed,' stuttered Manju, while Leila busied herself with the water decanter and Chandni coughed into her serviette.

'So, er, how do you occupy yourself, Chila? We don't see you around much.'

'Around?'

'You know, the Tamarind lunches, Nehru Institute talks, Beena's coffee mornings . . .'

'Ah, well,' said Chila, picking out a piece of bread from a back tooth, 'I have my rounds to do, really. It's a mad social whirl in Ilford.'

'Really?' Chandni said. 'You do surprise me.'

'Yeah, I'm rushed off my feet most days. What with . . . you know, visiting and . . . driving places, and that.'

Chila's mind was racing. She knew they would not appreciate the daily activities that she found exciting, visiting the brand new Tescos in Gants Hill where you got your groceries packed for you, having tea and samosas with her friend, Geeta, who worked in a jewellery shop and let Chila try on diamond and pearl tiaras when no-one was about, feeding old rotis to the swans at Snaresbrook Ponds, where she always had a good natter with the old ladies who ambled over from their residential home across the road. There had to be something else.

'Actually, I am being filmed for a television programme at the moment. That just takes up so much time.'

'You're an actress?' Chandni sat bolt upright, her nostrils quivering.

'You're not a model surely?' Manju said.

'My dear, such excitement!' said Leila. 'Do tell.'

'Um, well, it's both of us, me and Deeps actually,' Chila launched in. Deepak heard his name and turned round quizzically. 'A friend of mine, Tania, she's a director. And she's making a very important programme about . . . about people in love, and how they met, how they make things work. So of course, she asked me and Deeps to, um, give away our secrets.'

The women were really impressed, Chila could tell by the way they whispered to each other and giggled behind their hands. Deepak was looking a little strange, she thought, but that was probably because he had never heard her manage so many words in front of his friends. She could do it. She had proved it now.

'So, Deepak darling, we always said that profile was wasted on the stock market.' Leila waggled a playful finger at him. 'You must tell us when your screen debut is. We wouldn't miss it for the world.'

'Oh, we'll have a party when it's on,' Chila said, flushed with success now. 'I'll cook and we can all watch it together! That would be awfully good fun, wouldn't it, Deeps?'

Deepak nodded slowly, before draining his glass in one smooth gulp.

'You should have told me before mouthing off in front of everyone. God, you really showed me up, Chila.' Deepak was striding towards the car while Chila struggled to keep up, her slingbacks skidding on the pavement. 'You told me you were just talking to her about this stupid programme. I didn't know you'd agreed to be in it. And what right did you have to volunteer me as a bloody guinea pig, huh?'

Chila felt tears pricking her eyes. She had been doing so well and now this had ruined all her afternoon's efforts.

Deepak waited for her to catch up, his eyebrows a single slash, like a furry scar, across his forehead. 'This is typical of her,' he said almost to himself. 'Flashes her dimples and everyone bows down before her, without thinking. She's always treated you like her favourite pet. Throws a biscuit and you bloody jump, don't you?'

Chila concentrated very hard on not walking on any of the lines on the pavement. Maybe if she placed a sandalled foot exactly in the middle, he would calm down. It was working. He was walking more slowly now. Maybe she would risk taking his hand, to show this was just a silly row over nothing at all.

'Jaan?' she said quietly. 'I wouldn't have done anything behind your back. I thought you knew, you know, you and Tans being close.'

Deepak halted and spun round, catching Chila by the wrist. 'And what's that supposed to mean?'

For a moment, Chila did not recognize him. The features were familiar but someone mad and cold had borrowed his eyes, someone she did not know, who made her feel sick with fear.

'Deeps?' Her wrist was being bent back slowly. She thought she heard ice cracking. 'She's your friend as well,' Chila whispered, her voice breaking. 'I thought she'd ask your permission first.'

Deepak let her go abruptly. A single tear spilled down Chila's cheek, leaving a snail's trail through her foundation. Deepak saw it, and returned to his body.

'Oh, shit . . . oh, God, I'm sorry, baby. I'm sorry. I shouldn't have shouted . . . Come here.' Deepak enveloped her, holding her close, feeling her pulse flutter where her wrists lay helplessly at his chest. They were both shaking. Remorse rose into his throat, flooded him. God, he hated Tania. Hated the way she managed to throw her shadow from so far away. He had promised to protect this woman pressed against him, shuddering. He had promised himself he would keep his promises, from now on. He felt as if his survival depended on it. His salvation stood weeping in his arms.

'It's still early. Want to go shopping? Catch a movie? You choose. Anything you want, baby.'

Chila didn't look up at him. She was afraid she might see the monster still lurking in some fold in his face. She felt the bass of his voice through his chest, like the growl of an animal. She made up her mind they would not, after all, get a dog.

'Decided where you want to go tonight, honey?' Deepak crooned, smoothing a stray wisp of hair from her temple.

Chila spoke into his tie, her eyes closed. 'I want to see my mum.'

Sunita replaced the telephone receiver and pressed her hands to her temples. She had been trying Social Services for half an hour, and she had a direct line number. She now understood why all the chairs were bolted to the floor in government offices. If she wasn't so tired from lack of sleep, a night of pacing the upstairs hallway with Sunil throwing up in her hair, she would quite fancy picking up her orthopaedic swivel stool and chucking it at the next person who dared to walk in here and ask her for help.

She fished in her bag, pushing through old tissues, receipts, furry boiled sweets and a laddered pair of pop socks, and brought out her hand mirror. God, it was worse than she'd imagined. The cruel magnifying lens made each pore look like a lunar crater. There it was, the rugged terrain of her face, dustbowls under her eyes, mountains of whiteheads around her nose and a healthy thicket of black bristles sprinkling her chin. What was it about your hair as you hit thirty-five? One moment, you were moussing and gelling and teasing, the next, you were in a depilatory war, waxing and yanking and shaving as fast as possible, while the enemy crept all over you, setting up camp in the most unusual places.

That morning, Sunita had found her first white pubic hair. She had only discovered this after she'd taken it for a bit of panty fluff and attempted to yank it out. Akash had heard her yell of pain and knocked on the bathroom door, asking if she was all right. What could she have said? 'Don't worry about me, just dyeing my nether regions, out in a tick!' She had recently begun to spend more and more time in the bathroom. Firstly, it was the only room in the house with a lock on the door, and secondly, she needed to start the day with a good pluck. Which was the nearest she got nowadays to any kind of physical pleasure. She snapped the mirror closed and got up. She deserved another tea break.

'Excuse me? Miss Bhandari?'

Sunita looked up into a pair of amused brown eyes. She sighed inwardly. The young man noted this and smiled apologetically. He was quite cute, she thought idly; she liked a bit of stubble. Jeans, nice jacket, maybe he's Kashmiri, with those light hazel eyes and milky skin. And young enough to be her nephew, if not son. At least he hadn't called her Auntie.

'Could you see my colleague, Mr Ali? He's just over there.' Sunita was already picking up her bag.

'Actually, it was you I wanted to see. I'm Lakhvir Singh, from Hackney Disability Unit? We've spoken on the phone a couple of times and . . .'

Sunita dropped her bag, flustered. 'God, I'm sorry, I thought—'

'No, you would, me hovering around your desk like that.' He was on his knees next to her, picking up the debris from her upturned bag. 'Please, let me.'

Sunita winced as he folded up the grimy tissues, keeping one for the boiled sweets which he wrapped up and handed to her. 'Were you saving these?'

Sunita grabbed whatever she could and stuffed it away. Her knees clicked loudly as she hauled herself to her feet.

'You were asking for some policy information on home carers?' Lakhvir continued, producing an envelope from his pocket. 'I know it's hellish trying to get through and as I was passing . . .'

Sunita took the envelope, which was warm. This embarrassed her, for some reason. God, control yourself, woman! she told herself. Try not to look like some desperate menopausal harpy. 'That's really kind of you, thanks a lot. I've got so many clients coming in desperate for some home help with dependants, not sure what's available. Our local authority's pretty backward in this area. They seem to recommend tying old people to chairs so they don't touch anything and sending round some bad-tempered do-gooder once a fortnight to take the wrapper off the meals on wheels dinner.'

Lakhvir laughed, slapping his thigh. 'You got them sussed then! How do you cope, Miss Bhandari?'

Sunita put her hand over her chin, hoping the bristle wasn't too lively today. 'It's Mrs, actually. The sweets are for my kids.'

'I believe you.' He smiled.

There. That told him. Now he could file her away under M, Married, Mother, Matronly, Much too ugly to consider so thank God she's taken. She had forgotten how nice it was to be smiled at, without being asked a question about dinner or civil rights immediately afterwards. She pondered the unfairness of hair again: how unshaven men looked so yummy, while unshaven women looked like warthogs wearing lipstick. They should have done a seminar on that in the women's group. Something practical that would have helped her in later life. Like how to stop strange, rather good-looking men staring at you in an intense and unsettling manner.

'Mrs Bhandari,' he said gently.

Sunita's breathing quickened. The man was getting fresh with her! She almost wanted to turn round and check that Rosie from reception wasn't standing behind her, with her Wonderbra and slaw-jawed expression. No, he was definitely looking at her, and moving closer. I am in my favourite film, she thought, the one I haven't seen yet but which always has a scene in it just like this one. Take off your glasses, Miss Bhandari, and could you just shave your chin? Thanks . . . Why, Miss B, you're beautiful!

'It's Sunita,' she said, as huskily as she could.

He put his hand on her arm. Her flesh rose up to meet it, goosepimples galore.

'Sunita,' he said, musically, she fancied, 'do you mind if I just—'

'I am married,' she reminded him quickly, wishing she hadn't.

Lakhvir snaked a hand around her back and plucked something dangling from her sleeve. 'Sorry, it's been driving me mad since you stood up.' He held out a wrinkly stained pop sock which hung limply between them, like a shameful secret. 'Were you saving this as well?'

Sunita took it wordlessly as her heart jumped into a lift and asked for the basement. 'I'll show you out, Mr Singh,' she said brightly.

She was still stinging as she marched through the shopping centre, reliving every toe-curling moment. How could she have been so pathetic? So . . . predictable? She imagined him back in his office, surrounded by a group of grinning youths, telling them the one about the hirsute seductress and the pop sock, over and over again until they rolled on the carpet, begging for mercy. The humiliation Sunita could cope with. Somehow, it had become part of the fabric of her life, certainly through her work, dodging insults and sometimes fists from across her desk. It was the quiet storm she rode at home, every time Akash patted her rump, as if saying goodnight to a friendly beast, and turned over to sleep, while she lay awake in the darkness, willing her desire to roll over and play dead, and let her sleep too. What worried her, what made her walk faster and without purpose, was how easily she had responded to another man, without thinking. It wasn't even a big come on, more like a twinkly dig in the ribs. In fact, be honest here, Sunny, she told herself, the man was just being friendly. Is that all it took, a few kind words and a flirty grin and she would flip onto her back, like some eager puppy, legs in the air, wanting her tummy tickled?

She felt bestial, hungry. She passed a bakery and surveyed the array of enticing meringues and moist chocolate éclairs. That would do for a start.

She ate walking along, without tasting anything. She could not get rid of another flavour, something bitter coating her tongue. It returned every time she recalled Lakhvir's face as he was leaving. What was it that lay in the curve of lip as he said goodbye? She forced down a large lump of chocolate and oh God, did not want to remember but she did. It was pity. She saw herself in miniature in the orb of his eye. She looked grateful, even for mercies as small and misunderstood as the ones he had thrown down before her. It was only pouncing upon crumbs that made her realize she was being starved, slowly, to nothing.

She swallowed the last morsels of éclair and broke into a slow trot. She talked to herself, in rhythm with her footsteps. I have a husband who I wanted to marry and I love, I have two perfect children, I have a job, it's not what I hoped for but as much as I can expect, I am lucky, I should be happy, I ought to be happy, I will be happy. She stopped, feeling a stitch sew up her left side. She was in front of a boutique. DAZE said the neon-pink sign. She could feel that her breath, instead of slowing down, was getting faster. Not here, she panicked, not now. I don't even know where I am. There was a silver dress in the window, glittering under a spotlight. A mere slip of a dress for a slip of a woman. Spangles and sparkles, Sunita said, Nikita's favourite words at the moment, and went inside.

Sunita took a long hard look at her body in front of the changing-room mirror. Despite the hours in her bathroom, she had managed to avoid looking at her reflection for what felt like years. Her face she could manage, her extremities were tolerable. She had even painted her toenails, last winter for Chila's wedding. But that vast undiscovered country between her neck and ankles, that had been invaded and reclaimed by children, hair and cakes. It was not her home any more.

Where should she start? She traced the stretch marks across her belly and down her thighs, a relief map marking out dangerous journeys she had somehow survived. She took in the heavy drooping breasts whose nipple eyes stared at the floor, as if waiting to be told off for letting themselves go. There once was a waist here, she remembered, somewhere around here between these two bulging rolls. She circled the area where it used to be with her thumbs. She flapped the pouches on her underarms, fleshy wings, useless for flying. She jumped up and down a couple of times, and noticed which bits kept moving after she had landed. Most of them, she concluded. And what happened if she bent over, sideways on to the mirror? What shape did she make? A beanbag doing aerobics? A marshmallow attempting the hurdles? How much there was of her! Amazing really, what one's clothes disguised. Amazing that someone who felt so ravenous took up so much space.

'Are you OK, madam?' A startled assistant stood in the doorway, the cubicle curtain in her hand. She was trying hard to look Sunita straight in the eye, but only succeeded in twitching nervously.

'Oh, fine, thanks,' replied Sunita airily. She jumped again, this time trying to notice what happened to her buttocks in mid-air.

'Um, we would ask, if you are going to try that dress on,

madam . . . we would prefer it if you wore some under-garments.'

Sunita bent over to pick up the silver dress from the floor, causing the assistant to emit an involuntary whimper and back off hurriedly.

'No need to try it on. It's perfect,' she said. 'Do you take Visa?'

Martin got out his credit card and crossed his fingers as the assistant swiped it through the computerized till. He registered the satisfying beep of approval and waited for Tania's present to be gift wrapped. It was just a silly little gift which had caught his eye as he left the tube station. A snowstorm of the New York skyline, but not yer cheap plastic bubble containing a tired polystyrene snow flurry. This was state of the art kitsch: thick glass, avalanches of velvet snow swirling around the Empire State, the Twin Towers and, his personal favourite, the art deco Chrysler Building, an elegant spire of silver lattice and symmetrical chrome. It even played Sinatra's 'New York New York', one of their tunes, which always recalled for him a Soho coffee shop with condensation-steamed windows and cold finger-tips that tasted of hot chocolate.

He had promised her a weekend in New York at Christmas, but the way work was going, she might have to make do with a couple of bagels and a session with the snow dome. Still, he reasoned, as he made his way towards the Tisdale Centre, this would remind her that he hadn't forgotten. And women, in his experience, were not always impressed by the large, expensive gestures. Sometimes the small, cheap ones did just as well.

He recognized her laugh, or he might not have looked round. Of course, he could identify spoken Punjabi, but he somehow never associated it with Tania's voice. But there she was, sitting at a window seat in a café, deep in conversation with a frizzy-haired man whom Martin thought he recognized, or worse still, who just looked familiar because sometimes, Asian men did to him. There were probably a million innocent reasons why they were together and having a good time. But the easy flow of their banter disturbed Martin, particularly as some of it was bilingual, an odd guttural word thrown into the middle of a sentence which excluded him as effectively as a masonic handshake. This was a club he couldn't join. He had wangled the odd day pass, but life membership and bar privileges would not be forthcoming.

Martin was struck by the intimacy that a shared language could evoke, and how his writer's ear heard different tunes in each one. French always sounded dirty and indolent, provocative pillow chat, even if a couple happened to be arguing over who last unloaded the dishwasher. Spanish was passionate and slightly amused, as if the speaker knew it was obligatory to lose their temper about something inappropriate before the end of the sentence, and then forget about it two sentences later. Russian depressed him, in the way a good vodka hangover did, and Mandarin was noble and slightly condescending. He had heard Malayalam once, in a South Indian vegetarian restaurant. He chose it as his favourite so far, as the bubbles and rolling tongue plosives sounded like a large man farting in the bath. But Punjabi, he decided, he hated. It was crude, soil-bound, back-slapping macho shouting, no spaces to listen as Tania and the Bloke seemed to constantly talk over each other. They wouldn't be doing that if they had stuck to English.

The plastic bag containing the snow globe felt unreasonably heavy in his hand. If she looked over at him in the next ten seconds, he would wave and smile. He would go over, introduce himself, wait to be introduced back, and they would all have coffee together, like grown ups. After two minutes of watching Tania toss her hair and smoke in an unnecessarily dramatic manner, Martin stomped off back towards the underground station. If he hurried, he could catch a double Woody Allen bill at the Metro, *Hannah and Her Sisters*, followed by *Manhattan*. He was a big boy, he could see New York on his own.

Tania checked the top of Martin's computer; stone cold, which meant he had not been in the flat for hours. There was nothing left in the oven for her, which hurt for some reason, although he had cleaned up the kitchen and had even circled a couple of comedies in the satellite TV guide for this evening. She wandered around the flat aimlessly, stepping over her mess from the day. She needed company this evening.

Her long lunch with Akash had left her feeling restless and free-floating. It was her own fault; never have an unplanned meal with a therapist. What began as a post-mortem on the morning's drama turned into an impromptu confessional. It had begun innocuously enough. Although they had known each other for years through Sunita, it was always the women who had talked, managed the friendship, with Akash an occasional bystander, affable enough but never involved. They both had Sunita's version of each other to contrast and compare, privately, without wanting to upset the easy balance they had achieved. Akash found Tania to be just as clever and spiky as his wife had described, her lauded beauty was obvious, but what intrigued him was how she used it as a diversion, keeping the gawpers at bay. Tania, personally, had never understood what Sunita saw in Akash. He was good looking in a faded intelligentsia sort of way, he was smart and perceptive, naturally, but this passion and energy that Sunita had always described must have fallen away with time, like his hair.

However, after a couple of glasses of wine, or maybe because of them, she could see what Sunita meant. Once she began opening up, he was on the trail like a bloodhound, worrying her for more detail, sniffing at her for dates, smells, colours, how she felt. And he laughed a lot, encouraging her to embellish her anecdotes. In retrospect, they were amusing, she supposed. The way her father would line them all up for inspection, like troops, before going to school, and send them off with his motto, 'Be better than the person in front! No loafing, understand?' Her mother's secret stash of treats which she tied into the end of her sari pullau; when she unfolded it, sweeties and loose change and folded cuttings from magazines would fall out. No-one was ever allowed to read the cuttings, except the ones found in the last sari she wore when she died. Tania had hoped it would reveal some poignant insight into her departed mother's soul; instead she found a coupon for twenty pence off her next purchase of tinned fruit salad, and a cut out of some Hindi film star which her mother had written on in scrawly writing, 'Eyebrows like this please.' And the pointless day trips her father would organize on Sundays usually, when he would jump up from the table, rub his hands and say, 'We should see Watford. Watford is the place to go nowadays.' Never a theme park or a seaside, but a grey collection of anonymous suburban holes where her father would register at a local estate agent's, claiming he was thinking of moving to your lovely town and had they got anything in the hundred thousand pound region?

Akash had commented that this was her father's version of wish fulfilment, he longed for something bigger and better, and for those few short minutes in an estate agent's office, he was a rich man who had made it, who had choices. Tania pointed out that her father's actions had merely embarrassed his children to the point of hysteria, and given her a morbid fear of acquiring a mortgage. What she wanted to say was that it made her hate who she was, standing behind her mother in a cheap coat with too much oil in her hair.

'You should write some of this stuff down,' Akash had told her.

'Confessional work bores me,' she replied. 'That's why I've always chosen docs over drama, why I never use a narrator. The camera as objective witness, that's what it's all about.'

'Everything is subjective, Tania. Even for a voyeur like yourself. And your raw material is other people's lives.'

Tania leaned back on her chair, grinning. 'Snap,' she said.

She grabbed her handbag and decided: she would go and see Chila. She wanted to sit in a cardamom-smelling kitchen and eat home-fried snacks. Her tongue felt rusty; the halting Punjabi she had attempted with Akash had exercised muscles in her tongue and throat she'd forgotten about. Chatting to Chila was a good non-chemical sedative; half an hour's gossip about dado rails was just what she needed to relax. She thought about writing Martin a note but instead, placed her DV camera carefully in the middle of the dining table, before leaving.

Deepak scanned the row of pans squatting on the cooker, wondering where to start. He lifted up the lids in turn, checking what Chila had left him for supper. Aloo gobi, chicken with spinach, daal, rice and a tower of freshly made rotis. A Post-it note on the fridge informed him that inside waited a chocolate cake with his name on. Deepak went straight to the bread bin, pulled out a couple of slices of white bread, scooped up some chicken between them and ate it as he wandered from room to room, surveying his domain.

This was the first time he had been in the house without Chila, and it was only now he began to notice how much the place had changed. Gone were the heavy brown velvet curtains from the living room, and the lamp made from an old whisky bottle. It was all frou-frou frills and co-ordinated pouffes, and those stupid glass animals taking up some valuable shelf space. Deepak removed a couple of his trophies from the menagerie and put them on top of the television defiantly.

The back room wasn't much better. Deepak had fondly called this the Den, although the Knocking Shop might have been more appropriate in his bachelor days. This is where he had put his sound system, drinks cabinet, large floor cushions and low-level lighting. At one point, after he had invested in an electronics warehouse, this whole room was controlled by a single remote control. At the push of a button, the curtains would close, the lights would dim, a jazzy number would begin playing from hidden speakers and the radiators would turn up to full blast. 'Is it hot in here?' he would ask whoever, proffering more wine and waiting for the first layers of clothing to be removed. Then there was that terrible incident one night when he had managed to pull some incredibly classy Sloane, whose father also happened to own a few very promising franchises, and showed her into the room with a flourish. He pressed the requisite button, and suddenly it was Armageddon. Rock music screamed through the speakers, the curtains flapped in and out like epileptic bats, the radiators attempted to rattle themselves off the wall, and the lights dimmed, grew and then blew up. Selina/Sarah/Sophie did not even bother to remove the shards of light-bulb from her hair before she left.

Deepak laughed out loud, chuckling to a halt as he took in the velveteen wallpaper, the rosewood dining suite and chairs, the place settings ready at each chair. Did she actually spend time folding those napkins into swans? He sat at the head of the pristine, as yet unused table, a song running through his head vaguely remembered. Something about having the perfect wife, the perfect life, flowing water and no idea of what it all meant. He had been baffled by too many choices, that's why he was here. The initial amazement he felt at being able to attract so many women soon grew into a kind of contempt. It was all too easy. And if they tumbled so quickly for him, how many others had there been before him? He realized these were gross double standards, but the contempt had flowed both ways. As the notches built up on his bedpost, the bed itself grew bigger and lonelier. How he had ached for tenderness instead of tortured acrobatics, the sickness of longing and waiting for someone, instead of this endless, satiated, lazy pleasure.

He had tried to explain how he felt to Manoj who, having been married for five years by then, called him an ungrateful sod and asked him for any leftovers he might throw his way.

Surprisingly, it was Asif who had provided some comfort. 'Ah, ready to tie the knot, eh?'

'God, no. Just to have something . . . else, I suppose.'

Asif poured him a large whisky and put a fatherly arm around his back. 'All these lovely girls you have been seeing, gorgeous, all of them. Was there any one of them you would choose to be the mother of your children?'

'I haven't thought about kids yet.'

'Oh, yes, you have, you are right now! We only know truly what we want, when we imagine what we will leave for our children. You think my Leila was the prettiest girl on offer? The wittiest? The richest? No. But when I imagined her speaking Urdu to my son, making him our food, mixing with my family, she fitted. Like an old warm glove.' Asif laughed into his glass.

'Well, that's really persuaded me to rush down to the nearest marriage bureau and order myself something comfortable. Is a little bit of excitement, fun, spark, too much to ask?'

'For you, yes,' replied Asif sternly. 'It's too late for you. You associate the bad girls with the good times. That's why in an ideal world, both partners should be virgins. You know nothing else. You don't know if there is anything better, so what you have is perfect. You want to spend the rest of your life searching for the next best thing? Calling it love, this pain in the guts, when actually you might just have diarrhoea? Same symptoms, yaar.'

'You can find both,' Deepak said quietly. 'I did once.'

'And where is she now, this goddess?'

Deepak shrugged. 'Making someone else's life hell, I suppose.'

They both registered the overwhelming sense of déjà vu when he opened the door. It could have been the old days, the good days, when Tania would waltz past him swinging a bottle or a take-away carton, kick off her shoes and enjoy the feel of his eyes upon her while she reclaimed his space, purring. Now it was different. Now she stood like any other visitor on the doorstep; the woman he would have died for was now no different from any passing window cleaner or Jehovah's Witness.

Neither of them spoke for a moment, pondering, perhaps, the fickleness of it all. To have been so intimate, to have been able to walk away from it so quickly, to have believed as feverishly in something that turned sick and pale just months later. Maybe that was all there was, the momentary truth of a connection, the serial monogamy roundabout their parents would never ride on, fearing sickness and wobbly legs afterwards. What made people climb back on, knowing that they were wrong once and would probably be wrong again, knowing it would hurt, probably, eventually? You minimize the risk factor, Deepak answered himself, like the good businessman that I am, and you choose blue chip safe stock, so when you fall it's never too far or wholly unexpected.

It is safe here now, Deepak told himself, mantra-like, before he said, somewhat ungraciously, 'She's not here.'

'Oh.'

'Gone to see her mother. She won't be back till late.'

'I see.'

Tania turned to leave, longing for the safe haven of her car. If she could just get inside and strap herself in, turn the music up loud, all this would pass.

'Actually, I would like to talk to you. Have you got a minute?'

She hesitated, still not daring to face him. His voice brought back whispered conversations in dark, damp-sheeted places.

'It's about this TV thing you're doing . . . with Chila.'

It was work then. Work was allowed, facts and time-tables were permissible, they both knew that.

'I can't stay long,' she said finally, as she edged past him, careful not to let an inch of their bodies meet in the door-way. 'Martin's cooking me a meal tonight,' she added, as he shut the door behind her.

Deepak gestured at the small mountain of untouched food on the cooker. Tit for tat. See, I've got someone who loves me too.

'She's a good cook,' Tania said dismissively.

'She's a good woman,' replied Deepak.

They allowed themselves a look then, amused, cynical. Let the games begin.

'Martin's brilliant at housework too. I mean he actually enjoys ironing. He finds clean bathrooms thrilling.'

'Does he wear a frilly apron when he's hoovering then?' Deepak circled the settee, still keeping a distance from her.

'No, because he isn't one of those troglodytes who assumes personal hygiene is only for poofters.'

Deepak stifled a chortle and removed an invisible dart from between his shoulderblades. Banter as foreplay, their mutual weakness, the thrill of a matched opponent who predicts your every move. The skill of an evenly matched enemy who knows your Achilles' heel.

'And Chila isn't one of those ladettes who thinks saying fuck a lot and downing pints means she's a feminist.'

Tania moved to the armchair, perching on the arm. 'Martin's one of those rare men who really likes women. Even with their clothes on. And he makes me laugh.'

Deepak moved to the sofa, leaning on it nonchalantly. 'Chila's one of those rare women who enjoys being one. Even when she's wearing trousers. And she makes me horny as hell.'

Tania got up from the armchair, heading for the kitchen to grab a glass of water. She stopped mid-way, feeling foolish. She might not know where the glasses were kept any more. She could not bear the thought of opening the wrong cupboard or of having to ask him for a drink.

'So it looks like we both got what we wanted, then,' Deepak said to her back.

'What's that then?'

She could hear the smile in his voice: 'A wife.'

He touched her arm, gently, as she made for the door. Not like he had grabbed Chila only hours previously. No yielding soft flesh here, it was all hard-toned ready-for-flight muscle, and somewhere beneath his fingers, a pulse, hammering against a bloody drum.

'She doesn't want to do this programme, Tania.'

Tania laughed now, relieved. It sounded joyless; breathe him out, dead air. 'You're already telling her what she thinks. God, that was quick, Deepak. It took you months to do that with me.'

'You're using her. She's too sweet to see it and you know that.'

'Is that right?'

Deepak moved in closer, smelled perfume and smoke in her hair. Eau de Slut she'd called it once, wanting to see if he would silently agree. Guessing he would.

'You forget,' he said softly, 'I know you, Tania. Every inch. Doing favours isn't your job.'

She squared up to him, well-rehearsed speeches on autocue in her head. 'And granting them isn't yours. But then, that always was your big problem, Deepak. Getting to know someone and trying to own them is not the same thing. If she says yes because you've got bigger muscles than her, what she probably means is no. Why do you think women have to be such good liars? Especially our women? And how are you ever going to know the difference? Scared people never tell the truth. Do they?'

Deepak flinched from her, pulling his arm away. 'I don't need to fight you for her,' he said slowly, 'however many pseudo-feminist sayings you want to use to justify your career plan. I love her enough to let her make her own mind up. But I'll be watching you.'

And he did, as she flung the front door open and marched to her car, hair flying like some triumphant banner behind her. She always did like dramatic exits. He had rather enjoyed playing along, running after her in his bare feet on the damp pavement, calling her name, begging mock-forgiveness, astonished that enacting such clichés could be such fun. Now, he just felt cold. He shut the door and automatically picked up the telephone. He would check that Chila was OK, remind her that whenever she was ready, he would drive over, pick her up, bring her home, and lock the door behind them.

Tania

I NEVER BOUGHT INTO THAT TRUTH IS BEAUTY AND VICE VERSA crap. I'm waiting for proof that telling it like it is makes anyone feel good or better, and my theory was finally confirmed on day two at university when our current affairs tutor banged on about objectivity in reportage. So there's a war and you're there with your crew in pretend combats with a Kate Adie streak of dirt artfully smeared on your cheek. Where's your first location? When you get there, where do you first point the camera? Where the bomb lands or where it dropped from? What do you say to accompany the visuals? Hooray for our lads, the freedom fighters, or boo to the barbarian terrorists? What tone? Grave seen-it-all witness, here we go again, man's inhumanity, etc.? Or shocked not-since-Belsen horror, a catch in the voice, the soft toy lying/placed pathetically in the ruins? At every stage you make choices. You play God. Cue the Sun. The biggest lie is that we claim to have the real answers. But it is the perfect camouflage, if you want to be an invisible deity.

My mother believed that those gilt-painted statues on top

of the fridge were actual divine beings. She would talk to them like best friends, bow and cry to them, go to cover their ears if any of us said a harsh word in their hearing, ask them for blessings that they repeatedly ignored, like her health, and her children's future weddings. After she died, I wrapped them up and sent them to her sister in Bombay. I swaddled them in red silk and put FRAGILE – GODS WITHIN on the packaging. The only parcel I've sent to India that has ever arrived undamaged and on time.

The nearest I've been to a divine presence was on a beach in Greece with a saxophone player from Surrey. Yeah, he knew he was a walking oxymoron, which is probably why we got on so well. We drank two bottles of wine, and watched the sun sink over the endless, curved horizon as he played some Deep South kinda sultry composition, and life, for those few minutes, was blessed. I don't remember feeling particularly truthful, but something made bigger sense than me. I could have gone with it, but once I'd worked out that all it took to summon Him/Her/Them up was some retsina and a rather crap version of 'Summertime', I gave up on God/s for good.

Jonathan peppered his speeches with an assortment of divine expletives when I showed him the first rough cut of the documentary. Interesting how you can imbue a holy being with so many different meanings. Maybe that's what whoever it was meant when He said 'I have many names,' knowing future hedonistic generations would need them to use in times of stress, wonder and, of course, when having especially good sex. There were the Christs of glee when Jonathan saw the couple of spousal punch ups that I got in Akash's sessions, the Jesuses of amazement when I showed him the interview with the two sister-wives of the urbane Muslim businessman, who said they actually loved each other better than the husband they shared. And the oh Gods of envy when I ran through the various beaming, happily matched couples who, after a handful of chaperoned meetings together, took the leap of faith and fortunately landed, feet first, on their perfect match. And then he asked me about Chila.

'I mean, Jesus wept, Tania, she was the reason I wanted you to do this project. I mean, yeah, you've got some sexy stuff there, but the journey of it . . . surely she's the traveller we should be following.'

Of course, I couldn't tell him why she wasn't featured, why it had been so difficult to get her on her own, especially as she had refused to do the interview without Deepak being present. I mumbled something about availability to which he snorted, 'She's a housewife, for God's sake, how busy is she going to be?'

I thought I'd lost the whole thing then. There were hundreds of reasons I didn't want to do that interview, most of them featuring Deepak, his reactions, and the knock-on effect on my friend. My soft as butter, snug as a bug friend who is so desperate to be on television.

She actually rang me up last week (whispering quickly so she could finish before Deepak came out of the shower), and begged me to make her a star. 'See, I've told everyone about it, all Deepak's friends, and they were dead impressed, and I promised to invite them all to the – what do you call it? – showing, premium, whatever, and they've started inviting me to coffee mornings now and tomorrow I'm going to this Tupperware for India Street Kids thing and . . . I really want to do it, Tans. I'll be really good on it, promise.'

Like chucking a floppy-eared puppy into the storm. Martin once said, during one of our few nasty rows, that looking after Chila is the nearest thing I have to a conscience. But I couldn't explain to her that I was trying to protect her by leaving her out. Because then we would have to have That Conversation about why I felt she needed protection from her darling jaan, and how could I tell her that she was married to someone whose darkness had once filled me and frightened me in equal measure?

Shit. I have been through this so many times. That maybe I should have warned her off. Come clean. But why would her version of him be the same as mine? Truth is especially subjective in relationships. The number of girlfriends who tell me they've finally found the one, the witty, handsome, sensitive, yet manly man who will fill the gaping chasm in their otherwise accomplished lives, and I am introduced to ginger dwarves with halitosis, pot-bellied baldies with a nice line in toilet jokes, anorak-wearing Oedipal cases who blush when a bra advert comes on. And the majority of these averagely underwhelming men are stepping out with these incredible, ripe, blooming gals.

That's the real bastard about the biological clock: ovaries are such terrible judges of character. They get one whiff of a possible sperm donor and they're off, slipping in their own juices, pulling you after men you wouldn't have spat on a mere three years earlier. It's not that I don't like children per se, I just don't like what wanting them does to your brain. Apparently a female is born already containing all the eggs she will ever produce and once you hit thirty-five, they start dying off at a rapid rate. How fair is that? Apply the same rule to sperm production and you'd be falling over desperate-to-please men, wearing skimpy vests to reveal their fine child-producing frames, laughing uproariously at your jokes, showing off their cars with inbuilt baby seats, men who don't go green and twitch when commitment is mentioned, men who swap arrogance for Aran sweaters and nut roasts, because only those with time on their side can afford to be choosy and cruel.

Personally, I've always preferred my eggs unfertilized. Every month I wave bye-bye to them, one down, x number to go, shedding moons, resisting gravity and the tides. It's what I'm good at, what I've got used to.

In a weird way (and can I just say at this point the nearest gay experience I have had was a half-hearted snog with a drunk TV chat show hostess, only just worth it for the two-page story I flogged to a Sunday newspaper the next day?), Chila being with Deepak is almost like Chila being with me. My gift to her, although he'd say he wasn't mine to give. My personal leap of faith, the only one I've ever taken, believing that all that was good in him would be even better beneath the warmth of her unsullied sun. Goodness breeds goodness, fight fire with fire and all that. Maybe the sharp-fanged creatures we let loose together would become gambolling pussycats with Chila. I hope to God.

So Jonathan was getting more agitated, not helped by his ridiculously snug leather trousers and a few bottles of Chablis at his BBC lunch, and he comes to the brief section I filmed with Sunita. I'd planned to shoot a day-long interview with her, finally commit to tape the now epic story of how she and Akash met, yadda yadda, but when it came to it, well, she just wasn't there. Akash joined her for part of it, they told their story in a strange sort of dutiful manner, they even held hands, but it was like watching one of those crap carpet adverts. We love our shag pile and you will too. Maybe it was nerves. She let slip she'd had a couple of panic attacks over the last few months, stress of babies as per, so I didn't want to scrap the item and make her feel bad. I shot what I could, salvageable in the edit; with a bit of soft focus and some chocolate box music, they will look like anyone else in love.

I explained all this to Jonathan before he saw the unedited version (always have caveats a-plenty for him after a boozy lunch), and he watched it silently, chin in his hand, making those really bloody irritating grunty noises like some old bloke watching the boxing. And when it's over, he gets up and leaves the room, leaving me to hyperventilate into a paper cup and start flicking through *Guardian Media* for another job.

Then he comes back in, slaps me on the back and says, 'Brilliant! It's there, isn't it? It's all there. A spot of re-editing and we'll have a programme.'

I do a sort of half-nod, half-shake gesture, one of the useful genetic traits I've retained, the Indian yes–no head waggle, always lets you off the hook in a sort of mystical enigmatic way.

And then he says, 'I've had a word with Kirsten, the strand producer, and she agrees, go with the flow.'

'Right.' I waggled again. 'You mean, the same flow . . . of the journey . . . we were discussing. That flow.' Rule number one: always make them spell out what they want, because most of the time they have no sodding idea and they're hoping you will give them some definition that they can blame you for when it all goes pear-shaped.

Jonathan leaned forward, his eyes glittering. 'A therapist . . . married to her. It's perfect. Ironically funny. It's what they don't say that matters, eh? It's now. It's very now.'

Well, that cleared things up perfectly. I got on the phone to Chila in front of him and arranged the interview for the following week. I knew what I had to do. And Chila was so grateful she almost made me feel good about it.

Of course, just when I need a bit of TLC, Martin decides to behave like a slab of rare sod. Ever since I started this doc, he's been skulking around, chiselling away at his writer's block, tutting and harrumphing every time I try and get some feedback off him about my dilemma. (And contrary to popular opinion, it is a dilemma for me, using friends for fodder.) Scratch a new man and a prehistoric snake always slithers out. His testosterone levels are so high, he's choking on his own basic instincts. He wants to be happy for me, but how can he when I'm doing better than him? I tried to be as sensitive as I could, I tried explaining that me having a job and him not being able to get one did not mean I was standing over his bollocks with a mallet in my hand. I even tried to explain why I can't play the shucks, this is just a hobby game with him, not only because I respect him and expect more of him than that, but mainly because it made me sick, watching my mother contort herself to bolster my father's fragile ego.

God knows, my father had high ambitions: 'Only the best!' he would blare at us; 'You be the best. You will get the best.' Brave words from a man who never got off the factory floor long enough to see the sky, whose idea of haute couture was Crimplene trousers with the crease already sewn in, whose every effort to better himself just succeeded in making us ashamed of who we were. Smelly Pakis hanging around hotel foyers while he pretended to be checking out prices for the top-floor suite; jungle bunnies dithering in the Mercedes showroom while Dad begged for a test drive; the poor bewildered savages who found themselves, mistakenly of course, in the first-class carriages of trains, with Dad insisting the booking clerk had made a terrible mistake.

When I get asked about racism, as I always do in any job interview when they're checking whether I'm the genuine article (oppressed Asian woman who has suffered), as opposed to the pretend coconut (white on the inside, brown on the outside, too well off and well spoken to be considered truly ethnic), I make up stories about skinheads and shit through letterboxes, because that's the kind of racism they want to hear about. It lets my nice interviewer off the hook, it confirms that the real baddies live far away from him in the SE postcode area, and he can tut at them from a safe distance. I never tell them about the stares and whispers and the anonymous gobs of phlegm at bus stops, the creaking of slowly closing doors and the limited view from the glass counter (we never get as high as the ceiling), which all scar as deeply as a well-aimed Doc Marten. Maybe I would not have learned about them so early on if it hadn't been for dear Papa. Maybe I should thank him for that.

But funnily enough, it wasn't him I blamed. It was Mum. We were kids; duffle-coated, clean-nosed, well-drilled children whose dad had big hands and long strides. Mum was heavier than the rest of the family's combined weight; I could hear her ten-decibel hacking from the next street. This was not a small woman. But she shrivelled to the size of a wrinkled pea around her husband. Every bad idea he came up with (and there were many), was always hers. She stalked them, pounced on them and claimed them as soon as they went wrong, allowing him to shake his head and bellow, 'Your mother has bungled matters again!' Every good idea was usually hers, and given to him on a warm plate with a liberal dash of humble dressing. 'You see? How your father was right? Listen to him next time, all of you. Such a brilliant move, husband-ji. Thusi acha badh kithe . . .'

Oh, I knew the drill all right. Training began early in our house, not in the expected areas, cooking, shopping, cleaning, as Mother insisted I would have all my life to run after some man and she would rather I enjoyed my carefree virginal days. (Which I did, by visiting various cafés and sucking the face off some grateful sixth-former.) But what she taught me was more of a spatial exercise: how to take up as little room as possible. How to read the moods of everyone in the room and flow smoothly about them, adapting to their edges and hollows, silver and silent as mercury. How to walk in small steps, talk in sweet tones, pour dainty cupfuls, refill plates in the shake of a dupatta, smile and smile at visitors (for it would be them rather than my family who would judge me later on) and, most importantly, save any rages and rumbles for the privacy of my dark bedroom.

Strange that so many of us become doctors and business people; the women are so much more suited to the service industries. We aim to please. Any complaints, please see the manager. No tipping necessary.

Martin, moody scumbag that he is sometimes, is always bemoaning my lack of native culture. It must be disappointing for him; there he was, thinking he was getting the genuine article, looking forward to spatting with my family and having forbidden encounters in borrowed places, planning a romantic tour with me around the one-hut, dung-filled villages he visited as a student, and instead he gets someone who can drink him under the table and belch the alphabet as a party piece. I know a lot more than he knows I know.

Anyone with a bit of sense would guess that a comprehensive-educated kid from a blue-collar family in the East End is force-fed her language and rituals as a matter of survival, our defence against the corruption outside our front door. Anyone Asian, that is. Only anyone not Asian would assume that wearing mini-skirts and liking Italian food meant I was in ethnic denial. The roots go deeper than that, honey. Ask most of my girlfriends, ranging in hue from tinted copper to Dravidian blue-black; between them they run business empires, save lives on operating tables, mould and develop young minds, trade in non-existent commodities with shouting barrow boys, kick ass across courtrooms and computer screens. In the outside world, they fly on home-grown wings. Then they reach their front doors and forget it all. They step over the threshold, the Armani suit shrinks and crumples away, the pencil skirt feels blowsy and tight, the head bows, the shoulders sag, within a minute they are basting and baking and burning fingers over a hot griddle, they are soothing children and saying sorry, bathing in-laws and burning with guilt, packing lunch-boxes and pouring oil over choppy waters, telling everyone who will listen they don't mind, wondering why they left their minds next to the muddy wellies and pile of junk mail in the front porch.

I've seen it happen right before my eyes, the most frightening and speedy transformation since Jekyll and Hyde (the Spencer Tracy version, natch). One moment, my friend Meena was describing how she'd sacked three of her staff and organized a buy-out of a rival firm in her lunch hour, the next she was simpering her way around her husband, who stood at the top of the stairs, baffled by a piece of complicated equipment called an iron. She was so apologetic I thought she was going to do a Basil Fawlty and give the iron a damn good thrashing for confusing her man. If any of her colleagues had dismissed her, patronized her, ordered her, spoken to her the way the man she loves spoke to her then, she'd have wiped the floor with their battered carcasses. Instead, Meena smiled and said sorry.

I've seen it happen a little with Sunita, although she's hardly a high flyer; Akash was canny enough to clip her wings before she'd realized her potential. But I've seen enough to recognize it for what it is: our collective shameful secret. We meet the world head up, head on, we meet our men and we bow down gratefully, cling to compromise like a lover who promises all will be well if we don't make trouble. We hear our mothers' voices and heed them, to make up for all the other imagined transgressions in our lives. Everything else I can pick up or discard when I choose; my culture is a movable feast. Except for this rogue gene which I would cauterize away if I could. Unlike Sunita, I don't just wave the placards and wear the badges. Unlike Chila, I don't sit back and trust to the fickle workings of fate. I made a choice about the kind of life I wanted to have. When things go belly up, Chila always blames karma, Sunita blames her failed university career, I blame no-one but myself.

Jonathan was right, remarkably, when he said that choosing whom you love is the most political decision you can make. It was for all of us. We three girls managed the oft-quoted juggling act until it was time to find a man. See how I combine this bindi with that leather jacket and make a bold statement about my duality? Look! I can go to a rave one night, and the next morning be cooking in the communal temple kitchen! Watch how I glide effortlessly from old paths to new pastures, creating a new culture as I walk on virgin snow! And then it was time to cut the crap and own up to who we really were.

Chila didn't have much choice. Coming from the most traditional family and obviously not college material, they were lining up boys for her before she left school. Ironic, really, that the girl who most wanted to Do the Right Thing was considered defective material. Her parents assaulted the marriage markets on all fronts: the matrimonial bureaux where they find a perfect match by matching up your heights and income brackets, the notice boards in the temples and community centres where your personal details are displayed along with the times for yoga classes and the winner of the under sevens trampolining competition, and, of course, the gossip grapevine. God knows who said what about Chila, but judging by the men she was offered, her word of mouth was not great. Families would turn up at her folks' home dragging strange boys behind them, boys who had been shut up and hidden away and had limps and squints and bewildered smiles. They would stumble in, blinking in the daylight, wearing brand new too-small suits, sit staring at the sweetmeats while their parents pretended their sons were actually international tycoons disguised cleverly as idiots. I don't know how Chila kept her dignity. I hated her fucking family for what they were offering her, hated the other bastards for what they thought she was worth. And the amazing thing was, under all that pressure, Chila always said no. She would wait, she said. I don't know for what, we all thought. And look what happened.

For Sunita, it was always different. Her parents were considered the coolest around. Yeah, her brothers got away with murder, but her mum and dad always insisted she should get her education and then think about marriage, if she wanted. They offered to do some introductions, and even said if she found someone herself, they wouldn't mind (unless he was a black Muslim with no job, in which case they would kill her). The subtext was, choose anyone you like, preferably a Hindu Punjabi with prospects . . .

I would love to have interviewed her folks for the doc. Her dad insisted they call it 'Assisted marriage, no arranging in this house. We help, we advise and we leave it to her. Just like your upper classes, although I would never have put Diana and Charlie together. Whoever matched them needs a good slap.' I'm sure the reason me and Sunny have our spats is that I've spent most of my life wishing I had her parents. And with all that, the silly cow lets her pants do the talking and goes and chooses Akash.

And me? Well, I was somewhere in the middle. My father, for all his military bluster, knew that it was impossible to disguise our humble origins. Strangers might believe he was a millionaire in training, but amongst his own, his surname and size of house always defined who he was. So Mum and Dad attempted a few half-hearted introductions, but by then I was out of university, freelancing for local papers and being propositioned by an array of multi-coloured, multi-fascinating, fit young men. It was like being led to a feast and told your diet starts today, those stupid faddy diets where you can only eat one thing for the rest of your life. I'd only ever snacked on brown boy, and too much of that made me slightly nauseous. (That's the problem with biting the forbidden fruit; nothing ever tastes the same again.)

I did agree to a few meetings with prospective candidates, mainly because it was such fascinating material and a sort of rite of passage I felt I had to go through, like buying your first bra. There was plenty of interest, much to my father's delight, because of my mother's loud religious leanings, my qualifications, my reputation as a bit of a looker. On paper I was A1-plus suitable, and they breezed into our lounge, hoping for the best. Then I opened my mouth and within minutes they were scrambling for the door, snacks uneaten, scorching their mouths with quick cups of tea, telling Mum and Dad they would let us know.

The feedback was fairly standard: 'She is too modern' (too independent to do as he says and maybe a bit of a slapper); 'She is too Western' (speaks bad Punjabi and is definitely a bit of a slapper); 'He needs someone who will fit in with his job' (she has a job that will prevent her from supporting his career); 'We have a joint family system' (she will never agree to pooling her wages and spending her weekends going to kitty parties with us); 'He liked her but is looking for someone more like us' (he fancies the pants off her and finds this terrifying so would rather marry a buffalo with a moustache who won't go off with his best friend). Mum would weep and waddle around wringing her hands afterwards. My father would shout, throw things and curse the jumped up brahmins who thought they were better than us, curse the world and its donkey for giving him a proud heart and a thin wallet.

So I was resigned to this nuptial pantomime. I got to wear a nice selection of my favourite silk suits, and even looked forward to that moment when I would crack a joke and the creeping terror would slide across some helpless man's face. After all, any man who can't meet you without bringing his parents along is hardly the type to make your heart sprout wings and dance the tango.

And then one wintry morning, the tea is brewing, the samosas are fried and waiting, a smart car pulls up outside the house, Mum and Dad arrange themselves at the door-way (Mum always behind Dad as her size sometimes frightened young kids), they open the door and Deepak walks in with his family. My father was practically climbing up Deepak's parents trouser legs with gratitude that such esteemed and wealthy people would grace his house with their presence. My mum wheezed like some old faithful retainer, force-feeding them home-made nibbles and urging me with twitches and winks to walk forward, serve tea and be nice. And then came that moment, when I handed him a cup with a steady hand and looked up into his eyes and saw . . . the punchline to the joke we both found ourselves in. It wasn't his looks (though that helped), nor his money (I knew I was going to make as much as him), nor his clothes (although the Paul Smith suit was a relief after the polyester blazers and sensible jumpers I'd seen before). It was recognition, that we were both here out of obligation and some curiosity, that we could play the game and take the piss at the same time, that we knew this was an option, but hoped there could be something else, something different. That we wanted to believe we were good, and knew already we were destined to be very bad indeed.

My mother wailed and took to her bed when I turned him down. My father called me a fussy trollop and refused to arrange any further meetings. His father shrugged his shoulders and his mother blamed the greedy, ever-present blondes for spoiling her son's taste. And then we began dating. It had to be behind our folks' backs, because we both knew how the system worked. We would be allowed to go out for a few weeks, maybe months, and then a decision would have to be made. (Obviously, a few visits to the cinema and a couple of shared pizzas were more than enough to know whether you wanted to spend the rest of your days with this person.)

So we did all the usual things with unusual intensity: he brushed up my Punjabi, I ironed out his caveman edges and we almost stopped being surprised by how the same we were. He screwed money out of dark corners, I screwed people for stories on windy doorsteps; we loathed each other's jobs but screwing each other made us equal. We would compare carpet burns, kiss each other's bites better, revel in the blessed release of finding someone with whom we could play every role, mother, father, daughter, son, and maybe exorcize their power. Conceived in collusion, conducted in secrecy, played out in passion. Inevitable. Inevitable we would burn each other up and out, too alike to be happy, too alike to break up. And it was the inevitability, this feeling of being pulled along by some huge old energy until I fell neatly into my pre-ordained place that made me stop. I knew what would happen: we'd buy a house and become our parents. Like I said, scratch the surface . . . I got wise to what I'd become with him and I made myself move on. And let Chila move in.

So I've almost finished filming. I thought I'd do a solo

interview with Sunny, to cut in with the one she did with Akash. And then it will be me, Chila and, somewhere in the background, Deepak. I'm not sleeping too well. I close my eyes and see close ups and jump cuts. I will myself to fade out and credits but get distracted by Martin's gentle breathing next to me. He sleeps like a little boy, limbs akimbo and furry snuffles. But lately, when he's turned to snuggle into me, I back away. We haven't talked about this (I'm guessing he's put it down to pressure of work and possibly, he's right), but it's as if something else is in the bed with us. Ghosts on the pillow. I love him intensely when he's asleep – big blond giant, Viking of my heart – grateful that he's different enough to free me from my past. I can't tell him any of this when we're awake. He wouldn't understand. Sometimes, you just get weary with having to explain yourself all the time. And sometimes, the fact that he will never understand is perfect.

4

BACK IN VICTORIAN TIMES, THE BUILDING USED TO BE A workhouse, the largest in the East End of London. The wrought-iron gates enclosing the courtyard were, even then, black with age, rust gathering in the curlicues and half-moons of their intricate fretwork. The stone steps were pitted and yellow, like old man skin, maybe bearing the indentations of unwanted bandage-wrapped babes, thrown on the mercy of the state, no-name no-history children, baptized by abandonment to start all over again.

Fittingly, it then became a Jewish-owned warehouse; three generations of the Offenbachs lived on the premises, leaving Eastern Europe the moment they detected a sniff of sulphur gathering in the air. Bubby Offenbach would sit among the bolts and bales of material, shouting the news to his neighbour across the road, lamenting how the children forgot the synagogue to frequent dance halls with ear-crashing music, wondering if the gates would withstand another kicking from those passing men in black. His grandson took the decision to relocate the remaining brood to Woodford, now that they could buy a house as big as the warehouse itself. He knew instinctively that any roots the family put down would only ever be in shallow soil, so why the sentimentality all of a sudden? He explained to Bubby they would be living cheek by jowl with all his old friends (as near as a sweeping driveway and swimming pool would allow). Relocating the ghetto was all it was, and now their gates were higher and pulsing with deadly current, they could all get a good night's sleep. All the same, Bubby wept a few hot tears, as many as his lint-laden lungs would permit, when the Offenbach Brothers sign went down, and the Wahaab Brothers sign went up.

Imran Wahaab once enjoyed watching the flimsy clouds float past the golden dome of the newly built mosque, inhaling the familiar chillied aromas ascending from the restaurants below him. But somewhere in the Seventies, the steel shutters had to go up. The old gates creaked and groaned like his joints, moaning at the battering they received from objects lobbed by drive-by bullet-headed men, and graffiti was so tiresome to remove from his windows. He worried because now he could not check which way Jamila and Aftab went to school. There were too many diversions along the way. They came home with too many secrets in their school bags.

But gradually, as his eyesight began failing and his children had children, a wonderful and strange thing happened: the poky café-dhabas, populated by huddles of chain-smoking old men, acquired large plate windows and eye-scorching neon signs. The old men were ousted by young white people in scruffy clothes, who gratefully ate the same food at ten times the original prices and marvelled loudly at its good value. Buildings previously housing battalions of nimble-fingered women became music stores, supermarkets, boutiques, bars; reinforced glass and welded metal were replaced by open shop fronts, pavement tables, light and airy ceilings. Streets were rechristened with names like Imran's, and bilingual road signs appeared, thirty years after they were really needed.

How odd, he reflected, so much time and concrete spent keeping the world at bay, and now the world comes smiling and spending to us. So in 1992, Imran Wahaab took down his steel shutters. And in 1998, he sold his business premises to a young Bengali man who did not look like the entre- preneur he claimed to be – too much gel in the hair, too flashy a car to be decent – but who paid, like all the build- ing's previous owners, in crisp, fresh notes. Two months after the sale, Imran cashed in all his policies and finally retired back to Dacca, where he spent hours in the garden of his modest bungalow, tending a plot of blood-red brilliant geraniums.

The Buzz Bar was already heaving by the time Chila arrived with her party in tow. The repainted iron gates were festooned with blinking fairy lights and the courtyard fringed with lush palms in earthenware village pots. The space had been stripped to its bare essentials: whitewash over bumpy brick walls, exposed timbers, a concrete floor covered with rush matting and khelim rugs, and up near the rafters, at regular intervals, small painted green lizards with permanently surprised expressions.

'Goodness,' murmured Chandni in Chila's ear, 'he's spent all this money making it look like my deaf uncle's village!'

'Better not visit the bathroom tonight, girls,' giggled Leila. 'I for one don't fancy squatting over a hole after dinner.'

'Apparently it's the fashion,' Chila ventured, joining the long queue in the doorway. 'What's it called, jaan, the rusty look?'

'Rustic,' replied Deepak with a smile, kissing her head fondly.

'Oh, I knew that, sweetie,' Leila snapped back. 'It's just that they're going too far now. I mean soon it will go full circle. We will be over here travelling by rickshaw, wearing some awful cheesecloth monstrosity, and the Indian villagers will all look like people from American soap operas.'

Asif's voice cut into the women's chatter. 'That's happening already, yaar. Why do you think I bought all those shares in Star satellite? Murdoch's filling his airtime with wall-to-wall USA imports. In some places, the people don't have running water, but they do know who's sleeping with who in *Days of our Lives*.'

Chila tugged subtly on Deepak's sleeve. He answered her before she'd opened her mouth. 'It's an American soap drama, sweetheart.'

'We don't get that one on our cable box,' Chila whispered.

'Well,' Deepak whispered back, 'we'll just have to get you a bigger box then, eh?' and patted her hand.

They finally squeezed into the bar, immediately confronted by waiters dressed as bearers offering cocktails on raffia trays and pakore artfully arranged on banana leaves. Three large video screens suspended by saris hung from the ceiling, showing a collage of black and white Hindi movie numbers, kitsch Indian ads, and pop videos from the latest Asian underground bands.

'My God,' Manju said, 'is that what your film is going to be shown on, Chila?'

Chila realized that each screen took up almost a whole wall and her bowels suddenly liquidized inside her.

'Your face is going to be sooo big,' breathed Chandni, wondering if her recent surgery would withstand such close scrutiny. At least the trim and tuck she had done down below wouldn't be obvious to anyone else. Nature was drying her up, from the inside out, and she knew her husband had noticed. Of course it was worth every penny of his hard-earned cash, but even so, her womb contracted sharply with every step. The gold stilettos had definitely been a mistake.

'Well, that is stardom, surely,' chuckled Asif as he grabbed a drink off a passing tray. 'To be up there, everyone watching you! How does it feel, Chila?'

Chila couldn't think of anything to do except shrug her shoulders and dig her fingernails into Deepak's arm.

'I think you'll have to talk to her agent to get a quote on that,' Deepak said, making the women whoop in delight.

'Well, I think it's absolutely thrilling, sweetie,' said Leila, planting a delicate kiss on Chila's cheek. 'We're all terribly excited you invited us. The rest of the lunching ladies were most jealous when we told them we were coming to a proper film première. Such a refreshing change from all those Gandhi Centre do's where you end up flattering some sad old soak who was famous twenty years ago. And their canapés are disgusting.'

'You haven't even seen it yourself?' Chandni asked, wincing as she made for a suddenly vacant bar stool.

Chila shook her head. Her cheeks were beginning to ache with inane grinning. She was one of the club now and she had to keep up.

'Er, that's what happens usually, Tania told me,' she began. 'I mean, the film isn't ready until it's been stuck together and . . . and they get music on it.'

The women nodded sagely; the men had already grouped around the bar and were making loud calculations on the cost of the conversion.

'So Chila-bahen,' drawled Manju, 'does this mean you'll be leaving us for Hollywood? Or Bollywood even?'

Chila swallowed. They all adored her. They were grateful for being there. She reminded herself to send out her carefully selected thank you for attending notelets first thing in the morning. 'I can't see me dancing around trees, can you?' They laughed. Of course they would. 'Anyway, Deeps and I were thinking about starting a family. That big house needs some little feet running around. And we've had enough dry runs, if you know what I mean!'

Everyone laughed again, except Chandni, for whom the term dry run now had new and sinister connotations.

Chila caught sight of Sunita below one of the screens and waved madly. Sunita mouthed something and waved back. Chila relaxed in a second; she could feel the adrenalin slow its galloping through her veins, for the first time that evening feel the smile actually reach her eyes. Sunita motioned Chila to join her. She was in conversation with two other women, one, in a severe shalwar kameez, with short-cropped hair and thick NHS specs, dragging heavily on a bidi, the other in embroidered trousers with a Kashmiri shawl thrown over her shoulders. She batted the air animatedly, running long square fingers through spiky hennaed hair.

'Do you know them?' asked Manju hesitantly.

'Nice to see the lesbian contingent out tonight,' added Leila. 'I suppose we need someone to start the dancing.'

'You are too much!' tittered Chandni, attempting a few furtive pelvic floor exercises where she sat.

'Well, look at them, really,' said Leila crossly. 'Why is it so many of these young girls set out to make themselves look as unattractive as possible? No man in his right mind would want to go near them.'

'Maybe that's the idea,' said Chila unexpectedly. 'Or

maybe they're both married with five kids each. Maybe that's why they didn't have time to put make-up on.'

'Oh, my dear,' soothed Leila, 'I'm not shocked at all. In Pakistan I met so many women who were in love with their sisters-in-law or whatever. Hardly surprising when they have so little contact with the men. But they still got married, had children, kept everything going. One has to. It's perfectly OK to have a girlfriend as long as you realize it's just a hobby, really.'

Chila watched Sunita's companions and wondered what it would be like, to plan a future without including a husband. As long as she could remember, her tomorrows were filled with, built around a Deepak. To imagine otherwise would be like jumping out of a plane without a parachute, free-falling towards God-knows-where.

Manju nudged her. 'That one in the middle needs an emergency make-over.'

'Who?'

'The lardy lady with the growing out perm and her thinner sister's suit on.'

'That's my friend Sunita,' said Chila, a little too loudly.

'Is she gay?' enquired Leila.

'Cheerful enough,' Chila replied, and began pushing through the crowd.

Sunita did not register Chila at her shoulder for some time. She had been too caught up in Beroze and Suki's conversation, a shy spectator at an intellectual tennis match, feeling balls whizz past her ears – balls which, until recently, she would have been able to lob back with wit and confidence. Beroze was describing a recent case she had defended. A sweet old Pakistani granny had been caught smuggling pounds of pure heroin stashed in the inner tubes of her wheelchair. Her defence had been that her sons had forced her into it, that she had been too weak and frail to resist.

'I mean, this woman was terrified of her own children, had spent a life of dependency on the various men around her. All she had ever been was somebody's daughter, somebody's wife, somebody's mother. What free will did she have in this crime?'

'Sorry, I don't buy that bullshit any more,' responded Suki tartly. 'I meet women every day who on paper have no choices, but against every odd, they up and leave their homes, challenge their families, question their communities . . .'

'That's not the same—' Beroze began, but Suki ploughed on.

'Nahin, it is! We spend all our energy making excuses for not doing anything. Do you know how much effort it takes to stand still and do nothing, blame everyone else for your misery? Much more than it takes to actually change things, change yourself.'

'Shit!' Beroze said with a laugh. 'Remind me not to send any of my more desperate cases to your project. What do you do, slap them as they come in the door and say, What took you so long?'

'Um, well, I think everyone has a right time to do stuff, don't you?' Chila piped up perkily.

Beroze and Suki fixed her, then Sunita, with bemused stares.

'This is one of my oldest friends, Chila,' Sunita responded, moving a little to let Chila into their tight circle. 'Beroze and Suki were at university with me, even though they look like my daughters.'

Chila wasn't sure whether to laugh, as Sunita's observation was entirely accurate, but Beroze and Suki both pooh-poohed affectionately, which made Chila a little jealous.

Suki adjusted her specs to focus on Chila. 'Do you live round Ilford way?'

'Yeah, as it happens. Do you?'

'No I work round there. Thought I'd seen you about.'

'Oh, right. You don't work in Argos, do you?' Chila asked. 'I seem to spend my life there at the moment, just doing up the kitchen, you know how you just keep finding little bits you need and . . .' Chila trailed off gradually. Telling this to Suki was like talking into an unflattering loud speaker. Everything she said sounded too loud and horribly trivial.

Suki's cool brown eyes seemed to have acquired a slight glaze, although her mouth kept up its pleasant smile. 'No. Actually, I work at a project just outside the town centre. But Argos is pretty good value, now you mention it.'

'What project is that?' Chila asked. 'I don't know one round there.'

Suki swapped quick glances with Sunita who butted in, 'Um, the address is kept secret, Chila, for, you know, security reasons.'

'Well, how would anyone know where to find it, then?' Chila demanded, feeling rebuffed.

'Well,' began Suki, 'they would turn up somewhere like Sunita's desk and she would tell them. We tell the people who need to know, or they phone and we vet the calls.'

'It's a refuge,' Sunita said finally, gently, 'so it's not surprising you don't know where it is.'

'A refuge?' squeaked Chila. She had heard about them in the agony hour on the local Asian station. It seemed to be the answer to most of the questions from the desperate women who rang up, whispering in trembly voices from public telephone booths. 'You need to contact your local refuge,' Auntie Salma would tell them in soothing tones before switching to an ad for basmati rice. Chila imagined them to be dank, dripping places with mouldy blankets and bars on the windows. Auntie Salma always managed to make them sound like the last shameful resort for those people too weak to cope. But then she was only a boutique owner who happened to be a friend of the radio station manager's wife, and Suki, Chila decided, looked a little more sussed than her.

A waiter filled the ensuing pause by offering his tray of drinks around. Both Chila and Sunita grabbed the nearest glass available, Sunita downing hers rapidly while Chila wasted a few seconds trying to put her paper umbrella up.

Beroze turned to Chila. 'What you said, about everyone having their right time. That's so true, you know.'

'Is it? I mean, it is, yeah,' Chila responded gratefully.

Beroze continued, 'Suki here spends most of hers raging that things don't change quickly enough. I, on the other hand, know everyone eventually gets their day in court, metaphorically and literally speaking. We battle enough guilt, without beating ourselves up about not being braver and stronger.'

'In fact, why beat yourself up when you can ask a man?' Suki quipped.

Beroze ploughed on. 'When someone's had enough, they move bloody quickly, in my experience.'

Sunita cleared the creamy liquid from the back of her throat. 'Beroze is a barrister,' she said, surprised at how much the words hurt her throat, 'specializing in family law.'

'Oh, right!' enthused Chila. 'That's sort of what you do, isn't it, Sunny?'

Sunita hesitated, prickles of shame pushing through the skin of her neck.

Beroze sipped on her drink and added quickly, 'Sunita is on the front line. I'm the one who gets the glory with half the work load, but I suppose that's a fair swap, for all the essays I used to write for you when you were too shagged to pick up a pen, heh, Suns?'

'Oh shit, please don't remind me,' begged Sunita, really meaning it.

Suki adjusted her specs mock sternly. 'The department troublemaker,' she explained. 'We always said she'd end up keeping people out of prison or ending up in one. Was she a motormouth when you met her, or is that something she just did to annoy all of us?'

Chila caught Sunita's eye, saw something in her face halfway between pride and fear, conveying all that she was, all that she could have been, all that she carried with her now. For a moment she felt disoriented. It was always Sunita or Tania who had run to her rescue; when had things changed? 'Sunny's the brains in our group all right,' she said. 'But she's had to fight me for motormouth title. And of course, she was the first to bag a really nice bloke, so we were all dead jealous of her.'

'Ah, Mr Dreamboat Freud himself!' laughed Beroze.

'We just talked to him, Sunita. He's just the same!' added Suki.

Sunita looked over at Akash who was, typically, deep in conversation with a group of young men, listening with his head down, forefinger on his chin: her Thinker, cast in clay rather than bronze, every shadow and hollow familiar to her even with closed-tight eyes, like reading Braille. From afar she could see all he had to offer: wit, warmth, good profile, strong backbone, an angel compared to some of the brutes Suki encountered in her work, sifting through the shipwrecks of stormy relationships. Yes, he was the same Akash, and she wondered why, at this precise moment, she looked at him and felt nothing, when she ought to feel blessed. It was as if she watched herself watching the world going on around her. She listened in to Suki and Beroze's sparky banter, remembering how many hours she used to spend arguing ideals to the death, intoxicated by her commitment, astonished by her own undying faith.

'You see? There are good men out there, you just have to look a bit harder, that's all!' Suki finished.

'What?' Sunita jumped at Suki's voice.

'You found one, so did I, so—'

'Really?' Chila interrupted. 'Are you married, Suki?'

Suki's lips curled into a ironic bow. 'Put me down as a dyke, eh?'

'No no,' Chila spluttered, cursing Leila silently, 'I just thought . . . doing the job you do and all, you know, you'd get—'

'Bitter?'

'Yeah.'

'Far too clichéd for me, yaar. It makes me appreciate what I got. I leave the testicle crunching to Beroze here. My job gives me faith in everyone's ability to change. Beroze's, on the other hand, forces her to see everyone she defends as a helpless victim of circumstance . . .'

'Piss off!' Beroze said. 'And anyway, Miss smug I-get-it-five-times-a-night woman, I do have someone around as it happens.'

'The dating agency came up trumps, did it?' Suki enquired, relighting her bidi.

'No, met him in a bar. He's a graphic designer, trilingual, sorts out the whites from the colours when he does his own laundry, cooks blinding biriani.'

'And?' Suki held her breath.

'Oh, yes,' Beroze said, nodding, 'he gets down and stays down there for hours, without being asked, and doesn't even ask for the Listerine afterwards!'

Suki spluttered smoke and began hacking as she held onto Beroze.

Chila dug Sunita in the ribs.

'Did she mean . . .?' and Sunita nodded, tight-lipped.

'Well, you know our guys.' Beroze sighed. 'They expect us to worship at the shrine of their mighty weapon, but anything we have in our pants is dirty, smelly, chi-chi stuff which must be handled with fingers only, from a safe distance. And once a month, light the blue string and stand well back!'

Chila tittered uncomfortably, feeling her cheeks begin to glow. Of course she, Tania and Sunita had spent hours giggling about sex, until they all actually started having some themselves. Maybe it was something to do with growing up together, knowing each other's families. Yes, that was it, she decided, trying to tune out Suki's background anecdote which seemed to involve something plastic and a tub of tutti-frutti ice cream. How could you hear about your friend's sex life and then sit down with her dad and talk about the weather? But these women seemed to revel in it, what they did, how, how long, what they wanted and what they got. The idea that you could ask, that you could actually speak during sex, was at once alarming and thrilling to Chila. It made her feel naughty and powerful. She vowed to bring up the subject with Deepak at an appropriate moment.

Sunita was trying to conjure up a suitable fond memory of her tumbles with Akash, but found the images kept rearranging themselves into the jagged outline of her episiotomy scar.

'So where is this man with the magic tongue then?' Suki asked, catching her breath.

'Over there, talking to Akash,' Beroze replied.

They all turned as one to gawp. He was good-looking, spiky haired, nice smile.

'He's about twelve, isn't he? Knew there had to be a catch,' Suki said, and sighed.

Beroze drew herself up. 'He's twenty-three, and believe

me, girlfriend, you move to the next generation down and you will not be sorry. They've all grown up with sisters like me – notice I did not say mothers – and some of them actually like women, prefer women, because they've seen their mums go through such bullshit with their dads.'

'So it's a guilt shag, then,' Suki said.

'Not mine this time,' Beroze said, smiling. 'Anyway, I expect all this will be covered in your film, Sunita, which I can't wait to see.'

'I'm in it too,' said Chila defiantly, 'And it's not Sunny's film or mine. It's Tania's.'

'Right. Tania,' Suki said, looking meaningfully at Beroze. 'Her stuff's always, um, interesting.'

'I think,' Sunita said, slightly surprised at the sound of her own voice, 'sex is only part of a good relationship. People totally overrate how important it is.'

Suki chuckled. 'Yeah, and only people having bad sex or no sex say that.'

Sunita stood for a moment, listening to her own steady breathing, checking it was normal, and then turned on her heels and walked away.

Deepak was bored. He had discarded his business associates and their braying, harpy wives as soon as was polite, drifting around the room in search of whatever it was that would make the evening bearable. Despite the crush, he noticed that people had divided themselves into distinct groups, seeking out their familiars.

He gave the boiler-suited brigade a wide berth, earnest huddles of confident, chattering women – some of whom were surprisingly good-looking – who seemed to laugh longer and louder than anyone else in the room.

He hovered around the fringes of some media people who had requisitioned a corner plot, where the same words and phrases seemed to crop up: 'seminal', 'demographic', 'TX date' and, most often, 'wankerneverlikedhim/her'. He managed a half-interesting conversation with a young director who urged him to persuade the business community to support the arts, which he agreed with until he discovered her intended project was touring a play called *Sunil and the Big Spider* around infants schools in the suburbs.

For a while he chatted amiably enough to Akash, whom he liked but found irritatingly intense sometimes. However it was the presence of the other young men in the group that discomfited him. He couldn't work them out. They looked ordinary enough, normal beer-drinking lads, apart from the odd earring and tatty OM T-shirt, but they didn't know how to conduct a normal conversation. There was no mention of what jobs they did, how much they earned, current affairs, recent purchases, girlfriends/wives and possible kids. They mentioned football, but in a self-conscious, mocking sort of way. Instead they wanted to get personal. Within a minute of Deepak's arrival, they were asking him a million questions and actually waiting for his answers. They wanted to listen and let him do the talking, a habit which Deepak only associated with Chila. They laughed a lot, they had soft edges, and yet they cracked jokes which Deepak found clever and biting. Standing there stiffly clutching his wine, he felt as if he should slip them ten pence and tell them to go down the shops, treat yourself, don't run. Ridiculous, Deepak scolded himself, excusing himself, they're not much younger than me. But as he walked away he felt an unexpected tug of regret, remembering how he was ten years ago, buckling under the weight of his father's demands that he take over the family property business, deciding that if he was going to do his duty in his job, he would be as undutiful as he could in his private life. There had to be some part of him that didn't wear a suit. The schizophrenia didn't bother him; it seemed to be a requirement for survival among all his Punjabi friends. And then someone came along and danced mockingly along the fine line that divided his life so neatly, and forced him to choose.

Tania's ruby-red sari shimmered like some rippling beacon under the lights. Her hand ached from the hundreds of palms she'd pressed, her jaw from the millions of thank you for comings, her cheeks tingled from a billion fleeting you're so clever kisses. Martin was playing minder, coordinating arrivals into her orbit, refilling her glass, bursting with pride and envy, a heady cocktail which made him imbibe too many margaritas and allow his eyes to linger a little too long on Tania's perfect, bitable bosom. He always fancied her when she was unreachable and in ethnic dress; enjoyed knowing that when the world had done with praising her, he would take her home. And then he wondered if she ever felt like that about him.

'Mart,' she whispered, handing him an empty glass, 'make sure that bald guy with the blonde woman are put in reserved seating . . . Channel 4 people, and she always tries to leave early, so put her in the middle of the row.'

'In between two very fat people with big hats?' Martin suggested, but Tania was already air kissing a circle of new people. Martin finished the rest of his drink and went, via the bar, to find Tania's guests.

Deepak watched Martin disappear in the throng and tapped his foot restlessly. He wanted to go over and say hello to Tania, just to be polite of course. But he wanted to do it alone, not in line with the rest of her fan club. Everything about her seemed fluid tonight. She was all water, the way her head turned fanning her hair behind her, the slow undulations of her limbs, the uncertain smile that flowed in and out of the creases of her face. Only Deepak could spot that she was nervous as hell. He raised a hand, an anchor in the waves, a port in the storm. She saw it and waved back, teeth flashing, lighthouse beams, siren eyes. The past trickled away slowly through the gaps between their good intentions. It would not hurt, surely, to say good luck. He moved forward, only to feel a small hand tugging at his jacket.

'Jaan? Have you seen Sunny?' Chila's moon face was clouded with concern. 'She sort of ran off. I think she's a bit upset . . .'

'Ladies loos are the best bet,' said Deepak patiently, 'and I think that will have to be your job.'

'I've checked there, and I don't feel safe looking outside.'

Every other time, Chila's soft appeal and liquid eyes melted Deepak's reserve. Tonight, it made him want to shake her. Why couldn't she be like those other women here, who would march out into the darkness rolling up their sleeves, armed with a pair of nutcrackers? Tania had flipped her tail and swum away; he could see the back of her head in glimpses, obscured by the bobbing bodies of others. Deepak fastened his jacket and made his way towards the exit, not waiting for Chila's thank you jaan.

Sunita sat shivering on the upstairs terrace of the bar, which looked out over alleys and industrial yards. A jaundiced moon heaved on an inky raft of clouds. The stars looked tired, blinking against the passing aeroplanes and the illuminated pyramid of the Canary Wharf tower. Sunita's arms ached. She slowly rolled up her kameez sleeve, and examined the tiny criss-cross of recent cuts which segmented her upper arm. Although they stung now, she had not felt a thing when she'd moved the razor from leg to arm, deciding the hair on her calf should stay, and the skin on her biceps should bleed. Snip snap; so easy, so fascinating to see how frail her armour was. It wasn't planned. It happened in the frantic period between breakfast and leaving the house, when she had her precious private ten minutes in the bathroom. Nikki was wailing to be let in, she could hear Sunil splattering his cereal around in the kitchen. And more than anything, she wanted to feel . . . something. There, she said afterwards, I am alive, told you. She covered up the evidence of her still-beating heart with Mr Bump novelty plasters, opened the door and gave her beloved daughter a welcome hug.

Akash hadn't noticed. She made sure she wore long-sleeved pyjamas to bed, and although he kissed her tenderly every night, it was to say good night, I'm going to sleep now, a matey, nice to see you, come again kiss, a kiss that bound her to him and at the same time promised nothing. Ironically, one of the books lying next to the bed on his side was called *The Politics of Snogging*, a perky user-friendly tome with lots of cartoons. Sunita had read it in the bath in one sitting, while Sunil slept and Nikki splashed happily about at her feet. It was all common sense really, she thought, turning the pages, how a kiss isn't just a kiss after all. The chapter headings listed the Platonic Smooch, the Dramatic Mwaah!, the Maternal Pucker, the Passionate Pout, the Kiss-Off. Sunita closed her eyes and tried to categorize Akash's nocturnal nibble and opened them when she felt Nikki rubbing her soapy flannel gently over her inflamed arm.

'Hurt, Mama? I make it better,' Nikki said. Little girls starting so early, taking the pain for someone else.

'It doesn't hurt, baby,' Sunita told her, doing the same back.

That night she pulled out some hair from her fringe and carefully stuck them with spit over the covers of Akash's bedside books, the ones he often claimed he had to read before tomorrow and maybe Sunita should just go ahead and sleep. The next morning, she checked them, every hair unbroken, every book unread. So Sunita had started reading some of these books herself, never in front of him, sometimes at work in her lunch break, often on the tube, seldom when the kids were awake, always when he was upstairs in the study tapping away and she could sit in the kitchen, eating leftovers. It made her feel better to know there were people worse off than herself. Maybe one day, she could even help Akash in his work. What she really wanted was to find on some page, in some paragraph, a description of someone who felt exactly as she did. Then she would know she was not alone.

'Sunita? You OK?' Deepak hovered at the balcony door, unsure of whether to move forward. 'Chila's been looking all over for you.'

Sunita nodded and absent-mindedly picked at a scab under her sleeve.

Deepak edged towards her. He hoped fervently there wasn't going to be a scene. Surely this was her husband's job. 'Um, they're about to show the film. Everyone's being seated. Chila's saved you and Akash a place next to us.'

Sunita got up wearily. She turned to Deepak, her face now visible under the on–off flash of the fairy lights.

Deepak smiled at her reassuringly, thinking it was almost impossible to believe that his Chila and Sunita were the same age. He thought of his mother's friends, who seemed ancient to him when he was a boy, but whom he now realized were in their mid-thirties at that time. These same women had married with eighteen-inch waists and downcast eyes, and somewhere in between had ballooned to loud muscular matriarchs who seemed to enjoy clipping him round the ear and sending him into the kitchen for hundreds of pointless glasses of water. Why was it, once some women had married, they felt it was OK to let themselves go? This attitude, now we've got him, we don't have to bother. He imagined Chila three stone heavier in a food-stained cotton suit and was dismayed to find it was easy.

'Deepak, why do you love Chila?'

Deepak blinked rapidly for a moment. Sunita was next to him, almost touching. God, he hoped she wasn't going to cry. Women cried around him a lot, although he hadn't worked out why yet.

'Why?' he began. 'She's . . . very lovable.'

'And?'

Deepak shifted from one foot to the other. He would be really pissed off if he missed the beginning of the film. 'OK, because she's sweet and kind and beautiful and . . . she loves me.'

'A-ha!' shouted Sunita, making Deepak flinch. 'Yes, because she loves you! You see?'

'Not really,' said Deepak miserably, now avoiding eye contact altogether.

'The question is,' Sunita said, almost whispering in his ear, 'do you need her because you love her? Or do you love her because she needs you?'

Deepak looked at her then. A strange clammy sweat settled on the back of his neck. More questions. An evening of interrogation and now it was making him uneasy. Somewhere through a fog a small light flickered, just for a second, revealing rooms he had not known were there. Somewhere down a hallway, in one of those rooms, on a bed, someone laughed at him and rearranged silken red folds. He had been here before, it was just that he had forgotten when exactly. If he took one step inside, all would be lost. He would have to dismantle everything and start again.

'The first one,' he said, taking Sunita's arm, his fingers

not registering the bumpy scars which pulsed beneath them, a millimetre of silk away.

Tania sat at the back, way back, hugging a corner of the bar. She had wanted Martin to sit with her other friends, but he had refused so noisily she gave in, to his surprise. So he sat next to her, having made buddies with the barman and received a free jug of margaritas for his pains, his last sober thought spent in contemplation as he scanned Tania's unnaturally calm face.

Tania, for maybe the first time in her life, knew now what it meant to go with the flow. She watched all the people she loved, worked with, competed with, take their seats, chattering excitedly. She remained aloof, watching it all from her icy mountain top, resigned to whatever would happen next. So this is what it meant, this whole Zen thing, the quality she had always admired so much in Chila, to accept without rage. The only difference was that while Chila met the future with innocence, Tania had already prepared a likely script. There were a few possible endings. She decided to welcome any and all of them with equanimity. She sipped on her mineral water. She was ready.

The lights went down and a ragged cheer went up. A long sitar note vibrated through the darkness, the voice of a priest chanting the holy marriage vows over it, a translation on the black screen in white italic script. 'She promises that from henceforth, all other men will be but brothers to her. He promises that all other women will be but sisters to him . . . they will give each other's parents love and respect in equal measure . . . she will support him through his troubles, he will put food on their table for their children . . . from this moment, they will be known as one . . .'

The music snapped into a pumping garage beat with searing female vocals over it; a kaleidoscope of images and faces passing too quickly for anyone to cheer their appearance, fragmented photographs of erotic temple carvings, footage of anti-dowry marches, newsreel of the bandit queen Phoolan Devi addressing her gang of dacoits. Sunita caught a glimpse of her and Akash side by side. Chila saw her grin fly past, and clutched Deepak's arm, enchanted. It was as magical as she had hoped and, somewhere in there, she was immortal.

Then suddenly they were in Akash's consulting room. Mr Dhillon was describing how he and his wife met, his voice counterpointed by shots of Akash's books, the ticking clock, the fruit bowl, a hole in Akash's shoe. People began tittering, then whispering as the camera focused in on Mrs Dhillon's face, caught in an expression of undisguised disgust. Akash shifted uncomfortably and sneaked a glance round to see if the Dhillons were in the audience. Their conversation was taken from an early session, when things had been going well. The close ups came from somewhere else. It told a story, but not how he remembered it.

The scene switched to a marriage bureau office, shots of hundreds of Polaroids of happy couples on the wall. A pair on their first date, chatting nervously at a restaurant table, then pulling back to reveal a sullen grandma sitting at the next table, sucking on a cocktail. The buzz was creeping around the room. It was clever, witty stuff, slick, snappy cuts, subtle visual counterpoints, the camera an ironic eye, the quiet one in the corner no-one takes much notice of until it's too late.

Sunita was getting slightly queasy at the speed of it all, the thump of the music and the constantly changing angles.

'It's like one of those pop videos that my son watches,' Leila stage-whispered to Chila. 'When are they getting to your stuff, sweetie?'

On cue, Chila appeared in glorious Technicolor on the

three screens around the room. Leila led a burst of spontaneous applause. Chila sighed; if she had known the camera was going to be so close, she might have toned down the blusher and the gold eyeshadow. Still, her sparkly suit looked lovely. It was her face all right, but there was something about it, her expression, that she didn't recognize as part of herself. Before she had time to register this, she saw that she was walking around her kitchen, pointing at various recent purchases. 'This is a multi-chef. It's got this really amazing bit that grinds, so you can have fresh home-made masala instead of the shop stuff . . . and my Deeps really loves his desi food.' Chila sat on her hands, shocked at the sound that came out of her mouth. Was her accent that strong? Did she really do that silly Minnie Mouse giggle at the end of every sentence? 'This washing machine is computer chip controlled and it's got this bit that . . . well, you put shirts in and they come out almost ironed! With the number of shirts Deeps goes through, 'cos you know he's quite high up in finance . . . No, I don't know what he does exactly . . . funny that.'

The camera swung round and focused on Deepak, sitting reading the paper and throwing pistachios into his mouth. One of them missed. He looked at where it lay, left it, and turned a page. The giggles around the room were quite audible now. Chila looked up at Deepak, who was watching impassively; a tiny muscle shivered just above his right eye.

Then some other people began talking in the film. An angry man began shouting and throwing chairs and Akash was hiding under a table. The audience were aghast, their gasps audible and impressed. But Chila barely registered any of this. She was trying to eavesdrop on Leila and Manju's fierce whispers which had begun while Chila had been on screen. She heard the words 'Hilarious' and 'That wallpaper', and tried to refocus on the ongoing drama, her vision slightly blurring. She checked her watch. The film had only been running for twenty minutes. Maybe the best bits were to come.

Sunita recognized the mess before she heard her own voice coming at her in Dolby stereo. There were the tangle of discarded children's clothes on the kitchen floor, the pile of newspapers awaiting recycling, the rows of empty wine bottles (how had they managed to get through so many?), the unwashed dishes in the sink. She heard herself say, 'We were lucky to find one another when we were so young . . . and we were free to make our own choices, so there wasn't any pressure as such . . . I think we have a good life together . . . It's what we expected.'

Akash's jaw had dropped into his lap, his fists tight balls on his knees. When Sunita glanced back at the screen, for a moment she wondered who that sad-eyed, frumpy house-wife was sitting next to her husband, whose knee twitched throughout her chatter, whose fingers roamed aimlessly around each other, who prefaced every answer with a tremulous sigh. There was a faint roaring in her head, the whole of the sea in the shell of her ear. She knew who the woman was now. She made to get up and felt Akash's gentle hand on her back, soothing her, pushing her back into her seat.

He kept hold of her hand and kept watching as he said to camera, 'Of course, in my work you get to recognize the warning signs in a bad relationship very early on.' Close up of Sunita twisting her wedding ring round and round. 'The main problem is communication. Men tend to ignore the problems and hope they will go away.' Shot of Sunita vacuuming around Akash's pile of books. 'Women are more eager to talk, but first they have to be listened to.' Akash playing with his children while Sunita sits slumped at the dining table, staring into space. 'And if they're not, much of their anger and anguish goes inwards.' Close up of Sunita, but grainy, sound quality muffled, only half her face and no overhead light, as if she was unaware that the camera was there.

Sunita heard a familiar whimpering. She wanted to close her eyes now but could not. 'Whenever people ask us how many kids we have, I always want to say three . . . We should have had three. But we got rid of one . . . for the best.' Akash's hand slackened its grip on Sunita's. She felt him slipping away from her, limp and cold as a dead fish. 'I want to talk about it, but he's so busy and . . . you know what it's like—' The scene ended abruptly, seemingly in mid-sentence, freeze frame on Sunita's open mouth, slow fade to complete silence.

Everyone in the room seemed to be holding their breath. Sunita could feel people around her craning their necks to catch a glimpse of her face. And then, suddenly, the screen burst into life and colour: a wedding scene. The two awkward virgins who had shared a first date were now getting married, and the room relaxed, even managed a brief burst of grateful applause. This was the happy section. Blushing engaged couples, blissful married couples, couples emerging from counselling with a spring in their step, young men talking about their ideal woman being strong, independent and a true friend, young women laughing at a hen night, none of them even thinking about marriage before travelling the world and making their first million, old couples still in love after fifty years together, sharing their secrets: 'Don't take it all too seriously . . . Always make up before going to bed . . . Lots of sex is a good idea . . . Love your partner for who they are, not who you want them to be . . .' The audience cooed and sighed and felt reassured. It wasn't impossible, you could have it all. The bride's family cried as their daughter left them for her new home, and suddenly, Sunita remembered.

She remembered where the end of her sentence had gone. She had been drinking wine with Tania. They had finished filming, or so Tania had told her. Tania was being very sweet and understanding and asked her loads of questions and Sunita had started crying and, yes, the camera was on the table, and at the end of it, she had said, 'You know what it's like, Tania, because you know me.' You know what it's like – cut.

Chila thought she was safe now. The credits began rolling and she felt she could risk exhaling. But then, oh shit, here she was again, filling the screen, holding her wedding photo album proudly up for inspection. 'See, this is me and Deeps in a bush. It's really artistic, isn't it?' No-one knew what Chila said after that. The room rocked with glee as Chila turned page after page, her mouth moving, her eyes alive and proud, as she showed everyone the images from what she had always thought, until now, was the happiest day of her life. At the end of the scene, just as the last credit flew by, Deepak entered the room from the lounge. He saw the wedding album and barked, 'God no! Not those bloody photos. Put them away.' 'But Deeps,' began Chila. Deepak grabbed the album and stomped off, slamming the door behind him, to a few hisses from the audience.

Deepak's eyes did not waver from the screen. He was trying to work out where that cold snap in his eyes and baring of teeth came from, how Tania had managed to make him look so frightening, so ugly. The camera does lie, he told himself, it must, it is nothing but a distorting mirror.

The final shot was Chila, looking sheepishly at the door, then at the camera, giggling nervously and saying, 'Honestly, men!' Blackout.

The applause was deafening. Jonathan was on his feet,

leading an unsteady standing ovation, shouting, 'Director! Speech, speech!'

Martin hugged Tania wildly, too drunk to notice she stood in his arms stiff as a stick, her eyes still fixed on the screens which now played nothing but fuzzy electronic snow. 'Listen to that, Tans! You've done it, babes. You've bloody done it now!'

Tania remained where she was, collecting plaudits, embraces and several subtly exchanged cards from film and TV people who gave her the come up and see me sometime wink as they left, while Jonathan stood at her side like a proud father, beaming benevolence. Even some of Tania's rivals flashed tight, envious smiles as they passed, mentally binning the similar-sounding ideas they had intended to make, anxious to gather together and enjoy a detailed post-mortem with scalpels.

Beroze and Suki nodded briefly. 'Good work, Tania, much better than any of your other stuff.' Beroze smiled genuinely. 'You went for the whole picture. I mean, we're like any other bunch of people, right? We have our successes and our failures. It's all a lottery in the end.'

Tania nodded. She said thank you again.

Suki leaned into her. 'How do your friends feel about the film then?'

Tania paused. 'I just told the truth,' she said.

Deepak guessed she would be on the upstairs terrace, once he had ascertained she was missing and yet no-one had seen her leave. All three exits from the bar led to here. He knew she would seek air and darkness. From the top of the stairs it was easy to see anyone up there, with the neon light pouring through the glass doors. She was pacing along the terrace, almost lazily, her arms folded against the cold. Her sari pullau unfurled slowly behind her like a sail, the beads on its hem tinkling gently with each step. She did not cease pacing or look up when he swung the door open.

'What the fuck have you done?'

Pace, sniff, pace, turn.

'Aren't you going to answer me?'

She stops now. She looks at the floor. She shrugs.

'Are you so bitter, you have to mess up everyone else?'

She looks at him. His hands itch. She clears her throat, huskily. 'I shot what I saw.'

He shoots forward and grabs her shoulders. Not hard, enough to feel trapped birds fluttering beneath her clavicle. She is firm and unyielding to the touch, marble smooth, unbreakable.

'You saw what you wanted to see, you—'

'Bitch?' she offers calmly. 'Whore? Trollop? Rundi?'

Her stained lips around base Punjabi gutter terms. He is aware of her bare midriff in between blouse and sari. She feels heat coursing from fingertips to singing flesh. Narcotic familiarity. Red petals falling, poppy pods crushed, offering sweet selfish release.

'I had to do what was right. Like you did, Deepak.'

Hearing his name makes him loosen his grip. His hands trace a journey from shoulders to back to waist. The shock of skin makes him inhale sharply. He smells salt on her breath.

'Chila,' he stutters, 'deserves better than this.'

Tania nods, lifting her neck so her face tilts towards him, heavy flower on fragile stem. The world slips sideways; they shiver for a foothold. Her hands tremble as she reaches for his face, cupping his cheeks, infinitely tender, holding him up.

'Then why are you punishing her?'

Deepak raises his eyebrows into question marks. She tames them into relaxed curves, erases the line of discontent

181

furrowed deep between his eyes. Her knee slips between his, he holds it there.

'Punishing her for what?'

She feels seawater spring from her lashes: the storm approaches; she knows there are rocks and her feet will bleed.

'I only saw it through the camera. I only admitted it then. You torture her for being exactly what you wanted when you married. You blame her for your own choices. For choosing someone whose goodness would make you hate yourself. For not admitting you needed more. For not being brave enough to choose a fair fight, and picking a punch-bag. For wanting it too bloody easy, Deepak.'

Then they kiss, and the sky goes black as clouds cover the face of the moon, candles go out in sacred places and the stars make their excuses and leave. All the ties snap one by one with discordant twangs, duty, loyalty, family, security, but not, as one would expect, tradition, for their histories are littered with unsuitable lovers who inevitably come to tragic ends, drowned in pots in fast-flowing rivers, bricked up in shaded palace walls, stoned in blazing, heaving courtyards – at least, the ones that are caught. They do not know yet that this is part of who they have always been, that passion needs confinement to flourish, eroticism is fatally intertwined with restraint and that a rain-spattered sari will always win over a spangly scrap of Lycra.

They know none of this because they are lost on slippery pathways, in wet warm caves. And if they had opened their eyes, they would have seen Chila, Sunita and Martin watching them through yellow-tinted glass. They took three separate doors, they stand in three different places, they see no-one else except the silhouette that is sometimes one person, sometimes two.

Martin's version is filtered through alcohol and fatigue.

He sways to the rhythm of their deep kisses and knows somewhere, deep down, that this was always going to happen. He veers between having a sensible chat with Tania about this the next day, or sprinting down to the bar, grabbing the lemon-slicing knife and driving it through the third button of Deepak's designer shirt. He wanders back down towards the noise and smoke, descending the stairs into his own portable hell.

Sunita's lips part slowly of their own accord. A fluid warmth begins in her belly and spreads tentacles outwards, along sinews and nerve endings as her body slowly comes back to her. She feels herself rise and fall with their breath, feels the weight of her heart as it gradually heaves itself from its bed and begins a slow waltz around her chest, feels the ache in her limbs and the perspiration at her neck and the moan gathering in her throat as she moves with them but alone. It wasn't in a book, then. What she was missing was out there among the plastic chairs and the tin-foil ashtrays, the quiet eye of the hurricane, and she stands at its edges, being slapped and buffeted back to life. She takes the stairs back down three at a time, her scars aching gloriously, as they should.

Chila waits until she is absolutely sure before she starts crying. She gulps and hiccups and streams sticky liquid and lava grief, and the harder she cries, the harder they kiss. She wants to hold both of them, she wants to stand between them, her bookend loves. She only knows now what it was that she did not recognize on her face on that screen. It was fear. And now she knows what she was afraid of, what has always haunted her, what propelled every smile, every altruistic gesture, every cheerful acquiescence, every I don't mind, jaan. She has constructed a whole life around it. No-one must leave. No-one leaves nice people. I am nice. I will make myself nice. Someone should have told her, her mother, her friends, all those romances she read, all those films she watched, all those customs she upheld, that there are no guarantees. She walks down the stairs like her grandmother. On the balcony, the children play.

Spring

5

SPRING BUSTLED IN LATE TO LONDON, FULL OF EXCUSES AND
panting slightly, tweaking tightly furled leaves and reluctant
bulbs in its wake, gently shoving fronds and blades through
paving stones and crumbling brick, shooing away sulky
clouds and frost-breathy wind until finally, a shaky sun
wobbled into view, anxious to make up for its long
hibernation.

Mostly, it was business as usual. The traffic still slithered
its way in choky snakes through small gaps, the shops
replaced their Winter Sale signs with Spring Offers
placards, and the pelicans still breakfasted on pigeons in
Green Park. Diligent housewives, for whom the term was
not yet an insult or an anachronism, dusted, polished and
scrubbed, or instructed their Filipino maids to do so. Debris
and detritus were discarded with gusto, as attics, cellars and
outhouses were ransacked and cleared to let in the new air.
Crocuses nodded their leonine heads from flower beds and
pots, approving the bulging bin liners being carried from
front porch to hatchbacks, bound for charities or city
dumps. One woman's cast-off became another woman's

posh party frock, one person's hand-me-down another's perfect fit.

Which is why Martin moved out as soon as his window boxes turned green, taking only his computer and cookbooks, and moved in with Stella, a nurse from Finchley with South Italian blood. She was exotic enough for him to feel fascinated, and he had already decided that Italy was as far east as he would now venture in his search for love. Tania found his note three days later when she returned from a shoot. He left no forwarding address, so she too requisitioned an army of black bags and sent the rest of their relationship to the Mencap shop.

The gently warming earth and unseasonably flirtatious winds persuaded Sunita to peel off a few layers of winter woollies, amazed to discover that her body had been changing without her knowledge or permission. The blouses and jackets she had worn this time last year no longer fitted. The pouches and strained seams which she must have filled once now hung off her limply, like a former wrinkled skin. Against her face, the colours seemed faded and old. When she spotted flashes of unexpected colour amongst the weeds and junk in her garden, a red tulip winking at her through the rim of a rusty can, she dashed to her wardrobe. She opened it and faced an expanse of beige and grey, a veritable accountants' tea party of elasticated waistbands and sensible shoes. She flung the whole lot into her recycling tub, threw the children into a double buggy, checked the expiry date on her credit card and took the first available tube to town.

Chila knew that winter was finally over when she woke up and was not sick. The metallic fur on her tongue had disappeared, the ache in her breasts had abated, the dizziness that accompanied every sudden move had stopped. She sat up gingerly, sniffing the change around her, seeing it in the quality of light that filtered through the pink satin curtains, sharp and expectant, smelling it, a subtle tang of moss and the heady aroma of hyacinth as she flung open the window to see if Deepak's car was still there. She had missed him again.

She rubbed her stomach tenderly, whispering, 'Let's have paranthe for breakfast, eh?'

Deepak paced around the abandoned warehouse he had acquired just before Christmas. His father had counselled him not to invest: bad area, too much repair work needed. Viewing it through a sheet of sleet, Deepak had harboured his own doubts, but on a point of principle, i.e. his father said no so he had to say yes, he went through with the sale. And now, with unclouded sky flooding in through the frosted roof and dandelions appearing in mouldy corners, he could see nothing but potential. It was a good day, and he knew this evening would be even better.

Akash heaved a sigh of relief as he cleared away case notes from the post-Christmas bumper crop, his first as a fully qualified therapist. Every 2 January, the centre was deluged with fraught couples who had discovered under mistletoe and surrounded by turkey carcass that they really hated each other. There was nothing like a few days with close family in a confined space to bring the worms up to the surface. He checked his watch. The bursting buds outside his window seemed to beckon him, a thrush swayed contentedly in a high branch, its throat ululating sensuously. That decided it; he shut the filing cabinet and got his coat. He was taking the rest of the day off and could either go home and surprise Sunita or try and catch his therapist for a one-to-one session. He hesitated for just a second, wiped a fleeting image of some grainy footage from his back brain and set off for home.

*

Chila moved carefully around her kitchen, still not used to movement without the accompanying seasickness. She drew up the floral blinds and almost blinked at the sparkling surfaces that winked back at her. Mrs Singh knew her stuff all right. Mrs Singh was the cleaner that Deepak had hired as soon as Chila's pregnancy was confirmed, insisting no child of his would be threatened by his wife's obsessional devotion to housework. He had peeked at the doctor's notes during one visit and had been horrified to read that Chila was medically described as an elderly primigravida – an ancient mother, no less. Chila thought this was a tad unfair; on paper, she was thirty-five but at least she had managed to implant a seed in her ancient womb within a year of marriage.

Deepak had gone quiet for a few days after this information. Chila guessed by his dark looks and slammed doors that he was mourning the gaggle of nubile, fertile youngsters he could have chosen to bear his heirs. However, when he finally noticed that his silences and sulks were making Chila weepy and jumpy, he relented, for the sake of the baby, she fondly imagined, and instead showered her with unprompted favours. Neither of them could have guessed that Chila would turn out to be one of those rare unfortunates who get morning and evening sickness for twice as long as the three-month regulatory period. Half a year later, Mrs Singh was too permanent a fixture to demolish. It was the first of many grandiose gestures that had marked the last few months: first the cleaner, then a course of driving lessons and a spanking new Toyota when Chila passed her test first time. Next an extension into the vast garden, encompassing a sun lounge and a huge fishtank that covered an entire wall; and finally the gold credit card, a joint one naturally, which he encouraged Chila to use at every opportunity, although she had used it with caution, knowing he would have proof of every purchase when the statement came in.

He had constructed the very palace that Chila had created from catalogue clippings and blobby paste all those years ago, and now she did not even have to keep it clean. All she had to do was live in it. And wait for him. She took out a spray bleach and a j-cloth and went hunting for a stray smear or stain, giving up when she got to the dining room. At that moment, Chila hated Mrs Singh with a vengeance. Now she couldn't clean, she no longer listened to the radio. Now she had no breaks to look forward to, she had stopped watching tapes of her favourite shows, despite the spaceship-sized satellite perched on the new roof. Now she could buy anything she wanted, she realized how little she actually needed any more.

Chila padded to the hall and settled in the comfy chair next to the telephone, flipping through her address book, a rather smart leather volume which had replaced the Snoopy Fun Pad she had used for ages. She reassured herself by noting all the new entries over recent months: her luncheon circles, since she had formed a splinter group from Manju and Leila's cronies; the expectant mothers she had met in antenatal classes; the friends of her families who now invited her to all their functions as a respectable married lady; the ever-expanding circle of acquaintances from Deepak's business contacts. Her diary boasted similar successes; almost every day was marked with some celebration or dinner, weddings, namkarans where babies were given their names, engagements, ladies sangeet nights, Krishnaji's birthday, Baisakhi harvest bonfires, Diwali (already booked, although by then she would be bringing a baby to the celebrations), even a couple of funerals, from which now she could be excused, thanks to her delicate state. A whole year mapped out for her, the essentials of birth, marriage and demise, just as she had always hoped. Continuity, as satisfying as the pages rippling through her fingers marked out her days. And then she spotted Tania's number, next to Sunita's in the ST section. Chila's rule was best friends classified by first name, everyone else by sur- name. She automatically raised a forefinger, ready to dial one of their numbers, as she had tried to do so many times. Each time the same thing happened. She would shake, she would see a silhouette in neon on a windy terrace and she would rush to the bathroom to be sick.

Of course, today that would not happen because the nausea seemed to have left her at last and no-one could have been more attentive and generous than Deepak recently. She took a deep breath and dialled Sunita's number first. She heard the engaged tone and slammed down the receiver, relieved. She pretended to check Tania's number, although she knew it by heart, and slowly dialled the first digit, then the second, all the while steadying her breathing, rehearsing her tone, her opening words, then leaving a suit- able pause for Tania's apology.

Chila had already forgiven her for the film. After it was broadcast on television, the *Daily Mail* critic had called Chila 'a comedienne in the making' and the *Express* had waxed lyrical about her 'artless innocence and joie de vivre', which even Deepak had grudgingly admitted was a compli- ment. And as for the other incident, well, alcohol makes people do silly things, and who wouldn't fancy Tania, the belle of the evening, and that gorgeous sari. Besides, they had always been friends, even before Chila had come along, and the fact that Tania had not rung meant she really felt rotten about it. Not to mention Sunita, who probably took the whole thing very badly, what with being filmed secretly, and was too embarrassed to get in touch and it was all so silly and just one phone call could put it all right . . .

By the time Chila had dialled the fifth digit of Tania's number her hands were shaking so badly that she could barely aim her finger steadily. She could feel something rising from her chest and, as it grew, she knew it was not bile but something else sour and curdled, somehow mixed in a lumpy soup with Deepak's presents and his frequent business trips and his baffling erratic mood swings. If she made that call Chila would know everything from the first breath that Tania drew, because lies were so easy to smell on the breath of someone you knew too well, and the thought of knowing everything made her heave as she pressed the final number and from the downstairs toilet she could hear, faintly, through porcelain and water, Tania's voice on her answering machine telling her if she didn't leave a message, how the hell would she know who had called?

An hour later, Chila found herself sitting in her mother's Best Room (the one at the front of the house which was cleaned and locked like a museum until Company came), surrounded by chattering women and clinking tea cups and plates. Some of them Chila recognized from her childhood, her mother's unchanging circle of close cohorts who had recreated their own little village in the surrounding streets. These women had a shared history, albeit recent and woman-made, encompassing their arrival here, bewailing concrete and ever-pissing rain, setting up home, the long well-trodden road from one-room boarding houses to comfortable semi-detached houses with concreted over front gardens, and babies, which they still considered their paunchy married children to be. Now came the next stage, the best stage, the arrival of the longed-for grandchildren, all the glory and very little responsibility and, most importantly, the most convenient reason they all quoted for not retiring back to India, when in actuality, the India they all knew had vanished around the time of black and white films and enforced sterilization.

Some of them had brought their daughters, all of whom Chila had endured through many long evenings when the children were shut up in bedrooms with a TV, plates of Instant Whip and tinned fruit salad, and strict orders to 'play nicely', while noisy parties continued downstairs. The married ones regarded Chila with barely disguised amazement and not an inconsiderable amount of envy, their worst fears confirmed, that beauty and youth did not mean you would bag the richest, handsomest husband available. The unmarried ones sat open-mouthed and attentive, hanging on Chila's every word, gritting their teeth against their mothers' sharp nudges whenever Chila mentioned Deepak, which was often, thanks to her own mama.

If Chila's mother had owned a tiara, she would have been wearing it now. The crown of success felt good, having spent years in the balaclava of shame that she donned every time she was asked about her youngest daughter's prospects. Although she knew from her daily Gita readings that pride was not an attribute that would fast track her to Nirvana, she preferred to call it something much more simple and understandable: revenge. So every time Chila visited, she would make sure her friends knew about it, stock up on samosas, and wait for the crowds to arrive.

She ladled some home-made mint chutney onto a few side plates and cleared her throat. 'Did my beti tell you all about the new extension? It is like another house, it even has its own latrine!'

Chila chewed on her lip waiting for the ooohs of wonder to subside and her married contemporaries to stop choking on their vegetable pakore.

'Is that right, Chila beti?' enquired one of the large-portion ladies who seemed half-swallowed by the marshmallow-soft cushions of the sofa.

'Well—' Chila began the sentence which her mother thoughtfully finished.

'Oh, yes. And it has one of those vibrator fans. You know, the buzzing thing that comes on as soon as you sit, to keep the air fresh.'

If Chila had been able to reach her knees, she would have buried her head somewhere between them. 'Extractor, Ma,' she said faintly.

'My son-in-law has just built a swimming pool in my Manju's back garden,' Overbite Auntie said, smiling prominently. 'I said to him, Beta, why waste money? But you know' – she allowed herself a superior titter – 'he can afford, so why not?'

Chila's mother nodded, in that manner that Chila admired despite herself, which said both I agree and Shut your face, my turn next. 'Oh, a pool. Yes, my Deepak-beta is building one next year, but he is waiting until council agree to the jacuzzi and sauna extension also. Like you said, Devi-ji, if you can afford, why not?'

Overbite Auntie's cup trembled slightly as she replaced it on its saucer. The younger girls were enthralled. They had high hopes for a food fight before the end of the afternoon. Chila was momentarily confused. Deepak hadn't mentioned anything about a jacuzzi to her. Either her mother was lying or Deepak was and, depressingly, both were credible options.

'Acha bad,' Overbite Auntie whinnied back, 'some people like such things, but why bother when you can go on holiday five times a year? In a brand new Ranger Rover?' A double whammy, beautifully placed. One over-excited teenager almost applauded, before she remembered she was not supposed to be listening.

Chila's mother had never played poker; trump and bluff

were, as far as she was concerned, faintly rude lavatorial terms. But gambling she could do. When you had three daughters, you learned very quickly. She cleared her throat gently.

'I prefer the Rolls-Royce car myself,' she said confidently.

'Ma,' Chila began, mortified.

'Your son-in-law has a Rolls-Royce?' Settee Auntie asked, as Overbite Auntie had accidentally bitten her tongue and could not speak.

Chila's mother merely smiled and raised an enigmatic eyebrow, hoping she could think of an answer before she lowered it again.

Chila burst in suddenly, 'Actually, sometimes I think the house is a little too big.'

'Too . . . big?' Settee Auntie asked, bewildered. The other older women's faces reflected her concern; surely, when it came to security, one could never have too much.

'You know . . . I mean, rattling around in that huge place . . .' Chila trailed off.

Overbite Auntie made a late comeback. 'Does he leave you on your own a lot then, beti?' she enquired smoothly, all ears pricked now, radar on, wanting to find the first hairline cracks in the palace walls.

Chila's mother shot her a warning glance and after a moment, during which she looked like she might fling a pile of sweetmeats around the room, she grabbed the hem of Chila's suit and declared, 'Oh, yes, Deepak is a very busy man. Just look at this suit he had specially made for her.'

The room relaxed now. Chila sat very still as a few plump fingers stroked her sleeves, marvelling at the softness and quality of the silk. This particular Punjabi suit, in deep purple with delicate silver trim, was one of a job lot Deepak had ordered to accommodate her growing stomach. This one had room for Chila and her whole family, but she knew that was the point, to wear something that would swamp any hint of a bulge. She remembered being slapped on the hand for pointing at a woman beached on her mum's settee and asking what Bimla Auntie had eaten to make her so huge. When her mother had stuttered that Bimla didi was having a baby, Chila was slapped again for asking how it had managed to crawl in there when she couldn't see a zip.

Pregnancy was irrefutable proof that someone had Done It and therefore, over the years, Chila had noticed a number of imaginative methods employed to divert attention from this swelling of shame. Dupattas would be draped and folded and pinned over the offending region; aunties would turn up in marquee-size kaftans or simply leave their coats on all evening. On one occasion, a very large and shy acquaintance had insisted on using her very small husband as a shield, making him walk in front of her whenever she shifted location, shoving him in the right direction with her sari-swaddled bulge. Lately, Chila had noted that several young female pop stars, who had decided to celebrate their womanly independence by reproducing like rabbits, were positively parading their pregnancies at every available opportunity. They would appear on stage, in interviews, at parties, with the skimpiest outfits seemingly designed to flaunt their bumps at the world. 'Motherhood is sexy!' they chanted, thrusting their distended navels at the lenses, celebrating their newly acquired cleavages with low-cut spangly bras.

Chila did think, when she ventured a look down, that there was something wonderful and frightening about a taut pregnant belly. During the last seven and a half months, so many snatches of conversations she had had with Sunita came back to her, only now she understood the jokes and the groans and the terror and the joy. The classes at the local hospital filled in all the facts, but Chila wanted the gossip and the knicker-wetting anecdotes, not the embarrassed polite enquiries and sidelong glances she received from her mother and her friends.

'Chul!' Settee Auntie said with a sigh, 'She is looking . . . healthy.' Her eyes slid slyly to Chila's stomach and then quickly away. Some of the women coughed discreetly, averting their eyes and searching for non-existent crumbs down their blouses. 'God has smiled on her.'

'Oh, yes,' Overbite Auntie murmured, 'she has been veeerrry lucky.'

'Nahin Devi,' someone else butted in, 'we should all be happy, when one of us gets what we deserve, hena?'

There were murmurs of agreement, kisses, smiles, many of them genuine, a few muttered silent prayers as mothers reached for their daughters' hands and wished fervently and genuinely for the health and wealth of their sons-in-law, actual or yet to come. By worshipping their daughters' husbands, they were ensuring their daughters' happiness, for wasn't everything dependent on that? Knowing that a kind, decent man would be caring for their beloved girls when they were no longer here to check up on everything? Hadn't they seen what damage a goonda husband could do, trapping a woman like a fly in a web, free to play with her cruelly, as he knew his wife would stay, believing the misery of a bad marriage was preferable to the stigma and loneliness of separation? Didn't some of the women in that room know that themselves?

Chila looked around the room, love and hate arm wrestling each other across the best china cups. She knew they meant well. She felt suffocated by adoration and welcome. Although she knew her life had improved and expanded in so many ways, she could not shake off the feeling that somewhere, somehow, a part of her was, contrary to appearances, getting smaller. She shifted uncomfortably, and then gasped as a tiny body rolled over with her, inside her.

Her mother clucked with concern and handed Chila a glass of water. 'OK, beti?' she whispered.

Chila looked down transfixed as her stomach undulated like a choppy sea. The folds of the suit billowed into breakers and Chila gasped again as, clearly visible, slowly emerging from the purple silk, was the unmistakable imprint of a foot.

Her mother yelped inadvertently and dropped the glass, which shattered as it hit the centre of the coffee table, spraying half the guests with missiles of chutney-covered shards. A few of the women jumped up alarmed, optimistically clutching tiny napkins like shields against their expensive suits, knocking over chairs, which fell in domino effect until the last one hit Settee Auntie on the head, who had chosen that moment to try and stand up. She fell back, murmuring 'Hai RamRam!' as the cushions swallowed her up, leaving her trapped, legs and arms flailing like a podgy upturned beetle.

An eerie calm followed, broken only by a muffled popping sound as Settee Auntie was shoehorned into an upright position. All eyes were fixed on the one area where it was forbidden to look. Chila's stomach rolled and mutated irreverently, enjoying its defiant moment of glory.

'Blimey!' said one of the younger girls finally. 'It's like that film, *The Alien*, innit?'

Chila groaned, clenching her buttocks futilely, 'Make it stop, Ma!'

'Buche,' her mother breathed. 'Nothing on God's earth can stop that.'

'So much movement,' wondered Overbite Auntie, 'just like my Manju. And she had a boy.' It was her way of apologizing, a gift-wrapped prediction.

'Huh!' muttered Chila's mother. 'My first three kicked like elephants and we still got girls until Raju arrived. All we can do is pray now.'

Chila blinked rapidly. Her forehead began to burn. She pushed her mother's hand away, heaved herself to her feet and walked out.

'Beti?' Her mother was blocking her way to the door. 'You're not going yet? I've made biriani, your favourite, with extra ghee for you-know-who.'

'Who? The little prince in here?' Chila shouted, prodding her belly. 'Or the waste-of-space little girl?'

'Please, beti,' her mother whispered, her eyes darting to the door leading to the front room. 'They are all listening.'

'Is that all that bothers you?' Chila whispered back, angry at the wobble in her throat.

Too many things were making sense to her now. She, the last of three girls, the baby born before her younger and only brother, Raju. Her eldest sister, Rita, was welcomed as the firstborn, and had confirmed her high status by going to college and bagging a rich computer analyst who had whisked her off to California, where she spent her days doing consultancy work from home and watching the Mexican houseboys clean the pool. Next came Suman, whose startling beauty must have made up for her parents' initial disappointment, together with the fact she married a Scottish Punjabi laird, part of some strange aristocratic Indian clan who would divide their time between international business travel and shooting anything with hooves in the mountains. So by the time her parents girded up their loins for their third child, they must have reckoned, what with the law of averages and her mother's special guru-approved herbal diet, that their household would soon be graced by a tousle-haired little tyke who would carry on the family name proudly into the next century. Instead, they got

Chila. And what was worse, Raju was born a mere year later. Raju, whose galloping asthma and eczema guaranteed him total attention. No wonder she was left alone, with her catalogues, her Hindi films and her fantasies.

'You thought there was something wrong with me, didn't you? Is that why you didn't want me?' Chila asked.

'Of course we wanted you,' her mother said softly, 'but you worry more for girls. With boys it's . . . just easier.'

'Who says, Ma?'

Someone coughed inside, very near the door, precipitating a flurry of obvious clearing up activity.

'Come inside, beti, please?'

Chila thought back to those endless sessions where she was prodded and poked by those seeking to 'cure her'. All the energy her parents expended worrying about her future, while the present became a mere waiting area, with hard plastic chairs. She would go into that front room right now and tell all these young girls to go away and pack a bag and travel and read and climb mountains and see the view from somewhere very high and bright and maybe send her a postcard so she could remind herself of a different view.

She wanted to sit somewhere with Tania and Sunita, where there were no silver-plated knick-knack dishes with different compartments for peanuts and crisps, no nests of tables and plastic covering on the chairs – not so far away, not so different, but at this moment, it seemed to Chila, a few universes' journey from where she now stood. She wanted to tell her mother that she was right. There was something wrong with her. She should have been happy, and she wasn't.

'Beti. Chila . . . what is it? Please . . .'

This was Chila's cue. She would tell her now. She looked full on into her mother's eyes and paused, wrong-footed, because she saw there something baffling and unexpected.

Her mama was afraid. Afraid that Chila might utter words that would shatter the fragile throne upon which she sat, afraid that her daughter's confession would force her to confront her own demons of disappointment, afraid that her daughter's as yet unspoken misery would now keep her awake for the rest of her nights because she, as her mother, should have known, and if Chila spoke, the rest of the world would know too.

'I . . .' began Chila, feeling her dupatta heavy on her shoulders, yoke of ages, transparent as air, heavier than iron, a woman's modesty symbolized by a scrap of silk, izzat a mere textbook term up until now, a family's honour is carried by its daughters. Maybe because the strongest of the men would break their backs under its weight. Chila perspired with her own power. A sentence, a few syllables, a single tear – she could end this now and walk away from the rubble.

'Beti?'

One last time her mother asked her and Chila felt the shutters closing as she said, 'I feel fine, Mama. Don't you worry. Let's go and eat.'

Akash eventually located the Hoover under a pile of unironed clothes and began clearing a path through the house. He had sworn efficiently and without guilt when he had given up ringing the bell and let himself in to be confronted by the festering heap. It looked like the aftermath of a giant's tantrum, with breakfast plates mixed in with clothes, newspapers and toys. True, the house never looked actually tidy, but they lived in what he congenially imagined to be comfortable disarray. Only now did he realize that this was probably the state of their living space every morning, and that what he saw when he came home from work was the cleaner version of the dump in which he now stood.

His eye was caught by little scraps of bright yellow paper scattered apparently randomly around the rooms. On closer inspection, he saw that they were Post-it notes, which had been carefully stuck on various piles of debris. 'YOUR MESS', each said, except for a solitary note on a pile of books which declared, 'MY MESS – PLEASE LEAVE'. Akash exhaled slowly and flung his duster down. He made a cup of tea in a quickly rinsed mug and sat for a full hour before he realized Sunita was not coming back in a hurry. He put the Jam on high on the CD player and picked up his Mr Clean Bleach N Spray, vowing to tell his therapist all about his domestic emasculation at his next session.

Akash did not look up when he finally heard Sunita enter clumsily, negotiating the buggy through the narrow hallway.

'Hiya!' she called, a little too cheerily he thought, as he snapped his newspaper up to his face and pretended to read a report on inner city school violence.

'God, town was completely mad today,' she continued, her voice muffled as she bent down to release the children from their perambulatory restraints, 'but the buche were really good. They loved the tube as well. Course I had to bribe them with several packets of chocolate buttons so they need a wipe down . . .'

Akash ignored the implicit request and read the opening sentence of the report again, wondering when she was going to tell him why she had been in the West End when she should have been at work. It was not up to him to ask. He would use the analysis approach on her and wait until she felt she had to speak. That way he could not be blamed for asking leading questions. And not lose his temper, of course.

'Throw them in the bath for me, would you, Akash?'

Akash could not believe the complete lack of awareness she was displaying. Did she not realize she owed him an explanation? He lowered his newspaper slowly and wondered why there was a strange woman holding his son towards him like an unexploded parcel bomb.

'Sunita?' he stuttered.

Sunita stroked her boyish hair which barely skimmed the fur-trim collar of her very expensive velvet box jacket, which went remarkably well with her new slightly flared Lycra trousers and her soft leather cowboy boots. She smiled slightly, the tilt of her head revealing red and copper highlights shimmering in her crown. A tiny diamanté butterfly slide winked cheekily at him from above her left ear.

'Vidal Sassoon,' she said finally. 'They told me that the Gwyneth Paltrow was out, so they did me the Natalie Imbruglia instead. Everything else I bought was on sale.'

It was then Akash noticed the bulging carrier bags hanging precariously from the buggy's handles. His newspaper drooped mockingly in his hands. He knew he ought to speak, but at this moment he could not think of one sensible syllable to say.

Sunita began pulling clothes off Sunil, who gurgled fatly in her deft hands, his face a contented mask of encrusted chocolate.

'I worked out that I haven't actually bought myself anything since' – she was going to say Chila's wedding but she skated round it smoothly – 'for about eighteen months. A student did my hair at the salon. It's a bit shorter than I thought but I'm getting used to it. So pound for pound, I am a really cheap date.'

She plonked a naked Sunil on top of the newspaper on Akash's lap and began stripping Nikita, who still managed to keep licking her sticky fingers throughout the operation.

'They'll need feeding after bath, and best put some emollient in it – Sunny's skin's a bit dry. I'm going out in about twenty minutes so I'll just run up and change.'

It was only when Sunita was halfway up the stairs that Akash managed to shout, 'Where?'

'That benefit I told you about? With Beroze? You remember, sweetheart.'

He heard the bedroom door slam as Sunil gave a satisfied sigh and emptied his bladder over his confused papa's lap.

Akash soaped the children down on autopilot as they screamed and splashed in the foot-high bubbles of their bath. Next door he could hear Sunita singing along to the radio as she pottered around the bedroom. 'I'm so randy . . . randy randy randy,' she chirruped, off key he noted miserably. He seemed to have gone into delayed shock. Was there something he had missed lately? Something she had told him or he had done which had turned her into a designer-clad, over-sexed Natalie in the space of twenty-four hours? True, they had exchanged a few weeks of sharp, splintered words after the screening of that dreadful, exploitative film, which subsided until the bloody thing was shown on television and they argued all over again about exactly the same subjects.

He knew they were in danger of being trapped in some destructive co-dependent cycle and told her so, to which she had replied, 'Bollocks!' and then, 'It's really simple. I hurt, I wanted to talk about it, you didn't listen so I ended up talking about it to someone else.'

'But to *her*? On *camera*?' Akash had yelled back.

'I didn't know she was filming me,' Sunita had replied calmly, and that had more or less ended any detailed discussions about the whole incident.

Akash knew deep, deep down that most of his anger was fuelled by his own sense of failure. The shame he felt watching his wife cry helplessly into camera had been superseded by an overwhelming urge to shake Tania by her pretty little shoulders until her teeth rattled. But as neither of them had had any contact with Tania since, the wave of his bruter instincts had retreated, leaving him washed up on the shore, a nugget of emotional flotsam, rinsed clean but uncomfortably naked. He had tried to engage Sunita in a dialogue about Tania, hoping their joint sense of betrayal would bind them together, make them a team again, but she inexplicably refused to discuss her. Akash guessed the betrayal had been much worse for Sunita and he tried to respect that. His instincts told him that once Sunita had come to terms with what Tania had done, that would open the floodgates and together they could work something out.

That was yesterday. Today, he was not sure about anything except what he could see, and feel and hold: the fish-slippery perfect bodies of his children, the chocolate ring of scum accumulating on the sides of the bathtub, the slowly drying patch of urine on his favourite brown cords, and the sight of Sunita standing in the doorway, ready to leave.

'You didn't tell me you were going out tonight,' Akash said carefully, trying not to stare too hard at the short silver dress that clung to Sunita's not inconsiderable curves.

'I did actually,' Sunita said brightly. 'You probably weren't listening. It's written on the magnetic calendar on the fridge.'

Akash did not mention that he had not noticed there was a magnetic calendar on the fridge. 'I might have been doing something,' he said, reasonably he hoped.

'I usually am doing something when you have to work late or go to evening sessions,' Sunita said, checking her hair in the mirror above the sink, 'which is why the calendar is a good idea. At least we can liaise about things, keep the channels of communication open.'

Akash's ears pricked up, his Pavlovian response to any

phrase that he might have used himself when trying to win an argument. 'Pardon?' he asked, trying to keep the squeak of indignation out of his voice.

'If a couple can't co-ordinate the mundane tasks of daily life, there's little hope of them managing the bigger, more nebulous issues, wouldn't you say?' purred Sunita.

Akash dropped the soap then. He felt around in the suds for a while longer than he needed, hoping she would leave now. When he looked up again, she was still there, framed by steam and backlit by the yellow landing light.

Venus rising from that big shell, thought Akash, and then said, 'You've lost weight.'

Sunita shrugged. 'A bit. Haven't been trying. Don't care really, but I feel healthier.'

'The dress . . .' murmured Akash, fighting an urge to slide a soapy hand from her knee to thigh.

'Mama looks like a beautiful princess,' yelled Nikita happily, 'with spangles!'

'Don't forget the sparkles.' Sunita laughed and blew them a kiss before she skipped downstairs.

Later on, when the children had finally settled, which took an hour of cajoling, warnings and serious threats, a familiar soundtrack Akash usually heard in snatches from the safety of his study, he flopped down into an armchair, too tired to even think of picking up any of his papers. The children had drained him; he felt as if he had endured a session of dialysis and a hot enema to boot. He noticed he was sitting the way Sunita often sat in the evenings, slouched, legs apart, staring at a distant point somewhere near that large cobweb above the television. Maybe this was what being in touch with your feminine side meant, sitting shagged out and listless on a cushion, wanting desperately to be looked after, for just a few minutes. He leaned back and tried to relax his limbs. His hand brushed against something hard next to the armchair. He looked down and saw the pile of books, still with Sunita's 'MY MESS' Post-it note stuck to the cover of the top volume. He picked it up, and recognized it as one of his course study journals. *Psycho-Sexual Counselling: A Journey.*

'God,' he muttered, 'the Noddy version with big pictures. I don't know how she could—'

He stopped when he saw little scribblings in Sunita's familiar spidery scrawl in the margins. He squinted and held the book to the light, too exhausted to get up and find his reading glasses. 'Facile' read one of them, 'Over-stated' another. The remark on the inside back cover was bigger and underlined. 'Even three-year-olds know this stuff!' Then her initials and a date. Three months ago.

He flicked through the rest of the books quickly now. Some of them were his, some he had not heard of, with garish shiny covers and ridiculous shouty titles: *If You're Not Listening, Why Am I Still Talking?*, *Women and Fear: Dare You Read the Truth? Mind Sex! The Big O Revealed!* Sunita's running commentary in the margins looked more interesting than what was on the pages. If only he could read it.

Akash made the effort to find his bifocals and pour himself a glass of red wine before settling down again. He refocused, and Sunita's voice seemed to jump out at him from the well-thumbed pages. 'If I had known this twenty years ago . . .' was one, next to a passage about low self-esteem and how it influenced your choice of partner. Akash felt strangely unsettled, wounded even. A chapter on eating disorders was criss-crossed with red pen. 'ME AT SIX-TEEN', Sunita had written in capitals next to a description of a teenage binger. Why hadn't he known about that? 'I knew my mirror lied to me!' was her comment on a passage about distorted self-image. 'Good evening, madam, and what would you like to throw up tonight?' she wrote on the back cover, making Akash snort with laughter, despite himself.

They had laughed a lot together. Flashes of indolent evenings marked with pillow fights and fevered kisses came back to him, warm and full-blooded, with an aftertaste of cinnamon and maybe vanilla, decidedly vintage.

Sunita stormed through chapters, dismissing earnest Americanisms with pithy one-liners: 'Nothing wrong with guilt. Kept my mother busy for years'; 'This is a good theory unless you grew up in Ilford and only met men who wore tank tops'; 'I would love to shout I deserve good sex, but we have very thin walls and the man next door might take it the wrong way.'

Akash chortled and drank his way through the diminishing pile and was amazed to find, when he checked his watch, that two hours and two bottles had passed. He sat back, one book remaining on his lap. He felt, well, pissed, he had to admit, but satisfied, happy even. He felt as if he had spent two hours with Sunita on a student mattress, candles stuck in empty bottles of Liebfraumilch sputtering around them, while she pulled secrets out of him with gentle fingers, trapped in the web of her moon-luminous eyes.

How easy it was to remember what made you fall in love. How tragically easier it was to forget. They had never feared silences before. They would read companionably together for hours back then, secretly impressed with their grown-up restraint. Somewhere between then and now, the pauses between the talking had got longer and the silences had become deafening. Before, Sunita would catch his eye and ask, 'What you thinking?' Now they were both afraid to ask. Appropriate really, that they now spoke to each other via graffiti in a book.

Akash felt extremely grateful that he was reading her

observations alone, with no chance to demand further explanation. Indeed, how much was needed? – when he saw his name in bold letters next to paragraphs such as 'Sexual withdrawal, far from being a passive act, is in fact a deliberate and aggressive act, conscious or not', or 'Beware the eternally reasonable partner who seeks to make you into the unreasonable neurotic reactor', or, more worryingly, 'Listen, sister, if he ain't hot to trot, and he ain't got the cojones to even talk about it, you ain't doing him or yourself no favours by staying and staying schtum!!'

The final thin volume aroused Akash's curiosity: *Dark Lotus: The Mythology of Indian Sexuality*. He wanted to read this one. He checked the flyleaf: Hathi Publishers, Calcutta. She had purchased an imported book. He was impressed. The chapter headings were reassuringly predictable: 'Mother India – and her Son', 'The Role of the Hermaphrodite', 'Patriarchy Made Divine', and the final chapter, 'The Sita Complex', which Sunita had obviously read several times. There were plenty of YES! SO TRUEs dotting the margins, and heavily drawn arrows to certain sections with accompanying bubbles: 'My mother!', 'My mother again!' and 'OK, did my mother write this?' A few pages into the chapter, a whole section had been boxed off by a thick red line. Akash was somewhat irritated; this looked like wilful damage now. She could have used a pencil. He read:

> . . . and due to this, the deeply embedded image of Sita's sacrifice through fire to prove her worth, many Indian women subconsciously equate marriage and partnership with trial and suffering. Indeed, they expect it, welcome it as proof of a virtuous liaison, blessed by tradition. Stoicism in the face of extreme

pain is expected of the good wife (a belief possibly reinforced by the resignation and fatalism displayed by the mother or other close female relatives). Surrounded by forceful female role models, or loving harmonious parental examples, the myth will be challenged and replaced perhaps with other powerful Kali-centred female models (particularly prevalent in the South of India where matriarchal familial structures still persist). Left unchallenged, and indeed encouraged by dominant male partners, Sita will encourage masochism, martyrdom and the sub-jugation of self . . .

Akash read and reread this section, puzzling over its significance. Was this how she saw herself, the woman who just hours ago had shimmied out of the door in a silver handkerchief singing to the world she was randy?

'There ought to be a bloody chapter on the Krishna myth somewhere,' he muttered, reaching for a wine bottle and finding it was empty. 'We can't all be flute-playing charmers with the universe in our mouths.' He threw the bottle across the room. 'The Superman myth? What about that, eh?' he told a cobweb. 'Mild-mannered wimp, good with small animals and kids, jumps into phone booth and comes out with big muscles and his pants over his tights, ready to save the world . . . I think *not*!'

He got to his feet unsteadily. 'And wharrabout the biggie, eh? The new man myth. Oh, yeah. They really got us with that one, didn't they! You can cook quiche till you're shitting oven gloves and they'll still roll their eyes at some point and say Bloody Men . . . ow.' He closed his eyes. 'But we are . . . not the same.' He opened one eye. 'I see them every day, like Joe Jackson said, pretty women out walking with gorillas down my street . . . out of my office. Good women, taken all sorts of shit, take the gorilla's hand and forgive him. I'm a nice guy. And I still don't get the girl. I don't get it.'

He stared out of the window, curtains still open to the cloudy night sky. 'Sparkles, my arse.'

Chila sat in a dark corner, watching multi-coloured lights spin and strobe across the dance floor. She could see her escort, Shireen, at the bar, fishing in her embroidered shoulder bag for change. Shireen was one of Chila's most recent diary entries, the sister of one of her lunching friends, who was introduced to Chila as '*The* woman to know in East London. If there's something happening that is "happening", Shireen knows about it!' Shireen had that effect on people; they began talking in quaint Sixties hippy terms whenever her name came up, using phrases like 'right on' and 'cool babe'. Chila did not mind this (at least they weren't saying 'boring old fart' which summed up some of Deepak's business circles), and besides, after escaping from her mother's house, she longed to be somewhere anonymous and busy.

She watched Shireen pushing her way through the throng of enthusiastic dancers, holding aloft a long glass of white frothy liquid which she placed in front of Chila, and then rearranged her long thick plait which she quickly spiralled and pinned to the top of her head. Chila thought it looked as if a black cottage loaf had decided to perch on her crown. It seemed incongruous with Shireen's traditional loose-fitting suit. And then Chila remembered: the footwear. Always check the shoes to assess what sort of conversation you might have with another Asian woman, whether she was the type who wanted to discuss the price of gold and baby clothes, or talk about travelling round India and how crap men were. It was one of Chila's secret tactics in social situations, and it never failed. She knew what she would see even before she looked down. A pair of steel-capped Doc Martens peeked from beneath Shireen's baggy shalwar trousers. Chila sighed. She would have to keep alert then, and even though she had just arrived, she was trying desperately to repress a series of very large yawns.

'The barwoman was pleased with me, ordering a diet Coke and a pint of milk. You OK?'

Chila nodded before downing the glass in a few grateful gulps.

Shireen grinned at her and handed her a serviette. 'Milk moustache,' she whispered.

Chila giggled and wiped carefully around her mouth.

'That's better,' said Shireen, easing herself next to her. 'You've been really quiet tonight. I felt a bit bad, dragging you out.'

'Oh, no, I wanted to come, I really did,' Chila tried to enthuse. 'I mean, it's a really good cause and everything. What is it again?' She cursed herself for not doing her homework, for not admitting the real reason she was here was to avoid yet another night sitting on her own in front of the television, feeling her baby turn somersaults to the theme tunes of various soap operas.

'It's to raise funds for Jasbinder Singh's legal fees,' Shireen replied, before waving madly to someone across the room.

'Oh, right,' said Chila, no wiser, but wise enough not to let on. 'Jasbinder Singh, of course.'

'Awful case, wasn't it?' Shireen continued. 'But really symbolic of what's going on out there.'

'Oh, yes. Symbolic. I thought that as well,' Chila muttered, trying to check out where the nearest fire exit might be.

'I mean, did you read the papers?'

Chila nodded. 'Oh, yes, it was everywhere wasn't it?'

'Well no, actually, no-one bothered to report it, except the *Guardian*. At least, that's what I thought . . .'

Chila got up hurriedly. 'Baby on bladder, have to . . . you know.'

'Oh, right, yes, of course.'

Shireen got up to let Chila pass, and then suddenly, inexplicably, screamed quite loudly in Chila's ear: 'OHMIGOD! I have to dance to this one.' She climbed over a couple of chairs and ran, arms waving, right into the centre of the room.

As if on cue, dozens of other people around the room were also whooping like sirens, throwing down coats and bags and knocking down furniture in their haste to jump into the ever-increasing crowd congregating on the dance floor, mouthing the lyrics as they jostled for a space. 'But then I spent so many nights thinking how you did me wrong, and I grew strong . . .'

Chila stood dumbfounded; it was like a vision of mass hysteria, as more and more joined the pulsating group. They moved as one, boots and sandals and stilettos and sneakers stamping in unison, a forest of brown arms raised to the ceiling, silver bangles and red nail polish, manicured talons and work-worn fingers, clad in homespun cotton and gaudy silks, bare with ornate mendhi tattoos snaking around the wrists, fists thumping the air, palms open ready to applaud, singing with one voice, triumphantly, 'I'll survive! I will survive! Oh as long as I know how to love . . .'

Chila knew this one. It was really old. She remembered falling off her platforms to this song. She also remembered, if her memory of those youth club discos all those years ago served her correctly, that men never danced to this song. Whenever it came on, anyone male would scurry fearfully from the dance floor, before he was trampled by the stampede of baying women coming the other way. Of course, there were other songs that the men called theirs. Like 'Bohemian Rhapsody' (which they always insisted on singing and dancing along to, making Chila laugh), or indeed anything with lots of loud electric guitars. Chila had usually joined in the communal jigging with Tania and Sunita. She thought it was a nice song but she had secretly preferred the Bee Gees. On the one hand, it was quite re-assuring that some things had not changed. On the other, she had never really listened to the words before. Or at least, it seemed as if she was hearing them for the first time, at full volume in this belligerent high descant. And only then did it strike her. She swept the room; the bar staff, the DJ, the security at the door, everyone around her was female.

Chila was not surprised. It was happening more and more lately, this insidious segregation of the sexes. Odd, really, she had imagined that marriage would put an end to this division; no more giggles and whispers with other girls about the availability and motives of these strange remote creatures, no more longing for their forbidden company, no more what ifs. With a ring on your finger, everything would be above board and legitimate. You could move freely with a husband at your side, feel secure even around other men, knowing that they would be, henceforth, merely brothers to you. She liked that part of the wedding ceremony. It was a good theory, anyhow. But she found herself moving from sitting rooms to dinner parties to vast halls where inevitably, eventually, she would end up with the women. The men were always separate, or absent, like tonight. And mostly, no-one seemed to mind.

Ironically, her mother's friends seemed to see more of their partners than the so-called modern women with whom Chila socialized. True, her parents spent most of their shared time bickering, something they did unconsciously as they moved around the house, her father shouting crossly from behind the locked toilet door, her mother yelling like a fishwife from the front garden while she scrubbed the path. But Chila found it comforting. It meant they had grudgingly accepted each other and were grumbling about the fact that they were staying put. She could not imagine arguing with Deepak.

Briefly she recalled a group of young men she had met somewhere, whom she had liked very much. They were youngish, funny-ish, and unsettlingly friendly. More brotherly than her own brother had ever seemed. Where had she seen them? Then she remembered. Tania's film première.

The song finally ended to raucous cheers and whistles and, in reply, her baby kicked her swiftly beneath her ribcage. 'If you're a boy,' she told her bump as she started to make her way towards the exit, 'at least I can talk to you.'

She manoeuvred her way through the laughing women, her arms forming a protective shield over her stomach. As the last hurrahs finally faded, leaving an unexpected calm in its wake, she heard the laugh, a familiar honking which jerked her head up sharply and pulled her eyes towards a group gathered near the stage. Chila saw a tint of copper, a flash of silver, and began to move slowly towards them, reluctant, underwater steps, resisting the anchor of possible disappointment dragging behind her. Just a little further. Check her shoes, don't forget. And then the lights burst into flares on stage and everyone in the room rushed towards the front, and the familiar stranger was gone. But Chila did recognize the woman who was now on stage holding a microphone, waiting for the noise to subside. The spiky henna-haired woman with fashionably dowdy glasses from Tania's screening.

'Sisters,' she began, and Chila noted with satisfaction the woman was wearing baseball boots, 'we all know why we are here, to show our support both emotionally and I hope, financially, for a woman who has been through a hell few of us can imagine, but which is closer to us than we all think.' The audience quietened down immediately, tense, alert. 'On November the eighteenth of last year, Jasbinder Singh legally separated from her husband after twelve years of marriage, her husband, Gurpreet Singh, leaving Jasbinder with their two sons, Jaspal and Joginder. On December the twelfth, after a weekend visit, Gurpreet Singh refused to hand the children back to Jasbinder, claiming that his sons should live with him and his parents. When Jasbinder refused, and threatened to call the police, her husband took matters into his own hands . . .' Suki paused for a second, tightly gripping the microphone. Chila became aware of the silence around her, unnerving after so much noise.

'Gurpreet Singh told his wife if he could not have the children, no-one could, and that this was her punishment for destroying their family. He then locked himself in his car with his sons, doused himself and his children with petrol, and in front of Jasbinder, who was watching from a window, waiting for the police to arrive, burnt himself and his own sons to death.'

Chila closed her eyes and braced herself against the joyous tumbles inside her, her baby gambolling as the room held its breath. She became aware of cheers, thundering applause, and opened her eyes to see a small plain woman gingerly take the microphone from Suki's outstretched hand. Jasbinder Singh had the body of a young girl, and an unnaturally calm face, carved from stricken wood. The handclaps went on for some time. Jasbinder waited patiently for them to die down.

'Thank you everyone,' she began.

Chila had expected a harsh nasal twang, loamy with Punjabi soil, but Jasbinder spoke gently, only a lilt betraying her birthplace.

'Nothing can bring my children back. But I want justice. The courts tell me this was an act of passion, a tragic event. I want this event called what it was, murder. I have been blamed for this. People say it was my karma, my fate for leaving my husband. But no-one will blame him. Even in death, he has escaped. He is the lucky one.' Jasbinder struggled to keep her voice steady.

An almost tangible aura of energy, red hot, ready, passed from the watching women to the stage, holding Jasbinder erect, urging her on.

'This court ruling must be overturned, for all the other women out there, like me. For Leila Khan, who was stabbed to death when collecting her children from a custody visit. For Priya Kumar, whose ex-husband kidnapped her son and has been missing for five years. For Jyoti Patel, who let her ex-husband take her children on holiday and when he returned . . .'

Chila was almost running now, pushing aside bodies randomly as she fixated on the exit light above the double doors at the end of the hall. Mingled sweat and perfume made her gag, a sickbed smell, sweet and decaying. Staying here would curdle her hope, give her acrid breath and a squinted eye, make her look for the catch and expect the worst. Maybe it was already too late. She did not want to dance in big boots to old songs. She wanted to understand and to love, otherwise how would they survive, any of them? Who would her baby call Papa? She threw herself through the swing doors and ran straight into someone emerging from the toilets. She felt tinsel against her skin.

'Oh, my God, Chila.'

Sunita was cradling her like a child, cradling her child in her palms, possessively, short painted nails across Chila's torso, Sunita with a stranger's hair and dress.

'Oh, my God.'

Chila returned the embrace, taking in the tender vulnerability of Sunita's bare neck, silver prickles everywhere, tiny dancing stars filtered through brimming eyes.

'I'm sorry, I—' they both said, and then snorted snot and relief together, unwilling to let go.

'Why didn't you tell me?' Sunita hiccuped. 'Oh, my God, just look at you. I should have—'

'Me too, I should have phoned but—'

'It was all so—'

'I know, I know.'

They laugh and breathe deeply and laugh again and hold hands, sticky playground fingers, and weep without noticing, and Sunita can't believe, can't forget that there's three of them now, just like once before. She kisses Chila through purple silk, a big kiss from baby's favourite auntie.

Without looking up, she asks, 'Have you talked to . . .?' She can feel Chila shake her head. 'Nor me.'

They cannot say Tania's name. She leaves a chasm. SunitaChilaand . . . The trick is not to look down. Their loss would give them vertigo so they cling to each other, balance each other, hope for a new equilibrium to come, one day very soon. Sunita waits a moment. This time she forces eye contact. Oh it's so hard, knowing what she knows, not knowing what Chila might know.

'And how's Deepak?'

Chila smiles. She sees the lie and loves Sunita for it.

'He's fine,' she lies back.

Tania blinked in the unexpected spotlight as she opened the fridge door, grabbed the carton of cranberry juice and shut the door quickly, waiting for the blue gloom of the room to rearrange itself into shadowy outlines where her sofa squatted like some large beast in a soft pool of neon. She sat in her window seat, bosomy Indian print cushions encircling the window's bay, and watched the tail lights of miniature cars climb Holloway Hill, watched them disappear at the top, tipped off some invisible lazy conveyor belt. She sipped straight from the carton, a habit that had always infuriated Martin, which was probably why she was doing it, and wondered if she would spend another night watching the first flush of dawn rise over the hill and rinse the darkness away.

There were still Martin-shaped spaces all around the flat: the wall where his framed black and white film stills used to hang, the Marx Brothers around a piano, Woody Allen dressed as a spermatozoon, a concert shot of Spinal Tap, Jimmy Stewart frozen in ecstasy as he tries to tell the surrounding crowd that it really is *A Wonderful Life*; the top of the fridge where his cookbooks used to live (now inhabited by Tania's revealingly pathetic collection, *Gourmet Meals in Five Minutes* and *Cooking For One Can Be Fun!*); the acres of space left by the absence of his computer.

Tania did not subscribe to the theory that every time a relationship ended, the other person walked away with a piece of you, and vice versa, that each failed union took another chunk of your heart. That would mean most of the population would become colanders in a rainstorm, each soul a self-contained sieve. She did not believe it because she had been here before; with the regularity of reincarnation she lived and relived the moving out and moving on and, in the end, the walls always looked better rather than empty after a few weeks. But this time it was taking a little longer than usual, this time the insomnia had slightly outlived its welcome (now that the filming was over it was no longer useful), and she still avoided having Melody FM on in the car (those syrupy ballads were only for people in love or masochists who weren't). Tania thought all this was odd, considering the Martin-shaped space in the bed had been refilled before his pillow had gone cold.

She drained the last of the carton and left it on the sill before padding back to the bedroom. She sat gently on the edge of the bed. The candles were burning low in their mosaic-glass tumblers, fluttering like weakened moths against the fractured glass. He lay on his side, scissor-precise, hands clasped as if in prayer or namaste under his cheek, knees drawn up and together, prim as a nun. Even in sleep he kept himself tidy. Tania always made sure she watched her companions in repose. There were no masks in slumber, no rehearsed bonhomie, no practised one-liners, only the face one had as a child, before the world and other lovers chiselled away at unblemished skin. He must have been a beautiful baby, a spoiled boy with those eyes and dimples and anemone mouth.

Tania's first proper boyfriend, a history of art student, had told her she looked like a Picasso when awake and a Modigliani when asleep. The relationship lasted until she saw her first Picasso at the Tate. And he, the one next to her, whose neck she simply had to touch, was a six-year-old's drawing when awake, bold obvious lines, cartoon moods, out of proportion views. Amusing but not worth anything beyond sentimental value. And now, increasingly, she saw the delicate etching, the washes of colour, the fine detail, the bigger picture. It surprised her, it worried her, it kept her awake. It hadn't happened last time. It wasn't supposed to happen now.

Deepak opened his eyes and broke into a lazy smile. 'Aho bhanji!' Punjabi in her bed. So incongruous, so thrilling.

'Do me a favour,', she said, snuggling under his arm. 'Don't call me your sister. It's bad enough as it is.' That was supposed to have been a joke, but they both kept silent for a minute, shifting limbs to find what they had discovered to be the perfect fit.

'It's almost two o'clock,' Tania said, knowing what was on his mind. 'Do you want a coffee to wake you up before you drive . . .?' Home was the end of that sentence which she preferred not to say.

'In theory,' Deepak began slowly, 'I could stay now . . .' Martin's gone was the end of his.

They both pondered life in the wonderful world of theories for a moment before Tania said, 'And your explanation for being out all night would be?'

'Would be that I have found the person I want to spend tonight and several more nights with and therefore it made perfect, absolute sense.'

'Yeah.' Tania laughed and reached for her cigarette packet. 'That would do it. Well done.'

'A-plus-good-boy-shabash!' Deepak added in a mock Indian accent which always sounded more Welsh than authentic but made Tania snort smoke anyhow.

Between them, they had played all the members of their immediate families and some from the more remote extended branches too. Characters and anecdotes poured out of them, helping each other rearrange potentially depressing and embarrassing experiences into comic nuggets, seen from the same vantage point of love and regret. There is nothing more powerful than feeling mutually misunderstood.

Tania offered the cigarette to Deepak, who declined. Knowing why he had done so, she carefully blew smoke in his hair.

'What are you doing?' he said, ruffling his fringe in a

futile attempt to prevent the smell of smoke clinging to him.

'Say you were in a bar, with your disgusting chain-smoking friends,' Tania shot back.

This always happened during the last quarter of an hour, when they made clumsy, resentful small talk against the deafening ticking of a clock. Bickering was the best option, much safer than going into whys and wherefores, because in the end, what right had they to stay?

'And anyway,' continued Tania, 'you sleep separately, so what's the big deal?'

Deepak swallowed and shrugged slightly. It was back, swift and sharp, twisting his gut into a hard, tight ball. The guilt stayed away long enough for him to believe, for a few hours, that this was the right thing and he would tell Tania/Chila as soon as possible to put things straight. But whom should he tell first? And what, exactly?

Tania lay back on the pillow, her hair fanned out behind her, framing her face in old penny silk. Deepak's heart contracted, the nearest he would get to labour pain, this agonizing bearing down that left him gasping for breath. He had begun to realize that the heart did actually ache. It was a muscle after all, he rationalized, but unlike cramp, this pain did not pass with a quick rub or a hop around the room. It intensified each time he left her, which baffled him and made him furious. It was inconvenient. It made him say terrible things and then buy big, useless presents. It was the lack of control that made him feel so undignified, so delirious and so afraid of what he might do next.

He wondered how many others, at this very moment, were lying in tangled sheets preparing for a long cold journey home. Lately, he had found himself scouring scurrilous tabloid reports about serial adulterers or deter-mined individuals who had managed to maintain secret liaisons for several years, and reading these nudge-wink exposés, he felt torn between depression and disbelief. How had he managed to become another grubby statistic? And furthermore, how had they, anyone, managed to live like this for so long without going mad?

'Why did she stop sleeping with you?' The 'she' was almost whispered. Tania never said Chila's name. That way, she could almost pretend they were discussing someone else, someone they did not know, did not both love.

Deepak shrugged again. He was too tired, too ashamed to concoct a clever response or diversion.

'She seemed so . . . in love with you,' Tania continued, almost nostalgically. 'And then to reject you so quickly.'

Deepak closed his eyes. It was coming, sooner than he had imagined. She would find out and she would throw him out and then he would possibly die quite soon afterwards.

'It was my film, wasn't it?' Deepak was afraid to exhale. 'I can take it, you know. I take responsibility for what I did. For how I made you look, both of you . . . Just tell me, Deeps.'

Deepak breathed out and nodded. He opened his eyes to see Tania close to him, above him, inches away from him. Tears glittered on her lashes, transparent beads trembling, ripe and ready to fall.

'I never wanted that,' she said, her voice catching. 'I wanted her to see you clearly and love you still, not be in your power any more. I didn't want this.' She kissed him and it rained.

As he was leaving, she stopped him in the doorway. She looked bruised in the dusk, and tiny, dwarfed by a large T-shirt.

'She always wanted kids, you know. And I never have.'

'I know,' Deepak said, stopping with one arm in his over-coat, feeling ridiculous and exposed in her hallway.

'I mean,' Tania continued, helping him into his sleeve, 'if

you want a family, with her, a future, let's stop this now, while we still can.'

'Can we?' Deepak asked.

Tania ignored him. She was in practical mode. He half-expected her to spit on a finger and remove a mud speck from his cheek. She buttoned him up instead, her voice calm.

'If she wants to try again, maybe try for a baby, if there's a chance—'

Deepak put his finger to her lips. 'She doesn't. There isn't.'

There. No thunderbolts, no big fist coming down from the sky. Not yet. In the meantime, Tania could go on pretending she was merely offering comfort and he could pretend his wife wasn't weeks away from having their first child. It did not make much sense, there was an inescapable point when all would be revealed, but for once, for maybe the first time in his life, Deepak was living each moment with no thought of the future. He drove home and fell into a deep sleep next to a sleeping Chila, his back warmed by her growing, inevitable belly.

Akash only woke up when Sunita fell over him, yelping in annoyance. He sat upright on the bottom stair (how had he got here?) and fixed her with a rheumy red eye.

'Whatimeisit?'

'You're drunk,' said Sunita, trying to climb over him on her way upstairs.

He saw a flash of underwear as she lifted a leg. At least, he consoled himself, she still had some on. And what's more, they seemed to be her at home pants, large, comfortable ones with roomy legholes. This made him feel, momentarily, very confident.

'And you,' he said to her back, 'are such a bloody cliché.'

Sunita stopped and slowly turned round. She looked like some festive Amazonian, legs astride, hands on shimmery hips, gazing down at him from what seemed to be a great height. Had she grown taller? Or maybe, Akash mused, he was shrinking.

'What did you say?' Sunita said, through pursed lips, their edges blurred by faded lipstick.

'Cliché,' said Akash again. 'Dumpy, depressed housewife loses weight, gets hair cut, indulges in retail therapy, goes out on piss without husband. Left your job yet?'

Sunita physically jumped, her body actually rising a few inches though she managed to keep her feet on the stairs. A few hours earlier she had decided, with Chila egging her on, to give a month's notice at the CAB and enrol on a legal secretarial course. She had intended to discuss this first with Akash, but looking at him sprawled beneath her, oozing smarm, she suddenly changed her mind about consulting him on anything.

'I'm going to bed,' she announced. 'You can sleep down there if you want.' She did not know why she had said that. She tasted ashes in her mouth. The effects of the non-stop dancing had caught up with her joints, which groaned in protest as she ascended the last few stairs. She glanced down, and saw Akash sitting perfectly still, staring at the front door.

'Are you going to stay there all night, then?' she said, too loudly.

'I'd better keep my shoes on,' Akash replied woodenly.

'Why?'

'If you're going to leave me, I'll have to get up and walk around outside for a few hours and it might rain.'

Sunita's hand gripped the banister tightly. She felt inexplicably winded and confused. This was supposed to end like all the other recent spats, with a whispered sniping row in bed, and frosty muesli in the morning. But somehow, they had wandered into one of Akash's case files and were spouting the banalities that always signalled the beginning of the end.

Akash took her silence as assent. He knew he had guessed everything, curse his extraordinary instincts! Curse the unfortunate blend of red wine and his bloody big mouth.

Sunita knew she could reassure him now, laugh it off and hold out her hand, saying Come to bed and be my husband. But somehow, that would negate her extraordinary evening in which she had rediscovered her passions, her backbone, her legs, her equals, her beloved blooming friend, the world beyond with its cruelty and the compassion it engendered in return. She wanted to share all of this with Akash. And instead, he got drunk and talked about leaving. He had mentioned it first. It was his idea and he was kindly passing it onto her. So Sunita said nothing.

She went into the bathroom. As she locked the door, Akash laced up his shoes. As she wiped away her make-up, he plucked his coat from the hallway pegs. As she brushed her teeth, he found his keys. By the time she came out of the bathroom, he was gone.

Sunita

HE IS TWENTY-FIVE, FOR GOD'S SAKE. HE WAS IN NAPPIES WHEN I started senior school. He thinks the Bay City Rollers were an American football team. He can't remember Michael Jackson ever being black. He reckoned *The Female Eunuch* was a porn film or a German expressionist painting. He can't remember not equating sex with AIDS. He counts his parents as quite good mates. He believes that not belonging anywhere is a good and creative place to be. He says I make him laugh.

I suppose meeting him was proof that good deeds are repaid in some mysterious and unforeseen ways. When I promised Chila that I would hold her hand during her daily hospital visits (her blood pressure is going crazy at the moment and they're monitoring her blood sugar levels as well), I was thinking purely about her, my waddling friend, and my soon-to-be-born niece. We both reckon it's a girl, me because she's round all over, front and back, the way I was with Nikki. When I was carrying Sunil, I didn't look pregnant from the back, but from the front I looked like I'd swallowed a football. Chila keeps saying she *will* be having a daughter, repeating it like some mantra, although I've tried to explain that no amount of wishing at this stage is going to change what's already done.

Anyway, at the first scan I went to with her, Chila asked the radiographer if she would tell her what sex the baby was. I didn't think this was a good idea, and told Chila so when the woman left the room to consult her senior about this request.

'Let it be a lovely surprise!' I jollied her along. 'I mean, it's your first, so what does it matter?'

But Chila was adamant. She wanted to be prepared, she said.

'Oh, right,' I joked, knowing how anal she is about accessories and the like. 'Want to colour co-ordinate your towels and sheets, I suppose.'

She shook her head. 'I just want to know so I can . . . be ready. If it's a girl, she'll be all mine. If it's a boy . . .' and she wouldn't say much after that. She just looked, not disappointed but more perplexed.

So I was thinking about how to handle this, when the battleaxe in the green overalls came back in and said, 'I'm sorry, we can't tell you what sex the baby is. It's hospital policy.'

Well, I knew this was crap because just two weeks earlier, a woman on my course, Sally, had come in for a scan in this same hospital and had been told she was having a boy straight away. I sniffed the air. I knew something was fishy and it wasn't old guppy face who was shuffling some papers around and hoping we would leave without making a fuss.

'What do you mean, policy?' I asked her, and told her about Sally, using as many pseudo-legal terms and long words as possible. She had that Gosh, you speak good English look on her face that I can spot from fifteen paces after years behind that stained desk (which I am so happy that I will never see again). I could tell she was a mite confused, poor love, as Chila and I both happened to be wearing shalwar kameez that day and therefore messed up her rules, that the brown ladies wearing curtains are the ones you can patronize and baffle with policy.

'Well, um,' she stuttered, and by now I was enjoying this, 'in certain cases we do make exceptions—'

'So why not in ours, then?' I butted in.

'Well, you see' – she blushed – 'with our . . . Asian ladies, we tend not to reveal the sex. It's just, we had a number of the ladies afterwards requesting . . . terminations, when they found out they were carrying girls.'

Chila burst into tears and I felt a few blood vessels bursting somewhere behind my eyes. I can't remember what exactly I said, but it was loud enough to bring a few other people in gowns and uniforms rushing into the room. I recall the words 'blatant discrimination' and 'tarred with the same brush', which was probably not an appropriate phrase to use, given the circumstances. Also possibly 'my MP' and 'the highest level'. I ended, and I do remember this, with 'It's the bloody fathers you need to be re-educating, not harassing pregnant women who come in here expecting support!'

At this point, I was really enjoying myself. It was like the good old days at university on the marches and picket lines, and I was in my leggings and Doc Martens again and shaking fists at the sky, absolutely sure that I was powerful and beautiful enough to change the world.

And then he cleared his throat and said, 'Is there a problem here, Mrs Evans?'

And I shot back, 'Yeah, it's just too bad she doesn't know what it is!' which I have to confess is a line from some B-film I caught on Channel 5 one night and had always hoped I would have an opportunity to use. Here it was, and there he was.

Maybe it's something to do with the way doctors are so revered by my parents' generation, the magic profession which excused all other flaws ('Yes, Anil is four foot ten and bandy legged, but he's a doctor!' 'Yes, they have ten secret bank accounts in Jersey and sell out-of-date drugs to poor countries, but hey, they're doctors!'), but there is something special about someone who knows how to mend a broken body.

I mean, I didn't register anything special about him at first, this young Asian bloke in white coat, sort of nice face, sort of friendly eyes, in that awkward age bracket where they're too old for you to pat on the head and ask about their studies and too young to take seriously as an ally – in what was becoming a rather nasty situation. I expected him to shuffle his feet and scuttle round looking for an older white man in a white coat who would escort us from the premises. But the first thing he did was go over to Chila and comfort her. He told her getting upset was not good for the baby or her and asked if he could organize her a cup of tea.

Good move, I remember thinking, good doctor's instinct, good human being's instinct actually: seek the one most distressed. Then he turned to me for an explanation, even though Mrs Green Drawers was dying to get a word in. He asked me first, and by now I was getting slightly impressed. And when I told him what had happened, that's when he sprung into action.

Chila and I ended up in a nice plush office eating free NHS garibaldis while mysterious calls were being made elsewhere. The radiographer had by then flounced off, rustling her rubber gloves, and we had a quick visit from someone who looked like an accountant but whom we were assured was someone high up in Community Relations who muttered a few inanities about cultural sensitivity and responsibility to the patient, while Doctor Hero stood behind him looking faintly embarrassed.

We let him finish and Chila cleared her throat and said, 'It's OK. I've changed my mind, anyway,' which was a typical Chila way to end the whole affair, taking the path of least resistance, and then she asked if she could now empty her bladder of the five pints she'd imbibed for the scan.

That's when Krishan introduced himself properly and apologized for the whole mess. We somehow got into a long discussion about stereotyping and the damage done by well-meaning liberals which took in dowries, *The Simpsons* and the double-edged role of Third World charities, and suddenly half an hour had gone by, Chila was waiting to go home and he was being paged to go to Casualty. I left feeling I had clouds in my shoes and wondering why I hadn't noticed how bright the pansies were in those pots next to the sliding doors into which I had thrown up almost two years ago.

Of course I took it further. The whole scan incident thing, I mean. I started off mentioning it to one of my lecturers, who, funnily enough, made quite a name for herself in medical negligence cases in the Eighties. She put me onto some chambers contacts for advice. This no tell policy is quite prevalent in urban hospitals where they serve a large Asian population, but I had to find out through talking to other women, as the hospitals are strangely cagey about this whole area. And of course, I kept in touch with Krishan about my progress, not that he could help much as he was trying to finish his own internship and I'm not so naïve that I expected him to infiltrate the hospital computer files at the cost of his own job. But his support made all the difference. And just when I was at the point of going to the newspapers, imagining follow up exposés on *Panorama* and me sitting with Jeremy Paxman thumping the *Newsnight* desk as I told the whole awful tale, Chila brought me back to earth.

'You know,' she said one day as we were eating our usual post-blood test snack of tea and Walnut Whips, 'there's clinics you can go to where they guarantee you can have a boy.' She produced this cutting from one of the Asian papers. This place was three miles from my own front door. Some paunchy, bespectacled doctor guaranteed through his 'Special Methods' that any ladies out there could choose the sex of their child.

'It's done with test tubes, I think,' Chila said, sadly. 'And this place has a waiting list. He's got four other clinics round the country—'

I finished the sentence, 'And they're all full. Full of our women.'

Chila nodded. 'I don't expect many ladies go there asking to have a girl, do they?'

And there I was, back in the grey area again, caught out by the enemy within. There wasn't any point pursuing it after that.

'There's too many people's minds to change,' Chila told me. I argued that we have to start somewhere, and she said, 'With ourselves,' which startled me – impressed me, I'm ashamed to say. It just was not the kind of remark I ever expected from her.

'That's a really Buddhist approach,' I said. 'Been reading the *Tibetan Book of the Dead*, have we?' Probably a bit flippant, I know, but I was genuinely intrigued.

'Sunita,' she said, 'you don't learn the important stuff from books. It happens to you and someone gives it a long name afterwards. You should know that by now.'

I don't know what the official title is for what's happening to me but I know it started the night Akash walked out of the house. He came back of course, about half an hour later, tried to defrost his feet on my back and nuzzle apologies into my neck, but something had changed while he was gone, because he had gone. Made flesh the words, the threats.

My mum has always had this weird habit, she has never called my father by his real name (in fact, for years I thought his full name was Darling Sharma), preferring endearments such as jaan and ji and sometimes, when she was feeling fruity, husband-sahib. During my rebellious phase, when I was monitoring how many times my dad and brothers left my mother alone in the kitchen while they stared at the TV, I challenged her about this.

'Are you so in awe of him that you can't even use his name?' I asked her.

She laughed at me from behind a pile of unwashed pans. 'It is protection,' she said.

'What, scared that he'll get violent if you call him . . . What is it? D—' She put her soapy finger on my lips.

'We remind each other who we are, married to each other. Husband/wife. If I use his proper name, I am like anyone else he meets on the street. If I name him, I make him a stranger.'

It made sense in a quaint, superstitious sort of way. Every relationship has its own invisible boundaries, its own internal rules. For some people, it's never raising their voices in public; for others, it's not using the sharp knives when the cutlery starts flying. For us, it was promising not to walk out on an argument, to face each other and let the blood flow, and perhaps mop each other up afterwards. But he went. Maybe that means there are no boundaries any more.

A couple of years ago, the sound of that front door

slamming would have brought on a panic attack. The last time I thought I was having one was that night, the night of the film, when I had to sit in a room full of people patronizing me with their vicarious tears, when I stood in the darkness afterwards and watched a twenty-year friendship kissed to death. I had all the usual symptoms, the shallow breathing, the racing heart, the dizziness, and this time, I wasn't trampled by them, I reigned them up, drew them in and rode them like a madwoman, all the way down the stairs, all the way home. I do that a lot now. Akash said he was glad I was better, relieved my funny turns had abated. Maybe that's why he thought it was OK to walk out and slam doors, now I wasn't going to collapse in a heap and choke on my own breath. Maybe now I need him less, he loves me less. I asked Deepak something like that, that night, before the film out on the balcony. Did he need Chila or love her? He said both, I think. Not that it matters much now.

I know Chila enough to have guessed there is something haunting her, something that is nothing to do with the baby, the baby that was always part of her big life plan. You don't need to be psychic to guess the reason she is unhappy and that she's married to it. Before 'the incident', I would have just asked her point blank, however prying, however close to the bone. But now I'm frightened to mention Deepak, not knowing what else will come tumbling out. This is the time when we should have been closest, all of us. Instead, there's some invisible glass screen separating us, just the thinnest layer of transparent cold which glides smoothly into place whenever we approach anything intimate. I can see Chila, hear her, even touch her, but when we kiss, it's like brushing lips through a frosted window. When we try and talk about anything happening in our homes, the chill descends and we mouth polite chit-chat instead. Cocooned in secrets, both of us.

It's not just me. She disapproves of what I'm doing, I can tell, although it's all perfectly innocent and above board. Habitual really. After my morning lectures, and before I go off to do my shift at the CAB switchboard (the kids need nappies, I grovelled to my ex-boss), we trot along to the hospital for Chila's daily check ups. While she goes into one room to donate blood and urine, I sit in another sipping tea and chatting with Krishan. That's it, just talking. I have nothing to hide. I have said this to Chila outright.

'I have nothing to hide,' I told her at the end of the first week of visits, when I thought I saw her arch an eyebrow ever so slightly as I left her in the haemotology waiting room.

'Nothing to do with me, Sunny.' She smiled and then said, 'You're wearing lipstick today. And is that a new top?'

In fact, it wasn't a new top, just one that hadn't fitted me for a few years, and the lipstick was just to cover up a cold sore I thought might be developing. I explained all this to her very cheerily and she just smiled again, which I found a little infuriating. I actually sat down then, knowing Krishan was waiting for me and had arranged his break especially around this time, but I still took the time to try and explain, because – and I don't know why – I wanted her understanding, her approval maybe.

'Look, Chila,' I said, 'I'm at a very pivotal part of my life, do you see? I'm going through all sorts of changes, new career, new image—'

'New top,' Chila interrupted, which I ignored, for the sake of the baby.

'And,' I continued, 'I'm also trying to expand my social circles, be in touch with people who are sympathetic to the journey I am on. And besides, I've never really had any male friends, you know? The only men I've been close to fathered me or married me and it's about time I put that right.'

'So Akash is fine about this, then?' Chila asked. The screen descended silently, between our nailed-to-the-floor chairs. She obviously didn't get it, as is Chila's habit, so I persevered.

'I haven't told Akash because that would make it look like I *had* got something to hide. If he asked me I would tell him, of course I would.' I left out the bit about that being unlikely as we weren't talking much anyway.

Chila looked straight at me then. I'd forgotten how beautiful she's always been, and with this new baby-fullness ripening every feature, every pore, she did look divine, goddess-like even, the answers to old mysteries heavy on her brow.

'I always thought our husbands were supposed to be our best friends,' she said. The screen cracked slightly, a tiny fissure in an unseen corner, and I panicked, which is the only excuse I have now for saying what I said then.

'Oh, yeah, right. And is Deepak yours?'

It was unforgivable, I know, and I ended up driving her home, in her car, not caring about the cab fare back to work, because she looked so upset and tired and I wanted to do something, anything, for breaking the unwritten rule, that we look after Chila. I let her show me round the house, which is beginning to resemble a museum with its polished furniture and immaculate surfaces, everything matching and nothing used. I oohed at the fishtank and aahed at the conservatory and ate plates of deep-fried goodies even though I wasn't hungry, because we could almost pretend we were girlies again, catching up in a kitchen.

In fact, the only room that isn't pristine, isn't even finished, is the nursery. It's a gorgeous room, overlooking the football-pitch-sized back garden, with a huge bay window and a bumblebee-bulging wisteria which climbs round the surrounding wall. The walls are lemon yellow, but there are no carpets, curtains or toys, not even a cot, just a Moses basket and a blanket. I know Chila has been decorating babies' bedrooms in her head since we were both in short socks, so this struck me as extremely bizarre.

I asked her if her mum had been getting to her, those old-lady superstitions about not having anything ready for the baby before it actually arrives, in case all those mysterious unseen forces we call fate or sometimes God notice we are too happy, too smug at our good fortune, and decide to teach us a lesson in humility by taking it all away.

My mum used to scream if I ever began a sentence with 'Aren't we/I lucky that' or if I ever dared to praise anyone else in the family. Even something as innocuous as 'Does my hair look nice like this?' or 'That roll-neck jumper really suits Papa' would turn her into some wailing foghorn of doom. She would spit ferociously, hold her earlobes in penitence and loudly beg forgiveness from the skies: 'Nazar nahin lagthe! Don't tempt the evil eye.' Of course, being Punjabi, it came out as 'ewil eye' which somewhat lessened its dramatic impact, but her fear always alarmed me.

Was it so bad to celebrate the good things occasionally? Were we so ungrateful, so presumptuous, that one glancing reference to a possible blessing would bring a lava-wave of ancient wrath into our house, sweeping us away like spindly weeds? Maybe this was just my mother's way of teaching us to count your blessings. Unfortunately, all it taught me was to hope for the best, very quietly, and expect the worst, very stoically. Clearly anything good that happened was merely a fortunate, whimsical accident, a mistaken jewel spotted glinting in the dust which we might admire for a while, possibly hold for a moment, before They snatched it back, and then retired sniggering to the place I was convinced They lived, that shadowy alcove at the top of our stairs.

However, Chila maintained that the nursery remained bare because 'I just can't find the right kind of material, you know, that would go in a girl or boy's room. It's really hard, finding bisexual curtains.'

'Don't you mean unisex?'

'Same thing, innit?'

I laughed so hard I started choking. Chila was patting me on the back and trying to breathe herself, gasping, 'Don't! My bladder's not up to this!' and we clung onto each other for what seemed ages, just hiccuping and wiping tears and both of us knowing, without saying, that for this moment, it was the way it always used to be and how sweet it was to be back there, together.

And then Deepak walked in, carrying an absurd bunch of orchids which he nearly dropped when he saw me. We sobered up smartly, and within seconds Chila had snapped back into Mrs Hostess and was rustling up a fresh truckload of refreshments. It was a while before I could look at Deepak without feeling embarrassed. I was mildly surprised that he hadn't sprouted a forked tail and horns. I was looking for manifestations of evil somewhere on that handsome, groomed body. But it was the oddest thing; I felt sorry for him. He looked older, tired, strands of grey peppering his hair, no more strutting cock of the yard walk that I always associated with him, but a humble hand outstretched, a welcoming hug that lasted a little longer than necessary, as if he was grateful I was there.

'You look amazing,' he said to me a few times. I'd forgotten how long it was since we had seen each other. 'Been working out?'

'Something like that,' I muttered back, uncomfortable with this best-friends-again full frontal assault.

And then, 'Isn't she gorgeous?' he kept asking me, pointing at Chila, his arm around Chila, pouring tea for Chila, plumping up cushions behind Chila, devotion brimming his eyes. Chila took it all graciously. She even kissed him back.

I thought about that tree falling in the forest. If no-one sees it, it hasn't really happened. If I hadn't been there, would he have poured the tea? If he hadn't asked me about Akash, would I have said, 'He's doing really well. His own practice is up and running and we're thinking of moving to a bigger place'? I suddenly realized why we were all hanging onto these remnants of a friendship. We needed each other as audience, we confirmed each other's fragile normality. If they had come to my house, I would have served cakes too.

Deepak insisted on driving me back to work, knowing I was late. There was a third person sitting on the back seat during the whole journey, she whose name we dare not mention, and at one point I asked him to put the radio on, petrified the silence would force me to ask about her. Luckily, he chattered on, mostly about his newest purchase, some warehouse he's turning into a trendy shopping mall.

'Did you know,' he asked me, 'Hackney has a higher number of resident artists than any other London borough? It's cheap, there's large properties available which the creative self-employed need, and there's a good amount of urban regeneration funds being poured into the area. And what they need, the jewellery makers and designers and the like, is a workshop-combined-viewing-space, a place where they can work and sell from. And that's where I come in.'

I found this baffling. It was like listening to Margaret Thatcher campaigning for the removal of VAT on sanitary towels, unnatural and inappropriate. I'd always put Deepak down as a glorified landlord, like his father, doing up properties on the cheap, renting them for stupid amounts, selling them off finally to the highest bidder and starting again in another area where people wanted to live but could not buy. For them, London was like a huge Monopoly board, except they owned the bank and never went to jail.

'Blimey,' I replied. 'That sounds a suspiciously socialist concept, Deepak. Presumably you'll be charging a huge entrance fee.'

'No fee,' he said, 'No need. There's enough tourists from the richer areas with money who want to buy individual and authentic pieces, especially ethnic stuff. You can buy bindis down the Kings Road now.'

Bindis. That's what gave it away. When a man displays any sort of shopping knowledge, if it's not about cars and computers, you know he's been talking to a woman. It was her voice all right. It had to have been her idea – quirky, risky, one jump ahead. Suddenly I missed her fiercely, sitting there next to Deepak. I felt jealous, that all that fizz and fury and acid wit and dirty laugh belonged to him, rather than me, us. I hadn't forgiven her, but I wanted the chance to say it to her face. And I understood why he loved her, because hadn't we all? That's when I pretended I had to listen to the news, and we sat through a bulletin and the beginning of a play about Scottish drug addicts before he finally dropped me off.

As I was getting out, he grabbed my hand. 'I'm really glad you're back in touch with Chila,' he said.

'We were never out of touch, really, just busy,' I told him, wondering when he'd let go of me.

'You will be around, when the baby's here?' he said. 'She'll really need you then.'

I nodded and got out.

He rolled down the window. 'Promise me?'

God, he looked sad. I wanted to say, If you're going to leave her, you bastard, at least take some responsibility for it. But for a second, I had a feeling I was looking through some strange refracting mirror. I recognized that

241

expression, someone at the edge of a precipice, fingers clinging onto crumbling chalky rocks, exhilarated and frightened to fall.

'I promise,' I whispered, and didn't look back as he drove away.

I found myself avoiding the cracks on the pavement all the way to the office door, carefully placing my foot in the dead centre of every slab like I used to as a little girl. 'Nazar nahin lagthe. Let them be all right.'

Krishan reckons I'm going through a second childhood, or maybe catching up on the youthful rebellion I never had. It's true, I'm showing all the classic symptoms. I'm putting unnatural colours in my hair. I'm going out a lot and coming back late, reeking of crowded rooms. I have periods in the day when I forget that I have two children. I shave my legs daily in the shower and enjoy it. I've discovered where Kiss FM is on the radio. I spend increasing amounts of time either with people younger than myself, say at college, or with similarly badly behaved women who are sneaking out of the house with cigarettes and/or miniatures in their bags and two pairs of shoes, flatties for driving and stilettos for jiving. We're quite a powerful group, us wrinkly teenagers, us pre-menopausal minxes. And I keep meeting more and more of us, at benefits naturally, at the ICA for Indian cinema seasons, at selected clubs where the music is old enough for us to hum the tunes, and not so loud that we can't have a decent chat in a corner, at Asian comedy nights in out of town theatres, at obscure children's puppet shows where mythological papier mâché gods tell our kids the stories that we should have learned at our mothers' knees, had they had the time and we the inclination to listen.

I can spot One of Us from five hundred yards. My antenna is finely tuned now. She could be in jeans or a sari, have a bad perm or a sleek bob, be carrying a baby car seat or a briefcase (although it's usually both); she will usually be married or thinking about not being married or recently de-married; she will be a dutiful daughter, an efficient wife, an over-anxious mother. She will organize an evening out to a T, have food cooked and babysitter booked weeks ahead. She will step out of the house still applying mascara; she will have lit up before she reaches the end of the road. By the time she has reached the party, she is singing loudly and slightly mad.

We dance longer and wilder than anyone else, as the recently released always do, and the real teenagers, the ones with unsullied bodies and sulky beautiful faces, move away from us, appalled. I've seen the expression on their faces, somewhere between shame and fear. Women almost old enough to be their mothers are taking over their territory, upsetting the natural order of things, shaking their considerable booty around with no consideration for sensitive souls or low-flying aircraft.

'Shouldn't you lot be at home in a stained housecoat burning your fingers over a griddle?' That was all our mothers, after all. Sometimes I fast forward to my Nikki's adolescence. I see myself sneaking into the house with my shoes in my hand, and she is on the stairs, in owly glasses and a quilted dressing gown, with an alarm clock in her hand. 'Mum! What time do you call this? I've been worried sick!' I tell her to chill out and take time to smell the roses. She tells me not to drop her at school any more because her friends laugh at my swirly leggings and diamanté nose ring. I tell her to learn Italian and fall in love with someone kind. She takes Hindi lessons and at the age of twenty-one, after graduation, asks me to find her a nice Hindu boy from a good family.

This makes me laugh out loud, when I'm in the bath with her and stroking her nut-brown, perfect little body. (It goes without saying she will rebel against whatever I stand for. All my feminist friends have been landed with daughters who love dressing up in pink and take several Barbies to bed with them every night.) And sometimes, when I watch Nikki sleep, I count the teddy bears on her pyjamas and whisper the Gayatri mantra into her ear to keep her safe in the dark, and I get the other version of the future. I see a weeping Nikki on the *Jerry Springer Show*, underneath her the caption, 'Mom! You're out of Control and You Smell Bad Too!!' Nikki tells the audience how she's always wanted a proper mommy, just like her friends. 'You know, one of those plump ones with smiley faces who never complain and always have a hot meal ready, but she was too busy having fun,' she sobs, and the audience sobs too. And then I come on but no-one hears what I'm saying as they're booing too loudly and throwing chairs at me. I try and yell above the baying crowd. I want to tell them I do love my children and I always tried my best, but I wanted to make up for lost time, missed opportunities, to let my madness out in little controlled pockets while they sleep unaware in their beds, so I can come to them fresh, absolved, free from guilt, free from the smell I associate with so many of my mother's friends, the sour, damp smell of unfulfilled potential. But it all comes out in sick-making soundbites: 'I have a life too, you know! What about *my* rights, huh? Oh, blow it out your ass!'

And then I come to, sweating, and I kiss my babies over and over again and I promise them this is just for a short time, until I feel better, until I finally, properly, grow up.

Krishan told me I was part of a growing social phenomenon. 'It's being defined as middle youth,' he informed me over our last pot of tea. 'The baby boomer generation are refusing to grow old gracefully. They're redefining what being middle aged means.' Interesting he kept saying they when I meant us. 'Staying healthier, indulging in luxuries, competing with the twenty-somethings for entertainment. No more slippers and pipe by the fire if you're forty.'

'Thank God for that,' I replied. 'I don't suit a pipe but I do have a pair of pink mules. Do they count?'

'Pink mules? Definitely not.' He smiled. Such a good smile. The right amount of teeth, warmth in the eyes, never wavering. Where have all these gentle-men-boys come from? Where were they when I was growing up? 'Born Too Late for You to Love Me.'

My dad had that old song on some cheesy compilation record at home. It didn't even feature the original artists. Their famous hits were sung by their non-union cheap impersonators, but as it was the only English record we had, I played it until the grooves had lost their tread. That record was special because it was unique, the only alternative to Hindi film songs, and therefore glamorous, admired, enjoyed. A monthly trip to the cinema was like a mini-holiday. Being allowed to go on a week-long school trip to France felt like emigrating or eloping. The occasional youth club discos we begged and pleaded to be allowed to attend were the highlights of our year. Any boy we met who didn't have a Brylcreemed side parting and an eye-popping patterned jumper knitted by his granny was a demi-god, the dish of the day, the catch of the week – the boy who was different.

And now: clubs-pubs, mates-dates, cars-bars, holidays-hideaways, mags-fags, sex-shopping, bed-hopping, no-stopping, fusion-confusion – a cornucopia of choices, a smorgasbord of alternatives, as many avenues as there are aunties in the average family. I wonder if Krishan's mother tells him to count his blessings? Why bother when you start counting and run out of fingers and toes?

I could have tried to explain this to Krishan – I almost did, until I realized how I would sound: 'In my day', 'When I were a lass', 'Kids today, don't know you're born . . .' Besides, bitterness gives you wrinkles and the portrait in my attic is already looking pretty rough. Instead, I talk to him. I breathe in the possibilities like a succubus from his minty mouth. I arrange another night out with the girls.

'This can't go on much longer,' he said to me yesterday, out of the blue, and I almost dropped my custard cream. Luckily, since the dreadful Pop Sock Disaster, I am a little more restrained in my responses, so I calmly dusted off the biscuit, dunked it in my cup, watched half of it dissolve lumpily to the bottom, pretended this had been my original plan all along and sipped the tea which now had custard-scum floating on the surface. I coughed loudly for about twenty seconds and only then did I say, 'Pardon?'

'Well,' he said, 'Chila could have the baby at any time now. It's already cooked, as it were, this is just the basting period.' I love it when they use technical terms.

'Yes, of course, any day now,' I said, in what I hoped was a distracted, even bored tone of voice, while I imagined tying Chila's legs together in a double knot and shouting at the baby through her belly button to 'Stay in there, it's horrible out here. You won't like it!'

We let it go, chatted about Nikki's recent ear infection, the black-tie dinner he was attending that weekend with some old university friends. I managed to discuss a family wedding coming up without mentioning Akash at all. Krishan made a point of saying that he hadn't yet got a date for this dinner, although I know he's spoiled for choice. The Sangeetas and the Valeries and several nurses have cropped up in his conversation from time to time, always skimmed over, always dismissed. Quite early on I offered myself as an adviser, told him he maybe needed the perspective of a woman of the world, insider information with no bullshit. He grinned and said he had a very good idea of the kind of woman he was looking for. I bit my lip so hard that I may have left a scar, but I did not ask for further clarification. That was where I wanted to be, pregnant with possibilities, swelled with hope. With nothing defined, nothing over-stated, nothing decided, I felt safe, blameless, innocent. Just talking, like I said. Until yesterday.

Up until then, that room, with its grimy venetian blinds, worn leather chairs and dog-eared posters extolling the joys of vaccination and the symptoms of diabetes, was the most perfect and purest example of what it purported to be, the waiting room. Every time I walked into it and shut the door, I imagined that all around me the hands stopped on watches, the sand in hourglasses halted mid-trickle, clouds skidded to a scudding halt, fountains froze – a comatose world outside and in here, suspended, kept artificially alive, us. Nothing grows older while we are in here, nothing hurts, nothing changes. Bags down, feet up, kettle on. Count your blessings. Oh, I did. Every day. I want so much to see Chila's baby, I really do. Once the baby's home, there's no reason for me to come here again. The waiting is nearly over. A new life.

6

TANIA SKIMMED DOWN THE GLOSSILY PRESENTED FOLDER IN front of her, barely looking up as a steaming café latte was placed reverentially on the desk. She got to the last page, paused and looked up. Fay and Rory were both gazing at her with the expectancy of puppies waiting for a chocolate drop.

'What do you think?' they said, almost in stereo.

'Interesting,' Tania managed to murmur. She picked up her coffee and read the page again, feeling a familiar gloom descend.

'All these ideas have been approved in principle,' Rory chipped in. 'It's just a question of what grabs you most.'

'We saw the rushes of your last doc, the one about the white witches in Norwich. Have you got a title yet?' Fay asked, proffering a plate of expensive-looking sugary wafers.

Tania shook her head. 'No. Sorry, I mean, not for me, thanks, and yes, the working title at the moment is "Bedpans and Broomsticks", if Disney don't throw a wobbly.'

'Oh, that's brilliant!' Fay laughed. 'Because two of them are—'

'Nurses, well one's a care worker but she sees a fair amount of bowel activity.'

Rory and Fay both chortled a little too appreciatively. Tania was getting used to the sound of canned laughter in plush offices, to sashaying through smoked-glass doors which a few months ago would have been politely closed in her face. Polystyrene cups were a vague memory. Now she was served designer infusions in hand-painted pottery, the biscuits were usually monogrammed and sandwiches inevitably featured sun-dried tomatoes in some disguise. Ashtrays were produced if she wanted to smoke, which she did now. She had barely extracted her packet of cigarettes from her bag before a shapeless blob of ceramic was placed in front of her.

'My daughter made it,' said Fay apologetically. 'This is theoretically a non-smoking office. We've both given up and this was the only one around.'

Tania saw there was a shaky inscription around the rim in heavy-handed gold lettering, FOR MAMA. She returned her cigarettes to her bag, annoyed at the foolish tightening of her throat.

'I can wait, actually.' She smiled faintly. 'No problem.'

Fay twittered around with a coffee refill by way of an apology while Rory produced a sheaf of research material and unscrewed the top of his fountain pen hopefully. It still took Tania by surprise, the eagerness with which she was now received, the enthusiasm that her presence seemed to arouse in other people in the industry. Ever since her first film had been broadcast, *the* film, her telephone had not stopped ringing with offers of work. Within a week, she had signed on with a dapper young agent with offices in Chelsea harbour who assured her she would have her own production company up and running within a couple of months.

'All you need is some headed notepaper, a commission and a bag full of balls,' her agent had told her. 'Plus you're marketable. Asian babe kicking ass. Helps you got cheekbones too.'

Tania decided she would walk out if he suggested wearing a Wonderbra and hanging around Stringfellows, but she had to admit, he had impressive connections and the honing instincts of a shark. He had quickly organized some extra screenings in tandem with a couple of serious profiles in glossy magazines. Tania had sat patiently while she was photographed against a backdrop of saris and spices, amongst the crowds emerging from an Indian cinema and, on one occasion, in the bustling kitchen of a tandoori restaurant, her image reflected back at her in wavy miniatures from the gleaming steel vats that surrounded her like burly metal minders. She took it all with good grace. She ensured she counteracted the obvious visual imagery with pithy street- wise soundbites: 'I'm a director first, an Asian second', 'I care about my audience's IQ, not their race', 'Your talent is your calling card. No-one calls Woody Allen a Jewish film maker any more'. It was easy enough. They were lines she had been practising in her mirror since her teens, the distillation of a thousand award-acceptance speeches she had rehearsed in her parents' cramped, steamy bathroom. They were the crystallization of a million pillow chats with Martin, when they would shape their glittering careers out of candle smoke and coffee fumes, as distant and diffuse as clouds. Now she had arrived, apparently, atop a shaky pedestal, sniffing the rarefied air and alarmed at how high she was, how far down it was to the ground.

'So!' Rory beamed, rubbing his hands together in a matey

sort of way. 'Anything take your fancy on that list there?' Tania braced herself against the back of her swivel chair.

'Well, let's see. They're all mockumentaries really, aren't they?'

'Are they?' asked Fay eventually.

'By that I mean, they're all fly-on-the-wall, let's film some ordinary people doing stuff and shape it into a story afterwards sort of genre.'

'Oh, yes, absolutely,' breathed Fay, relieved. 'It's what everybody wants at the moment. Real people are much better actors than professional actors, ironically. You can't get an Equity member to reproduce what we get for free.'

'Indeed,' murmured Tania, smoothing out the corners of her sheet, 'and of course you don't have to pay real people much either. So let's see. We have *Sweat!* set in an East End Turkish baths, *Slap!* set in a Newcastle perfumerie, *Wax!* set in a Welsh beauty salon, and an as yet untitled project set in a Birmingham sewage works—'

'We're not absolutely sold on that one,' interrupted Rory.

'No,' agreed Tania, 'you won't get many old people watching something called *Turds!*, I suppose. And calling it *Shit!* would just be too much of a gift to the TV critics, eh?'

Fay and Rory's smiles had wavered slightly. Rory patted his hairline absently, leaving an imprint of inky fingertips on his temples, the smudgy footprints of some small creature who had scuttled into his hair for cover.

'Is the exclamation mark compulsory?' Tania enquired cheerfully. 'I'm just thinking graphics here. Of course, we could have a really funny theme tune, lots of tubas and whoopee cushion noises, just to warn the viewers to expect lots of pratfalls, because they do love seeing innocent people making complete arses of themselves, don't they?'

A palpable hush filled the room, interrupted only by the cappuccino machine coughing politely in a far corner.

'Right, well,' said Rory, standing up, 'good of you to come in.'

Fay snatched the misshapen ashtray off the desk and shut it firmly in a drawer. She was trembling as she brushed Tania's hand in a vague attempt at a handshake.

'You are still with Mark Stein at ITA?' she asked, tight-lipped. Tania could see Fay was itching to call her agent at this precise moment.

It was only when she found herself on the pavement outside, her mobile ringing frantically inside her bag, that she realized what she had done. She flicked the phone on and held it away from her ear as Mark launched into a barking monologue.

'I don't need to tell you that you won't be invited back in a hurry. What is it? PMT? Or just thought you'd piss off a few people who might want to employ you for the next few years. I mean, I thought you knew what their output was. I never said this was going to be *Pano*-sodding-*rama*, did I? There's nothing wrong with being populist, in fact, in this present climate, there's a lot right with it. Tania, you still there? Hello?'

Tania began walking slowly, wishing she had a hand free to peel off her jacket. Her hair felt matted, oily worms clinging to her neck. It had been overcast when she had set off that morning, unremitting slate grey, migraine weather. Now, a paper-thin wash of blue sky arched above her, a tie-dye sun bled yellow and orange at its centre, the birds were singing arias in the treetops and she felt sticky with tension. She had a fierce urge to jump into the car and drive until she hit the coast.

'I'm still here, Mark,' she answered.

'Listen up, Tania, you're only as good as the last thing you made. You've had a great start, a fabulous start, but difficult geniuses aren't in fashion any more, not even in

Hollywood. When you're handling other people's dosh, they want to know you can smile and shoot film at the same time. Don't blow this.'

Tania paused outside a travel agent's window. Mauritius looked rather inviting. 'I'm just not interested in doing that nudge-wink exploitative crap any more, Mark.'

'Oh, yeah?' his tinny voice rasped back. 'Worked pretty well for your first film.'

'Like I said, I don't do that stuff any more,' Tania replied quietly, before cutting him off.

She studied the Mauritian tourist board poster again. A sun-kissed couple with violently white teeth ran hand in hand along a deserted beach. The sea was an unnatural shade of violet, so clear she could spot the shadowy triangles of fish basking in the shallows. She could afford to go anywhere in the world at this moment, although, she realized with a jolt, not on a Club 18–30 holiday any more. She studied the vibrant display of faraway places more carefully. There seemed to be three distinct groups of holiday makers: couples, joined at the hip, matched with romantic getaways in Rome, Paris, New York, the Caribbean, India; families with two children, splashing happily in Spain, Tunisia, Greece; and then the euphemistically named Discerning Traveller, which meant anyone over fifty, who could choose to be shuttled safely to any location, provided the walks weren't too long and there was access to a mini-golf course. The small print informed Tania that to travel alone would cost more; the single supplement provided an expensive reminder, a warning to those who dared to venture somewhere gorgeous without a partner.

Automatically, Tania dialled Deepak's mobile number and exhaled in relief when he answered.

'Me,' she said.

'Hi, you.'

'Can you talk?'

'Yep, just waiting to go into my accountant's office. How did your meeting go?'

'It went.'

'They don't deserve you, so sod them, eh?'

Tania cradled the phone to her cheek, wishing it was a cocktail, a conch shell, his hand. It was increasingly like this; whenever her work was going well, she felt invincible, her life was a straight path bordered by manicured fields, chocolate box pretty, no diversions. Right now, she did not, officially, on paper, have a job, although it was merely a question of sticking a tack into a list of options. But without a contract, a schedule, she was lost. Actors called it resting, the gaps between employment. Tania thought that was a stupid name for this exhausting limbo in which all the snags and flaws in her smooth-seamed existence became magnified and ugly. The pattern blurred as she felt herself unravelling. She had to stop this quickly.

'I really would like to see you tonight, Deeps,' she said. There was a brief pause, far away she heard office chatter, the rhythmic hum of a printer.

'Tonight?' he asked curiously.

They both knew this was unusual, Tania requesting an unscheduled appointment. Normally, she would waver about times and dates, preferring to keep things fluid, a veneer of casual reluctance.

'I think that's OK,' he said finally, both of them smiling unseen into their mouthpieces.

'Ten-ish?'

'Ten is perfect,' Tania replied.

She spent the next two hours being effortlessly impressive. She held court at her agent's office, dispensing charming apologies and sugar-coated demands until Mark and his assistants were gambolling at her feet, creasing up at her cruelly accurate impressions of Fay and Rory, pissing themselves at her punchlines, gasping at the glamorous gall of it all, what Tania did next. It was what they expected, after all, why they had taken her on. Cheeky bit of exotic, her intellect a huge plus, photogenic enough to be flirted with, brainy enough to backhand the compliments with panache. So satisfying, to meet someone who sent the clichés tumbling like dominoes.

'The Yanks would love you!' Mark enthused. 'You look Mexican. Tell them you're Asian and they'll expect some bird from Vietnam, say you're Indian and they'll ask what reservation. When they twig you're from the land of Ravi Shankar and holy men, they'll be creaming their Calvin Kleins.'

'Is that a good thing?' Tania asked. 'I thought they liked easy to read packaging. You know, WASP, Jap, redneck, Latino . . .'

'They like whatever someone tells them the next big thing is going to be. Why shouldn't it be you?'

Why not indeed, mused Tania as she surveyed the Thames from eighteen floors up. While Mark paced the room talking animatedly into his mouthpiece (this agency was rock and roll enough to afford cordless telephone headgear), Tania counted the pleasure boats riding the river below, painted matrons out for a watery stroll, wearing tourists like artificial cherries on their whitewashed hats.

Years ago, she, Chila and Sunita had decided to be chicks about town and spend a day on the South Bank. Tania had nurtured some vision of them all strolling around the open-air book markets discussing Sartre, maybe taking in a controversial photographic exhibition in one of the theatre foyers, rounding off the evening with a play, something gritty with lots of swearing written by an angry Northern adolescent, and a bottle of wine afterwards, which they would sip silently, watching the moon rise above the illuminated dome of St Paul's Cathedral. Instead, they indulged in a vulgar shopping spree (financed by the remainder of Sunita and Tania's termly grants and the contents of Chila's Post Office account), had tea at the Ritz, cocktails in some frou-frou parlour in Covent Garden and ended the evening by singing drunken Abba songs as they wobbled along the Embankment, arm in arm, beneath the necklaces of lights that adorned the sweeping nape of the river. Is this how the very old feel, wondered Tania, when they recall their younger selves and encounter a startling, healthy stranger?

She then remembered a vague friend of her father's, a jolly Sikh man with a pristine waxed beard, who had grown up streets away from her father in Ambala. They had pounced on one another at some wedding, overjoyed at the reunion after so many years, and Jolly Sikh Uncle had been duly invited round for dinner. It was only then that Tania's father discovered that his former street urchin companion was now an extremely wealthy jeweller. It pained her even now, remembering her father's blustering attempts to disguise their lowly status. Suddenly, he was not a factory floor foreman, he was a 'tip-top manager type in the export department'; their terraced house was apparently 'our town dwelling only, we go to a bigger place at weekends near Surrey'; and their clapped out Ford Cortina was 'the only car with a strong enough suspension to transport my fat wife!' Her father's friend absorbed all this without comment, though Tania spent much of the evening gagging on her Bombay mix and sitting on her hands to stop them flying to her ears. Indeed, Jolly Sikh Uncle had seemed too tired to argue. He had accepted their hospitality warmly, said little, ate a lot, even gave Tania's brother the keys to his Mercedes when he asked if he might sit inside and test out the radio.

'So far we have come, me and you!' her father had exclaimed loudly at one point. 'Who would have thought, hah? Both of us in England, living the good life.' Tania had stood up at that point, wanting to leave the room before her father claimed she was a genius physicist or an astronaut and demanded she do a floor show.

But then, Jolly Sikh Uncle had carefully unbuttoned his shirt, one at a time, his platinum cufflinks glinting in the light from their Spanish lady table lamp, bared his chest and revealed a raised purple scar bisecting his sternum.

'I have made two million pounds. I have had two heart by-pass operations. My next million will probably kill me,' he said quietly.

Tania's father slapped his knee roguishly. 'OK then, when you get it, give it to me, hah?'

Jolly Sikh Uncle shook his head. He picked up a glass bowl of peanuts from the table and offered them to Tania's father. 'When we were boys, back in Ambala, you asked to share my moongphooli once. Remember?'

Tania's father nodded his head slowly, a softness uncreasing his face. 'Hah, I remember, sitting on the roof of your house after kite flying. Our hands were cut to ribbons. We put ground glass on the string so we could cut down the other boys' kites. My mother slapped me for that. What a memory you have!'

'And what did I say to you then?'

'You offered me the bowl and you said . . . you said, I wish these were diamonds.'

Jolly Sikh Uncle inclined his head. Tania had thought he

looked like an old grizzled lion, dignified in his dotage. Then, he had emptied all the peanuts onto the table, produced from his inside pocket a velvet pouch and tipped an iridescent avalanche of diamonds into the bowl. Tania had yelped in amazement. Her mother had reeled backwards into a chair, fanning herself with a paper plate. Jolly Sikh Uncle picked up the bowl, which seemed to vibrate with white sharp heat in the dimmed room, and handed it to her father.

'Tendon-sahib, believe me when I say, I wish they were peanuts.'

Peanuts and a necklace of burning bulbs. Tania knew they were connected, belonged together. She felt sand shifting in her back brain. There was an answer there, if she could just dig deeper. Her happiness depended on it. She closed her eyes waiting for revelation.

'There's a film here with your name on it.' Mark was standing in front of her. 'Heard of the Jasbinder Singh case? Woman whose kids got barbecued by her ex?'

'I read about it.' Tania stared at him blankly. Part of her was still in an incense-smelling sitting room counting treasure.

'There's a few people chasing this one, but you could do something special here. The bigger picture, and so on. Prime time heavyweight slot. Fancy it?'

Tania shrugged. 'I don't want to do any more Asian stories.'

'Why not?'

'You know why, Mark, we've discussed this. No more grubbing in the ghetto, I'm mainstream now.'

Mark sat on the edge of his desk wearily. Tania waited for the explosion, but instead, he massaged his temples with his fingers, collecting his thoughts. His tall, skinny frame folded into right angles, save his left leg which pointed bonily to the floor, a flamingo in deep contemplation. Tania noticed the tidemark of sweat on his collar, the thinning hairline. He was about the same age as her. His sharp, inquisitive features made him look younger, but he looked up with wise, beady eyes.

'The ghetto got you where you are today, Tania. It's what makes you different. And a good story is a mainstream story, end of story.'

Tania stood up defiantly. 'Why does everything I do have to come back to me? People like me? My family? My background? Our dirty linen? I'm an artist not a bloody social worker. Nobody asks Scorsese to only make Italian mob movies—'

'No,' Mark cut in sharply. 'He chooses to do them because he knows he can do them better than anyone else. He started out telling his own stories and their success gave him the power to choose. You can't see the join, Tania. You can't separate what you're good at from what you are. But you can use it to get you into a position of power and take it from there. First, you've got to know your voice, and then you've got to like it. Get it?'

Tania steadied her breathing. 'Are you Jewish, Mark?'

Mark laughed. 'Are you joking, asking a question like that to someone called Stein?'

'Does being Jewish inform your every daily activity? Do you wake up, check you're still circumcised and hum "Hava Nagila" all the way to the office?'

'I don't have to,' Mark replied, getting up stiffly from the desk. 'I know who I am, so I've got nothing to prove. Bloody hell, I'd have never started this conversation if I'd known you were going to be so defensive.'

'Who's defensive?' said Tania, defensively.

'Fine.' Mark sighed and returned to his executive chair. 'Go do a nice film about lady golfers in Weybridge. At least it will be funny, exposing them while you give away nothing. You're good at that.'

Sunita finally managed to coax Sunil's arm into the sleeve of his top. She zipped him up quickly and sat him next to Nikita on the settee. Nikita had pulled her hood up and was concentrating on tying her toggles, humming along to the private choir in her head. Sunil watched his sister, wide-eyed, and carefully dragged his hood over his head, grunting with effort. They sat together, legs splayed, like two malevolent shrouded pixies, plotting devious deeds in their secret language.

Sunita paused, halfway through collecting toys from the floor, a bubble of joy expanding her ribs. Tiny perfect people, flesh of her flesh. Whenever she looked too carefully at their vulnerable bodies, when a bruise bloomed from a tumble, when they started, blinking owlishly, at a sudden noise, when they watched her applying face cream like astonished spectators at a circus, she was winded by an urge to swaddle them in bubblewrap and place them on a high shelf, away from predators and pollution. The responsibility, at these times, was overwhelming. Her life beyond their immediate sphere seemed banal. And the relief when she left them to fly through the door with essays and plans was enormous.

I am a good mother, she told herself as she stuffed a couple of Tellytubbies into an overflowing toy box. I will not feel guilty, she told a plastic dinosaur sternly. If I am happy, they are happy too, she reminded an entire family of Pretty Ponies before they were unceremoniously shoved under a cushion.

'I like your song, Nikki,' Sunita called over her shoulder, interrupting the musical babble coming from the settee. 'What's it about?'

'Poo!' shouted Nikki firmly.

'Oh. That's, er, lovely,' replied Sunita, remembering from some book that Nikki was right in the middle of her anal phase and she really ought to encourage her to explore it fully. 'Is it a talking poo? Does it sing to you from the loo? Maybe it has a special name, eh?'

'No,' said Nikki, 'I want a poo now!'

Sunita tuned into the noises coming from upstairs. The shower was still going and, as usual, Akash had the radio on full blast.

'Beti, Papa's in there, can you wait a minute?'

'*No!*' cried Nikki, 'it's poking out right now!'

Sunita suppressed an expletive, scooped Sunil under one arm and frogmarched Nikita up the stairs. Nikita complained loudly all the way to the landing about how the poo would come out right now and spoil her Spice Girl socks. Sunita pushed at the bathroom door and found it locked. Akash never locked the door. He paraded about semi-nude on principle, claiming the children ought to feel comfortable about their bodies. Sunita rapped on the door impatiently.

'Akash? Nikki needs to go to the loo. Why have you . . .?'

A cloud of steam hit Sunita in the face as Akash threw open the door and disappeared quickly behind the shower screen. Nikita settled happily onto the toilet seat while Sunil emptied a plastic bucket of bath toys onto the lino and banged them together, satisfied. Akash stood with his back to them, soaping himself vigorously. The muscles in his neck and back pulsated softly as he reached around himself, water coursing down his spine, the valley of his long strong back. Sunita surveyed him critically through the misty shower screen. Diffused by droplets and steam, his body looked as it did when she first discovered it, greedily and with some gratitude. The shock of his naked skin at such close quarters brought her up sharply. Here was reality; the family unit, hermetically sealed in domestic vapours. Her daughter's knickers on the floor, her son's fat fists around yellow ducks, Akash's emerging love handles, soap-bubbled smooth – the ballast in her days, bearing no connection to the woman who sat in waiting rooms, twirling the ends of her hair and smiling.

Sunita raised her voice over the blare of the radio: 'I'm dropping the kids off at Mum's soon.'

Akash glanced at her for a moment, squinting through the haze, and nodded before turning his back on her again, holding a flannel to his groin protectively.

'What's up with you?' Sunita called. 'We've seen it all before, you know.' She extended a playful hand around the screen and made a grab for the flannel.

Akash caught her arm with his free hand. Water soaked her sleeve. 'Please!' he shouted.

Sunita withdrew as if she'd been stung. She patted her sleeve with a hand towel, smarting. 'Don't you want to know what I'm doing today?' she asked.

'What?' Akash turned the volume on the radio down with a quick, irritated flick.

'I said, do you want to know what I'm up to?'

Akash shrugged. Needles of water bounced off his raised shoulders, ricocheting like bullets. 'Why?' He smiled sadly. 'Got something to tell me?'

Sunita replaced the towel precisely on the radiator. 'Phone's ringing,' she said quietly.

'I'm not going to hospital today, Sunny,' Chila sounded muffled, mumbling through cotton wool.

'Why?' blurted Sunita, and then, 'I mean, anything wrong?'

'Deeps is taking me to a consultant in Paddington. She's

an old family friend. I'll have all the tests there.'

'Oh. OK then.' Sunita sank onto the stairs, dis-appointment dragging her limbs.

'Sunny? Is that OK? We can still go tomorrow.' Chila was sorry for her. Chila was apologizing for not attending her own hospital appointment.

Sunita rested her head on the telephone receiver, feeling foolish. Days of meandering chatter in steamy bathrooms stretched ahead of her. It was good enough for most people, she told herself, so why feel cheated now? Before she had read all those books, she had considered herself one of them, one in an amorphous mass, wedded to collective compromise. That was the trouble with dabbling in therapy, she now realized; she had the vocabulary to dissect, justify and validate every feeling. Every desire was reasonable because, after all, there was always a reason behind it. Before she would have said, with stony stoicism, Why not me? Now she asked, saturated with dissatisfaction, Why me?

'That's fine, Chila. I've got loads to do anyway today. Give me a ring later on, let me know how it goes. Acha curie?' The Punjabi balm – never failed, erased all polite English niceties.

'Acha bhain-ji.' Chila smiled. 'Later.'

Tania checked her A–Z again, and gingerly manoeuvred her jeep into a small gap between a three-wheeler and the burnt out chassis of what was once a BMW. She was less than a mile from where she had grown up and this area was un-familiar as moonscape. Long ago, some visionary architect, who had no doubt lived in a traditional mews house the other side of town, had decided to reinterpret the East End ideals of family and neighbourly doorstep chats. And came up with five lozenge-shaped tower blocks, facing each other in a surly pentangle, each floor sharing a common balcony which ran the length of the building and overlooked what he fondly imagined would be verdant communal gardens filled with the cries of cheeky-chappy children, dropping their aitches and swallowing their glottals as they spun hoops through their patch of urban paradise. The grass was still there somewhere, visible in tufts beneath litter and mud, while the play area itself had been concreted over, supporting metal skeletons of rocket-shaped climbing frames and swingless bars.

The address Tania had scribbled on an envelope seemed to bear no relation to where she found herself. She exited the car, double checked the alarm was on, and walked towards the entrance to Jubilee Tower.

Finally she stumbled onto the third-floor balcony, rasping for air. She wanted to stop for a breather, but knew if she did she would only have a quick fag, so she forced herself to quicken her pace, checking the numbers on the uniform row of red front doors which seemed to stretch out for miles ahead. There were splashes of individuality here and there, a hanging basket of yellow pansies, nodding dogs peeking through net curtains, even a welcome mat which sat defiantly between two mock Greek urns outside a newly painted door. But mostly, the inhabitants had chosen anonymity over greeting; only their washing gave them away, hanging from overhead racks above the front doors. Someone here had a newborn, miniature Baby-Gros in lemons and blues suspended like pastel starfish in nets. Many of the residents must have been old, judging by the number of flowery pinafores and huge shapeless vests that fluttered like tattered flags on parade.

Somewhere in the distance, Tania's eye was drawn to a flash of colour, a beacon of green, a pasture amongst the concrete, emerald-belligerent. As Tania walked towards it, she knew she was in the right place. The shalwar kameez rippled slowly in the breeze outside number 1209. A playful puff of wind inflated the kameez, momentarily inhabited by a Rubenesque headless woman with heaving bosoms. Tania rang the bell and crossed her fingers.

'Who is it?' A woman's voice, firm, slightly accented, suspicious, came from behind the net curtains. The door remained firmly shut.

'Hello,' Tania began, 'I'm looking for Jasbinder Singh.'

'Who wants her?'

Tania felt increasingly that she had walked onto the set of a Seventies cop show. She had an urge to reply, Tania the Ferret don't take no as answer, you slag! but instead smiled, aiming it in the vague direction of the twitching lace, catching the faint outline of a spiky head.

'My name's Tania Tendon. I'm a film maker and I was wondering if—'

The door swung open and Tania recognized Suki immediately. The hair was shorter, the glasses were bigger but the expression was exactly as Tania remembered it, vaguely mocking, as if she had been expecting her.

'Oh, hi. Suki, isn't it? We met at my première . . . at the Buzz Bar . . . a while back now.' She kept leaving gaps, hoping Suki would pick up the conversational baton and at least attempt a slight trot.

Suki stood square in the doorway. There was no mention of a cup of tea.

Suki's lip curled slightly. She had seen Tania approaching and had ushered Jasbinder upstairs straight away. She had wanted to laugh out loud, watching the Armani-clad princess tottering along the balcony, out on a 'slumming expedition. Strange; she had quite liked Tania, admired her even as she'd observed her operate on the incestuous circuit where they all converged eventually. Tania's reputation preceded her. Difficult, abrasive, arrogant were some of the adjectives used, but as they were mainly attributed to men, or other rivals, Suki had never taken them seriously. Her own ambition and attitude had earned her a few expletives over the years; mouthy women tended to upset people. They would have all been labelled witches once. From what she had seen, Tania was ferociously bright and sussed with it, and being beautiful as well was just greedy, but not her fault. (Suki had worked extremely hard on loving herself. The theory was just about catching up with the reality of her mirror, so she could afford to be generous.)

In fact, it had been Tania's friendship with those other two women that had impressed Suki. It softened her, contradicted her machiavellian image, bestowed upon her a certain tenderness, a seam of common sense. After seeing Tania's film, Suki was so shocked she had not been able to speak. In her world, populated by unthinkable betrayals and violent revenge, loyalty was all. And to rub it in, the woman had talent.

'Jasbinder's not here. Can I take a message?'

Tania changed tack. She was used to dealing with slammed doors, except they were usually being slammed by men, who would always, after a few minutes, unlock all bolts and defences and wave her in.

'Well, I hope you might be able to help, Suki.' Always use their name, it encourages intimacy. 'I know you've been part of Jasbinder's support committee—'

'I run it. We set it up.'

'Yes, of course, sorry, and I was wondering . . . I would really like to talk to her. Off the record, of course.' That was stupid, she scolded herself, using journo-speak. God, why did she want to talk to her? She had not considered this detail up until now. 'I think her story deserves to be told. I'm not sure how at the moment. But I know I could give her the kind of platform she needs. I mean, I'd take my cue from her.'

Suki blinked once, waiting.

'Um, well, do you have any idea of what her response might be to this?'

Suki folded her arms languidly. 'Well, I know what mine is. Piss off.'

Tania did not flinch as the door banged inches from her face. She stood with her nose pressed against the wood, and then almost toppled over as it flew open again, with Suki in front of her, spitting as she spoke.

'You have got a bloody nerve, haven't you? This must be a good story to get you out of Soho, sniffing round like some culture vulture when it suits you! This is someone's life, you know, and you're not stealing it so you can make your name on Jasbinder's back!'

Tania lurched backwards, her heels slipping under her. 'I . . . no, listen . . . I really do—'

'Save it, eh? You've made it clear who you work for. Anyone who shits on their friends isn't going to care about a stranger. You don't live here any more. And this stuff is not for tourists. Go home.'

Tania did not wait to watch the door closing again. She began running, and only paused when she reached the ground floor, wheezing through burning lungs, taking shaky steps across the forecourt towards her jeep.

She did not register the patch of charred ground in the far corner of the car park, nor the few bunches of Cellophane-wrapped flowers laid on it, nor the weather-beaten, dull-eyed soft toys that had been fastened to the green wire fence beyond. Tourists had been here; a few malevolent ones had ripped down the sympathy cards, stamped on the carnations, urinated on the teddies like dogs marking out their territory. But others had merely stood at the spot, shaking their heads at the blackened concrete, weeping at the memory of the fire, closing their eyes to blot out the image of a mother watching and screaming from the balcony of Jubilee Tower.

'There's baby's head . . . spine . . . fingers, nice long ones, bound to be artistic, eh? . . . Oh, I think baby's got hiccups, see the little jumps? . . . Not much movement at this stage, there's not much room in there now . . . OK, Chila?'

Chila couldn't tear her eyes from the flickering blue screen, watching her child attempt watery kung fu kicks which she felt, a second later, beneath her skin. She had kept all the scan Polaroids and had stuck them with fruit-shaped magnets to the fridge. She had the whole sequence now, starting with the indistinct blob that had looked like a small blue-burning planet in an endless black galaxy. She had watched the blob acquire a tail, a forehead, hooded eyes – an alien comma, peeled as a prawn; seen hands and feet sprout and limber, vertebrae stack themselves as tidily as newly washed plates, features emerge from blank living canvas, a personality profess itself through thumb-sucking and sly somersaults. And now the person itself, ready.

For Chila the novelty had almost worn off. Nine months was a long time to spend in someone's company every second of the day and night. For her, it was a chance for a quick chat, accompanied by helpful visuals. Deepak however, could not stop gazing at the screen, awe-struck and occasionally slightly afraid.

'He looks squashed. Oh, look at his leg, it's . . . Does that hurt, Chila? . . . He's turning over . . . Is that his . . . ? Look at the size of . . . Well, that settles it, he's bound to be a son of mine,' he concluded.

'That, my dear Deepak,' Dr Stroud informed him, 'is the umbilical cord, so don't pat yourself on the back too hard. From this angle I can't tell the sex—'

'We don't want to know,' interrupted Chila.

'Quite right too,' said the doctor, wiping the sticky gel off Chila's stomach. 'No problems, it's all looking quite normal.'

Deepak leaped up suddenly, pointing at the screen. 'He's stopped moving! He hasn't moved at all for at least—'

'I've stopped scanning, Deepak. That's just a still, the last image before I switched it off.'

'Good,' blustered Deepak. 'Of course.'

'Deepak's only been to one scan before this, the first one,' Chila explained mildly, as she slipped into her shoes.

'I see marriage hasn't changed you much,' remarked Dr Stroud drily as she pushed past Deepak towards the bin and whispered to Chila, 'I delivered him, so I can get away with being cheeky.'

Chila sat up. 'Yes, I know. So what was he like as a little boy?' she asked with a shy grin at Deepak.

Dr Stroud wondered what this sweet creature was doing with the son of one of her oldest friends. The number of times Asha had bewailed Deepak's romantic escapades. 'He thinks I'm stupid, Sheila! He thinks I don't know what he's up to. But I can smell cheap perfume on his guest towels. I've seen the lipstick marks on his glasses. Unless . . . You don't think he's wearing lipstick now, do you? Bhagwan! I tell you, anything is possible when you go off the rails. I want to see him married before I die!'

Asha had complained of being on the verge of demise for most of the time Sheila had known her. Like many of the wealthy women she had treated over the years, hypochondria was another way of passing the days and feeling important. Still, having never had children herself, preferring merely to bring them safely into the world, Sheila always tried to understand. And silently thanked her own celibacy for keeping her far away from this maelstrom of worry and confusing passions.

She loved Deepak, out of loyalty, but she liked Chila more. She sat down on the couch next to her.

'Oh, much like he is now. Charmed the birds off the trees and into his pedal car. I think poor Asha had given up hope of ever seeing a grandchild.'

'Let's leave Mum out of this,' cut in Deepak, fidgeting awkwardly with his jacket.

Chila tried to imagine him as a schoolboy, in grey shorts with a stripy tie and jam around his mouth. She did try, but she could not quite grasp the concept of Deepak being a child. She simply saw him in miniature, same hair, same stubble, zipping around in a pint-sized sports car with a couple of large-breasted blondes sitting on the bonnet.

Deepak had always been cagey about his past experiences and Chila had never wanted to push him, finding the idea of him with other women upsetting and distasteful. She had no history, brought no ghosts with her as they got into bed. Which meant everything he did was unique, ground breaking, perfect. How must it have been for him? she wondered. How could he have deemed her special when he'd seen it all before, done it all before? Maybe she ought to make some provisions for after the birth. She had once seen some chocolate bodypaint advertised in Cosmo; it seemed a great idea, combining her two favourite activities in one handy jar. It had been months since Deepak had been intimate with her, virtually since the confirmation of her pregnancy.

'We don't want to disturb the baby,' he had said, as if he expected it to bang on Chila's uterine wall and ask them to Keep it down.

Chila had read enough baby books to know that there was no medical reason to abstain. And now she was having difficulty sleeping, lying awake while the baby did its nocturnal disco routine, she found it strange, the physical proximity and the desert of bed between them. She couldn't discuss any of these feelings with Sunita. Talking with Sunny could be dangerous, they both knew that. The baby had brought them together, held them in tenuous balance. Beyond the scales loomed an unknown darkness, full of glinting secrets and softly breathing premonitions. If Chila ventured out too far, her fear dragged her back, gratefully. She had to deal with what she could see. He was still with her. They were still married. They were soon to be parents. Within those certainties, she would still try her best. She decided to ask Deepak to go via Tescos on the way home. Tonight she would cook, and clean her own kitchen afterwards. And plan something very special for dessert.

Tania drove mindlessly for an hour, automatically stopped at red lights she did not register until minutes later, took bends and negotiated junctions with the blind instinct of a homing pigeon, and found herself driving along the street of her childhood home. Nothing much had changed; still the same short row of terraced Victorian houses, wedged between two dual carriageways, and at the back of them an old railway yard where dying engines were taken to be spannered, hammered and eventually melted down for scrap. There were still children rushing up and down this rabbit run, a rainbow coalition of bikers and runners.

The last time Tania had skipped along here, hers was one of only three Asian families in the street. Her former house looked well-tended, in fact better than when they had lived there. Someone had planted sunflowers in the tiny front garden and the window sills and door had been newly spruced up in a dazzling shade of lime green. A woman emerged from the front door, indigo-black in a vibrant zig-zag wrap and matching headscarf. From the folds of her robes, a small child peeped out with lemur-luminous eyes, clinging with arms and feet to her front. Somalian, Tania guessed, and watched her scatter what looked like old cooked rice onto the path.

Tania inhaled painfully. Her mother used to do this, donate leftovers to the city sparrows. 'These chirie love my biriani,' she would say proudly, resting her bulk on the upturned milk crate, hoping she would actually catch the birds eating her food. Tania used to dread arriving home from school, with her gaggle of friends, and finding her huge mama parked like a polyester-draped juggernaut in their front garden. 'We've got a back garden, you know,' Tania would hiss, trying to heave her back into the house, wishing she had a normal-sized mother whose embarrassing behaviour would at least be less visibly comic.

And now, almost every front garden in the street had been turned into an extended patio. It was mainly women in bright robes and saris who sat right outside their front doors, chatting, hanging washing, wiping down children, reading, shelling peas, oblivious to the honks and fumes of the nearby major roads. Their boldness had also encouraged a few white OAPs to venture into the once hallowed space of the front lawn and just sit, to watch the baffling multi-coloured world go by.

Now Tania could see that this was perfectly understandable, logical even, coming from places where life was lived outdoors, communally. It was an act of bravery, considering the weather here. Tania had never thought of her mother as courageous. But she did know how cowardly it was to deny someone the simple pleasure of sitting under a pale sun to watch the sparrows eat. Grief gripped her in a huge tight fist. She wanted to bury herself in the billowing waves of one of her mother's voluminous housecoats, her favourite pre-school game, to make a tent and invite everyone to lounge in the shade of Mama's gargantuan thighs, Chila, Sunita, Deepak, even Suki, gather them all in and create sanctuary. There had to be somewhere she could call home.

Sunita groaned as she rounded the corner into her parents' road and saw the dozens of cars parked around their house. They definitely had guests, judging by the make and state of the vehicles. Their rich friends drove BMWs or Mercedes, with personalized number plates, usually an approximation of their offspring's names. She spotted a 5EE MA, an AN1 1 and a P00 N4M, wedged in between the other poorer friends' cars which were generally from the Datsun family and all had extremely worn upholstery, where too many family members had been squashed together in the back. She picked her way through the bumpers, annoyed her mother had not mentioned this when she had dropped the children off this morning. If she had known they were having company, she might not have chosen today to wear the red mini-dress and black bomber jacket which a gushing sales assistant had claimed made her look like Cher with a pre-surgery bustline.

As she reached the driveway, she could see the party going on through the open curtains. Dusk had fallen quickly, in the time it had taken her to walk from the bus stop, and the illuminated window framed the revellers like actors on a spotlit stage. The guests flitted from table to sofa to the drinks cabinet, a huge globe on wooden wheels which split at the equator to reveal bargain-cheap wines, expensive vintage whiskies, and sweet pre-mixed cocktails for the ladies. The dividing doors to the back room and kitchen had been opened out, and Sunita glimpsed her parents loading starters onto huge china dishes. She stood on the lawn for a moment, taking a mental snapshot of the hubbub, humming-bird-bright saris, men in sober suits, the more dashing ones in pyjame kurthe with shawls hanging casually from a shoulder, engaged in their old dance of greeting and eating, slower now, older, but the same old steps, a rhythm which had pulsed quietly in the background of childhood, a river which continued with or without her.

Sunita felt as if she stood on the banks, poised, watching others borne away happily in the current. It was so easy, to just drift, to laze in the undertow, like Chila, instead of leaping against the waves. She remembered Uncle with Patterned Jumpers and his lecture on reincarnation, and wondered if he was inside. She thought he might like to know that she had come back as a salmon.

Amongst the throng she spotted Akash cheerfully offering round snacks on silver trays. He had turned up for a party that he hadn't thought to mention to her. Sunita prickled with irritation until she remembered their conversations nowadays consisted of a few surly grunts over the bodies of their squirming children. He would look good: the dutiful son-in-law. She would look exactly how she felt right now, like the absent mother in the scarlet dress. She rang the doorbell, took a deep breath, and plunged inside.

Mata-ji sat in a comfortable armchair with a hot-water bottle concealed under her cardigan. She was not up to standing much nowadays, and besides, she liked watching the youngsters enjoy themselves. Sometimes people forgot whose mother she was. She supposed that they did all look alike, the ancient ones in their white saris and tightly knotted buns who limped and sighed and wheezed behind their children at functions.

Mata-ji was one of the lucky ones. Her daughter-in-law was a gem, never made her feel like a burdensome widow. She even had her own room and fan heater and her radio permanently tuned to a station that played non-stop bhajans. Not like some of her unfortunate friends, whose sons used them as unpaid babysitters and cooks, whose daughters-in-law locked up the pantry and phone when they left them alone in the house. One family had done the unthinkable and placed their grandmother in a home of some kind. It was the final proof that chaos had arrived. It was called Sunny Pastures, but looked like a hospital and smelled of cabbage and cats. Mata-ji had been there once to pick up her friend on the way to an engagement ceremony. How awful it was to be in a place full of old people, reminding you wherever you looked of your own crumbling body. How terrible to receive your children as visitors once a week, if you were lucky, and spend the rest of the time being called Dear and Lovey by busy women in nasty clothes. Mata-ji had felt her friend's shame as her own. To be old in this country was punishment enough. To then have to do bingo and ballroom dancing with other toothless persons was simply torture.

Mata-ji massaged her feet, emitting tiny grunts of pleasure. Nikita and Sunil, who were tottering past with handfuls of sweetmeats, dropping a trail of sticky pink crumbs behind them, paused and watched the floor show.

Nikita giggled, spraying her front with flecks of barfi. 'You sound like the guinea pig at nursery, Buree Dadima. He's called Henry.'

'What is it? You are hungry?' shouted Mata-ji. Her great-grandchildren had shocking accents, their parents spoke Punjabi like memsahibs, even her own son sometimes forgot a phrase and reverted to English occasionally. Mata-ji hoped fervently that her son at least still dreamed in his native tongue. Personally, she would hate to fall asleep and hear people whining in that funny twang in her head.

Inside her head was possibly the most pleasant place to be, where she danced like a nautch-girl and rolled around under mosquito nets with her dear departed husband. She spent many a happy hour recalling their gymnastic love making in various hot locations. It was what gave her that beatific expression that passing youngsters called wisdom. If only they knew. She felt sorry for them; all this busy-busy lifestyle and pressure of work, so little time to enjoy. Of course she had worked hard all her life, but her tasks were finite. When a pan was clean, it was clean. When the prayers were over, it was time for bed. Everything had had its place, and nothing had interfered with that. When she had broken all her bangles on the stones around her husband's funeral pyre, crashing her wrists against flint, even then, she had felt fulfilled. She had given all of herself to him. He was on his way, on to the next stage. Now she was alone and free to recall him whenever she wished. At this very moment she was on a wooden cot somewhere near Amritsar, and he was coming towards her, carrying his tenderness with him, like a diya in his palms . . .

'What you thinking, Buree Dadima?' Akash knelt next to her, automatically taking her hand.

'Kuch-nahin beta. Nothing special. Where is Sunita?'

Akash pointed her out reluctantly. Sunita was offering a silver tray of drinks around the front room, ignoring or possibly oblivious of the curious glances that followed in her wake.

'Why has she forgotten her trousers?' Mata-ji demanded.

'Um, it's a dress. It's the fashion nowadays,' Akash muttered, hoping Great-granny wouldn't notice the bondage-style boots as well.

'When the peahen starts strutting, the peacock must beware.'

Akash shifted uncomfortably and heard his knees crack like walnuts. 'Sorry?'

Mata-ji worked her dentures into a better position. 'She doesn't dress for you. What's the matter?'

Akash focused on a loose thread on his cuff. He was

afraid to look up. Buree Dadima had a way of wheedling information out of everyone; they were taken in by her snowy hair and mischievous, deep-set eyes.

'Oh, nothing. It's nothing. You know, now she's studying again, she's just . . . experimenting.'

Mata-ji snorted into her chunni. 'Ex-per-menting. So many long words and you still understand nothing.'

Akash was tired. The children were on a sugar-high, he had lost two clients that day and was frankly not in the mood for deciphering obtuse Indian quips.

'Buree Dadima, it was different for you. All the rules have changed. We have so many choices.'

'What is choice? Hah? You stay or you go. You love or you don't love. And if you find another, in few years you will be back in same place, with choices. Even the gods had arguments with their wives.'

Akash sighed wearily. 'It's much harder being a man, believe me.'

Mata-ji snorted again, then chortled, then broke into an asthmatic laugh, hacking like an old boiler, slapping Akash's shoulder as she struggled for breath. She wiped her eyes finally, waiting for the phlegm to settle. 'He Bhagwan! That is a good one. Now I know the world is upside down.' She patted his cheek affectionately. 'Easy to love in the harvest. It is how you love in the famine, that is what counts.'

Akash smiled patiently. 'And men are from Mars and women are from Venus.'

Mata-ji stopped smiling. 'Don't be stupid. Now get me some food. Good boy.'

Sunita rinsed out some glasses in the sink as her parents co-ordinated bubbling pans at the stove. They were a good double act; her bumptious, short-legged father banged lids and cracked jokes while her mother glided effortlessly through the chaos, smiling at his punchlines as she maintained order with a flick of a wrist.

'Beti, you must be busy nowadays,' her father shouted over the hiss of the pressure cooker.

'It's all the studying she's doing,' her mother added, tucking her sari end into her waist.

'Of course, studying. You don't forget to eat properly, brain food—'

'Like almonds, fish, lots of milk—'

'You've never liked milk—'

'The trouble we had to get you to drink your thoo-thoo—'

'Hah, she would hide her bottles—'

'Under her bed!'

Sunita had never really noticed before how they finished each other's sentences. They were slowly fusing into the same person. Even the way they negotiated each other's bodies in the small space was fluid and unconscious. Sunita had always been the envy of her friends. 'Your folks are so cool,' they would say, when the term had been fashionable. 'Yeah, suppose so,' Sunita would reply nonchalantly, bursting with pride inside.

The dramas and tensions that some of her friends played out in their sitting rooms sounded like suburban fairy tales: dominating fathers, fearful mothers, curfews and threats, dramatic and exciting second-hand, but only at a distance. Now her pride was mingled with unease. How had she managed to get things so wrong? She didn't even have the excuse of unhelpful role models. They had weathered all Sunita's sea-changes with cliff-face stoicism: her decision to marry Akash, failing her exams, ending up at the CAB. They had not even referred to her bright red mini-dress. Their acceptance humbled her, but Sunita feared it was conditional. How would they react if they knew about the toy-boy doctor in the neon-lit waiting room?

'You haven't mentioned my dress, you two,' Sunita said lightly.

'We don't need to.' Her father smiled, and her mother finished. 'Everyone else has done that for us!' They sniggered companionably.

'Let them gossip!'

'It keeps them busy, eh?' How she loved them for that.

'But you are looking tired, beti . . .'

'Are you getting enough sleep?'

They were either side of her now, smoothing her short hair, rubbing the small of her back.

'Is there anything we can do?'

'We'll have the kids at the weekend—'

'Hah, we can cancel that kitty party—'

'So boring, the same faces every Saturday—'

'Or take the kids with us—'

'Hah, they love dancing to the harmonium—'

'So talented they are.'

Sunita broke away slightly. 'Really it's fine! I'm fine! Stop fussing, will you?'

Her parents fell silent. They cocked their heads, bird-like, to one side – the same side, for God's sake, Sunita noted bitterly – and folded their hands patiently.

'What? What are you waiting for?' Sunita said unnecessarily loudly.

'Hello, Akash beta,' her mother said quietly. Akash was standing in the doorway, his eyes fixed on Sunita, a look of disillusionment on his face.

'I'll lay the table,' Sunita muttered, pushing past them, pulling her dress over her thighs as she brushed past Akash.

He looked down at the plate of food he had selected for his wife, and began eating it, tasting nothing.

*

'That was delicious.' Deepak smiled and pushed his wiped-clean plate away with a satisfied smile.

Chila stood at the helm of a flotilla of serving dishes.

'Is that all you want? There's more . . . of everything.'

The mountain of food in each dish was barely dented. Maybe she had gone a little over the top: three different meat dishes, four of vegetables, plus the rice, naan, salad. The five courses of starters had been a mistake. Luckily the downstairs freezer was almost empty. She began doing Tupperware calculations in her head.

'Here, let me,' Deepak offered, and began loading plates into the dishwasher.

Chila felt giddy with pleasure. This was it; this was what happy couples did. They performed the simple everyday tasks together, like a team. It was so easy. Just a small gesture of goodwill, like cooking a special meal, and look how much you got back. Give and take.

'Any dessert?' Deepak called from the depths of the dish-washer.

On a whim, Chila waddled to a cupboard and grabbed a jar of chocolate and hazelnut spread. She held it uncertainly towards him.

'Chocolate spread?' he said, puzzled.

Chila laughed breathily. 'Why not? We don't have to eat it . . .' She pushed away a slight niggle about the nuts. They would have to watch the sharp bits, and maybe lay a towel on the bed.

'Shall we just admire the jar, then?' Deepak said, standing now, hands on hips, amused.

'No, I thought we could . . .' She caught sight of her reflection in the glass-fronted oven. All she could see was stomach, stick limbs extending from the sides, a tiny head somewhere above it. What was she thinking? She ought to be knitting bootees, really. She cleared her throat. 'I've got ice cream.'

'Great!' enthused Deepak, and returned to stacking dishes.

Chila finished her second bowl of Cornish vanilla and lay back on the sofa with a sigh. Deepak carefully placed a couple of cushions behind her back, flicked on the TV and handed her the remote control.

'You choose tonight, jaan,' Chila said warmly.

Deepak scratched the side of his nose. 'Actually, jaan . . . I have to pop out for a while.'

Chila gripped the remote like a weapon. A strange tight cramp pincered her abdomen.

'What did you say?'

Her voice sounded deeper than usual, Deepak noted, his fingers bunching in his pockets. 'It's some problem with the warehouse . . . I can't get out of it.'

Chila sprang to her feet. Deepak had not seen her move so fast for months. The cold snap in her voice chilled him instantly.

'You're not going anywhere.'

Deepak's confusion almost made him laugh. 'Sorry?'

'You will be. You're staying with me tonight.'

Deepak began walking blindly towards the door. Rage and guilt grappled with his limbs, every step was an effort. He would not look at her. He could hear her heavy footsteps behind him.

'I know where you're going!' she shouted. Where had she learned to bellow like that? 'She was mine! Not yours! You're supposed to want me!'

He felt something fasten on his back. He swung round, arms flailing, knocking into something solid yet yielding to his fists, drum-tight yet spongy to his blows. When he opened his eyes, Chila was on the floor, on all fours, animal-like, teeth bared, panting. He thought she might spring at him. His hands flew instinctively to his neck.

She hissed at him, spittle dotting her lips. 'She doesn't love you.'

Deepak choked on something hard and spiky. He knew if he opened his mouth, his wails would topple walls, he would vomit up the sickness that had brought him here, leaving a gutless, empty skin. He wrenched open the door and almost ran down the tree-lined sweeping drive.

'Leave it,' rasped Deepak thickly, as he buried himself in Tania's hair.

'It might be work,' she breathed, feeling her way through the darkness of the bed, over skin and sheets until she found the receiver, gasping as Deepak began a slow descent over her belly.

'Hello?'

'It's Sunita. Is Deepak there?'

Deepak felt her stiffen beneath him, not an arch of passion. Suddenly there were steel fibres beneath the muscle. She atrophied beneath his hands, each pore snapping shut, tight.

'Sunita? Sunny? I don't believe—'

'Is he there?' Sunita cut in, expressionless.

Tania held herself very still. 'Why should Deepak be—'

'Tell him his wife's in labour. Now.'

'She's what? . . . She's . . . I didn't know.'

The dialling tone.

Tania sat up, she fell out of the bed, something sharp entered her thigh, she fumbled for the light switch, scrabbling across the wall with freezing fingers.

Deepak recoiled in the sudden wash of light.

'What . . . what's going on?'

Tania stood naked before him. She clung to the wall behind her for support. There was a small cut on her leg. Against the white wall, she was as darkly stark as the desert, so many shades of gold and brown. She looked at him, profound with loss. A hot wind began blowing him away, grain by grain. Her voice, when it came, was parched, parchment dry. 'Get out.'

Chila

OHMIGODOHGODOHMUMSHANTIOHMIGOD . . .

It's OK, it's going . . . I can breathe between the waves

I'm thirsty . . . I want water . . . Sunita?

You should have warned me, you sod. . .

I know I wouldn't have believed you . . .

Yes, I know the story about you crapping yourself, don't remind me . . .

My legs hurt . . . Can you? . . . Harder . . . What socks?

What delivery bag? I didn't have time . . .

I haven't even brought a toothbrush . . .

Yes, I packed it two months ago, then I forgot where I'd put it . . .

Don't make me laugh! . . . Don't, really . . .

Oooooooww

No, it's not a contraction, I'm laughing and your bangle's got caught in my drip . . .

Don't pull it! . . . Nurse! . . . That's done it . . .

Don't pull, I said! . . . Oh . . . oh . . .

Ohgodohgodohshitcontractionthistimeohh . . .

I want drugs, whatever you got . . .
Yes . . . and that . . . an injection? Will it hurt?
What's so funny? . . . Sunny? . . .
Now you've got hiccups? . . . Have some of my water . . .
Don't look down there . . . it must look awful . . .
A flower? Fuck off
I don't want them to cut me
Tell them, Sunny . . .
Won't this hurt the baby? The pushing . . .
Yes, what we're made for . . . I suppose . . .
Hot now . . . take off my socks . . . horrible colour
West Ham? Really? . . . fancy . . .
Nice dress . . . you tart . . .
Joking . . . you got the legs . . . red suits you . . .
I want to get up . . . Why?
What monitor? . . . On baby's head? Take it off!
Cutting her before she even comes out . . .
or him . . .
Distress? . . . No bleeding wonder . . . wouldn't you be?
Did you tell him, Sunny?
What did he say? . . . Is he coming?
Did he say Of course?
You're lying, I can always tell . . .
Who did you speak to, Sunny?
Was he there? With . . . Look at me . . . look . . . 1 . . .
OhMamaMamaMamahelpmeiwantmymumshit . . .
Are you holding my hand? Am I hurting you?
Why are you wrinkling up your face like . . . ?
I'm meant to be crying, not you, silly moo
It's OK . . . you don't have to tell me
I know where he was . . . where you found him . . .
I know . . . always known . . . known forever amen
Thought it was a phase, a germ, be better soon
Every time he screwed her I got a present . . .

She must have been good for me to get a conservatory
And I thought Nutella would get him back . . .
No, he's not been with any Spanish woman
It's chocolate spread . . . don't ask . . .
Oh god, there's something coming . . .
Coming down . . .
Stop this now . . . I want to get off . . .
You can't? . . . Why not? You're the fucking doctor . . .
Nonononononopleasenomorestopitstopstop . . .
Feel what? . . . Where? . . . There? . . . This? . . .
Here? . . .
Whose head? . . . Isn't that my hair? . . . No? . . .
Put my hand there, Sunny . . .oh
oh
Yes, I can . . . wet . . . lots of hair like . . .
He's not coming, is he?
She's stuck . . . He's stuck there . . .
No, not in traffic . . . not him . . . The baby's stuck . . .
I can push now? What do you think I've been . . .
I can't do this, Sunny
I'll be ripped apart . . .
Again . . . hah!
This is nothing . . .
This is something he can't do
I can do this, Sunny . . .
Go with it, I know . . .
Yes, I feel it coming and go with it . . .
Like surfing . . . No, never been . . . want to . . .
You and me, we'll go somewhere . . .somewh . . .
OhohohohohicandothiswantMamaTaniaohohoh
Have I split?
Am I bleeding?
Nearly yes . . . yes just few more seconds . . .
Said what?

Who?
Her? Her name?
Did I?
Fancy . . .
This is it now . . .
I want to push when I'm ready don't tell me
Who's at the door?
Why is he shouting?
Yes . . . I know him . . .
I know him he's my husb . . .
OhohTELLHIMTOPISSOFFNOWGETHIMOUTOFHEREohoh
Who's crying?
Sunny? No, it's You . . .
You're here at last . . . give me my baby . . .
There You are
No, don't cry, Mama's here . . .
Where have You been?
You've come far, I can tell
You're so slippy . . .
Oh Your mouthtoesfingersohmyheart
Mine
I dont know, haven't looked
boy or girl
who cares?
Mine

7

SUNITA SAW HIM AS SOON AS SHE LEFT THE WARD. HE WAS sitting in the visitors' area near the lifts, elbows on his knees. She was going to walk straight past him but his head jerked up at the sound of her boots on the floor.

'Is she OK?'

Sunita took a long hard look at him. She could now. No more peeking through a veil. Pop idol gone to seed, she thought, all those charming features sagging with night grime and shame, all those white hairs shining in his beard. She did not even feel angry now.

'She doesn't want to see you,' she said, turning on her heels.

'I'm the father!' Deepak shouted, immediately regretting it. Even to him, it sounded hollow. He had bitten every one of his nails off. His stomach alternately rumbled and crunched into painful knots. He had vertigo every time he stood up. No-one close to Deepak had ever died. His acquaintance with bereavement was minimal, formal. So he did not recognize anything that was happening to him.

Only his fear motored him on and if he stopped, he knew something terrible would happen again.

Sunita turned round slowly. The night's events were catching up with her. She was anaesthetized with fatigue, but strangely calm, viewing it all from a quiet heightened plane. How peaceful it was, out in the open at last, no filters or blinkers, no hiding in corners. The birth had thrown into relief all the banalities, the secrets. She could lie down right now and sleep for a week.

'I saw you, that night, on the balcony.'

Deepak had to rummage for this memory in a messy cupboard. He had covered his trails so often, it was hard to distinguish the real from the fictionally convenient.

'Yes,' he said simply.

'Is that how long it's been going on?' It. A euphemism for an event she would need a dictionary to describe fully.

'Yes,' he said again.

'Wouldn't it have been better for all of us if you'd just married Tania in the first place and left us what we had?' She had said her name, there, for the first time since . . . It. No sour taste, no urgent need to spit. Babies bestowed such benevolence. Every world leader should be made to watch a birth, Sunita thought.

Deepak was thinking about marrying Tania and wondering why there were no fireworks dancing across his vision. 'I wanted to marry Chila,' he said softly. 'I want to see my baby.'

Sunita shook her head. 'They won't let you in there. She's left specific instructions.'

He called out after her. 'At least tell me, a boy or girl? Please?'

'Chila has a son,' Sunita said, without looking back.

Tania spent most of the day cleaning. She stripped every last shred of bedding and put it on pre-wash extra in the machine. She threw away all the half-burnt candles, removed each flake of wax from tables and floors, collected every newspaper and magazine, every wrapper and carton, even books she knew she would never read, or reread, and put them in next door's recycling bin. She moved every piece of furniture and hoovered every square inch of floor, she dusted until reflections sprang from every plane, she defrosted the fridge and disinfected the pedal bin. She disconnected the phones and double locked the front door. Then she got into a shower and stood beneath scalding water until her skin turned red and prunish. She put on a plain white T-shirt and sat in the middle of her perfect flat, waiting for nightfall.

She only became aware of the knocking after a picture actually fell from the wall near the door. The sound of splintering glass reached her through a claggy fog. Somewhere inside the fog someone seemed to be calling. It sounded like her name. She tried to move and found her legs had decided to go for a short holiday and leave some useless pieces of wood in their place.

'Tania! For God's sake! I know you're in there!'

Her lips cracked slightly as she tried to form a word. She registered the soft tearing with curiosity. She picked up a leg and moved it efficiently. Then the other. Now they were in an approximate position, all she had to do was heave herself up. She thought she felt sand beneath her feet as she reached the door. The banging was so fierce, it seemed as if the wood was breathing up to meet her in shallow violent breaths. She looked through the security eyehole. A shouting man. She did not recognize him, which was a very good thing.

'Tania? Please open the door!'

Tania's brother would have slapped her when the door

finally opened if it had not been for the blood beneath her feet.

'What have you . . . ? I've been knocking for nearly half an hour. What's going on?'

Prem pushed his way inside, dragging her with him, and made her sit down on the sofa. He took in her vacant eyes, the criss-cross cuts on the soles of her feet.

'Are you on drugs?'

Tania shook her head. She hadn't seen anyone from her family in months. She saw no reason to break her silence for this almost-stranger.

'Your phone's been off . . . Shit, this is too weird, I can't believe . . .'

He ran to the sink, wet some kitchen paper and carefully wiped Tania's feet, picking out shiny slivers of glass.

'So you know, then. Is that why you've done this? A bit bloody late to feel bad about it, if you don't mind me saying.'

Tania cleared her throat which hurt quite considerably. Her voice came out as a whisper. 'Has something happened to Chila's baby?'

Prem paused mid-wipe. 'You have definitely taken something illegal, haven't you? I want to say for the record I have never approved of your lifestyle, but I thought at least you had a bit of common sense.' Prem was big on common sense. He had begun a pension scheme at twenty-two, had almost paid off the mortgage on a five-bedroom house and had established trust funds for his children before they were potty trained. The fact that he had not had any contact with his sister for almost a year did not prevent him from having opinions about her behaviour. And now, what did it matter? He was virtually the head of the family and, as such, he had to begin as he meant to go on. He may have disliked Tania, but he had a duty to allow her back into the fold, given the circumstances.

'Get dressed. And bring some plasters.'

Tania stood up automatically. 'Where are we going?' she asked timidly.

Prem stared at her bewildered. 'You don't know, then? To the hospital. It's Daddy.'

Chila jerked up from her bed at the sound of muted snuffling. She leaned over the portable cot at her side, licked her finger and placed it in the tiny space between the nose and mouth of her son. Satisfied he was still breathing, she relaxed back into her pillows. Even though he had slept almost constantly since the birth, she had not managed more than a few snatched minutes' sleep, afraid to doze off in case he needed her.

She shifted her body around trying to get comfortable. She registered pain, but mildly, from a distance; she knew there were savaged areas that were in need of urgent repair, but they could wait. Overwhelming every other sensation was a profound sense of completion. She, Chila, catalogue-cutting dumbo and mistress of the *faux pas*, had done something wonderful, had produced a piece of heaven, a morsel of perfection.

She looked around at the other new mothers on her ward and could not understand why they were not letting off party poppers and hanging fairy lights and swinging from the buzzing fluorescent bars in joy, in acknowledgement of the amazing thing they had all done. She wanted to be garlanded with necklaces of jasmine, offered silver trays of Turkish delight, have liveried maids brushing coconut oil into her hair, someone to push her drip for her when she made that long and terrible journey to the lavatory. Instead, the ward was suffused with somnolence, sighed with the heavy, lazy air of a stable of cows. Her mother had told her, when she had visited her with boxes of sweetmeats and the smug expression that grandmothers of newly born boys always wore, that in India, she would be treated like a princess.

'You see, a new mother is made to stay in her bed for forty days. No getting up, only eating the finest food, full of sugar and butter, nothing to do but wait for blessings and feed your son.'

'That's nice, Mum,' Chila replied, 'but I'll probably have to do the Tescos run as as soon as I get back.'

'No no no!' her mother gasped. 'You will get a chill in your womb and your milk will dry up! Bed rest only! You get your husband to do it. This is the one time he can't say no.'

'And if I asked you to do it, Mum?'

Her mother squeezed her hand. 'I am always here. But it is not good for anyone to come between a new baby and his parents. Now you are a family. You don't need me any more.'

Chila had wisely decided not to tell her mother that Deepak had not even seen his son. She had received several visitors on her first day; Sunita of course, at every visiting hour, bearing gifts of fruit and magazines and stupidly large balloons. Her parents, a few of her parents' friends, a couple of girls from the supermarket where she used to work and some of her ladies' luncheon group, all ooohing over the baby and remarking on how much he looked like his daddy.

Chila watched the fathers come and go to the other beds in her small ward. The African woman opposite poured tea for her quiet tall man every visit. They didn't speak much. He would hold the baby, she would watch him, they would smile at each other occasionally and nibble companionably on biscuits. There was a jolly red-haired woman who had produced an almost bald baby with a dusting of hair like paprika. Her husband would bound in with three flame-haired children who would fight over their new sibling and eat all their mother's chocolates. There were two women who did not seem to have partners. One was a young girl, no more than a teenager, who would hold her baby for hours, gazing at her with a kind of bewildered amusement. And the other was a much older woman, maybe in her early forties, who had been on the ward for two weeks following complications after a Caesarean. Every item she had for her baby was designer made and colour co-ordinated, and she was visited by groups of smart laughing women who took over her bed and took turns reading out the horoscopes from glossy magazines.

The apparently single mothers did not disturb Chila as much as the Indian woman in the bed near the window. She was small and mouse-like, and spent much of the day huddled in a nest of blankets, snacking on obviously home-made food from Tupperware containers. But fifteen minutes before visiting time began, she would carefully sponge down her face, apply powder and lipstick, vigorously brush her hair and plait it expertly, put on a small red bindi, and await her husband and young daughter. Maybe it was the way she prepared herself, with such anticipation, or the way in which her plain face was transformed into a flower, opening petal by petal when her family entered the room, or simply the fact that she was Indian, but Chila found it unbearably fascinating to watch. It was the normality, the ease of their connection, that rendered her an observer. Chila felt at times she was watching a movie, a replay of her happy family ideal. When she had seen herself in Tania's film, she had felt a similar jolt of disassociation.

After the screening, she had felt adrift, powerless; she felt she deserved to be exposed. But now, something was different. Now she could watch the mouse and her brood with a kind of curious detachment, nostalgia even, a longing layered with sadness.

'You know,' her mother had said to her before leaving, 'at home we say, when a woman gives birth, she has one foot in death. It is a dangerous time. But when she has given birth, she gives birth to two new people, the baby and herself.'

Sunita had agreed with this. 'In psychological terms, that's pretty damn accurate,' she had nodded wisely, helping herself to another handful of jelly babies (Sunita was big on playground sweeties at the moment). 'For a woman, your whole sense of identity is transformed when you become a mother. The I becomes a We, for ever, and of course that has profound implications for your primary relationship. It's amazing really, how much truth there is in our mums' witchy sayings.'

'Like never leave the house if you have just sneezed,' added Chila sharply, 'or don't wash your hair on a Thursday.'

'Um, yeah,' Sunita replied hesitantly.

'Or don't step over anyone on the floor or you'll stunt their growth,' Chila rushed on. 'A woman with a second toe bigger than her first will dominate her husband, left-handed people bring bad luck, never count the number of chapattis anyone eats, keep away from widows because they're cursed, aren't they?' Chila's voice wobbled as she finished the sentence and she lay back, exhausted.

Sunita stopped in mid-chew, the severed head of a small green mannequin in her hand. 'That's going a bit far, Chila. Some things are common sense, others are just silly superstitions. In fact, when India was a matriarchal society—'

'Oh, stop it!' Chila shouted, her voice bouncing off the white high walls. 'No more sodding fairy tales! No more stuff you've picked up in books! It doesn't help when it's really happening!'

A couple of the other mothers looked up sharply. Their visitors paused their conversation, throwing curious glances over their shoulders. Chila's son stirred milkily in his cot.

'Chila . . . I'm sorry,' Sunita began.

Chila threw Sunita's hand off hers and leaned forward. Sunita shrank from her. She could never remember seeing anger or bitterness shadow her friend's face, but there they were, contorting her features, expelling her voice as an unfamiliar hiss.

'I'm glad for you, Sunny. You've got it all and a side helping as well when it suits you. But don't tell me what I'm feeling. Don't pretend what's happened is part of some big plan to make me into a superwoman or crap like that. You've got choices. I only had one and he's shat on me. And our baby. When you can feel it, feel something even like it, then you can talk. Otherwise, shut it.'

Chila lay back and turned her face into her pillow. A plump, quizzical nurse appeared, hovering at the end of the bed.

'Is she OK?' she asked chirpily.

Sunita shook her head.

'I think maybe she's tired. Are you tired, dear?' she said unnecessarily loudly near Chila's ear.

Chila's response was muffled by pillow but audible nevertheless: 'Sod off.'

The nurse ushered Sunita apologetically off the bed and drew the curtains around it in one smooth gesture.

'Nap time for Mummy, I think.' She winked and waited by the bed until Sunita had left the ward.

It was the smell that broke Tania's stupor, that familiar mingled odour of floor polish, disinfectant and distant over-boiled vegetables. It brought back childhood days spent in out patients with her mother, who would wring Tania's hand as she pulled anxiously on her inhaler. Tania had more reason than most to hate hospitals, but it was not the nearness of death or illness that bothered her, it was the impotence, the handing over of control to an army of well-meaning cogs in a slowly fragmenting machine.

'This hospital will kill me,' her mother used to moan paradoxically, always aghast at the amount of time she had to spend climbing steep Victorian stairs, queuing for tickets 'like in a supermarket at the meat counter' in the chest X-ray department, flicking through ancient magazines, waiting. Sometimes, in desperation, her mother would collar anyone in a uniform with an Indian face and plead with them in Punjabi, hoping the old school connection would hasten her appointment. There were usually apologies, sometimes a friendly chat, but never any favours. And strangely, her mother never seemed surprised at the constant rejection; indeed, she seemed to expect it, another test from the gods which she would accept with grace and a large amount of coughing.

Following her brother along the echoing corridor, Tania slowed down instinctively, half-expecting to hear her mother's steps behind her, a slow, heavy shuffle, the swish of material around her legs, her familiar refrain, mock-scolding, 'Always too fast, Tania. Too fast you are.'

'This is it,' Prem said, assuming an important dramatic pose which annoyed Tania intensely. 'Don't be shocked by all the wires and stuff. They're trying to find out how much damage the stroke actually did. Oh and Tania—'

'What?' Tania spat, expecting a lecture.

'He's completely unresponsive, at the moment. Just to warn you, you know . . .'

Tania opened the door carefully. Her father was lying poker straight on the bed, hooked up to a battery of bleeping machines which flashed intermittently, green darts piercing the gloom of the room. Tania sat down uncertainly on the plastic chair next to the bed. It had been a long time since she had been this close to her father. She wondered how she could have ever been frightened of this soft, sagging face. Unconsciousness had erased every crease of disappointment, every angle of anger. Only one small part of her memory of her father remained, resting in the deep vertical line that bisected his bushy greying eyebrows, an exclamation mark of bitter triumph. Even like this, he seemed to be whispering, Told you!

Tania carefully placed her hand on his, shocked to find the skin warm, jolted by the contact. It seemed days rather than hours since she had touched another body, and the intimacy of skin on skin brought her up sharply with an almost physical pain. Fragments of the previous evening came back to her, sharp mosaic pieces, a possessive arm over a pristine sheet, the shrill alarm of the telephone obscene in the darkness, her nakedness against a chilling wall. She suppressed a sob and felt a prick of shame as Prem laid a gentle hand on her shoulder, because she did not know for whom she wept.

'The doctor says he can probably hear us.'

Tania sniffed and nodded as she fumbled for a tissue.

'We found him like this in the morning, so we don't know when . . . we don't know how long he's been like this . . .'

Tania had seen her father's room in Prem's house in the days when she still paid the occasional visit. It was tucked away in the corner at the end of a corridor, almost shouting distance away from the other bedrooms and the downstairs family rooms. 'He wants to be self-sufficient,' Prem had explained, and obligingly fitted an en-suite bathroom at considerable cost; after all, he had argued, it would ultimately add value to the house. No-one in Prem's family had objected when her father chose to take his meals in his room on a tray, babysat by satellite television. No-one had thought it odd that her father would lock his door for hours on end and could be heard clearly from the kitchen below, pacing the room with his regular military steps. 'Dad's funny ways!' Prem would grin, knowing Tania could not argue this point. Her father had always been, at the very least, prickly and eccentric. But ultimately, she knew she had no right to criticize Prem, to question her father's position in his son's house, because she had never been involved, never taken an interest in their arrangements.

'Tania is always so . . . busy,' her mother's surviving friends would mutter, making it sound like her diary was filled with baby-strangling appointments. Their meaning was clear and understood by everyone. As a daughter, she had failed. Oh, she may be top dog, big boots in that far off TV land, but here, where it mattered, she was nobody.

Her father moaned suddenly, making her jump and momentarily let go of his hand, which fell lifelessly onto the bed.

'He does that sometimes,' Prem said almost fondly. 'It doesn't mean anything apparently.'

'How do you know?' Tania flashed him a look. 'How do you know he isn't in pain?'

'It's just a muscle thing . . . or something. The doctor said—'

'The doctors say whatever will stop us from getting upset. He might be trying to tell us something,' Tania almost shouted.

'Look,' whispered Prem, his voice suddenly hard, 'he's been saying quite a lot over the last nine months since you've seen him, and that was only for half an hour.'

'Stop it!' hissed Tania, getting up, away from him.

'Oh, yeah, you don't want to hear it but you know as well as I do you've not exactly kept in touch, have you? And now you're having a go at me? Who's been looking after him?'

'I wondered how long it would be before that came up.'

'Who's been putting up with the cantankerous sod while you've been gadding about with your arty-farty friends, eh?' spat Prem, 'Not to mention what else you've been up to,' he added pointedly.

Tania's ears pricked in alarm. 'What's that supposed to mean?'

Prem deflated suddenly. He rubbed his hands through his hair and brought them over his face, trying to drag away the tension with his fingers. 'It's a very small world, Tania, our world,' he said wearily. 'I don't know what you're after. I've never known, really. I hope it's been worth it, Tans.'

Tania watched him leave the room. She stood staring at the door for a long time afterwards.

The receptionist greeted Sunita like an old friend. Simone had noticed, like everyone else on the desk, how often the attractive Indian woman with the funky haircut called in for Dr Bedi. There wasn't much she missed: certainly not the new clothes, the spring in her step, the wedding ring. Of course, it was none of her business and besides, nothing new. Nothing like proximity to death to get the old hormones going. She had stumbled across more secret assignations in store rooms and offices than she cared to recall. People would do the strangest things in the name of passion. They had all been at the desk on those occasions when a sheepish man would be admitted with something unmentionable stuck in a cavity. 'I was having a shower when I slipped and fell backwards onto the Hoover.' 'I jumped out of bed naked and tripped, impaling myself on this frozen chicken.' 'I thought the hamster was back in its cage.' Simone never judged anyone. Firstly, she was too damn busy. Secondly, she had seen too many damaged bodies wheeled into here. The affordable pleasures, however momentary, were all anyone could hope for.

She told Sunita, 'You're in luck today, he's just gone on a break.' And away she went, wings on her heels. Simone returned to her computer screen and treated herself to another digestive.

After a couple of knocks, Sunita pushed the door open hesitantly and peeped around it. Krishan was sleeping awkwardly on the small two-seater sofa, his calves and head dangling from either end. Asleep he looked even younger. Sunita had an urge to brush some hair from his forehead. This wasn't right, feeling so maternal, or maybe it was, given what she'd just experienced. She knelt down near his head and he immediately opened his eyes.

'You're early.'

'Chila's had her baby.'

He sat up now, alert. From dead sleep to wide awake in two seconds, a requisite for a junior doctor. 'Everything OK?'

Sunita hesitated. There was no point mentioning Chila's outburst. No doubt it could be explained away by a thousand different hormonal reasons, but at this point, that was no consolation.

'Yeah, fine. A boy, seven pounds two ounces, no forceps, slight tear, went to the breast straight away.' Sunita felt herself gabbling.

Krishan grinned. 'Well, thank you for the medical precision, but is she feeling OK? Are you?'

Sunita wasn't sure how it happened, but one minute she was describing how they took turns at the gas and the next she was howling like a banshee into his chest. She was frightened at the sound of her own wailing, an old animal sound that did not belong to her body, dragging with it from the sludge glimpses of yellow wallpaper, a descending gas mask, a beer can ring on her finger, waking from a numbing night on a trolley, feeling emptied and bereft, blood flaking from her thighs like dead petals.

'I lost a baby,' she said finally. No, tell the truth. 'I got rid of a baby. Once. At eight weeks.'

Krishan said nothing. He held her tighter. She could hear his heart, steady, strong.

'I know I had to do it. It wasn't the right time. We had careers to plan. We had families who could not have coped with the shame. But I lost my career. My family have never stopped loving me. What was it all for?'

She couldn't see. His stethoscope was pressing into her cheek. His T-shirt sported a damp sticky patch but he didn't seem to mind.

'Listen, Sunita,' he said. 'You do what's best at the time. If I started regretting some of the decisions I've had to make over a dying body, I'd never survive.'

'But you save people!' Sunita cried, pulling away from him.

'Not always. I do what I think is best in the circumstances. Hindsight is useless. Predictions hardly come true. What is there, but the moment of decision?'

Sunita wiped her nose on her sleeve and stared at him. 'Are you sure you're only twenty-five?'

'Are you sure you're only thirty-four?'

Sunita sniffled, 'Actually I'm thirty-five. So sue me.'

Krishan took her hand gently. 'You're an amazing woman. I mean, woman, mother, kitten, vamp, carer, joker, liar, soothsayer—'

'Wife,' Sunita interrupted.

'Wife, yes. All of them. Don't take this the wrong way, but I'd be proud to have you as a mother. Or a daughter.'

'Or . . . ?' Sunita asked.

Krishan leaned forward and stared into her eyes intently. His hand slowly rose and cupped her cheek tenderly.

This was it, she knew. All these weeks Sunita had wondered about this moment and of course it happened when she had no make-up on, reeked of sweat and had a considerable amount of nasal fluid smeared over her face. She waited for crashing waves, trains going through tunnels, fountains spurting into life, violins, anything. And she was back on a balcony, witness to another kiss, sacrilegious and defiant enough to shock her back into life. One kiss leads to another. Now she knew, if it had not been for Tania and Deepak, she would not be here, now, like this. And it came to her with the velocity of epiphany, the illumination of angels, the simplicity of snow. She looked back at him bare, unafraid, and knew finally what she wanted and what she deserved.

Chila couldn't help laughing as she watched her son root blindly for her nipple. His eyes were closed but he smelled his way, twisting his head until he found the perfect aim. He latched on with a speed that almost alarmed her, fleshy clamps, gummy pincers, releasing a warming tingle until she flooded for him, relieved. With her free hand she slipped her forefinger into his palm, a tree trunk against the tiny branches of his fingers which curled around her with creeper-like tenacity. Swaddled in his blanket, he made the shape of a small canoe, the kind she had seen floating down the Ganges trembling under their cargo of burning candles and fresh flowers. Only on the television, of course. Strange, she called herself Indian when she had never been there. And her parents rarely talked about Africa as their regret at leaving overwhelmed any joy of remembrance.

She would take her son to India, she decided. She would buy one of those baby backpacks she had seen the posh woman in the bed opposite displaying to her friends, and one of those hats with flaps for the ears, and visit the Himalayas, her favourite backdrop for any Hindi film song. She would play him all kinds of music to sweeten his soul; Lata, of course, all the old Seventies soul stuff, even 'I Will Survive', because she felt he ought to understand there were many different songs and ways of singing them. She would teach him to be kind to animals and to be a rock for his friends, she would feed him simple, wholesome food straight from the earth; organic was more expensive but she could probably swing a discount at her old supermarket. She would encourage him to talk at an early age. She longed to talk with him; at him would do for now. They would have passionate open conversations, none of the pained silences and fumbling sentences she remembered having with her parents. She would massage his growing body with almond oil, and the force and love she poured into him would help sprout strong, lithe limbs. She would never smack him, but have a tone of voice that would let him know where his limits were. She would kiss him every day, take him to temple every week, to the theatre every month, on holiday somewhere warm and gentle every year. She would rewrite the book on motherhood, because every new mother could. Perhaps, she pondered, she ought to start thinking about a name.

Deepak turned on the ignition of his car just so he could have the heating on full blast. Although it was a warm day, he felt as if he had been squatting in a freezer. He wrapped the fraying overcoat he had found in the boot around himself and held his hands up to the air vents, hoping the stale warm air would somehow unthaw his sinews. The car resembled a skip; the back seat was covered with empty take-away cartons and old newspapers. Two bunches of wilted flowers, a basket of over-ripe fruit and a clutch of bedraggled soft toys filled the front passenger seat, lying where Deepak had hurled them in desperation. Occasionally, a blue helium balloon with IT'S A BOY! written in white piping around the rim floated slowly across his vision, until he batted it to the back seat with a sharp slap. Since his son had been born, he had spent almost all his time in this same spot in the hospital car park, opposite the Maternity Unit entrance. He had only left for two brief periods: once to grab some food, and the second time to collect his passport from home. Each time he had come back clutching flowers, toys, fruit; meaningless gifts. He opened the glove compartment to check it was still there. He took it out, double checked the expiry date and winced at his photograph, which gave him the air of a shifty travelling salesman. It was only after Chila's eighth refusal to see him, to even accept a hand-written note, that he had thought about the passport.

It didn't make sense of course, nothing did. Since that midnight telephone call, everything he said, did and saw had taken on a disconcerting sepia gloss. The moment before Tania had picked up that telephone, he had confidently assumed where he lay was reality, the room in which he reclined, the pillow under his head, the body beneath his fingers. The moment after, a breath later, a blink of an eye, and it was gone, all of it, as if some huge hand had plucked him up brutally and held him high above the landscape, a vast empty plain, and in its centre, the room, the bed, the pillow, tiny and insignificant.

He had always imagined that when the moment of truth finally arrived, as he knew it would, it would come with terrible fanfares and the crumbling of walls. It would be a cleansing with fire, pure and savage. He was not prepared for this, this monochrome limbo, a gradual draining away of vital colours which left him weak-bodied and with a mind that raced like fever. He soon realized the black and white fragments that occasionally intruded were newspaper clippings, read long ago. Fathers who took their babies – Stole Them! said the headlines, but then they would, wouldn't they? – were men who looked like him. They had wives who looked like Chila. They all loved their children. Love made people do terrible things, he knew that now.

He finished off the last dregs of some cold coffee and tossed the cup onto the back seat. He turned up the heating another notch and wondered vaguely if there was a hat lurking somewhere in the debris of his boot. Then he remembered: one of those fathers, an Indian father, had done something terrible in the name of love. A snapshot of a charred car crossed his vision fleetingly. He suppressed a wave of nausea and burrowed deeper into his coat. A savage. An inhuman act. No-one could argue with that.

Deepak leaned forward for a moment to adjust his coat and sighed when he looked up and saw her walking towards him, head bowed, deep in thought. Now he was hallucinating, he noted dejectedly, although he had to admit, she looked amazingly real. A bit thinner perhaps, her hair needed a wash, and that tracksuit did nothing for her, but yes, a good likeness. It was only when Tania actually looked up and he saw the fear in her face, that Deepak realized she was real. He opened the car door quickly, almost barring her way.

Tania's first instinct was to run, but there was something in Deepak's expression that rooted her helplessly to the spot. A blast of hot air seemed to inflate him in front of her. He brought with him the smell of old food and rotting leaves. He looked as if he was running a temperature. He looked as if he would chase her until he caught her if she dared to run. So instead, she held herself upright, with effort, and tried to make polite conversation with someone who only hours before had been part of her, inside her.

'You've seen her, then,' Deepak said, feeling somewhat annoyed. 'How is she? How's my son?'

Tania edged away from him slightly. 'No. I haven't seen her.'

Of course she was going to protect her. They all did that. Deepak felt foolish now. How could he ever have imagined that anything he might offer would intrude upon their friendship?

'Tell her I want to see her, Tania. She'll listen to you. She must have forgiven us if you saw her.'

Tania managed a small pinch of pity for him. She did not expect some kind of explanation now, not having seen him. He was too far gone for that, and frankly, she didn't care. She closed her eyes and watched the luminous green lines of bleeping machines snake across her lids. She opened her eyes and Deepak was holding the car door open, inviting her inside.

He has gone mad, she thought.

Deepak thought for a brief second that Tania was going to refuse his plea. But then she glanced into the car and seemed to jump slightly. Maybe she could see how hard he was trying, see the sad remnants of his sorries strewn over the seats. Maybe she needed to talk too. But he felt elated when she threw him a brief smile and walked around to the other side of the car. He swept all the fruit and toys to the floor, clearing space for her. When he spoke he sounded almost cheerful.

'Not too hot for you, is it?' he asked.

Tania shook her head. She stared straight ahead while he talked. Deepak talked for almost half an hour, barely pausing for breath. He was grateful that she allowed him to do that. In fact, her silence encouraged him to say much more than he intended. He began by apologizing of course. The pregnancy, well, that had happened the night of Tania's film and there hadn't been any further contact since then, so he had not been lying in the absolute sense of the word and he wanted to tell her, oh, so many times, but he knew the minute he did that, she would leave him and that was something he could not cope with. Not then. Now it was different and they both knew they had been extremely stupid and these things happened when two people felt lost and lonely at the same time and they both had, hadn't they? And they both knew that Tania was one of life's copers and didn't really need him whereas Chila . . . and at this point Deepak had to pause because Tania had batted the blue helium balloon so hard that it had burst with a loud pop and they watched it deflate slowly, until it wheezed to the floor and settled comfortably on Tania's shoes. Then Deepak went on to say, a little sheepishly, that he had been having all sorts of strange thoughts, how hard it was to not see his own son, to miss out on those first few vital days, and Tania had nodded then, understandingly he thought, but he hastened to add that this situation could be resolved quite simply, if she, Tania could arrange something. After all, Tania and Chila were best friends.

Tania had smiled again. She seemed to wipe her face a lot. Then she had rooted around on the floor and asked him if he had a tissue, maybe on the back seat, or in the boot. Deepak had looked, and so had she, furiously, ferreting in his glove compartment and among piles of rubbish, and eventually he had found some serviettes that had come with his take-away fried chicken and he had wiped her cheeks himself, overwhelmed with gratitude.

'Tans,' he said, feeling clear-headed for the first time in days, 'you probably don't want to hear this, but I do love you. I always will. But it's not enough, is it?'

Sunita found Akash sitting at the kitchen table surrounded by files. He smiled hesitantly as she came in and sat down by him. She could smell garlic and tomatoes. A bottle of wine stood opened on the counter.

'How's Chila?' Akash asked.

Sunita nodded, a slow, world-weary nod, the nod she had seen so many of her aunties do around her mother's kitchen table, the all-encompassing, we've seen it, done it and got the T-shirt nod which made her feel very old and wise suddenly. Akash nodded back, satisfied, then got up to tend to a bubbling pot behind him.

'Where are the—' Sunita began.

'Asleep,' Akash murmured, blinking against the rising steam. 'I bunked off early and took them to Whacky Warehouse with Selina's kids. Should have seen Sunny in the ball pit, he was a right goonda, chucking them all at the big boys . . .'

Akash barely looked up as he added a sprinkling of herbs to the sauce and stuck an experimental finger into the pot, burning it, as he always did.

Sunita watched him, transfixed by the ordinariness of it all. Home and hearth, what they had all whispered about, all three of them, even Tania, under duvets with torches, over milkshakes in cafés, shouting over bass lines at smoky tables, endless phone calls, millions of hours spent in hope and analysis, of what their lives might be with Someone Else. Was this peculiar to women, this constant projection in minute detail of a twinned future? Did men spend this amount of time and energy creating their perfect lover, fine tune the details to shades of wallpaper and names of future offspring? Sunita liked to think they did, that this was not only a female disease, it was just that women were honest enough to admit it. Maybe that's why they were all so constantly disappointed, disillusioned, disenchanted, that was the word. Because fairy tales always ended with a wedding. Whoever began a love story with 'They had just got married . . .'

She rose slowly, feeling slightly light-headed, and stood next to Akash, uncertainly. He looked up quizzically. His face was flushed from steam and possibly wine; curls hung in baby tendrils from his temples. Catching him unawares, it was not so difficult to glimpse, somewhere in there, the nineteen-year-old in faded jeans who had promised her everything from a candlelit mattress.

'What's up?' he said finally.

Sunita took a breath, inhaling a fair amount of garlic fumes, which made her splutter in an undignified hacking manner until Akash handed her a glass of water and watched curiously as she gulped it down, her mind racing. She would do what all the books had advised: honesty, tell him how the lack of communication in their marriage had led her to seek comfort elsewhere, albeit emotionally, and that Krishan – oh, those eyes – was merely a symptom of a much deeper problem that had to be aired in a civilized and frank manner, and if it meant she had to unpick all these strands, of herbs in a pot and children in ball pits and inter-twined families and the steam-flushed face of her husband, then, surely, that was what must be done.

'Akash,' she began, and she took his hand.

Tania swung open the door, nodding her head blindly as Deepak reminded her to talk to Chila as soon as she could, thanking her again and again, telling her he would have his mobile on, waiting for her call. She walked away quickly, not seeing where she was going, and only when she was sure she was out of sight did she check her sleeve. It was there, the thing she had spotted and wanted and decided she would get, at any cost, even if it meant sitting in his car for an hour and a half, suppressing a constant desire to attack him with rotting fruit. She drove home via Tower Bridge, and parked recklessly on a double yellow line. She ran along under the absurd fairy-tale turrets until she reached the centre of the bridge.

'For you, Chila,' she whispered, as she took Deepak's passport out of her sleeve, wrapped it in a plastic bag with the jack from her boot, and threw it into the green-grey waters below.

Tania

I KEPT ASKING MYSELF AFTERWARDS: IF I HAD HAD MY CAMERA with me when it happened, with all of us there for the first time together, would I have filmed it? It would have been an interesting test. It's one of the basic rules of thumb, along with never revealing sources and always fiddling expenses forms, you should carry your chosen weapon with you at all times. The camera or the notebook or the audio recorder. The best stories arrive unannounced, sexy happenstance, as I'm in the one profession where the unexpected is always welcome. I thought I would be better prepared. Maybe I'm getting rusty. Maybe I just don't care enough any more. As it happens, I don't need the footage. It's all here in my head, every flicker, preserved.

I know it was a bit of a futile gesture, flinging his passport to a watery grave but it suited my mood at the time. I shouldn't have had the Verve playing on my car CD; it sounded too much like a soundtrack and I had to fill the frame with something appropriately dramatic. Afterwards I parked up somewhere, I still don't remember exactly where, but there were pigeons and the smell of frying bacon, and did the Care in the Community shuffle for hours through the streets. It was odd, seeing the fear on people's faces as I approached them, watching their freak radar swivel them away from my trajectory, enjoying their confusion that such a pretty gal in a designer tracksuit should be dribbling and muttering her way through their patch. After a while, I actually began to enjoy it.

The Madness of a Seduced Woman – was that a song or a book? Hell hath no fury, You done me wrong and killed mah dog . . . I ran through all the phrases I could muster to try and name what was propelling me along the pavements. I recalled some country and western song titles which, despite everything, made me laugh, in a braying dislocated way. 'I Gave Her a Ring, She Gave Me the Finger', 'Walk Out Backwards so I Think You're Coming Back'. Except I did it out loud. Very loudly. I howled and keened and rent my fleecy top and I didn't give a shit. I spat out gobs of bile until I went hoarse, I shouted whatever I remembered in no particular order: a leg resting on mine, my brother's Adam's apple bobbing in his throat, a baby punching its way out into the world, glass winking in my heel, my dad's surprisingly clean fingernails. Do you know how little we scream, as adults? Children do it all the time, never alarmed or worried by the decibels they produce. I frightened myself for the first few seconds, then I got used to the roaring and the skin tearing in my throat. Then I turned it into some kind of song, a mantra my old ma would no doubt call it, and I told my story to myself, to finally believe it, because no-one else would. Not then.

The only regret I had afterwards is that I had almost become another bloody statistic. Yeah, I've read all those reports about our propensity towards cracking up and self-harm, how we are more likely than any other group to do what all good girls do, dispose of our mess without bothering or blaming anyone but ourselves. But this did not feel like an apology. In fact, I've never felt so powerful as I did for those lost hours, sobbing my secrets to the pigeons. All that time and energy I've wasted trying to keep control, when giving it up, giving into the chaos I've always feared, was so . . . Deepak was just an excuse really, the bogyman who I could claim led me astray. I can get lost on my own perfectly well actually, carry my madness on my back, owning it, whistling a perky tune. All the winds of the world in a knotted knapsack, ten miles to London and still no sign of Dick. Best way really, for now.

If I could, if it was possible, I'd track down every blip on that graph of misery, every woman who has used her creativity and cunning to try and dispose of her own beautiful body: the ones who loop festive saris over wooden beams for their nooses; the ones who concoct witchy cocktails from their bathroom cabinets and lie down in convenient places to avoid startling the neighbours; those who fill soapy baths and clutch their cheap disposable razors in clean brown hands; the ones who write out loving farewell notes in big three-year-old frightened writing; and especially those who decide on a whim that they will punish the world by punishing themselves and make their exits furiously, messily, but still alone. I'd let them in on the big secret, show them the hair-thin line that separates anger from despair, giving out from giving up, black-faced, demon-killing Kali from demure-eyed, long-suffering Sita.

No, I haven't suddenly found religion although, strictly speaking, by now I should have undergone some kind of guilt-blasted conversion, if only for appearances' sake. Oh, Lordy, the local mafia have bought ringside seats for that one. I've met covens of moustachioed masis around my dad's hospital bed, where they gather to eat his futile, freshly bought grapes and contribute what they feel is an important part of the healing process, hours of tuneless wailing and breast beating, pausing only to spit occasionally in my general direction. To them it is perfectly obvious why my father lies in unconscious limbo, it may as well be written on the chart at the end of his bed. 'Broken heart and loss of faculties due to bloody ungrateful daughter who has not even the decency to say sorry. PS We were right then, huh?' I am convinced the main reason they turn up with such frequency is that they do not want to miss the moment when I finally crack and fling myself upon his body, tearing out my hair and begging Bhagwan to take me instead!

What they do not know is that we have an understanding, me and Dad, we've made a pact. We stick to what we've always done, because to behave otherwise would be gross hypocrisy and worry us both unnecessarily. So that's what we promised each other, when I whispered in his ear and saw, I know I did, the tiniest tremor of an eyelid in response. I won't cry and he won't die. We can sort out the sub-clauses when he finally decides to wake up.

The day or so after my wild woman of wonga impression remains slightly blurred. I vaguely remember driving home, singing some old Hindi song in a no doubt atrocious accent. I remember ringing up my agent Mark and telling him to cancel all my work projects until further notice. And then I was waking up, fully clothed, on the kitchen floor, with birds madly carousing outside and sunlight warming my bones like a spotlight. Then I went shopping. I parked up outside Riz's music shack on my old stomping ground and just got out and walked. I've done the ethnic ramble loads of times on camera, but only lingered long enough to angle my profile perfectly or raise an ironic eyebrow at a piece of kitsch. This time we were all there, mum, Sunita, Chila, holding imaginary hands, fighting over Big Mac-sized bindis, sharing headphones to listen in on a tune, running fingertips over fabrics cascading from their bolts like waterfalls. There was no sense avoiding it any more. So it hurt, having them all there, but they always had been, gossiping and wheezing amongst the daals and industrial-sized tins of tomatoes.

I was expecting to be recognized. Mostly I was ignored. Obviously none of them read any of the magazines or newspapers that claim I am now officially the voice of Brit-Asian Yoof. Actually, no, there was one woman, an old lady in a voluminous billowing suit who stalked me around Asha's Tip Top Mini Mart, staring in that unapologetic way that old ladies do. She finally grabbed my wrist at the check-out and demanded 'Are you Tendon-sahib's lost daughter?' I told her yes. I didn't know how else to answer her.

Anyhow, Dad seemed to approve of most of my purchases. I scan the beeping screens around his bed to assess his responses to me, to my questions. Each one shows the same programme, the intensive care test card of black shot through with a continuous green line, the story of his body unfolding as he breathes. I edit out the rhythmic everyday pulses and watch for the unexpected leap, the irregular contraction that tells me he has heard me. There were definite jumps of appreciation when I held up the armfuls of silver bangles I'd chosen and jingled them near his ear, making them choon-choon softly, Mum's theme tune as she waddled around the house. He enjoyed the alarm clock I'd found, encased in white plastic domes, whose alarm is a muezzin calling the faithful to prayer. He held very still as I waved packets of spices under his nose – not the red chilli powder or the coarse black pepper, obviously, but he seemed to recognize the ground cinnamon, the garam masala, the special chana masala mixture that he likes sprinkling on fresh fruit. And when I broke off some leaves of fresh coriander and crushed them beneath his nostrils, I saw them wrinkle, I'm positive.

It was day four, I think, when I decided that Dad needed a shave. Long ago, when he wasn't embarrassed to have physical contact with me, I used to sit on his lap, counting the white hairs in his stubble.

'You gave me that one,' he'd say as I pointed. 'Your mother did all of those. Your brother made the hair come out of my ears.' I was fascinated by how quickly these bristles would reappear after his morning shave. If I stared hard enough, I felt I could almost see them emerging, pushing their way through his soft brown skin.

'Does it hurt?' I asked him.

'Nothing hurts me,' he would boom proudly, and I believed him then.

I'd watched him shaving so many times that it was easy to remember how he liked it. The old-fashioned way, of course, a soft brush, warm water, a hot flannel, a curving cut-throat razor. I wanted to do it. It is a good sign, that his hair is still growing. It means that despite his silence, his body continues to thrive. I'd just lathered him up when my brother swept in laden with gifts, dropped whatever he was carrying and knocked me and the razor across the room. If I'd managed to hold on to it I'd have carved an explanation onto his nuts, but in any case, he was off on one, spluttering and foaming as he paced around the room, slipping on the carpet of squashed soft fruit beneath his feet.

'I can't believe . . . I know you've sunk pretty low but . . . Do you think anything you do will make any difference now? He can't change his will, he's not capable and I will personally drag you through the courts if you dare—'

'I don't know what's in Dad's will,' I told him, 'and I don't give a shit.'

I got up then, picked up the razor and sat down again

next to Dad. His monitors were steady, laconic beeps. Why would he be surprised that me and Prem were fighting again?

'Then what were you ...?' Prem finally shut up when I began scraping the blade over Dad's cheek, watching the salt and pepper filings collect in the white foam.

'I presume he's not left me anything,' I said, not looking at him, hearing him exhale noisily.

'You can't change anything,' Prem said finally, and then, 'Why are you doing all this now, Tans? You don't have to.'

'I know. Maybe that's why I want to. Not that you'd understand that, bro.'

By the end of the first week I had become used to the routine. I no longer experienced that swoop of disbelief in my gut when I walked into Dad's room and found him comatose. I think the TV screens helped; another long edit, I told myself at first, Dad on freeze frame until I cut this altogether to make sense. Now I'm just bored with reverting to convenient cinematic tags to justify the whole sodding mess. Before I would have comforted myself with the certainty that, some day in the future, this would inspire a wonderful film, a seminal scene, a dramatic anecdote. Not now. Now I crave anonymity, privacy. I guard my grief jealously, like a pearl. I flinch at the news, I avoid tragic headlines, I follow babies and small dogs in the street with moist, protective eyes. I now yearn for goodness, for resolution. My mum once told me that was what karma truly meant, to experience at some point all you have inflicted. So saying sorry doesn't make much difference, I suppose. And actually, when it came to it, I didn't have time, none of us did.

I hadn't imagined for a second that I would bump into Chila or Sunita at the hospital. I assumed that Chila would have been discharged after two days at the most and that it was pointless trying to contact her, either of them, because there was no explanation I could offer that wouldn't insult their intelligence or make me look less of a twat.

That's not to say I didn't hope for a brief unplanned encounter in a corridor for the first couple of days, that I would round a corner and they would both be there, cooing over a bundle, too suffused with joy not to welcome me back into the fold. That was the Hollywood version. Then I woke up, thought about how long, how many lies, how could I? The Hackney version begins with an expletive-littered screaming match and ends in a fist fight, with all of us holding handfuls of someone else's hair.

They did that for me, you know. Both of them. I'd limp back to them after another playground rumble and they would groom me like two maternal monkeys, checking my teeth and hair, producing tissues to dab away any blood and spit, putting me back together neatly before returning to our families, because we all knew what hell there would be to pay if our parents sniffed any scandal clinging to our uniforms. It was simple really, only having to choose between two worlds, home and everywhere else. And in between was the long walk home, and the three of us, rebuilding the crossing on each journey. That's what I missed most; it's not some mysterious mother-country ancient bond, it's nothing to do with being oppressed, menstrually synchronized womb-en or any of that crap. It's just that there aren't that many of us who built that bridge, walked it together. Our parents ignored it, our children won't even see it. Some of us will never get off it. I missed them, my fellow travellers.

So when it happened, about ten days after Dad had been admitted, I had stopped hoping that I would ever see any of them again. Actually, I was feeling heavy and hopeless myself. We had just had a meeting with the consultant,

Prem and I, who'd informed us in hushed but strangely impersonal tones, that our father was never going to improve, and what course of action did we want to pursue? We had been told when he was admitted that there was little point in operating. There had been such massive brain damage that even if he survived the operation to remove the clot, which was unlikely, his 'quality of life' afterwards would be minimal. Prem had become belligerent and shouty, his normal reaction when faced with anything that doesn't run according to plan, and insisted that 'You will operate and you will save him! However he ends up, he is still our father!' I had waited a few minutes until the alternative options were established. 'You could choose to keep him as he is,' the consultant had continued smoothly, almost like a sales patter, laying out the choices like carpet samples, what you lose in shade you gain in shag pile, madam, 'but it is merely a matter of time, maybe weeks, before he dies. Or you stop his suffering now.' And now he was advising us to make a decision.

All three of us instinctively looked towards Dad then, or rather at the bank of machines. Which was the actual switch that one had to merely flick, to end it? Ironic, really, I thought, all those times in my childhood when I had prayed that my embarrassing, bellowing, fabricating father might be fitted with a volume button, and finally, I am given the chance. I briefly remembered some bizarre news item, where a spate of sudden deaths in the intensive care department of a hospital was finally solved when detectives watched the ward cleaner doing her rounds. She would unplug the life-support machines to plug in her Hoover. That was more the sort of exit that suited Dad. Darkly comic, preventable, dramatic. Not his smart-ass daughter, she who once claimed there was no such thing as absolute truth, faced with the finality of On and Off.

So that day, as I made my way to the main exit, intending to snatch a hurried cigarette, my head was full of fuzzy feedback and funerals. I wouldn't have recognized them, anyway, standing together just beyond the automatic doors, their heads almost touching. I had been looking for two girls, one dark and dumpy, hovering hesitantly in her space, never quite owning it, waiting for permission to proceed, and the other taller, long hair in need of a good brush, a plump, sturdy arm around her companion, ready for fight or flight. So I pushed right between them, muttering an apology, barely registering the confident, curvy woman with her gleaming bob and her softly smiling, lotus-open friend, standing proudly, glowing with pleasure as she rearranged the blankets around her new son.

'Tania,' they said together, an involuntary gasp tinged with what I choose to remember as pleasure.

I turned. My limbs turned to liquid, the world looked molten and yellow. I heard what sounded like a war cry somewhere far away. Triumphant and fearful, I stretched out a hand slowly. And then he was there, only for an instant amongst us, scattering us like seed, and when we came together, Chila, Sunita and I, Deepak and the baby were gone.

We actually stood staring at Chila's empty arms before we registered what had happened, before we saw Deepak's car reversing crazily out of the car park and screeching onto the main road, leaving an echo of angry blaring horns. Chila opened her mouth agonizingly slowly, cavernous grief, a grotesque silent yawn, and before her guttural wailing began, I was running towards the car park exit, dialling on my mobile phone as I sprinted, gasping instructions to the police. I did not need to wait for their questions. At this moment I knew him better than anyone else. I knew his car number-plate, his likely haunts, his credit-card details, his favoured hotels. I knew the routes he preferred, the friends he might choose to visit in an emergency and who would lie for him, no questions asked. I knew where all his distinguishing marks were hidden. I knew I shouldn't have known any of this, but it was done.

A crowd had gathered by the time I returned, panting and cursing my inefficient lungs. Nurses, security guards, appalled visitors and frightened patients were milling around uselessly, uncomfortably silent, transfixed by the sight of Chila and Sunita, sitting together on the floor where they had fallen, Sunita whispering continuously to Chila, holding her as if she feared she might float away. And Chila, shivering and mute, glacial with shock, staring at the empty baby blanket fluttering gently in her hands. I marched the voyeurs away, instructed the necessary officials on what had happened. Yes, we knew him, yes, he must have been hiding behind the soft drinks machine, yes the police had been alerted and were no doubt on their way, and no, there was no need to hover with banalities because all we could do now was wait. Then I sat next to them both on the floor, took each of their hands and completed the circle.

We didn't say much, at least not to each other. Sunita and I tried to deal with the police. Fuelled by anger and despair we talked at them simultaneously for the first fifteen minutes, only halted by one young PC's nervous enquiry, 'Are you her lawyer and press agent or something?'

Chila only spoke once, to insist we did not inform her family yet, and then asked if she could go home.

We sat together in the back of the police car, listening to the robotic instructions coming over the radio. I expected urgent barking news flashes: press statement imminent! Roadblocks in place! Airports covered! But outside, it seemed the world turned laconically; burglar alarms sounded for no reason, drunks slapped each other in gutters. Maybe kidnappings were routine around here, I thought bitterly.

The WPC on the front seat turned round and said, almost apologetically, 'Don't worry, love, it's all under control. He won't get far . . .' and tailed off, embarrassed by her own well-meaning platitudes.

I snaked an arm around Chila's waist and pulled it away quickly, feeling dampness. The front of her shirt was transparent with moisture.

'He hasn't been fed,' she said dully, sticky with her leaking milk.

I searched in my bag for tissues while the WPC tried again. 'Your little one, love, what's his name? We need to inform—'

Sunita butted in, her voice harsh, accusatory. 'She didn't have time to give him one.'

We sent the WPC away. She had a whole support team standing by, she argued with us, counsellors and doctors and men in uniform with batons. She reassured us they would all be ready if we needed them, outside in the squad car, our protection. As Sunita muttered as she shut the door, 'More like the bloody morning-after pill.'

I quickly gathered up any baby accessories I spotted downstairs and shut them inside a kitchen cupboard. We turned on all the lights and put the heating on full blast. Sunita insisted Chila take a shower and led her, meek as a lamb and doped up on some druggy cocktail the hospital had made her take, to the bathroom.

I made a call to Suki. I managed to blurt out what had happened before she followed her first instinct to slam the phone down, and then she gabbled advice and lists and numbers at me until my head span and I had to beg her to slow down.

'I want to know what we can do now, right now!' I asked her.

'Be there,' she said. 'He can't go abroad, the baby's too young for people not to notice.'

'But what if . . .' I couldn't say it. I thought it. A burning car, Dad's funeral pyre, hot blood flowing in a delivery room, the expanding heat in my head.

And then I heard Chila and Sunita descending the stairs behind me and finished off quickly, promising I would call later. But I couldn't stop shaking. I shook all the way into the kitchen, couldn't hold the kettle to fill it at the tap, spilled coffee all over Chila's pristine counters. By the time I attempted to sit down at the kitchen table, my limbs were doing their own epileptic boogie, knocking against the table, comic morse code, making the laminated coasters jump in sympathy.

Sunita leaned towards me. 'Tans?'

Even Chila looked up from her lap momentarily, confused at the intrusion into her grief.

I tried to brace myself against the chair back and felt it jar rhythmically into my back. I grabbed a table leg for support and it seemed to quiver in my grasp. It might have been funny if it hadn't been so grotesque.

'I'll be fine,' I managed to gasp, wondering why my teeth were chattering, cursing whoever, whatever was pulling my strings, making me dance like a marionette on acid. Sunita came and stood behind me. She gripped me around the shoulders, trying to absorb the tremors.

'It's OK, Tans,' she said quietly.

Of course it wasn't, but thankfully, she didn't insult me by turning all maternal. It was far too soon for that. She held me with the practised efficiency of a care worker. We both knew I had no business making such a scene when I wasn't even the patient. Look after Chila, as always, her firm grip seemed to be reminding me. And I tried to tell her I wanted to, although it came out sounding like some strange East-European dialect. I would look after Chila, as soon as I had managed to forget about Dad and desertion and dead babies. And then I saw Chila looking at me and I knew. The purity of her, every inhibition scorched away, bleached bone clean. I knew nothing could stop her asking me now.

'Why did you do it, Tania?' she said simply.

I felt Sunita's hands tighten their grip on my back. My jaw trembled so furiously that I felt bones clicking somewhere in my skull.

'I . . . I . . .'

'Do you love him?'

I shook my head. That was easy, it did that all by itself.

'Did you love him?'

I ached all over, I wanted desperately to pee, I wanted her forgiveness but I could not lie, not this time.

'Yes,' I said, and as I said it, I felt the tremors receding. 'Yes, I loved him. I really did.'

Chila almost smiled, I grieved for how much older she looked.

'I don't think I ever loved him,' she said calmly. 'It was the idea of him. I . . . wanted to do what was right . . . and good. You know?' Oh, we all knew.

My breathing began to steady. Sunita's hands were making small gentle circles on my back.

'But you should have told me, Tans. Or he should,' she continued, in that same fatigued whisper. 'When I saw you both . . .' She paused, searching for words. 'Saw you . . . kissing . . . out there, out in the dark. I had the chance then, you know, to stop pretending. But I didn't. None of us did, did we? Why, Tans?' She used my nickname.

My hands stopped their restless fluttering and lay limply

in my lap. I wanted to tell her this wasn't the ending I had envisaged for us, the fall-out of that ill-timed kiss under jaded stars. We could have all been nobler, braver, stronger, good. But in the end, was it any better, to excuse the desire and destruction that had torn us apart? That was me too, all of it, all of us; destroyers and preservers that gave us this dark, dogged strength. Without it how would we survive?

But I didn't get a chance to say any of this, because we all heard the key turning in the lock of the front door and we inhaled as one, turned as one, rose as one to greet Deepak as he walked calmly towards us. Behind him, through the open door, I glimpsed the flash of whirling blue lights, the silhouettes of a careful advancing army. I can't recall his face at that moment. I fixed on the baby in his arms, the first time I had seen him, wrapped in a car blanket, all there, breathing, blissfully asleep.

Chila uttered an involuntary cry and ran towards him, snatched him away, and he fitted, perfectly I thought, into the crook of her arm beneath her breast.

Sunita placed herself instinctively between Chila and her husband, legs wide, hands on hips, almost spoiling for a fight. I sat down again, clung on to the chair like driftwood, thankful for ballast.

Deepak glanced over his shoulder, the siren blue revealing hollows and contours in his face. He raised a hand to them, the waiting officials, a cowboy's mocking salute, thanking them. For what? For waiting? For finding him?

Chila had almost stripped the baby down to his nappy, feverishly checking over his body, palpating the tiny ribcage, the plumped up thighs, the malleable wobbly head. God, babies are too small, I thought. His frailty almost made me dizzy.

'Chila?' Deepak said.

She would not look at him, raise her eyes from her ministrations.

'I just wanted to see him,' Deepak said.

Sunita snorted loudly, her hands bunched into fists.

'I don't want to be the man you think I am, Chila. I was always going to bring him back.'

Chila shook her head slowly. She was already far away. Deepak took a step towards her, an old man's shuffle.

Sunita and I exchanged a brief look, saw in each other's faces, despite everything, compassion, regret, a flicker of resignation. Too much suffering, time to lay down arms, maybe, soon.

Deepak made one last attempt. 'I wanted to see him, that's all.'

Well, that's when the proverbial doo-doo hit a rather large fan and it all went off, gung-ho coppers and blaring loudhailers and sirens so loud they woke the baby up. As Sunita quite rightly said afterwards, what was the bloody point when it was all over anyway?

'I expect they'll file it under Domestic,' she intoned, Eeyore-like, much later, when we had completed all the statements and endless form-filling, and had sat round for ages just watching Chila watching her son, the only person who had managed any sleep in forty-eight hours.

We had an extremely efficient timetable of naps worked out, so one of us would be with the baby while the others tried to rest, but we ended up all crashing out on Chila's king-sized bed. I woke up stiff-necked, dribble patches on my clothes, reeking of sweat and relief. The baby was spreadeagled in the centre of us, limbs far-flung, an X marking the spot, a farewell kiss.

I was not embarrassed until then, the morning after, and I snuck out of the house with my shoes in my hand while the household stirred behind me. Chila's family were due to arrive, Akash was on his way bringing food and children, the family machinery was cranking back into motion and I didn't fancy playing Spare Part Auntie at the party. Besides, I had my own family to visit.

It only struck me when I drove back into the hospital car park that Chila and Sunita had no idea that my father was ill. I don't know if they'd be interested. I suppose I will tell them, if they ask.

Since then, there's been a couple of telephone calls. Chila called me once. To thank me, for Christ's sake. She couldn't talk for long, Anand was crying for his feed. I recognized her mother's village twang issuing orders in the background. It sounded like she'd requisitioned half the neighbourhood as on-site nannies. Chila mentioned putting the house on the market and something about a trip to India. She said she'd get in touch again but hey, babies keep you busy.

Sunita rang up for Suki's number. I was with Suki at the time. We sort of hang out together. She's got some interesting friends, bit intense some of them but I'm happy to drift along, chewing the fat. I've met Jasbinder Singh a couple of times too. Amazing woman. Haven't mentioned anything about a film. Yet. So when Sunita called, I passed the phone to Suki and the two of them chatted happily for twenty minutes while I hovered around pathetically, trying to listen in.

I gather Sunita's working hard for her first-year exams, Akash is whisking her off for a romantic weekend to Barcelona immediately afterwards, Nikki's lost her first tooth. Life goes on, in a fashion.

We're still waiting for Dad to make up his mind whether to rejoin us or move on. Never say die. I don't anyway. The doctors say my father is effectively dead but they don't see what I see on those screens. It's a question of interpretation.

And it is possible to love without expecting anything back. They say you feel that for your children. One day, I'd like to ask Sunny and Chila about that too.

8

FROM A DISTANCE THEY LOOKED LIKE A FLOTILLA OF SWANS, gliding between the cedar trees, iridescent flashes against the granite of stones and monuments. The sun shone cruelly, inappropriately, as others huddled around sleek, low, black cars, shaking their white plumage, clucking respectfully, shedding white shreds of tissue from sleeves and bags, waiting. Some were sitting on the grass, as there had not been enough space inside for the unexpectedly huge crowd. They nested in small plump groups. Old women removed their shoes and massaged their feet, sighing with the breeze, waving away the tissue snow and playful midges, angling their stiffened backs towards the sun.

'They look like they're on a picnic,' muttered a wife to her husband as they swept by, armed with a trowel, a small rake and basket of bursting bulbs. Mrs Keegan had never been happy about the arrangement, having a crematorium within the graveyard grounds. People should have the option, one or the other. Sharing facilities was just penny-pinching and probably disrespectful. She wanted to visit her brother's grave and mix with the other regulars who came to dig and plant and remember. That was the difference. They chose to remember, they kept the body and didn't fry it and send it off into the air up a chimney, nothing left to remind you or bring you back for a chat. And the way they wailed! As if they weren't drawing enough attention, dressing up in white clothes like they were off to a wedding. She tugged on her husband's arm to hurry up and quickened her pace past the cars, towards the chipped angel in the far north-west corner where her dwarf tulips would just be exploding into red and yellow fractured cups.

Mr Keegan slowed down a little. He had never dared say, but he looked forward to these foreign cremations. There was always a good turn out, they seemed to have a lot of friends, the deceased, and it cheered him up no end, seeing all those cream and snowy silks instead of the usual black stiff suits, which always reminded him of scavenging crows. True, they made a lot of noise. It was upsetting sometimes, the dramatics, the flinging themselves around. But he wondered if it wasn't better that way, to let it all out and not be ashamed, rather than the choking, muted snuffles that his wife occasionally allowed herself, as she dug around in the soil, telling the headstone what she'd been up to that week. I mean, what was the point of that? It's not as if they ever did anything very interesting, and Mr Keegan reckoned they had more important things to consider on the Other Side than Mrs Keegan's corn operation, or their projected caravanning trip around Norfolk. No, best to have it done and dusted, he concluded, and why not make it a festive send off? That's the way he wanted to go, with a brass band and a piss-up. Not that she'd let him.

He paused as a crowd began to filter out of the memorial hall, led by three young women. He reckoned they may have been sisters, or maybe it was the bleached white suits against the warm brown of their skins, but they stepped together, precisely, almost touching. He realized, with a faint shock, that one of them was carrying a baby, couldn't have been more than a few months old. That wasn't quite right, surely, bringing a young one to such an occasion. But he was a bonny chap, gurgling away. Mr Keegan thought of his own grandchildren and wished hungrily that they were with him. He turned away reluctantly. He could see his wife in the distance, kneeling down at the feet of the angel, already yanking out weeds with military precision. He adjusted his belt and set off along the path to join her.

'I didn't realize your dad had so many friends,' Sunita whispered to Tania as they made their way slowly towards the cars.

'Nor me,' Tania replied. It took a long time to reach the main body of the crowd as she paused to namaste to some faces she vaguely recognized, accepted embraces and murmurs from others she did not know at all. People began instinctively to throng around her, the three of them at the centre of a dazzling mass, slow-moving sails circling their island.

'So many people,' Chila breathed, squeezing Tania's hand.

She muttered back, 'Thank God I can get away with calling them Uncle and Auntie because I don't know any of their names. I should know. I should have asked.'

'You're doing fine, Tans.' Sunita patted her. 'Better than Prem, anyway.'

Tania's brother brought up the rear of the crowd. He was supported by his wife and an elderly man who was having some difficulty holding him up.

'Bas buche, enough,' the old man kept soothing him, wishing Prem would angle his wailing away from his deaf aid. He'd seen it too often, the way the children would fall apart like this, after years of wanting to escape their parents. But then, hadn't he left home at seventeen, and then left India itself without a backward glance? He felt the sun beating down on his bald patch and sweat begin to prick through the skin. Only a short walk, he thought, and he could sit down on the grass and wait. Not long now, to send his old friend off, to set him free.

Prem straightened up when he saw Tania. She looked so different with all that hair pulled back so severely, so straight-backed, scrubbed clean. The crowd parted smoothly to let him pass and he stood behind her, feeling calmer. He had done his best. His son would do the same for him. Some things would never be broken and he took comfort from that.

Somewhere, imperceptibly, a cog turned, a lever swung, sparrows shivered on their branches, a whiff of smoke, a memory of it drifted on the still warm air, and the gathering fell silent. All eyes swivelled towards the roof of the square-topped building.

Sunita gathered her dupatta around her body, planted her feet squarely on the ground, imagining roots taking hold, wanting earth, seeking solid ground. The sun felt good. Spain would be hotter.

Chila held Anand closer to her, smelled the milk and soap in his downy hair. She felt light as air, solitary. It was so strange to be standing with the old ones, aged couples holding hands, taking part in the old ways, and feel so new and unfamiliar. It wasn't so bad, to be here alone. Not better, just different. It was monsoon season in India, the travel agent had advised her. Chila had replied that she didn't mind rain.

Tania watched the first few flecks of ash spiral from the chimney's mouth. Around her, muffled moaning began, bodies shifted, gently moving her, taking her with them. She gave herself up to the tide, gracefully, gratefully. Then more smoke, spattered with grey-black debris, coming faster and thicker, eager to escape the brick maw and billow across the unbroken sky.

'Go on . . . go!' Tania said, exhilarated, raising her arms above her, scattering the sparrows from the trees, who fluttered through the grey snow and beyond it, singing their journey as they flew.

Eat, Drink and be Married

Eve Makis

Anna's head reels with plans to escape life behind the
counter of the family chip shop on a run-down
Nottingham council estate. Her mother Tina wants
nothing but the best for her daughter: a lavish
wedding and a fuly furnished four-bedroom house
with a BMW parked in the driveway. She thinks Anna
should forget the silly notion of going to college and
focus on finding a suitable husband. Mother and
daughter are at loggerheads and neither will give way.

Anna's ally and mentor is her Grandmother Yiayia
Annoulla. She tells Anna stories about the family's
turbulent past in Cyprus, the island home they were
forced to abandon. Yiayia practises kitchen magic,
predicts the future from coffee grains and fills the
house with an abundance of Greek-Cypriot delicacies.

Anna longs for the freedom enjoyed by her brother
Andy but spends time appeasing her parents, dodging
insults from drunken customers or going on ill-fated
forays with her petulant cousin – the beautiful Athena.
It is only when family fortunes begin to sour that
Anna starts to take control of her own destiny . . .

'HEART-WARMING, FUNNY, TRAGIC AND
UPLIFTING . . . THE STORY HAS A FEELGOOD
FACTOR TO EQUAL *MY BIG FAT GREEK
WEDDING*'
Narinder Dhami

0 552 77216 X

BLACK SWAN

A SELECTED LIST OF FINE WRITING
AVAILABLE FROM BLACK SWAN

THE PRICES SHOWN BELOW WERE CORRECT AT THE TIME OF GOING TO PRESS. HOWEVER TRANSWORLD PUBLISHERS RESERVE THE RIGHT TO SHOW NEW RETAIL PRICES ON COVERS WHICH MAY DIFFER FROM THOSE PREVIOUSLY ADVERTISED IN THE TEXT OR ELSEWHERE.

All Transworld titles are available by post from:

Bookpost, P.O. Box 29, Douglas, Isle of Man IM99 1BQ

Credit cards accepted. Please telephone +44(0)1624 677237, fax +44(0)1624 670923, Internet http://www.bookpost.co.uk or e-mail: bookshop@enterprise.net for details.

Free postage and packing in the UK. Overseas customers allow £2 per book (paperbacks) and £3 per book (hardbacks).